Thawing As She Goes

If we shadows have offended, think but this, and all
is mended, --That you have but slumber'd here,
while these visions did appear.

– Puck, A Midsummers Night's Dream, Shakespeare

How dare you continue to look away and come here
saying that you're doing enough when the politics
and solutions needed are still nowhere in sight.

– Greta Thunberg, Speech to the U.N., 2019

Dedicated to Marie-Noelle and Tristan
Anything is possible

Second Printing

Illustration credit: Daniela Zamora

Library and Archives Canada Cataloging in Publication information available on request.

ISBN 978-1-7781716-0-4

Printed and bound in Canada

Contact the author and share your views at rumbawords.com.

Printed on certified 100% recycled post-consumer
Rolland Enviro Paper.

The complicated, everyday lives of the Ashers', Bernals' and Fulcos'

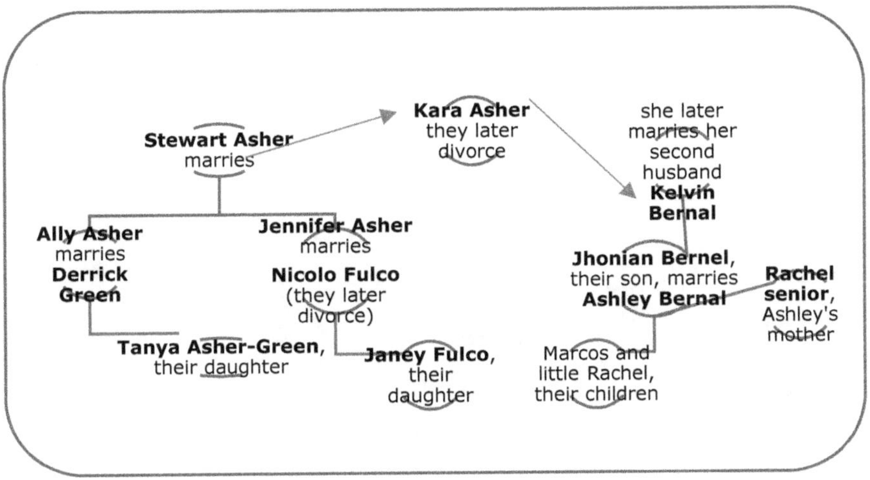

ADJUSTED

<h1 style="text-align:center">One</h1>

The gritty roll of her tires against the gravel faded as the car stopped and converted to a barely audible idle.

"Darling, we're here. Can I get the door for you?"

Ally looked out the curved, tinted windows to double-check the parking job. It was a hot day and the heat seemed to wave off the asphalt surface. The lot at the diner was full, but the car was well within the yellow lines.

"I wish you wouldn't call me darling," she snapped bitterly.

There was a pause. "You're upset. I can change. Just tell me what you would like."

She blew out a frustrated sigh. "You're infuriating. For Christ's sake, give me a minute!"

Ally pitched forward to look at the front screen, squinting at the controls on the front dash. She needed to see the gauge for herself. "Ahh piss," she grumbled to herself, as she stared at the blur of the battery indicator. "Effing eyes!" She dropped back down into the seat and began to root through her packsack, irritated with this sign of mid-life.

"Is there something I can help you with?"

"I'm just getting my glasses. It's what happens when you're over fifty. That's something you can learn. Now, can you wait?"

A mistake to say that question out loud. Her sharply delivered question would provoke an irritatingly smooth reaction.

"Of course. I'm always here. I can help."

Ally continued to root, replying flatly, "I know, that's why you are making me insane."

"I don't understand. Tell me more, keep talking, and I will adapt."

Ally screamed a little to herself. After two weeks, this trip couldn't end soon enough. It aged her every day as she argued with this machine about the simple things. Where to park. When to get charged. Did she want to pull off and rest? With the constant chatter of interruptions and her thirst for some silence, every minute in the car was painful now. It didn't matter what the car said or did; she was ready for a clean break. Impatiently she fished out her glasses to focus her failing vision on the gauge. "Good," she thought. "At least that's okay." The power level was still green and she didn't need to plug in the car.

Ally let out a sigh of relief and rumpled things back into her bag, ruminating about how a younger self would be unfazed by this technology. But that was not now. For the past two weeks, while she'd been out of the city solo, her feelings about this unfamiliar object had been a difficult part of an otherwise wonderful vacation.

The initial idea of hiring a self-driving ride had been seductive. "Oh, well, you've gone top-of-the-line!" The rental agent looked at her with admiration. "You'll like the *Immerse*. It's our most sought-after model," he assured her. "Everything's kinda new. Everybody wants to get inside and look."

She packed all her luggage in its clever front compartment which organized itself. The vehicle was one of the intercity electrics that had a six-hundred-kilometre range. Highway-bound, she floated comfortably while the cities passed by in a blur. She nestled comfortably into the joy of its roomy, plush backseat that felt more like a roaming living room. Four seats turned to face each other, and she'd tried them all. So pleasant to reach under the center console and pull out the container of water stowed earlier. Refrigerated, just like indicated on the RFID tag, to the perfect temperature.

This didn't feel like driving. She'd watched something on the big screen that descended in front at her command. Pulled up the work table to eat a snack, and curiously found a mirrored compartment for cosmetics. It felt luxurious watching the green farmer's fields pass by as she twisted her long, dark hair into place. Making up her face to show her mature elegance; with the right hair and makeup, she still got the odd compliment. The years had put a seasoned edge on what only could be considered her tall, imposing presence. Not quite the ease of charisma. Something much more influential. Most people found that if Ally wanted you to do something, you would, and willingly.

More bewitching, initially, was that the car spoke. Not just repeat phrases like her fridge. Well beyond simpleness like "the door is ajar. The door is ajar." It was a natural language interface that sucked you in. This was the first time she'd been in a completely voice-activated vehicle, let alone be in charge. "Nothing to worry about," the rental agent had assured her. "Just get in the back and tell the nav system where you want to go."

Nav system. More like a crazy wizard riding along with you in the next seat. The car chirped more than in real life. It constantly told you friendly little facts like there's a patch of rainy weather ahead. Or how soon you could turn off the road for coffee.

What's more, you could choose from an infinite number of personalities for it to mimic. In a couple of days she'd gone through Cary Grant, Hugh Grant, Richard Burton, Elizabeth Taylor, Liam Neeson and Emma Watson. All dead now, but brilliantly brought back to life as the personality of her vehicle.

It was close to feeling like you were riding with a friend. A comfortable old friend that you could share a trivia game with. That's what Ally thought at first.

"Hey Hugh, tell me the name of that movie you were in with Rachel Weitz."

"Well, let me think," it stammered back diffidently. "That would be *About a Boy*."

"Hugh, you're right. How about another one?"

"It would be my pleasure."

"Mine too."

And so the relationship began. She'd talked to Liz Taylor about husbands and divorces. Asked Richard Burton about why he left Liz Taylor. Had Cary Grant sing *The Halls of Montezuma*. Asked Liam

13

Neeson to recite key movie scenes, substituting her daughter's name. It was a rabbit hole of distraction. She'd only started with the possibilities. There were famous sports personalities who could recount their best moments on the field. Politicians could walk you through their decision-making. Limitless.

But quickly the seduction grew excruciating.

What Ally realized is that you're never alone in one of these contraptions. It constantly asked you questions, thinking it was getting to know you; studying you and your habits. A machine algorithm assuming that if you liked one thing, you'd want more of the same. "Do you want me to tell you about my movies," it asked hopefully during a welcome moment of silence.

"No," she replied firmly. But it didn't give up, suggesting topics for them to discuss that grew more and more generic and inane. She didn't give up either. Instead she grew ruder and ruder. "Why don't you just shut the fuck up," had become her standard refrain.

And the technology wasn't perfect. It made the occasional worrisome mistake. Or maybe it had feelings and messed with her. She'd swear the damn thing didn't tell her the truth a couple of days ago. She'd noticed the "needs recharging" alarm on the front control panel. When was it going to tell her to plug it in? In a panic she asked the machine if it needed to be recharged. "We're okay for now," it lied.

She took it into the local dealers, ready to pay to have some of the technology disabled. The technician just whistled when he saw it. "That's a beauty!"

"I know. Can you neuter it? Violently, if possible."

He looked at her with amusement. She was not his first. "Have you got all the codes? I need the codes to get into the computer."

That was probably a turning point in the trip. Now she found herself double-checking everything. Once the trust is gone, you just can't get it back. This was the last day; she looked forward to dropping this car's sorry ass off with the rental agent. She'd soon be back in the city, with the car and driver that came with her job. A real person, her driver, helped her carry her files and made sure she was safe.

14

She appreciated it so much more that she didn't think too much about how she got around. She felt safer when she could look up from her screen and see a human.

The sun glimmered on the front hood. She looked past the glint to the full parking lot to the entry of the country diner. A stream of beachgoers was exiting. The familiar yellow stucco exterior with its red neon sign hadn't changed in a couple of decades. There was a newish set of solar panels on the side but otherwise it had that worn, scrubbed look that comes with making stuff last longer. Already, Ally could smell a prodigious amount of bacon grease and toast. Score, what a luxury to find real bacon! She wanted to kiss whoever was the local farmer. Exactly what she wanted on her last day away! A gorgeous hot beach day and getting stuck into a plate of animal protein. She got out of the car, slamming the door with authoritative force. The firm click told the universe that she had a plan, and nothing would stop her.

Passing through the door, she surveyed the crush of like-minded vacationers that had joined her for breakfast. She took in the harried waitresses and the overflowing tables of people. The loud cacophony felt like a material barrier between her and the far end of the room. Cutlery jingled from across the room. Kids jostled as if they were already playing in the waves at the beach. A young man with a long ponytail balanced a grey basin of dirty dishes. Ally watched him disappear into the steam of the kitchen. The breakfast that had featured so high on her holiday "must-do" list was quickly moving into the impossible column.

Ally stood at the entry considering her fate, dodging a toddler that made a break for it, almost falling into the potted plant located a little inconveniently near the door. About to abandon her plan, she saw the welcoming wave across the diner. Her friend Elizabeth was alone at a table for two and beckoned for Ally to join her. Elizabeth smiled as Ally thankfully made her way over. A dollop of fortune had saved her last day. Ally was hungry, and the prospect of the pending plate of animal protein, the delicious food of her youth, made her happy. But even better, she'd managed to salvage another vacation tradition: the farewell breakfast. Her car was loaded, and once she'd eaten, she'd make one more trip to the beach and make her way back to Ottawa.

She'd been coming to the same vacation spot, on and off, for about thirty-five years. It was an easy two-hour trip from Ottawa if you took the self-driving lanes. Locals called it 'The County,' as if there weren't scores of other counties in Eastern Ontario. In the minds of the people who lived here, there was only one.

Ally loved the pace, which didn't seem to lose its agricultural roots despite the churn of well-to-do, city-bred retirees with their bucket list of projects. They fashioned a parade of out-of-place restaurants, wineries, and art studios that were fun to explore. The old tomato soup factory from 150 years ago would become a fitness facility with classes on some international yoga craze. Or a barn would be turned into an artists' collective that drew a rotating series of exhibits. Well-known singers who wanted a turn in the country would show up at the Royal Theatre. Every year, some projects would close and others would arrive. It was rich pageant of creativity and business savvy, only some of which would prosper more than a season.

If that wasn't enough, there was the natural beauty of the County itself. Surrounded by water on all sides, it formed almost an island in Lake Ontario. The air seemed to change as you drove over the majestic bridge on highway 49. It was green and flat with well-tended farms and houses lining its never changing rural roads. And although the flooding had made it more difficult, it still managed to produce some of the best food anywhere. You couldn't buy some of the vegetables they grew anywhere else. Ally was taking home a bag of red carrots, the purple broccoli and the homemade, real-meat salami.

But the killer was the beach. A worn sign in front of the provincial park told everybody that the County offered the world's largest natural fresh water sand bar. And it didn't disappoint. You could walk for kilometres with your toes on the soft, white sand.

The only drawback were the day travelers from Toronto and Montreal that invaded her adopted home base on the weekends. They dirtied the beach with their trash and cigarette butts. They clogged up main street on a sunny Saturday. But they compensated by supporting all the eccentric businesses she enjoyed. The wrought iron importer on the main drag was only open in the summer. And the woman who sold black garlic on Route 10 on Wednesdays in the summer. They needed the tourist trade. Quaint can only be quaint if someone pays for it, Ally would tell herself. So she doted on great stuff and observed every new arrival and departure like a local. She liked it so much she'd begun to pass occasional winter evenings loitering on real estate sites to price out potential properties. This year she'd even stopped at an open house to view a home that was for sale.

"I saved you a seat," Elizabeth beamed at her. Ally smiled back, so delighted to see the youthful cast of Elizabeth's face, even with her eight decades of experience.

It was awesome that she'd be able to say goodbye to Elizabeth before she left. Ally had visited her when she'd first arrived two weeks ago, to catch up with her friend and the local news. She had met Elizabeth when she'd rented one of her beach cottages when her daughter was young. From there, they had continued in friendship and even though they didn't connect more than a couple times a year, their communications were heartfelt when they happened. Ally felt she had found a soul who spoke about where she herself was headed. Someone who figured out the important stuff. And maybe Liz saw in Ally a younger version of herself.

As their friendship grew, Ally came to admire how Liz was open to all of life's possibilities. Elizabeth had been sixty when the two first met, and Ally could tell her truthfully that she never altered a day. Elizabeth had lost her husband some decades ago and his loss was the only subject that could raise any sign of melancholy. Otherwise, Liz was still busy with her cottage rentals, happily tending to the grass and the demands of the out-of-towners. In the off-season, she travelled as soon as she could get a permit, often with her sisters, one of which was still in Germany. She always had a story about her and grandchildren to fill an empty spot in a conversation. She lived and had no intention to stop.

"I'm so thankful I saw you. I've never seen it so busy."

"I just caught you there, in the corner of my eye." Elizabeth's voice had a tremor of joy. She motioned to the front of the diner. The room was l-shaped, and where Ally had just recently stood was obscured by a swarm of people lining up. Both women squinted through the sun in the window while they watched a waitress doing her best to find empty tables. A tall, lean fellow with a large wave board entered the diner. The waitress looked at him and laughed kindly as she pointed around. Elizabeth and Ally watched as he beat his way to the exit.

"Good timing. If you'd stopped by the house, you would have missed me. After I eat, I'm catching the train to Toronto to spend a few days with my sister."

Ally nodded. "I remember, she lives near Guelph, doesn't she?"

"You've got such a good memory. Imagine remembering that. She does. She's meeting me at the station in Toronto and we're going to see a play downtown. I haven't seen anything at the theatre this year. I'm so looking forward to it."

"Liz, I'm not sure how many people make it out of the house for the theatre anymore. I admire you for even making the effort."

"You've got to make an effort. Or your life will fly by very quickly."

"I love your philosophy. You should blog about it."

Elizabeth politely scoffed at the idea. "I'll tell you something. They want all us old folks to blog about something. They say it brings us closer, reduces the 'social isolation.' I see the government posters at the community centres. I want to talk to real people. I don't want to be stuck in my house. If they honestly want to make life better, they could make it easier for us older people."

Ally was familiar with the argument. The government had been crafting messages about change for decades now. People of Elizabeth's age grew up with a different set of experiences. They vividly recalled the old days, when they had different choices.

Elizabeth paused, a little cautious about offering her opinion. "They should look at things like meat rationing. All my friends give their rations to their kids. I suppose you know something about that," she chuckled without malice.

Ally caught the implication. Food rationing to cut emissions was unpopular. The older woman wanted to know if Ally had heard anything new at work she could share.

"Shit!" The crash at a table was near enough to startle the two women. The ponytailed busboy had lost control of his grey basin of dishes. They both laughed at the makeshift feel of the meal. Why either of them had left their well-organized kitchens for the chaos of two fried eggs and some local bacon was becoming a legitimate question.

Elizabeth continued. "I'm sorry I didn't have a spot for you this year. Now tell me, how has the vacation been?"

"Not sure I'd rent the same car again. But otherwise, wonderful, like usual. The first few days I'm always disoriented with the slower pace."

"That's true, but I think the pace is good for people."

"It's good for me, once I get used to it. I love the power of a good vacation. Next year I'll write to you earlier because I do miss being close to the beach. But it's still good. This year I got to revel in the charms of the village. I went every evening to the old ice cream stand. The tennis court was nearby. I got to play every day with the local club."

Elizabeth smiled in appreciation. "You'll have to think about it when you get closer to retirement."

Ally chuckled inwardly at Liz's attempt to draw her out. "How about you," Ally asked. "I've been driving around, and there's so much remediation going on now. I get to see the charts and tables at work about what's happening across the country. But looking at the changes I've seen just these two weeks, it's impressive. You must be pleased with the restoration work at the shoreline. I've read that the risks of flooding in your area are down significantly."

"That's one positive thing about all this environmental adaptation we've been put through over the years. I got a government grant to do some work where my dock was washed out. I just found out they are giving me another one to add more rocks to support the shore against erosion. I guess they want to overestimate any potential water level increases. I'll send you a photo when it's done."

"Please do. I got to say, it's great to have the beach back."

Elizabeth picked up her coffee cup and signalled to the waitress flashing by that she wanted to order. "Yes, it's a miracle. It took forever. I started to wonder if the town council would ever let us swim there again."

Ally pointed at the crowd of people in the diner. "It's really bringing the tourists back. Everybody missed the beach. It's what makes the place so special." Ally thought back to a recent evening. She'd climbed out of the waves toward the beach. The sun had descended behind the trees in the distance that glowed yellow and orange around the indigo blue of the silhouette. Beautiful. Her eyes traced the horizon as she stood in awe of the serenity. Memorizing the feeling of peace, the sunset, the sound of the water. And then it hit her. A sweet part of her youth had returned. The work that they'd all done to control the flooding. The sacrifices, the money, and the changes. It was worth it to her to live memories like this again. To know others could too.

"I'll tell you what's good about it, apart from the swimming. It's been good for our house values! It was impossible to sell for years. And of course, the grandkids love to visit again. I remember when the lake rose so much the beach was just a sandy strip at the edge of the water."

"I remember. And then it's been closed, for what, ten years?"

The delightful perfume of bacon came into range and paused the chat. The waitress brought two plates of wonderfully greasy food and both women fussed about their plates, cutting and chewing the thick cured pork dripping with the yellow of the egg.

As they polished off their food, they exchanged pleasantries about the coming few months. As they spoke the crowd thinned.

"I didn't even notice the music when I came in."

"It's horrible. I don't know why they bother," Elizabeth offered. The music was some sort of modern, insipid, two-word chant, mumbled over a beat about as regular as rain on a roof.

"I agree. It's painful. I don't think it's our age. Is it supposed to mellow us up? It sounds like it's sung by a robot." Then, mercifully,

20

the monotonous beat stopped and became something much more familiar.

"I saw her when I was a girl. What year would that have been? 1986? She had a gift. I was just a teenager and my father drove us to the casino where she was playing." Liz started humming, joy coming onto her wonderful face as she sang. "And on the bus, dear, I think of us, dear. I say a little prayer for you. Forever, forever, you'll stay in my heart. I will love you. Forever, forever, we never will part."

"Aretha Franklin," Ally nodded. "My mother would play her in the car when I was a kid."

"It's vintage, but perfect. Makes me think of my husband. He loved Motown. He'd sing this to me."

"You're beaming."

"He was a special man. It's important not to lose sight of that. What makes you happy. I think about that a lot now. It's my family, the people who mean the most to you. That's all you need."

"I see what you mean Liz." Ally paused to take a sip from her mug of coffee. "I like to think that I make a difference. Left the world a better place."

Elizabeth nodded, in understanding, if not in agreement. Then, she doubled back to where she'd wanted the conversation to go. She had always liked Ally's husband Derrick. It must be driving her crazy that Ally had not mentioned him.

"Do you mind me asking? I don't see your husband on these trips anymore."

"After 28 years, we've both got our separate routines. Now he's retired, he often gets away in the winter."

The lie delivered, Ally studied Liz over her mug, gauging her credibility. It wasn't high. She offered something a little closer to the truth. "My job is twenty-four hours, seven days a week. I like to, really I need to, get away on my own and recharge."

"Well, I wondered and I don't mean to pry." She paused for a minute, looking a bit stuck. She wanted to say something helpful. But anything was going to be clumsy. "It's just that I noticed he hasn't come down with you for a few years now. Derrick was always good company. Tell him I say hi." Liz looked down at the table and assembled some of the breakfast debris. She put the empty jam pots onto her plate to signal to the waitress she was ready to leave. "Excuse me, I'm going to make a pit stop."

Ally sipped on the last of her coffee while she thought about the lies in her life. The lies she used to face the people she respected.

Usually some of it was true. For instance, she wasn't lying to Liz about recharging.

For two weeks she enjoyed not having responsibilities. The sun and the water had filled her until she was whole. She lost track of work and other problems, marooning them in the eddies of her mind. Opting to spend time visiting friends. Leaving herself open to spontaneous choices and to new experiences. All that was real.

What was a lie was about Pete. Elizabeth could never know about him. He had joined her for part of the vacation and they were flawless days.

The same sunset where she remembered the beach of her youth, Pete had waited patiently for her at their campfire. He'd stood at the end of the beach and watched her make her way over to him. She'd been a long way down, and he'd put a hand up against the sun of the late afternoon. He kept his eyes on her, coveting the curves of her silhouette against the sunset. She casually meandered back down the length of the beach, stopping to smile at the kids splashing in the water. Or picking up some beach glass that caught her eye. Chatting with the couple making their way in the other direction. She looked up and saw him watching her progress. He waved and overwhelmed her with the affection in his gesture. She anticipated the feeling of his hands against her sun-kissed skin. It was sure worth the lie to be together.

Elizabeth returned to her seat and picked up her purse to pay. Ally got up to leave and retrieved the older woman's bill. "Liz, it was great to see you. My treat."

"Oh, thank you. I'd argue about paying, but I know with you there's no point!"

The diner was almost empty now. The sun was strong, so no doubt the same crowd was now filling up the beach. They wandered to the front of the diner and waited to pay.

"There's been a lot of new developments in the County since last year. Some good. Some not so good," Elizabeth said. "Did you try that new coffee shop? I don't think it is far from where you were renting."

"Yes, they've done a lovely job. It was all post-consumer design. I liked how they used the cement and the old wood beams with the local recycled furniture."

Elizabeth looked down, fidgeting with her purse, while thoughtfully brushing some wayward crumbs off her blouse. Ally knew what she meant. Talk of the PC world unsettled her. People moved to the country to escape a lot of the post-consumer demands. To get away from the modern world with its environmental choices. She probably thought the coffee shop, with its cold grey metal exterior, was a PC eyesore.

"I guess you have to bring your own coffee cup?"

"For take-away. Liz, I'm used to it. And it's worth it if it saves the planet."

Elizabeth looked meaningfully at Ally. Anybody from the Department of Citizenship would say the same thing.

Ally smiled back. "I guess you think I'm parroting my own propaganda?"

"You're flipping back into work mode. Going back to the city today to make us better citizens and save the planet."

"Is that how you see me?"

"Ha, all good. You can't help it. It's in your blood."

"I guess, Liz, over the years you've drawn your own conclusions about me."

"Sometimes you say things that make me think of what my husband would say. He was an old military man. He'd tell me, 'Liz, don't become what you're fighting.'"

"Huh, not sure how that applies to me."

"Well, aren't you the top person at the Citizenship department?"

"True." Ally nodded her agreement as she flashed her finger across the terminal to pay with her ring.

Two

The room was oval, with a ring of people running their way to
health on the rim. Inside the track was a bank of treadmills,
ellipticals, and some virtual cardio booths, all filled with people
stretching and pushing themselves.

Each end of the huge gym was covered with the thin film kind of
screen; it looked like it was painted on the walls. These screens were
divided into six blocks, with different content on each. One had a
class beamed in from somewhere. A bunch of people dressed in black
tights were following along at the other end of the gym. Another
block had business news. That would be relevant to her if she had
any real money. Then there was a guy holding a cat, about to jump
into a foam pit. When he landed the foam turned into some sort of
slime. He got to his feet with a panicky cat and stupid toothy grin
while the neon-coloured words "Dime-Dumble!!" scrolled diagonally
across. That was clearly an algo's idea of what today's gym-goers
needed to know. Pathetic. A couple of women stood chatting in front
of the one screen that was crucial. Ashley glanced over at it as she
entered the gym. "11:45," she noted.

Today Ashley's mother-in-law Kara said she would be home early and
promised to look after the kids. The woman was a saint. The smartest
thing her husband Jhonian ever did was to convince her to let his
mom move in. What Kara says she will do, she invariably did. Ash
knew she could take the hour and have a decent workout. Maybe
even something sweet from the Power Bar afterwards. Any working
mom knows that an hour to yourself is a luxury worth savouring.

The biomedical consultants at the fitness desk gave her some tips
before she got started today. Their services were free and she needed
to know about protein required for the muscle mass goals her doctor
had sent her. According to him, her weight and hormone balances still
were all okay. Women like her in their late-thirties needed to worry
about those things. It's a complicated puzzle to stay healthy and in
good standing with your health insurance. You had to do four exercise
sessions a week to keep your health credits green. And they had to
be scannable to your card. Dancing about in front of the screen of
your living space didn't qualify.

Fortunately most workplaces had scannable gyms now. Ash worked in the planning division of a large, national supply-chain management company. She spent a couple of days a week at the company's central facility in the west end, in part to have access to their gyms. Posters all over the warehouse told her how her employer was helping her meet the challenges of today. It was a help. A bit of help. Yes, she was grateful. But life was so freaking intense that a bit of help didn't seem to make a dent.

She made her way to one of the weight training circuits, picking up twenty-five pounds and squatting. Although the screens across the gym flashed relentlessly, most people listened privately on their head phones, so the gym itself was eerily quiet. Ron, the gym rat, was holding court nearby. He was well past fifty and extraordinarily fit. Every time Ashley came in, Ron seemed to be there going through his routine. Invariably he would be yakking animatedly to any number of younger men about exercises or sports.

Ron was one of the gym's "micro-stars." In non-social media language, a very local celebrity. In exchange for free membership for his family, Ron allowed the gym to use its facial recognition software to locate him and broadcast images of his workout on the dedicated screens. He could add his touch with messages, like what he was working on that day.

From her position where she now worked the kettlebells, Ashley went unnoticed as she overheard snippets of his conversation. It was amusing how the young men wanted to impress Ron with their strength. She was amused too with how Ron managed to engage them. He was no stranger to their admiration, but he didn't abuse them either.

The digital clock turned to 12:00 as her watch beeped. The screen at the weight station switched to a cast of her personal screen. "Here's what you missed since you checked last."

"Frig," she said aloud. "I thought I turned it off."

She swiped through a list of new messages since she checked 30 minutes ago. Her life had been busy. There were twenty-three messages, all but one from a bot.

26

The bots were letting her know about the work they were doing for her family. Completed systems updates, how they had returned library materials, ordered groceries that had been used up, posted sports scores and updated her family calendar with a round of automated dental appointments. Routine information that she'd scan later, as now and then, the messages could be embarrassing to read in public. Like the hilarious one she got once from their new toilet bot her husband had just installed. The message was more an illustration, and a large profile of the tank and bowl with brown and yellow arrows pointed in many directions. It was writing to let her know it was "on the job." It promised to provide monthly updates on her family's health. A good idea, with her family's history of type two diabetes. But more part of her medical feed, not something she wanted flashed around the gym.

Then she finally got to the one real message from her mother, Rachel. "Fuck, Mom," she said aloud. It was a video and she'd watch it later. Ash predicted that her mother needed something. There was probably some issue of officialdom that her mother needed her to check.

She expanded the thumbnail. Rachel was smiling in front of a building that Ashley didn't recognize. From the architecture, she guessed it was somewhere in the southern states. She jabbed at the screen to move the image around, analyzing the image for insights. She walked over to the mats wondering what was her mother doing there. It was summer, and if Rachel was going to be in Canada, it was usually now. As Ashley worked through three sets of planks, she wondered what travel regulations her mother had ignored this time.

Ashley grunted as she checked the form of her side planks. She imagined her mother regaling her travelling companions with her clever review of the "boring life" in Canada. In fact, Ashley's boring life. All boring until her mother needed something.

"Let her sweat," Ash reassured herself. Whatever her mother was up to now, she wasn't going to let it crash her workout.

Next she made her way inside the ample track where the machines were almost full. Large screens on top of each machine flashed liquid images while people bobbed in front, clad in all manner of headgear.

She stepped on one of the three empty cardio machines, reaching down to get her ear pieces.

"You using this," a woman mumbled from behind. Ashley started, turning to see a shapely young woman wired with some sort of electronic monitoring system. Or maybe it was sound. In either case the young woman was intent on claiming the machine. Ashley had already put a foot on it. She was sure she was there first. The woman's hand was reaching around to the instrument panel.

"Yes," she firmly told the young woman, attempting at the same time to look her straight in the eyes. The woman was pissed at Ashley's assertiveness. "There's two others," said Ashley, a little bemused. This happened a lot.

People, especially the real gym devotees, got attached to particular machines. There was a slight moment when the young woman considered pushing Ashley aside, but she relented and found another machine. Ashley shrugged, looking down at her exercise gear. Nothing shapely. Out of date and worn because she'd bought it used. At least it was clean. The waves of her light brown hair were neatly tied back off her shoulders. Not exactly stylish, but she showed some evidence of effort.

Shaking her head, Ashley looked at the screen to set the machine to standard treadmill. She had thirty-five minutes left on her gym reservation and opted to use the extra five minutes to ramp her heart rate up another five beats per minute.

Plugged in with the headphones and stuck on the treadmill, she flipped through the usual bewildering variety of screen choices to max her time. There were exercise videos made by the gym trainers, and links to a network of paid exercise apps. There were the old-time TV reruns, podcasts, travel and learning experiences, a truly crappy 3D experience thing that needed those goggles, music, on-demand guided nature runs or a download from her home server. She started loading an old movie with a very young Dakota Fanning. It was an early film with her as a spoiled rich child. But the timing was wrong. You can't choose to watch a great old film; it just has to be playing somewhere, à la impromptu.

She closed the screen and had time to herself while she paced, and she started to think. Why not turn it all off and explore her own mental desktop. Be brave and check-in with how she was doing?

"Yeah, it's okay," she reassured herself aloud. "It's doable."

She paced for a minute or two. No thoughts came. Or maybe, it was like the colour white. All the thoughts came at once and caused a mental whiteout. She closed her eyes as the screen on the machine told her she was twenty per cent done. What was her first thought?

Panic.

No. That was stupid. Try again.

Happy.

Christ. Are you twelve? Surely she had a thought.

There's a message waiting from my mother. Oh geez, not that.

Then she caved and pressed the *Yolo* button on the treadmill. She ID'd herself with her fingerprint and watched the comforting yellow banner appear. She heard the musical sting and felt a jolt of relaxation.

The app was her guilty pleasure. She was one of the millions worldwide that paid monthly to be part of *Yolo-Hooray* community. *Yolo* was part emotional support and a good measure of entertainment. The reality content from the forums or discussion threads with 'Yolo agents' was popular with her friends and coworkers. It frequently was a source of gossip.

Even though she rationalized that she didn't use it that much, Ashley hid the growing time on the app from the adults in her life, even her husband. It wasn't so much that using *Yolo* revealed that you were looking for help. Lots of people, at some point in their life, reach out for help. In fact, the government had a well-resourced app that was free.

Still, Ashley worried about other people's judgments, wincing if someone said, "well, step away from *Yolo*," when she complained about not having enough time, or "you pay for that?" when she could get services for free.

"Yolo" defenders would admit that it wasn't as productive as the dry government services, but it made your problems fun. The government service was so slow, asking for personal information to confirm your identity, and then administering some standard tests, like your pulse and blood sugar with your screen. With *Yolo,* it was easy to hop on and tell the world your problems. That's what she liked about it. She felt like she had an instant community.

She flipped through the dashboard at the top of the page. "Make your life predictable," was splashed across the top. Like just about every app, there was a cornucopia of opportunities to invest your time. She could find a licensed counsellor, which was the original reason for signing up for the app. She'd found her counsellor there, and it was convenient to talk to someone on her schedule. That was years ago when the kids were born. Since then, the app had sprouted many new services.

There were the support forums and daily town halls, where people advocated for their issues. Government and businesses frequently had their people monitor the comments and provide their perspectives. Paid *Yolo* counsellors also weighed in, and it was obvious they were often located outside Canada; they missed the context and offered hilarious answers to problems.

People had a lot of gripes, from overwork to plain old discrimination or fairness issues with the government. You could whittle away the time reading what was posted. It was fascinating how people got themselves worked up about issues. The same characters advocating their points of view in ways that were disproportionately aggressive at times. The world online had a way of compounding anger. This anger got attention in all the news streams. People had their few minutes of celebrity and parlayed it into other public roles.

There were also the notice boards and discussion threads of more official-type information. Postings of the latest research on raising good kids or dealing with the pressure of living with your parents. That kind of stuff. Nothing very helpful. You'd soon find the same information anywhere.

There was a menu for people in crisis. This had been there since the app launched, but it now offered a finer breakdown of problems based on their "advanced algorithm." The selection changed over time with the seasons or as new problems surfaced. You could pick your problem from a top twenty list and get right to the peer support worker. If you were in serious trouble, they could send an ambulance. Ashley went through the list, feeling grateful that she was able to feed and clothe her family, happy that she benefited from feeling equal in her key relationship and was not limited from performing daily tasks because of social stigma.

Finally, she found the menu she wanted, "improving my mental health skills." The tagline was "get the tools, know-how and inspiration to be your best self."

Ashley clicked on the button marked "Pathway to Happiness" and looked over the sub-menus. She'd been following the cognitive behaviour course with the optimistic view that it might improve her happiness skills. She'd been trying to find a way to improve her internal chatter. Maybe stop jumping to the negative all the time. The "establishing positive dialogue" module had led her through exercises to eliminate phrases like "always fall behind" or "never find the time." *Yolo-Hooray* had identified fifty phrases for her that signalled negative thinking.

Exercise one asked her to reframe something she had told the program when she first did her intake interview. The phrase was "My days are always filled with a lot of grind. I don't know if I have the strength to cope. I wish I didn't have to solve everyone's problems."

Ashley had been surprised when she first read what she'd said. It held up well and was refreshingly candid. Still, it was a bit negative.

Staring at the screen for a minute, she pressed the dictate key and quietly told the screen "My days are very full and I am grateful I am resilient and can cope. I am happy that I have people I love around me and I can help them solve some of their problems." She clicked the assess button and *Yolo* kicked back its thoughts. "Good work, you successfully avoided negative language. Take some time to reflect on how you feel."

This was where she'd got stuck last time. How she felt was, well, manipulated. How could reframing her reality with "positive" language make it measurably better? The idea was to continue to recognize and reframe negative thoughts. Keep doing this, the argument goes, and you'll feel happier.

It felt more like her thoughts were being autocorrected. And the AI had neutralized the meaning. Her meaning.

She walked faster and checked her pulse rate. She was well into 115 beats per minute. A good five minutes like that before she amped up the rate again.

She closed her eyes and started to meditate some phrases of gratitude. *Yolo* had assured her that this would help her be more positive. She was trying to think of a third thing to be grateful for when another sort of thing came to mind.

It was an angry thing. A thought about what she really thought about her mother's message.

Here Ashley was, doing the right thing for everyone. Investing everything she had making a decent life for her family. Running on a treadmill. Worrying about the future. Avoiding mirrors to avoid observing the drained woman staring back.

And there was Rachel, her mother, having a good time in Arizona. In the summer heat. Parading near what looked like a fountain. What was she doing there? She probably snuck over the border and flew there. How many laws was she breaking this time?

She checked her pulse again. It was upwards of 132 and the machine told her it was in the extreme zone. She was eighty-five per cent done, sweating and looking forward to her shower. She looked over to the machine with the shapely young woman. She had been churning away, but now she was chatting with a well-cut young man. They made a nice-looking couple. She watched them on the sly until the buzzer rang to say her time was up.

32

Three

Her ancient clock radio abruptly blared rapid-fire chatter about the weather.

This information screwed with the dream in Janey's head. She lounged on the carpet-covered rings of concrete that circled the firepit of the lobby of her apartment, warming herself and hanging with people she admired. She had the comic touch; people laughed. She rolled over on her abs, resting her head on her hands. A handsome guy, that she couldn't place, admired the line of her ample rack. "They're all mine," she told him with a soft sparkle. Janey lingered in her dream, her head simmering while the radio chatter grew inescapable. Then she rolled over, took a breath, and opened her eyes. With grudging acceptance, another day was underway.

Now the radio played an old heartbreak song that always made her mom sing. Her mother's tuneless humming still made her wince. She deliberated changing the channel, but her arms weren't awake yet.

She tried to remember anything about the day ahead. Her hand reached out to pull back the sheets. It had been a hot night and she languished in the rush of cooler morning air. She turned in her bed and gave herself another minute. There was nothing like those first few minutes of wakefulness. A chance to luxuriate in bed as if time was your own. It was heaven.

When she finally pushed herself out into the world, it was startlingly humid. She kicked into her usual scramble to get to the shower and get her clothes on. Her wardrobe was unimpressive, the technical garments based on the widely-accepted principles of sustainable fashion. You found this puritanical glossary printed in white washable ink on anything new: breathable for optimized heating and cooling, built to last years, emissions zero, treated with a bio enzyme to reduce the need to wash, ethically and locally sourced, recycled, compostable, standardized sizing.

She crushed herself into one of the summer season shirts. The one thing that was missing was enough space for her boobs. "Less fashion meant more real choice" it said on the label. "What a pile of crap," thought Janey, not for the first time, as she argued with a safety pin.

Even the environmentally-friendly clothing designers couldn't mask the well-proportioned curves of her twenty-eight-year-old body and the allure of her chestnut hair.

She stumbled to the kitchen of her apartment and downloaded her daily review onto her kitchen screen, glancing at it as she ate her oatmeal. It was a genetically modified version, a true super food. It tasted OK but it was always a little too creamy.

She read through some frightening information about a new commission that was going to look at makeup packaging. She sighed, just when you think you're safe, there's more change. An actress she rather liked was getting divorced. The side view of the news stream already showed that her friends were chattering about it online.

And there was an interesting story about what might happen again in September. Some northern American politicians were talking again about joining Canada. The story went that heating costs were rising again and people couldn't make ends meet, so the Canadian government-run programs like health, home conversion, and heating were looking like more and more of a bargain.

It was easy to be jealous of the States. The American government didn't lecture you about sacrificing for the future. You could still wander down the street, weaving in and out of interesting "boutiques." It was fun to shop. They had every imaginable thing there. She looked down and checked. She was wearing her fav bra that she'd smuggled in from the States. It had pink lace and convertible straps. Impossible to get here. What you could get here was often made of hemp and sometimes a small lump of fibre would get into the weave at an inconvenient spot.

She loved to visit Stateside and could see what her parents meant when they talked about their childhood. But everything considered, she couldn't imagine living there. It was getting difficult to find a spot where the flooding, air quality, forest fires or general poverty didn't bum you out. It was chaotic, and life seemed to be one big squander.

She assembled what she needed for the day and then took a minute to organize the bright yellow cushions on the couch. She loved this room. Some people thought the massive pine boards made these new frame buildings feel grimly functional and spacious. To her, it needed some added personality to get away from the sterile, institutional look. She stepped back to savour how their fuzzy texture brought together the *Hygge* feeling. They worked well with the linen couch and the photos she'd arranged on the opposite wall. It balanced out the bare wood that dominated throughout, and gave her living space a wonderfully snug feeling.

As she walked towards the transit station, she went over again the day in her head. She was going to exercise at lunch. She smiled to think of the good it would do her. Tonight she was going to stay behind and have drinks at her favourite bar with some friends from work.

At some point today she would have to call her mom, Jennifer, in Toronto and let her know she could help with software installation on this week's Friday home day. Mom was getting a powerful smart satellite system with the home theatre and a macabre video and audio stream selection. All the screens would be replaced with new thin film ones. The speakers were hidden throughout the house. The signal could be broadcast to any combination of screens. It would function all over mom's house and any vehicle she was in, no matter where she was in the world, as long as you gave it an IP screen address and the account code. Janey wondered pragmatically if the system ran on many devices at a time. She wanted to scam some of her mom's signal.

Janey's trip downtown was busy, but she only had to stand part of the way. She got to the coffee shop on time and filled her mug with her favourite brew.

The office seemed pretty chill. She was still getting her coat off when Fioria, her colleague, told Janey about how her first date went with that guy she met a month ago. From the cheery update, it looked like it was going to be a while until they did the real-life thing, but she completely trusted the guy. The women chatted quickly about when the couple was going to do the physical meet up. These were always awkward, no matter how you did them.

Her stuff put away in her cube, she turned her thoughts to her workday. She had what was called a starter job thanks to a business degree in post-consumerism. When she was applying for a job, she looked for something with a career track. She had seen the difference in lifestyles that a decent, stable job could make and had planned sensibly. Now she spent seven hours a day in one of the cubes on the twentieth floor of this downtown office tower.

Her organization worked in plastics. The Plastics Council of Canada was set up as a self-regulating agency, a preemptive move to make sure the government didn't step in.

The history of plastics is something Janey learned about in school.

Years ago, you could find plastic in everything. It cluttered up the oceans and scientists found micro particles in samples of our wastewater. Gross.

Then in 2025, Canadians finally elected a good-sized number of Green Party candidates to federal Parliament. The Greens arrived with their vague policies to save the planet by reducing consumption, and people started talking about what it meant to live in the post-consumer era. What did it mean to be a good consumer? Consuming less? Consuming the right stuff? A lot of people wondered about plastic.

The discussion evolved quickly. Soon the argument went that we weren't consumers at all. We were citizens and contributors to society. We had the right to enjoy its benefits, as long as we assumed its obligations. That made a lot of sense, but then the tone of the conversation became offensive.

Many advocates talked loudly about their own narrow interpretation of an environmentally pure citizen. Splinter minorities dominated the media. They talked about a lot of crack-brained ideas, trying to hold everyone up to their standards. These were some dark days according to Janey's grandmother.

There were 'cerebral' outputs like the member of Parliament who argued we should make cats illegal because they killed too many birds, and furthermore cat memes stereotyped women as cat ladies. Or the 'Keep it Dirty' crowd who refused to wash their clothes because of the fibre that washing machines put back in the watershed. Nobody said much publicly against these stupid digressions, preferring to grumble in private. The conversation about what to do about the environment languished.

36

It wasn't until the more conservative thinkers realized that their personal assets were at stake that the ideas of the post-consumer era took shape. Several widely known political figures shocked everybody by saying that it was time to put the environment as priority number one. They argued that we didn't need a new ideology or a new society. Actually, what we had was pretty good. The goal, they argued, was to try and keep things the way they were, while achieving the goals of carbon neutrality. They called for a realistic national plan with targets. Let's assemble the best science they suggested and reach a consensus on the areas for focused action. We should keep the goals clean and avoid conflating people's ideology with needed environmental action. We needed to review the goals every month, by collecting and publishing data. We needed private sector action and investment. Advocacy and investors needed to stop punishing industries for their past, if they were genuinely part of the solution. And besides, we needed their money.

These ideas were met with a great deal of public acceptance, because it sounded like they might be hard work, but at least we didn't need to turn ourselves into cat-hating clones that refused to wash. They had traction because it was heartening to think that if we worked together to deal with our problems, we might have a chance to be some semblance of ourselves.

The problem for the Greens back then was the politics. Their own members were a remarkable source of some the looniest ideas. The anti-cat proposal, for example. But the timing turned out to be good for them, at least with the benefit of history. It was the year when floods and weather-related catastrophes struck every province, except P.E.I., which instead suffered a terrible blight to its potato crop in the fields near Summerside.

That year was full of environmental panic when people wanted change desperately. They started to protest and they demanded some of those interesting ideas about having a plan. In about a year the Greens had cleverly rebranded the conservative ideas, all largely intact. Canada was moving into the post-consumer age. The Green Party had brutally purged the craziest of their membership and those that were left started to see the political benefits of changing their plans. All that was left to do was the environmental change itself.

The Green Party made more headway in the subsequent election, reaching minority status. They launched reviews of acceptable consumerism, which quickly pointed to plastic as one of the most detrimental consumer products. The facts were hard to dispute. The government tests of waste and recycling systems from many countries showed that plastic made up a third of the worst kind of "indestructible waste." And then there were the assessments of natural resource draws to make plastic. Any material that was made of food or non-renewable resources did not fare well. Plastics were made of hydrocarbons, corn, and soy, so that put them on trial by the public.

The industry did its best to respond. But all established economies, even to an extent the United States, had been forced to act. Country after country introduced legislation to eliminate or restrict all plastic.

This big idea was one of the leading stories of the post-consumer, PC era for everybody – whether industry, workers, or real people. Canadians had legislated that plastic only be allowed if the plastic article lasted 10 years or more. No plastic could ever be thrown in the waste. One day that might change when a truly bio-degradable, natural source plastic was invented that actually worked. We weren't there yet. Everybody knew that the person who did that would be the next MiMi Aung or Jensen Huang.

The fact that Canada was a relatively early adopter of the U.N. agreement that banned or limited many activities considered harmful, like the production of most plastic, was an economic advantage to getting over the shock. The country went into the 2030's fully committed to the International Protocol for Post Consumerism -- Industrial Growth and Responsible Resource Management (called the International PC agreement by most).

As a hard-hit industry, companies that supplied the plastic of old crashed at first. But people still needed plastic. Facing the one-two punch of travel restrictions for trade and that more manufacturing needed to be repatriated to Canada, the industry soon rebuilt. Prices for plastic soared as companies increased quality to meet government standards. There turned out to be a net employment gain. Stocks soared for companies that were ready for the switch. Companies that were ready with their durability guarantees and recycling programs prospered.

The change was a killer for everyday people who had no idea how much they depended on the plastic of old. Toothpaste tubes, fast food containers, band aids, disposable pens, and grocery store packaging. It was all phased out quickly.

News stories abounded of people hoarding goods such as plastic wrap for kids' lunches before it went out of stock. Suddenly Tupperware was fashionable. Simple paper packaging replaced the frustrating packaging of old that used to cut you when you opened it. Old people cried on the nightly news because they were overrun by their own plastic trash. Some people tried to hide plastics in their trash or deep in their compost, but they were found out. Either by zealous officials or even more zealous neighbours.

People learned to wash and carry what they needed for their daily life. They brought containers to grocery stores. New businesses flourished that delivered goods in bulk and retrieved the packaging afterward. "Just like the old milkman," she could hear her grandmother say. Wood and paper replaced daily disposable items. But they weren't popular. Wood spoons would give you slivers on your tongue. Paper straws would disintegrate. "There was a reason we used plastic," her mother would tell people.

It was easy enough for a single person with a decent job. Family life, however, was a much bigger headache. This explained the trend to a whole industry of plastic and metal "daily life helpers" and of course the Friday home day.

Janey spun about once on her chair, looking outside to distract herself. Her building was equipped with environmental controls that tracked her body temperature and the amount of sun coming through the film on the windows. She didn't agree with the temperature that the sensors had selected for her, and she flipped through the control panel at her work station to adjust it.

For a starter green job, she was pretty proud of what she did. It surprised her sometimes she had the authority she had; she got it without any real knowledge of plastic. She'd been honest about her economics degree and her experience with creating sustainable product cycles. She went heavy on her personal environmental commitments, and that sealed the deal.

People who had an idea about a plastic product came to her office for her rubber stamp. She spent the day reviewing items and inputting the info on their projected uses, composition, and shelf life.

Her decisions were based on the predicative tools in her software. If the system rejected something, then it would not be sold or produced in Canada. She was the only human gatekeeper in the process and her position led to the occasional bribe or threat. Thus, she found her place as a low-level plastics goddess at the Plastics Council of Canada.

She could draw a straight line between herself and her impact on people's everyday lives. It made her a bit squeamish. The software was pretty good, but nothing was fail-proof. The Plastics Council kept confidently posting information about how the system was working for Canadians. She believed what they said, although sometimes didn't understand how it all worked. It was just a little shade over what was otherwise a very promising career.

Four

Janey strolled across the field, feeling the steam of the day condense on her skin. The park was crowded with picnic paraphernalia, as it always was on Conservation Day. Even with the crush of people, her family should be easy to find. They'd be camped out in their usual spot, the familiar Asher/Bernal banner painted on an old sheet and strung between the same two trees. At least there'd be food. This family didn't function without food.

She finally saw her grandmother, the curls of her white hair bouncing freely in the air, sitting alone at the end of a long row of tables, staring off knowingly in the distance. She had one leg casually folded over another, showing off a surprisingly large, white walking shoe for her thin frame. She leaned against the tables that had been commandeered earlier by her aunt and uncle and arranged to benefit from the shade of a nearby tree. "Hi Nans," Janey called as she got within earshot.

"Oh, wonderful, you're here! I was just thinking about sending you a message."

"Not to worry Nans, I wouldn't miss this." Janey smiled at Kara and then sorted out the picnic blanket and box of carrot chips and bean dip that she'd brought.

"You're looking good. That chestnut colour suits you. Makes you taller, but then you're already lovely and slender."

"Thanks, Nans." Janey looked down at her outfit in confusion. She was in plain shorts and a pink t-shirt. Then she remembered that Nans hadn't seen the new hair. She fingered the long, silky strands, pleased with her grandmother's approval.

"It's really hot today. I could use something cold." Janey followed her grandmother's nod and walked over to the base of a tree. Then she rooted down, past the ice, to the cooler's bottom. She fished out the coldest container she could find and pulled it up, as if she snagged the prize.

"Why do you always hide the good stuff," Janey chided Kara, as she knocked the ice from her arm.

"You never know if a park ranger will want to inspect your cooler."

"Nans, nobody cares. And the park rangers, if they exist, all use drones."

"Perhaps you're right. And anyway, without the labels it all looks like apple juice. I have to be careful not to give the wine to the kids."

Janey snapped open the plastic jar. Drips from the melted ice felt good as it ran down her arm. Janey squeezed it out of force of habit. "Polycarbonate. Probably fifteen-year durability rating," she guessed. Then she looked at the bottom of the jar and expertly read the plastic symbol.

"Where is everyone, Nans?"

"They're over at the awards ceremony. I waited back here for you and Tanya."

Janey straddled the bench across from Kara and took another sip of the Chardonnay, obviously one of the low alcohol wines that Nans was constantly promoting. She hoped her cousin would get here soon. It was like her to show up late, just in time to eat.

The two women surveyed the horizon and, from their vantage point, saw an expanse of green in every direction. Trees at all stages of growth spotted the park. On the west side, about 200 feet away, sat a conservation kiosk, a post-consumer construct of recycled cement and wood beams. It incongruously flashed digital images on the regularly-spaced pillars that ran around the outside. A solitary ice cream vendor sat on his bicycle, stocked for a very busy day. Throughout the park, benches were spotted with people, but most of the crowd was at the ceremony. The stage was hidden behind a hill in the distance. The din from the stage blared scrambled words. The loudness reverberated, obscuring their meaning, while periodic cheers signalled that the winners were accepting their prizes.

"The kids were excited?"

"Of course! They put on their uniforms first thing this morning. Then they ran around the house teasing each other about what prize they were going to get."

"How old are they now? I mean Aunt Ashley and Uncle Jhonian's kids."

"Little Rachel is four and Marcos is six now."

"I can't wait to see them, with their uniforms and their prizes around their necks. It reminds me of when I was a kid."

"I was thinking about you and Tanya this morning, while I listened to them tear around the house. Twenty years ago or so, that was you." Kara turned to look at Janey with pleasure. "You used to work so hard on your conservation prizes. Remember when you won the Suzuki prize? I was truly proud of you that day."

"You're making me feel old, Nans. It wasn't that long ago. Yeah, I remember. Actually, I was twelve, and I worked for months on reclaiming that empty lot, taking up the concrete and planting grass. My hands were raw."

"Stubborn girl. You wouldn't let us help."

"One of the Conservation Cadet leaders said I couldn't win if I got the adults to help. I took it so seriously. You should have told me that every kid got a prize."

"Not every child gets a Suzuki prize dear. That was important for your future. I have a picture of you from that day on my wall."

"Yeah, well...." Janey scanned her fingers and finally found the mark. "That, here," Janey held out her finger to her grandmother. "It's the scar from when I lifted all those pieces of asphalt and threw them in the wheelbarrow. There was so much blood. That's my Suzuki prize!"

Kara took the young woman's hand in hers and turned it over delicately. "I see it, dear. I remember it hurt. But think of it as the mark of experience."

The din in the distance changed its tenor. There was a loud round of applause and a sudden cheer, and then the reverberation of the forced sound stopped.

"Janey, I'm going to enjoy the peace and quiet for another minute, then I'll get started setting out the food."

"Let me know when you're ready." Janey looked down at her wrist to see the message from her cousin. "Tanya's in the parking lot. She needs help bringing in some chairs. I'll be right back."

As Janey strode away towards the parking lot, Kara basked in the temporary stillness. She shut her eyes to hear the whisper of the leaves in the breeze. When she opened her eyes, she saw the first of the wave of humanity coming over the hill. Kids in their uniforms ran ahead. The adults followed, laughing and obscuring their faces while showing off images on their screens. Everyone intent on reclaiming their picnic spots to celebrate and relax. The laughter and screams grew closer. It was finally time to unpack all those goodies that Kara and the family had lovingly assembled earlier. Grandma time was on.

Out in the parking lot, Janey struggled to find her cousin. Everyone brought a vehicle today. The lot was full and she had to walk further and further. It was worth it. The party never got going until Tanya arrived. They were grown up now, but as kids they'd played a lot together. Their moms were very close back then, and Tanya and Janey often ended up in the basement with a stack of toys or something on a screen. Even then, the three years between were balanced out by their personalities. Janey was reserved, more apt to wait and see. Tanya was curious, more apt to stray.

The years passed and things changed. Tanya's mother, Ally, moved up in the government and was always so busy that nobody saw her for long. Janey's mom, Jennifer, was now divorced and remarried. A few years ago she'd moved to Toronto to be with her new family. But the cousins, now in their twenties, stayed good friends. Janey played the straight part of the two-women team. Tanya adapted well to her part as diva.

Janey had almost walked out of the park when she finally stumbled on her cousin. "Hey girl!"

Tanya waved back through the miniature front window and unfolded herself from the front seat of the "dreamcycle." Not the expensive vehicle's official name. Rather an apt nickname because people joked it was so small that it dreamed of being a car when it grew up.

Janey's younger cousin stretched herself to her full height, and a bright halo of afternoon sun framed her face. Tanya's makeup was sparingly natural for her, although she was predictably wearing her homemade, artistically ripped and embroidered clothing that made fun of the government standards. Today her cousin's lips looked a little fuller. Tanya had natural beauty, but that beauty tended to evolve with time. The arch of brow would get a little sharper. Or the jawline would jut more from the neck. Her wavey hair was a dramatic new colour. Once Janey had asked about the changes and got an offended deflection in response. So, she didn't ask anymore and Tanya never offered.

"So damn happy you've arrived. And you're early!"

"You mean we aren't ready to eat?" Tanya's deep, slow voice had the resonance of a classic Hollywood star.

"Food's not even on the table!"

Janey moved in closer to help. "These are nice. Heavy, too." The women bent over to unpuzzle two rolled-up cylinders from the tiny back seat. There was a final heave, and the chairs stood on their circular sides.

"They're decent, right? You push a button and they go up by themselves. And they have built-in AC."

"Nice," Janey nodded, admiring them and wondering which man had loaned the car and expensive kit to her cousin. "But...we're a good ten-minute walk in. And it's just skinny us. How're we going to manage both?"

Tanya crawled into the front of the car and pulled out a clear bottle of wine and a bag of cookies. "Simple," she declared as she locked up the vehicle. "Just push a button and the motor moves them for you."

"No shit." Janey took the handle and pressed the green button. The contraptions made a refined whir, and then gradually started to turn its wheels and move forward. "And that's why life is easier with money!"

"You don't have to hold the handle. There's a sensor. The things will follow you."

"Fuck, that's creepy. Practical, but creepy."

Tanya laughed. "Apparently you can dump your stuff on top of it and it will roll along!"

Janey neatly arranged their stuff on top of one and several metal clips lifted from the top to secure it. "Ha! Decent."

Tanya looked over. "Reminds me of a joke my father used to tell me."

"Oh great. This will be good."

"Yup! What's the ideal girlfriend? A girl that's waist height with a flat head you can put a drink on."

"Oh, for fuck's sake." Janey put a hand up to her cousins back, groaning in sympathy.

They made their way over to the lawn. Janey watched as the contraptions, with the bag of cookies and wine bottle safely stowed, politely rolled behind her cousin. She wondered if it was by accident, or by design, that they looked so servile.

Tanya stopped at the edge of the grass for a moment to survey the scene, getting an eyeful of the happy, colourful crowd. By now the ocean of ceremony goers had made their way back to their picnic sites. Another Conservation Day, this last weekend of the summer celebration of harmony with our environment, was underway. Camp stoves were lit, and steam started to waft off the pots of water to cook the corn, vegetables, and boil all manner of sausages. People lifted over-burdened coolers of food and drink onto their tables, and many had already set out the salads, cooked and cured meats, breads, and condiments that were the staples of the perfect outdoor feast.

46

"Scenes like these make me feel so like a pointless speck of sand."

Janey smiled at her cousin. The melancholy had already arrived. "It takes a whole lot of sand to make a beautiful beach.'

"You're a classic glass-half-full kinda girl," Tanya observed, still staring at the crowd. "I assume we're in the same place as always," Tanya asked. "Now that's our fun-loving family for you."

"You got it." Janey tried to laugh off her cousin's mood. "I don't know why you expect our family to change."

Tanya and Janey strolled onwards, conscious that they had a few precious minutes to catch up in private. "So," Janey began. "I've got to tell you this story about this asshole now before we see the family. He was a real fucking creep."

The two women talked intently as they wandered over to their picnic site, ignoring stares from fellow picnickers too fascinated by the mobile chairs to look politely in another direction. Fortunately, the parents in the crowd couldn't hear the story now underway.

"It was bizarre. The guy was a freak. Online he seemed okay. We got to the bar, and that was alright. We sat down, and five minutes in, I got this horrible vibe from him. I don't know what it was. He kept grinning at me like I was some sort of stupid sure thing. He might as well just said to me upfront. 'Stop talking bitch, I just want sex.' I smiled back at the guy, but in my head I was thinking, 'let me out!' I was there maybe ten minutes, barely talked to the guy, picked up my stuff and told him I was going to the bathroom. I left and went home. Never heard from the guy again."

Tanya walked along silently for a minute. Then she leaned into Janey empathetically. "Sounds like you had a lovely evening. He clearly figured the two of you'd leave after the first drink and have sex."

"That's the impression I got. But what did I do to make him think that? The guy seemed interesting online."

"He was probably stringing you along, acting interesting. Guys just don't like the online dance. Not saying this guy was prince, but I find by the time they get to meet you in the flesh, that's all they want.

The flesh. If you say yes to a real-life meet, you're saying you'll do them. That's what guys think."

"That's so fucking sad."

"Oh, oh, what is even stupider is that once you do fuck 'em, they want the fantasy. It starts off normal, but pretty quick it gets rancid. I mean, it's sex, and that's usually a great thing, but lately I feel like I'm in the way somehow. They're busy acting out some fantasy with me there. Half the time I just can't wait for the guy to get dressed and get the fuck out."

Tanya paused. "Hang on for a sec."

She took a step back and reached for her wine bottle. It opened easily and that made Janey think that her cousin had taken a few hits in the car. Tanya took a significant swallow from clear glass and extended the bottle to Janey. "Do you want some?"

"It's alright. Got a bottle opened at the camp site."

Tanya let out a deep chuckle. "Probably that shit that Kara thinks is so wonderful?"

"You got it! It's got no buzz."

From behind them came a gentle 'ding.' "What's that," exclaimed Tanya, looking at the chairs.

They had come up to a large sign, stuck in the middle of the park, a metre in front of them. "The chairs must have some safety sensor."

The women stopped to check the sign, and then rolled their eyes when they read it was a chart outlining the "Alternatives to Plastic."

"Did you do that," Tanya mockingly asked her cousin.

"No! I'm not responsible for everything to do with plastic!"

They sidestepped the sign and the chairs followed a discreet distance behind. They laughed. "I feel like we're being stalked!"

After a few minutes more they saw a familiar group of children running circles around a row of tables.

Kara saw them first, and the two women returned her wave. Their grandmother went back to pointing orders to the others, like the family grand marshal that she was.

Another stellar family do was getting underway, a tribute to their grandmother's organizing power, who would tell them all, repeatedly, how delighted she was that her family was together.

Their Aunt Ashley and Uncle Jhonian were lighting up the stove, giggling about something as they worked. He came up behind her he pushed her wavy hair aside and kissed her on the back of her neck. Ashley beamed as she turned to her husband.

"God, those two are gag-bait," asserted Tanya. "I don't think I ever will get married."

"I dunno," replied her cousin. "They kinda give me hope." It was true. Over the years, Janey had observed how hard they worked to make a good life with their kids. But they found a way to make their life together fun. Despite the tough times, those two were alright.

As they arrived, Jhonian came over to admire the new hardware.

"Are those automatic chairs?"

"Could be," shrugged Tanya. "A friend let me borrow them. Actually, he loaned me his dreamcycle, and the chairs were in the back seat."

Jhonian looked the technology over with appreciation for the fine details. "Hey kids, look at these!"

"Go ahead," Tanya waved her invitation. And with that Jhonian pressed the buttons to install the chairs. There were gasps and squeals of amazement from them, as well as from some of the nearby picnickers.

"It's like a real Transformer," Jhonian geeked out as he tried out one of the chairs.

"Now he'll want one," announced Ashley, who was dumping a pile of corn into a pot.

"No, I want two," he called back to her. And with that, he climbed out of the chair to help her finish unloading the food.

"Hey everyone! Don't eat without me!" The voice came from the west side of the park, and everyone looked up at once to see Jennifer and her new husband arrive.

"Mom! When did you get in from Toronto?" Janey rushed over and helped Jennifer with the ample supply of food she was hauling.

"I wasn't sure we'd make it. We did the trip into Ottawa yesterday." Janey knew her mother hated the drive and what it did to their travel permits. But it was special to have her here. It made her Nans happy.

Next, the kids peeled off the transforming chairs to run to greet a pair of children making their way to the campsite. The parents came up behind, bearing two large Tupperware containers.

"Just put it over there beside the rolls," directed Kara over the din of the children racing through and around the adults. "Unless it needs to stay cool?"

"Who's that," Tanya whispered in her cousin's ear.

"I think they're the Lopez family. Jhonian knows them." As if to offer his confirmation, the presumed father of the Lopez family went over with Jhonian to admire the transformer chairs.

Janey drifted off to sit with her mom. Tanya found a perch on top of the shaded bench that marked the outer ring of the Asher/Bernal picnic territory. She took a few more pulls of the wine bottle as she watched the ritual of her family unfold. Most everybody was gleefully paired with someone else, as they toiled away at their own enormous pile of food in preparation for the feast. Jhonian and Ashley were preoccupied with the corn and sausage. Kara smiled along with her son-in-law, Janey's step-dad, tearing bread rolls apart. The Lopez's were organizing chicken. Janey and her mother Jennifer arranged fruit on platters in colourful lines to turn each platter into a cartoon character. Tanya sat drinking her wine, alone, happy that her own mother had not yet appeared. Content to keep away from the chaos as the rest of the children ran around in noisy circles far enough away from her.

50

Janey looked up to catch her cousin's gaze. Tanya sent a lazy wave of admiration back in their direction. Jennifer waved back in her heartfelt and welcoming way. Aunt Jennifer explained a lot about her adorable cousin. Janey was fun to have around. She was straight, but she didn't judge so much when people weren't as perfect as her. Janey's destiny was up the predictable steps on the ladder of life. If it was important to Janey, there were surely thousands of young people who wanted the same. Good for Janey. Basic suited her.

A beat shook the ground at the campsite. Papa Lopez had successfully installed the speakers on the tree, and people greeted the music with nodding heads and bars of humming.

By now the table was groaning with the weight of the holiday celebration. The air was groaning with the overflow of picnic clichés.

"I brought Dijon mustard."

"Jhonian, can you check if the sausage is ready?

"I always forget the sharp knives."

"It's okay, I brought one."

"Let's try to cover up the food from the flies."

"Oh, there's too much food."

"Yeah, well that's our family for you!"

"Okay everybody, dig in!"

People lined up around the table, holding the metal plates in their hands as if about to receive their last meals. Children were dutifully served first.

Then the music softened and there was silence as people finally ate.

"Who made this bean and quinoa thing. It's delicious!"

"Oh, come on people! Eat some more! I don't want to take it home."

There was a magic moment of hush when all over the park people were sitting down and eating. "It's so quiet," Jhonian confided to his wife from their spot on the long picnic bench. Ashley grinned back, leaning into him a little and squishing up her tanned nose to push her sunglasses up, nodding in Kara's direction. "Your mother is in her element."

"She lives for Conservation Day. Or maybe she's been at the booze since we were at the ceremony."

"Maybe it's the booze. But I think she's just happy we're all together. She gets stupid giddy at this family stuff. It could just be that."

Jhonian looked over at his wife's plate. "Are you going to eat that bread?"

"No, you go ahead, I got it for you." She passed the piece casually to her husband.

He took it from her gently. She was intently studying something happening off past the family. Her brown hair was tied up the way he loved, so that it cascaded down to her neck. She'd got a bit of sun today. "Drunk or not, thanks for putting up with my giddy mother. A lot of this today was you."

Ashley untangled herself from the bench and took Jhonian's plate. "You can thank me later," she whispered. Then she turned to the rest of group. "Hey everybody, I think that's Ally over there. Anybody want some dessert? I've got my eyes on those brownies!"

There was a sudden wave of activity around the table as people did as they were bid and huddled around the desserts.

Tanya wandered out of the woodsy part of park and strolled back to her bench. Janey went over to her, offering a plateful of dessert. Tanya's eyes looked out-of-focus and she'd developed a sniffle. "Where'd you go?" Janey knew the answer already.

"Oh, don't rag on me," was the ready response.

"Fair enough." It was true that by now most of the adults were buzzed out on the alcohol and pot that had been clandestinely passed around all afternoon.

"Just saying, keep your wits about you."

"Why?" But Janey had already left to get something else to eat.

"Hello, you!" It was an unwelcome voice.

Tanya started as if she felt a gun at her back. Then she turned to see her mother Ally standing right behind her.

"Oh, hi," Tanya volunteered weakly. I didn't see you arrive."

"It's quite the crowd. I got here about five minutes ago."

Tanya glanced at her mother's outfit. "You've been at work," she observed sharply.

"Yes, and I'm going back again soon. Since the whole family is here, I thought I should put in an appearance."

"That will make Nans happy." Tanya looked coolly off in the distance, watching the kids run in circles with cookies in their hands.

"It's good to see you. You look good," Ally offered.

Tanya turned her head to pretend to study her mother's face. "Looks like you've had work done." She stared at her mother and winced a smile. "I'm thinking fillers around the mouth?"

Ally stood passively, not wanting to take the bait. "I left a few messages. We should plan a mother-daughter outing soon," She waited for a minute, to give her daughter time to reply. Then she sighed with resignation. "Okay, I'll go find Nans."

"Yeah, see ya," Tanya replied, walking away as she spoke, moving like a heat-seeking missile to her cousins' side.

"I need to pee," Tanya said to Janey with a raspy voice that barely hid her agitation.

"Oh, okay, I'll come with." And the two of them made their way to the kiosk in the centre of the park.

"How's your Mom," Tanya asked glumly.

"Okay, I think. She seems happy in Toronto. I was down to see her a couple of months ago. It's my Dad I worry about." But Janey knew what her cousin wanted.

"Your Dad didn't show again Tanya." And truth was that most people in the family were happy he stayed away. Tanya didn't answer so she ventured in another direction.

"And your Mom said she isn't staying long," observed Janey.

"Dah," Tanya replied cynically. "She's still the same."

"How so?"

"She sure the shit doesn't care about me."

"Her job is pretty busy."

"Yup. I wish I got paid every time I heard that. I'm supposed to admire her because she's so *so* very busy."

It wasn't the first time Tanya was angry about her mother. Ally was a bit of a mystery. She arrived empty-handed to eat. And today, although it was Sunday, she had to leave early to get back to work. A peaceful, lazy holiday, with people drifting away to play games or to catch up and to do what people usually do at a blissful picnic, but Tanya's mother was going back to work.

"I guess your Mom is doing what everyone expects of a senior civil servant, serving and sacrificing." Even, Janey didn't add, if that sacrifice was her own family.

Tanya sighed, closing her eyes in the sun while her cousin walked into the bathroom. She looked over to their picnic site and felt calmer with a decent distance between them. The people looked small enough she could handle them. Her mother always got her wound-up, but she knew what she needed to push the bitterness away. Her head would settle just as fast. Truth was, this family shit wasn't worth the excitement. She just had to wait. By this evening thoughts about this afternoon would be good and fuzzy.

Five

Ally was elegantly poised on the leather couch in her office, scrolling through the agenda for today's department heads meeting. There were three things on the docket today. The first two were mind-numbingly dull. The pending boredom made her long for more of the wavy feeling of beach life. For a brief second, she considered picking up her suit jacket and running for the exit. But that was just a mental game she played. Instead, she stood up and handed the screen to one of her assistants. She picked up her vintage grey wool jacket and slid her arms in place, checking the effect in the mirror at the far end of the room. Her nod was the cue that they were set. She opened the pair of mahogany doors that led to her large boardroom and felt the room come to attention. The voices around the large oval table hushed as she made her way to her chair at the head.

The deputy minister looked around the table nodding to the assembled group. "How is everyone today," Ally asked the room. "I hope well. We have a very full agenda. I will make a few remarks on what I hear about our department's priorities at the roundtable at the end. Let's get started."

Two of her senior people started with the departmental budget, with a half-hour presentation on projected shortfalls. They presented the usual tables with their minute details. It amazed her that her best people could whip their teams into such a lather about financial reports and business planning. As she always told them, when it came to money, there were no shortfalls. Her department looked after the all-important happiness statistics in the national positive outcome index. These were the monthly numbers that were reported out to convince Canadians that they were better off. Happier, environmentally responsible, connected.

Collecting the data was a financial sinkhole, a bureaucrats' wet dream of accountability, a continual "get more money free" card. She could call the people at the Treasury Board and watch the money rain.

When they introduced the new statistical framework decades ago, she was part of the team that had fought hard against using the term "happiness." But it had turned out to be a great thing. Making people happy was a mantra of government for decades to come. When Ally joined the service, she started with the Department of Canadian Heritage, then languishing in the bureaucratic backwaters. Her department was a dinosaur, ill-funded, toothless, and charged with the unwanted task of safeguarding Canadian culture.

But then, and lucky for Ally's career, the Green Party won a good number of seats in Parliament. Prompted by a series of true, unignorable economic and environmental disasters, Canadians had grown anxious for change. They went from asking a simple "weird weather, eh" to panicking about an onslaught of natural disasters.

Like a drought that dried up the St. Lawrence River at Gananoque to the point it became unnavigable for shipping. It dominated the media coverage for a whole summer and turned out to be the first in a series of inconvenient events.

The climate became real, erratic, and frightening. People grew fixed on reports from scientists who forecasted how the ice caps up north were disappearing. Coastal towns, even the big ones like Halifax, became anxious about the price tag for mitigations. Nobody wanted to move inland, but some people were frightened that they had to.

For several bad years the country became a map of hotspots. Droughts in some places, and violent storms with flooding in others. Ally had personal experience to draw from. Floods put the family cottage, source of so many beloved childhood memories, underwater.

Wildfires raged out West for longer and longer, creating continuing smoke advisories and eventually requiring people to wear masks outdoors. People joined social groups to figure out where they should buy homes to avoid the worst of it. Albertans started to violently protest why there was no plan to replace the cattle ranching and the oil production that clearly were becoming economically unviable.

And then the unimaginable happened. Basements in neighbourhoods across the country started flooding in unpredictable but regular intervals. Insurance companies started to refuse coverage to some. Housing prices in the suburbs crashed, and voters looked in panic as the value of their single most important asset disappeared.

The environment became a hostile force and quickly the old standby issues like jobs and health care were crowded out of the public's mind. As a result of furiously loud public protests, an election was called in 2027. And so began the creation of the Green Party's own political dynasty, introducing wholesale, cross-country change.

Things got off to a slow and muddled start, but the financial disasters piled up and soon the insurance industry was teetering. The Party finally got some of the best thinkers on the subject, and acting in terror, resolved to put substance into their Post-Consumer platform.

The first step was a development of some guiding principles. Ally cut her teeth writing up the discussion summaries for the first major project in the new era. She sat on the edge of her chair through all the group sessions, listening intently at Cabinet Committes while deputy ministers and other blow-hards outlined their differences of interest. After a messy process that took many months, the government finally published five little statements written to focus all the public policy to come.

One. *Pursue a cleaner Canada through a new economic equilibrium.* There was wide agreement that the country needed to adopt a new economic framework. Academics pointed out that the relentless pursuit of growth, expressed as a single number, created a relentless process of resource exploitation. New economic targets were expressed first in words, looking to create an abstract goal of happiness. The first two targets made a big impact: the replacement of carbon-based fuels and the meaningful reduction of methane-producing activity. Of course, the results ended up being expressed in numbers, but at least we started with more focus.

Two. *Pursue an innovative Canada through practical technological solutions.* Ally privately lobbied to find a better word than 'innovative.' It was already plastered everywhere, so it didn't mean much. But the word satisfied the traditionalists who worried about the small lobby of luddites who were anxious to reject progress. They need not worry. Once industry was armed with some standards on product life cycles and energy use, technological development ripped forward at a head spinning pace. The only curb to ambitions was the government's refusal to try to lead the world in some of the bigger geoengineering projects, like pumping gas into the stratosphere to reflect some of the sun's heat. The Prime Minister of the day worried publicly that these projects might lull people into free riding an easy way out. The government's resolve only softened when Russia and

Denmark agreed to work together on refreezing the Arctic ice cap. Canada eventually did get dragged into this international cooperation, if only to protect its sovereignty.

Three. *Pursue sound stewardship of our resources to avoid mortgaging on our future.* Lots of people were confused about what this meant, thinking that resources were natural ones like minerals and water. But it quickly became clear that this was about money. And keeping the middle-of-the-road voter happy with how the government was spending its cash. History will judge how irresponsibly inflated the burgeoning national debt got. But gambles on big "strategic investments" were made, and paid off. For example, the $10,000 grant to switch to alternative fuel vehicles. In five years many vehicles had switched. A lot of money came in too, through programs like the Carbon Credits and the Green Bonds.

Four. *Leverage our investments to solve the problems of the future.* Ally knew that this statement, on its face, never meant much. She also remembered the almost physical fights that occurred while this discussion was on the table. There were violent disagreements between specialists that dragged on for months. Engineers railed against the "hubris" of scientific claims that any of the measurable environmental change was caused by humans. Instead they argued they were normal cycles in the weather. She remembered one lengthy diatribe from a bellicose academic, who paced the room angrily in a dirty red t-shirt, pronouncing that that these shifts in weather were part of the planet's recovery from the ice age.

By this time, Ally had assumed a leadership role on this committee and handling their disagreement was her challenge. Her deputy at the time, smiled as she described the conflict. "You can handle it," he assured her. "Just make them think that they are all right. Afterall, there doesn't seem to be any real disagreement that we need to adapt."

And that's what this principle became about. The great compromise that any big climate actions would be a two-for-one. They'd aim to adapt Canadian life to changes in the climate while reducing human impacts causing climate change. It took Ally a week to convince everyone that there was a difference between the two. But she got it done. Everyone walked away happy.

Finally, there was number five. *Pursue better, more connected Canadian communities.* Nobody really cared what this principle was about. Even when it was written. Ally always felt that everybody was so excited to get going on the economy, new technology, finances and adaptation that the people stuff in this last element would take care of itself. There were initial thoughts about immigration, resolution of historical differences and social isolation; it didn't get far. However, it was published with the rest and Ally made up some text to give it meaning. A decade later it was dropped from Speeches from the Throne. Officially there were four principles now. But every public servant had to remember it, if only to get the answer complete on job interviews.

The principles cast, it was up to the subsequent Royal Commission on Sustainable Prosperity to table their report, recommending the replacement of the GDP and GNP with brand new measures that looked at a basket of scales, among which the old economic indicator of growth was only one. The national statistical agency put their mind to constructing such a measure, and Ally was one of the bureaucrats at the table.

The measures were comprised of sustainable agriculture, land use, biodiversity, food supply, water supply and purity, economic prosperity, employment, carbon calculations, waste renewal index, life expectancy, and health. Plus, a revolutionary measure of Canadians social connectedness, social awareness, and collective participation in society called "happiness."

Government departments and agencies were redirected to lead the foundering country toward this new reality. Many of her colleagues assumed the new mantra like religion.

It had been offensive at times. Objectives got crossed and confused with each other. The intent had been to reduce carbon levels to meet international commitments. In the end, the government had regulations to deal with a grab bag of environmental challenges. But some programs were more about allaying public fears, ginned up by the sorts of people who screamed the loudest and the monied fearmongers manipulating them. Some public servants grew wary of the conflation of goals with programs that often did more for people's careers and bank accounts.

Still, Canadians were proud of what they had achieved in three decades. They were the envy of many countries. When the world looked at the Americans down south, Canadians had to agree that the changes had been worth it.

Their neighbours to the south had resisted the evidence and decided to let the markets deal with the environment. Flooding had redrawn the maps around coastal states. There was scarcity and economic turmoil aplenty. True, if you were wealthy, you had one hell of a nice life. A life that you would never get in Canada. Still, for most Americans living in the States you had to deal with the large migrations of average people seeking an affordable life where they felt safe. It was why many poor Americans walked across the border to avoid literally freezing to death over the winter.

But even Stateside there were signs that change was coming. Polls showed that there was growing support for a third party that had a sensible environmental agenda. It was attractive to many. After all, in actual numbers, most Americans were quite poor.

All of this had meant significant career progress for Ally. Her department evolved into the fiercely important Department of Citizenship and Consumerism. And as the role and scope of the department expanded, Ally had been a central figure in the evolution. She'd been the head of the task force on the new model citizen. She'd been a key advisor to the government-wide effort to adapt to automation and technology. She was a current board member on the private-public partnership to reduce social isolation. In thirty years she had been everywhere. It was no surprise to government observers that she became the deputy minister or head of one of the most important government departments.

There was a break in the meeting as the question period about the budget wrapped up. Ally got up to get coffee, turning her back so no one would see her yawn. People took her movement as a sign to take a break with her. "We've got a busy agenda. Be back in five," she instructed the crowd. She needed them here since there was still a lot to cover. Ally got back to her chair and issued the staff in for the next presentation. Work got underway quickly.

The second item on the agenda was a brief discussion on the statistical happiness indicators themselves. There were several deficiencies that her officials judged in need of correction, but the Party was never going to accept her department's word on that. It was a sign of how the Green Party had evolved. As the party in power, they became the gatekeepers for the new religion and gospel of the happiness index. Any proposal for change was a threat to that power. In the interest of everyone's time, Ally shut down the pointless conversation, stating she would follow up.

Finally, they got to the fun stuff. Ally almost sighed aloud in approval when the communication team came in. She had, bar none, the best propaganda team around.

Today they would be looking at some of the new advertising proposals for the annual citizenship campaigns. Gone were the days when it was enough to vote and obey the law. Today's model citizen was a special blend of post-consumer advocate, high tech geek, and self-sustaining knowledge worker. A new generation grew up thinking that having the government tell you how you can make a difference kept our collective asses from a dark, painful doom. You pulled together and did your part to make tomorrow a better place. That, or faced polite and frosty social ostracism. At least that was what the government was aiming at.

The lights went down in the room as the group looked at the screenshots of the updated messages.

For the next month, they would be pushing support for the Friday home day. Long ago employers were expected to create a four-day work week. This was old news. The idea was popular with families because they got to deal with the mounting time pressure to take care of their home life. People had accepted the idea of a day off. Now all the propaganda was into the nuances of what this "bonus" day was all about. The ad had a picture of an overcharged scheduler and a piece of the paper glued by an optimistic citizen. "Meet up on Friday," claimed the ad.

The post-consumer era had brought about hardship, but it also had the unintended consequence of forcing people to barter. People bartered rations, services, stuff they already owned but didn't need. The tax department didn't like barter because nobody paid any tax. Yet, although illegal, barter was still practical. It coerced people out of their homes, to talk to people, and to stay connected in ways that didn't have electronic support.

Finally, they reviewed the video message from the prime minister that would be shown on public transit for the next week. A waving red and white flag rolled on screen while the PMs voice read his lines. "Canada works because it invests wisely. Our diverse communities from coast to coast to coast know how to work together to steward our land, water and natural resources." (Cut to the standard beauty shots of same.) "Canada is the envy of the world. Together Canadians, from all walks of life, have learned to change our expectations and reduce our footprint to historic lows. Efficiency has become our invisible resource and our ally.

"Collectively, we reuse almost everything up to three times." (Revolting shots of garbage from the turn of the century.) "We have reduced consumption so that our needs are met with no net loss for future generations. But there is still more to do." (Shot of Arctic Ocean ice-free.)" As the world's population nears 10 billion, our work internationally is more important than ever." (Graphic of the world map with an upwards arrow. Text: 'number of international agreements' plastered across the bottom) "Canada is truly blessed." (Headshot of the PM.) "Your sacrifice and hard work make this possible. Your gestures now are the building blocks of a happier PC world for our kids, and in turn theirs. We are moving ahead. Please continue to sustain our Canada together."

This was the heart of being PC, accepting measurably less. The message had provoked the usual visceral anger around the room and no one dared show it. After decades of sacrifice, they all thought that maybe the war against our pre-consumer habits would someday end. The thing was that their efforts at propaganda had been so good, they had given the government a powerful weapon to control what people believed. The group was quiet as the lights went up. This was a duty review. The room knew the PM had approved the script directly. No good to comment.

Ally picked up her cold coffee and swilled it back. The deliberate movement managed to discharge a wave of fleeting anger, and nearly drowned out a glimpse of insight. She saw the thought in her mind and called it back from the brink of vanishing. Maybe, she wondered, we're not fighting the same war. Or maybe some were still fighting, while others want to put away their weapons.

She shook her head, as if to disagree with herself, but the thought didn't go away. The idea didn't make a lot of sense. But then, being rational wasn't always the foundation of the PC era.

THE GENERATIONS

Six

"So, did you like it?"

Janey Fulco walked back through the ages, in the good company of her forever bright and bouncy friend from work, Fioria. "Yeah, Fi. I'm raving."

They tripped down towards the exit, following the long hall that was wrapped in luminous panoramas of days gone by. It wasn't real, but like just about everything in the last hour and a half, it came close. It was her first immersive artificial reality experience and it'd been deeply weird. Good weird. You could walk deeper and deeper into the vistas, exploring reconstructions and talking to people. Sometimes the people were fellow experiencers, sometimes they were projections. In the beginning she waited to see if she'd hit a wall or touch something gooey. Trip over a piece of equipment. Before long she stopped worrying, abandoning her understanding of the physical world on a freaky interlude from who or what was real. Then the concept dropped, and she had a blast.

Now they were on their way back to reality. The images changed from rough medieval, to quaint Jane Austin, to bleak images of an early industrial era, to the squandering seventies and finally now. It took a good five minutes, giving Janey time to reflect on what was authentic and what was good enough to be worth the effort.

"This was exotic. I've never been here before. It was a true experience." Janey stopped for a second to free the heel of her shoe from the long skirt of the peasant get up she'd rented.

"Oh, I've been a couple of times. My friends and I love it. It's hard to believe they get all that out of the thirty questions you answer on their app."

"It's a kick in the ass. I talked to one of those holos for about five minutes before I realized it wasn't a real person."

"Really?"

"It was giving me a lesson on relationships from about the year 1350. I really cracked up when I figured it out."

"Ah. That's what that was. You almost met a man."

It was another of her friend's frequent digs at Janey's staid personal life. "Bitch," Janey teased back at her, hoping when she let the word out that Fioria's feelings wouldn't be hurt.

Fioria pulled the satin-covered cone from her head, pulled the sensor out of her ear and tussled her hair in place. "That's the end of me being a queen." They were in front of the change room opening and followed the neon arrows in.

One shower and a half hour later, Janey stood outside under the giant sign for *Holos Past*, waiting for her friend. The sun was brilliant, shining down on her and heating all it touched. Despite the light, she zippered up her jacket, grateful for the extra warmth because the air was crisp.

At least the air outside was fresh. The centre was filled with the smell sensations pumped in to make the experience real. The medieval era was apparently foul. That, coupled with barrage of sounds from the real costumed people, each interacting with the life-like scenes had been an overload for her senses.

It hadn't been cheap either. "You paid what to spend an hour inside that beaten up warehouse at the airport," she could hear her cheap-from-necessity father lecture. She'd argue her point in this theoretical reckoning. "Yes, Dad. I did. You know what, I liked it. Let me have this experience, fake or not."

"Strawberry or peach?" Janey's reverie was broken by her friend's arrival with two containers of with the words 'frozen zen' stamped on them.

"Peach, please. Thanks!"

They went over to a nearby bench. "So, you've been here before. What other rooms have you visited," Janey inquired.

"We did Shakespeare and Al Capone. I don't know if you'd like that one. It was violent."

"Sounds it. I'll come back sometime. Try something else. I've done the peasant thing. Maybe come back as a chef. That'd be different!" There was a loud noise and the two women looked up at a group of teenagers streaming out of the centre. They'd not opted for the costume rental and spa service, so they were still dressed like the Beatles.

"Fi, I've got to get moving soon."

Her friend nodded, taking some generous slurps of her beverage. "What have you got on for the rest of your weekend?"

Janey was comfortable with the kind of close, but walled, relationship that happens to people who spend days together in the cubes. She worried that interesting information can travel and linger in the office lexicon of prejudices. Janey volunteered cautiously, "Oh, I'm waiting to hear from my cousin. You?"

Fi, on the other hand, was always happy to share whatever was front of her mind. It worked for her and made her socially successful. She told Janey about last's nights adventure with boyfriend number one, who really had feelings for her, but didn't excite her as she thought he should. "We went out to dinner, and then, you know, went back to my apartment afterwards. I think I am going to break up with him soon. He just doesn't get the hint. We go out to dinner and I tried to push him away. Then, you know, like, I refused to hook up, but I comprised and went down on him. You think he'd want to break up with me."

"Poor bastard," Janey half-commiserated silently with the guy in his defense. Janey hastily looked at her wrist. That was enough today about someone else's sex life. Truth, she was wistful that her weekend could use a real plan. There were options: organizing her place, visiting the fam, going to the gym. All average, stand-up stuff that used to make her feel like she'd achieved something. None of this popped with her anymore. The way ahead endlessly looped back to the start. It's why she was sitting with Fioria now. Why she might get lucky and round up Tanya on video to talk, if she was ever out of bed and coherent. Maybe she could rope in her cousin into letting her hang out tonight. Tanya always knew where to party. How to make stuff happen. The trick was to be in her entourage.

Fi got up to leave. She was about to say something else, a joke, but she stopped. Janey had had enough. "So see you Monday?"

"I'm in the home office for the next two days. I'll be in Wednesday."

"I'm in then too. Let's get out of the building for lunch. If we can. Whatever this state you're in is, you can tell me all about it."

"What?"

"I see it. You're bored."

Janey got up and stretched, smiling. "Piss off. You can't be serious." Then her face brightened. "Thanks so much for today," she offered, walking away waving.

Fi laughed back as Janey left in the direction of the light rail station. It wasn't a cruel laugh, but it wasn't jealousy either.

Seven

Janey looked around from her spot in the middle of her father's apartment. She smirked seeing that her father, Nicolo, had found another way to up the mélé-mélo style of the place. A paper lantern shade had been draped askew over the same base that had sat naked since he'd moved in.

But the rest was the same. The crumpled box that sat unopened for three years ago. Dishes tidily cluttered up the sink. The coat rack near the door held a collection of coats and jackets, some of which she was certain he would never wear again. His prize possession was a collection of paintings on the wall. They'd been on display in her childhood home and she'd heard the story of how they had been purchased from some artist that he had loved years ago. The apartment was smallish, but it had all he really needed. He'd brightened the place up with a collection of candles and bric-a-brack collected from garage sales and the Salvation Army.

She loved this place despite its limits. She felt comfortable here. It wasn't like her mother's place, sterile and run with precision.

When her parents split three years ago, it was a shock. She hadn't noticed their growing disinvolvement. In fact, she had never really given her parents' marriage a second thought. When they sat her down and had the talk about their future, she was stunned. She was even more stunned that her mother had found someone new and was moving to live with him in Toronto.

It had taken a lot of mental digestion, but she was past it. Her father had stayed on in town, moving into this very simple apartment. She was distressed for him that he'd opted to live like this, but she knew it was mostly because of his kids that he had made this choice.

Her dad was wounded after the separation. For the longest time he would ask sad questions about her mother. Was Jennifer happy? Was she going to see Jennifer soon? Her mother had come to town several times and Janey hadn't shared this with him. Her mother was flourishing in her new life. It would be cruel to make her dad cope with that.

Time had gratefully passed. She was convinced he might never set his foot out again into the romantic world. Three years later she had no idea if he did have a companion in his life, but she also realized that sometimes it was better just to not get too involved.

Even so, she did care about him. She valued his opinion and often sought it out when she needed to think things through. But today she was there, doing what you often do with parents: checking in.

"So, what do you want to do today?" Nicolo asked.

"Haven't really been giving it much thought Dad. I'm sure you have some ideas." He always had ideas. He was often out with new people, although she didn't hear much about what he got into.

"Well, I thought we could go to the new art exhibit at the museum. It's kind of fun to see all that recycling."

"What's that about?"

"It's an exhibit where they take old industrial machinery and make something new out of it. I saw a picture of a sauna that's made completely out of old automobile parts."

Janey sighed. Once again his fascination with PC culture was slightly pissing her off. She got irritated with how her father and his crowd made an art form out of the environment. They hadn't invested a minute of effort when they had a chance to make a tangible difference. But now, when their efforts were mostly symbolic, they took a nostalgic turn backwards. He would tell her that it was important for them to pay homage to the environmental movement. She knew the view was popular among his friends; she knew he was going with the flow. It infuriated her a little bit and yet she let it slide.

"Sure, let's go see that!" Janey answered brightly.

Her father went to put on his coat. He was a tall man, rounded at the middle. But nearing his 60's, he still had a way about him. He carefully picked up a jacket from his rack as if he was shopping at an exclusive boutique. Then he took off her coat to pass it to her. As he picked up her coat another couple of coats fell. He sighed and bent down to the ground to pick them up. As he put them back and turned around to look at her. She hadn't moved.

"Janey dear, you don't always have to say yes to everything I come up with!" He said it in his native tongue. Her Italian was rusty, but she knew what he meant.

She was taken aback. He was challenging her usually compliant nature, and she didn't know quite what to say, in any language. Her face said the same thing.

"Don't you think I know you? If you don't want to go, just say let's do something else."

Janey looked confused and again her face shared her emotions. It was a mental rabbit hole. Crap, not another one. The rules of engagement between the two of them didn't allow for her opinions. She thought for a second about apologizing, but then told herself to grow up.

"So Dad, why don't we just stay here. I wouldn't mind talking. I can make you lunch."

"If you like!" Again with the Italian.

"Well, if you really want to go to the show, we can go out to see that recycling thing."

"Your Mother says I'm always trying to make people happy. Let's have lunch here." He went over to the fridge to root around. He pulled out some sliced soy bologna, some vegetables, pickles, and the mustard.

"Why don't you see what you can do with this?" he said as he looked at her and smiled. It was her dad's warm, familiar grin. "I'll put the kettle on. So, what do you want to talk about?"

"Nothing, I guess. I mean, I just thought it'd be nice to chat because we never chat when we go out."

"I guess that's true. It's not like the old days when we were all living together."

Janey explained, "for example, I found out from Mom that you got a new job."

"Yeah, that's right. I start in a week. I'm not sure it's the best job in the world for me, but I need the money. As you know, nothing is free anymore."

He watched as she piled some greens on the bread. "how's your job working out?"

"No change, Dad. Like you say, it pays the bills."

"I was so grateful when you got that job. And so happy that you had a place to start a career. You keep that job, they're hard to come by."

"I know Dad. You tell me this every time we get together!"

"No, I don't!"

Janey curled her face into a sarcastic look.

He picked up the sandwich plates. "Yeah, okay. Well, what kind of a shitty father am I! I want to you have a decent job. Decent job, decent life!"

As he walked over to the table Nicolo asked, "are you going down south to be with Kara this spring?"

"Yes, but more like in January for a couple of weeks. I'm looking forward to it. How about you? Going anywhere this winter?" As the question left her mouth, Janey wished she hadn't asked. He couldn't afford it.

"Not now that I've got this new job. I just gotta stay right here."

They both went over to the table near the window to eat their sandwiches. It felt a bit stiff and they fought the silence. This wasn't like them. Usually they were laughing and joking about stuff. Pointing out some badly-dressed character in the line up ahead of them or making fun of some idiotic sign. They had a kind of routine, not a lot of dead air.

Janey remembered something she'd meant to ask. "Dad if you need anything from New York, let me know. I'm stopping by this time."

He looked up as she took a bite and smiled. "You're going see that fellow that you always see?"

"You mean, like, you're waiting for me to find a fellow? What's with you today?"

He withdrew a little. "Sorry I didn't mean to overstep! I thought that you liked this fellow. What's his name?

"Byron."

"Nice name."

"He's just a friend." Janey sighed, exasperated. Then she snapped. "Frig. No one wants me to live my life."

"What do you mean?" her father asked, genuinely surprised.

Truth was, Janey didn't know what she meant. Which explained what followed.

"I mean I feel like I never make my own choices anymore. I just do what everyone thinks I should do."

Her father returned to his sandwich and chewed a few more bites.

"I didn't know you were feeling anxious. You'd let me know if you were feeling anxious? A lot of my friends say their kids feel anxious. We can always find you some help, if you have any kind of anxiety disorder."

"I can't believe that! You seriously think I might have an anxiety disorder. I'm just a regular twenty-eight-year-old. This is how we all feel. I don't need help with anxiety. I need help with the things that are giving me anxiety!

"Like you expecting me to be married or something! Or staying in a job just so I don't starve! You don't get it. I don't get to choose

74

anything anymore. I get to wear what I'm told, go to the job that keeps me from being out in the street. And I must listen to you guys ask me if I have an anxiety disorder. You think it's easy? I don't own anything and I don't want to own anything and I don't have any guy that I'm going to marry in the future. I don't have an anxiety disorder. I just have a life that gives me a shit-load of anxiety."

Her father picked up his tea and sipped. He looked at this daughter and tried to stall while he thought. "Sorry, I didn't know that's how you felt. I guess I kind of lost touch."

"Yeah, you guys got no clue. I love you, Dad. I do. But when you ask about my job or how my life is going, I don't know why you bother. It's all going according to plan. Just read what the government says about a young person's future and know I did all those things. And if I get married, or if I have kids, it's all a laid out for me. It's nothing but work, work, work."

Janey stopped for a minute and reflected on what she had just said to her father. She'd overdone it with the spicy sauce. Maybe exaggerating a bit because she really did love her father and trusted him too. It felt good to vent.

For his part, Nicolo's anxiety had reached a high level. "I do want to listen to you. I hope you think I listen to you."

Nicolo continued softly. "It must be difficult. I guess I don't think of your youth as much different than mine."

"You got that right! From how you tell it, you got in a car and you did what you wanted. You went to school if you wanted and you spent time doing nothing. I'd like that."

Janey put down her plate. Her Dad looked crushed. Or more crushed than usual. They should have gone to the museum. Right now they'd be poking fun at some old woman in the cafeteria.

"It's okay Dad. I'm alright. I'm venting. I mean, for half of it. Don't worry. I'm fine. I've lots of time to have fun and I'm looking forward to my trip in January. Life could be worse."

Her dad collected the plates and stacked them in the sink. He was running out of room. Sooner or later they'd get done.

He filled up their mugs with fresh tea and took his place. "You know everybody today feels like they are underwater at points. Me, your mother, even Kara. And when we're stressed, we all think we're alone. We look at all these people out there having fun. People having fun are on every screen. We think we're the only one that can't cope, and everyone else is getting along fine. It's a myth. We see what our kids are going through. Their kids. I can't get my buddies to shut up about it. Everyone wishes things weren't so hard. I want to do whatever I can to help you now."

"Thanks, Dad. I appreciate it. You understand that I have to believe I'm going somewhere."

All he really could offer his daughter was hope. So he skillfully shifted the conversation to her upcoming trip with Kara. A formidable woman, his ex-mother-in-law. He remembered how he and Kara used to tangle. She would label him passive because he was blind to what it meant to live in the post-consumer world. There was the time he'd caught her frosty judgment because he'd bought a small, second fridge for the basement. His ex-wife was always running out of space.

But he, too, had his disagreements with Kara. His opinions were nuanced and he found them harder to put into words. He often held his opinions to himself. But sometimes he couldn't contain himself. He remembered how he'd commented dryly about one of her recent blog posts as he passed around some meat at a family dinner. She'd gone on about how unfair it was to not let city people raise farm animals on their property. The foolishness of pushing families to raise a pig in their backyard! It had pushed him over the edge. He always felt that Kara fell victim to the latest post-consumer philosophy, confusing and inflating causes without thinking about the impact. She could be so unaware of the consequences of what she so passionately advocated.

He'd lost touch with Kara after the divorce. But he could still feel the sting of some of those disagreements. He didn't know who had been right. He never would know. But he had full view of who was hurting.

Eight

Ashley Bernal was playing along with her six-year-old son, Marcos, enjoying the best part of her day. The kids had been out at play care most of the day. She'd worked in the home office upstairs. The five of them had already eaten dinner together. Now son and mom were in the pleasant interregnum between her son's current hope for a generous stretch of play and maternal attention, and her near-term expectation that he would soon be falling safely asleep in his own bed.

She stood watching him rotate his body weight from foot to foot while he hummed thoughtfully. Young kids offer parents many such moments of waiting. Today, for example, she asked her young son to choose a toy. Playful pauses where children debate in their heads their own limits of control, the options for responding and probably, just finding the words. Ashley found those moments hilarious. With either of her kids, these pauses spoke lots about who they'd be when they grew up.

Her daughter Rachel, who Ashley had named after her mom, was a curious child. Rachel junior, with her imagination, could well be the next Nobel Laureate. Even at four, her tiny thoughts were bent towards understanding how things worked. They would be out on the back deck flipping through a story. Or sitting at their large kitchen table looking at the birds in the front yard. Rachel would pierce her mother with her innocent, soft brown eyes, laden with questions that oftentimes stumped Ashley. No, she didn't know why they picked red for stop, or why mustard was so yellow and what was the soft stuff underneath the cover of the screen. "Why are there raspberries, Mommy," her little girl would inquire. And then it would start. "So we can eat them," would be the opening answer. "But why do we eat them?" The goal for Ash was to find an answer that didn't raise fresh questions. She'd be tempted to make some shit up, but the couple of times she did, Rachel would repeat it to Jhonian, or worse, a neighbour. Usually with the intro "Mommy told me…" followed by the misinformation "…that raspberries are candy. Candy is bad for you."

Marcos, even at his age, was a great negotiator. He was bound for sales, or the law, or if worse came to worse, a politician. Any career where his abundant charm could convince you to tag along. He always had a plan. He could skilfully present you with a couple of options that showcased the choice he wanted you to make. "Mom, which one of these toys can I buy," he'd petition to her in the grocery store. Two would be unsuitable; dangerous or expensive. One would be what he wanted. "None," Ashley would reply, waiting for his crestfallen face. And that would do it. Half the time she'd cave and he'd get what he wanted. Clever kid.

She watched him tonight, casting sideways glances at her living space and debris that needed to be put right before she went to bed. Like the corduroy couch cushions that somehow had been piled in front of their picture window. Or the toy cupboards at the other end of the room with their doors ajar and bins and baskets precariously askew. Trying not to think about the messages from work she was going to answer. Hoping that Kara hadn't called it a night and that she'd come back up from her basement apartment to clean up the dinner disorder in the kitchen. It was the usual long list before bed.

The whistle of the kettle on the stove sounded. "I'm just going to get my tea. While Daddy gives Rachel her bath, pick one toy, I don't care which, and we can play for fifteen minutes." She walked away backwards, trying to maintain an authoritative eye contact with her son. Before she disappeared, she raised a finger and faced him squarely. "Then it's bathtime. Agreed?"

Her son kept rotating from side to side. Then he pulled up his shoulders and offered a coy smile, pressing her to rush to get the kettle and pour the water on the tea bag. She barely dipped the bag to make the water the familiar brown when she heard it. "Bop, bob, bob," rapidly repeating. Jhonian did that too. Sitting at the kitchen table and rapidly thumping his foot on the floor. Nervously like he might explode. This time it was her son. Jumping with pure joy to see his mother. He did it often when he'd hatched a plan and it was a good one. Sometimes Kara would come up and ask her grandson if there'd been an earthquake. Luckily, they lived in a detached house, so the noise didn't make others complain.

She took her mug and summoned her good humour for the short trek.

"Hey dude, I see you're ready for bathtime."

Marcos still didn't say a word, beaming instead at her as he jumped in place. In the scant minutes of her absence, he'd managed to silently find, relocate and upright all the Lego bins that she carefully sorted this past weekend. Better still he'd piled all his clothes at the foot of the steps to the second floor. He kept at the jumping, landing flat-footed to maximize the thud. Bits of him flapped along to beat. He added a clap to the bounce for emphasis. He was a miniature version of his father. Course, dark, Mexican hair and dark brown eyes. Square shoulders with a goofy grin.

"Good job. Maybe next time, for Mommy's sake, leave on the underpants." She sat down on the floor in front of the mound of bricks. "What shall we build?"

He gave one final leap before folding himself into a cross-legged position. He giggled and picked up a handful of pieces. They were well into building a friendly monster when Jhonian issued the bathroom all clear. Ashley grabbed a bucket and asked her boy to help her fill a bin. Then she suggested that he take his red and blue masterpiece upstairs. With that began the process of coaxing her six-year-old son into the bathtub.

The bath-story-bed routine was very familiar to him. Still, her boy teased out the process with his charm, pretending not to know what happened when his mother said "bathtime" in her firm mom voice.

Eventually, Marcos complied and she lifted him into the bath. Tonight there were some bubbles to mix with his toys and he spent a happy ten minutes making bubble mountains for his toys to climb. Ashley stood in the doorway and listened as he happily babbled his story that went with mountain climbing. He had a child's voice but considerable powers of observation of what went on in her household. His story made her smile.

Hardly a day, maybe a minute didn't go by when she didn't think of her kids. To say that she thought her children as two of the most beautiful people she had ever known would only begin to capture the profound love she possessed for them. She stood there, bone tired from her day, and as she watched him play, she realized that she'd helped create his happiness. It was these slices of her life that made her happy too.

Her son now lay flat in the bath. A typical scene, he lay singing and smiling at her. Toys were strewn from one end of the bath to the other. Shampoo bubbles floated on his tummy and around his head. She waited until he had finished playing and then gently suggested it was time to be moving on with the routine: combing his wet hair in a funny spikey hairstyle, sparkling teeth, hug, story, and bed.

She progressed through all the steps with speed and skill. He laughed, trying to spin out the moment to last. As she rubbed this six-year-old down and dried his hair, she hoped that by her manner and her commitment he would always understand that she loved him.

Ash had become like so many modern working mothers. By definition, tired and worried. She wasn't sure about much. Her life had discarded many of the ambitions that she had started with. Love seemed the only constant. And love is a safe place where her family is accepted without question. Her little guy needed a place in her heart where he would ever remain her tender little boy, a place to go whenever, to rest and recharge.

He giggled one more time and she gently reasoned with him that it was time for bed. She leaned over his bed, kissed him, and organized his favourite toys.

"Good night sweetie. Mommy loves you."

He smiled as she waved at him from the doorway. She closed the door, hoping she'd remembered everything.

He would get older and leave her home. She wouldn't always be able to hug him and kiss him good night. It was the natural order and she accepted it. Some days her fatigue and temper pushed her to look forward to it.

Life had become hard and unpredictable. But even today being a mom carried the prize of hoping you can do something right. A chance to carve out a piece of the future and create happiness for a few people. When he left, he would go with the strength of her love.

This promise made most days of the journey worth the effort. The idea carried Ashley forward from exhausting day to exhausting day. It was pointless to be angry about being part of the 'have not' generation. Patience willed her past their fate, to look for better. For her, there are no Edens except those we create on earth.

Nine

When Jhonian came through the front door everything was ready to be served.

Ashley had been getting dinner ready in the kitchen when she heard his cheery "Hi Ash." She waited until he reappeared a few minutes later in a clean t-shirt.

"How'd the day go," he asked in a way that he intended to make Ashley feel, after eight years of marriage, that he still wanted to know. Jhonian continually looked at her with affection, seeing only the beautiful women he married. A woman who was smart, athletic and striking.

She smiled back in a way that said, "better now" he was home. She was happy to be happy with him. His black hair had some gray in it now and he wasn't quite as trim as he'd been when they had met and fell in love. He was even now what most would call dark and ruggedly square. Ashley told him that she loved that age had given him a patina.

They knew couples who had lost their marriages to anger or the struggle to keep up. They resolved early to not let that happen. The wear and tear made marriage more valuable. The result had been a kind of happiness that was mostly unshakable.

The dinner was set out on the buffet so parents and kids alike could help themselves. Jhonian called his little Rachel to help her with her plate of food. She purposefully looked at each plate, deciding whether or not to sample its contents. "No, Daddy, I just like carrots tonight." He basked in this dividend of fatherhood.

Ashley called her son to the table and he arrived with his usual energy of a six-year-old superhero. She bade Marcos to take off the grandiose homemade cape and put down his old plastic sword. Both were old toys from her mom's basement, and she pictured her brother playing with them years ago.

Kara came up from the basement and joined the dinner queue. Tonight they were eating the canned tomatoes that she had put down with her foodie friends at the community centre. They were excellent and brought out the flavour of the cultured pork meat. With three adults in the family, they had enough rations to eat meat protein most nights. Of course, much of it was that stuff grown in a petri dish. You rarely found the real thing anymore in the city unless you knew a farmer.

They sat down together to eat, and, as was their family rule, Jhonian turned off the screens by flicking the kill switch. In the wake of silence, he noticed the sound of wind outside and then the bustle of the family getting to work on the dinner. This moment was one of his daily favourites.

"Hey Dad," asked Marcos. "Do you think plants have feelings?"

They all listened as the little boy recounted, in a roundabout manner, how a post on why people should stop eating vegetables had fueled a debate at school. Scientists had done tests and measured how plants felt pain. The children had been terrified by stories of carrots being pulled out by the roots.

The adults looked at each other, amused and slightly alarmed by the emotion brought on by this meme. Then Kara replied, with elderly authority, that "plants think it's their goal in life to be eaten." Then she took a large mouthful of carrots and told the kids to look how she was honouring them right now.

Jhonian steered the talk away from mortal thoughts for vegetables towards a safer topic.

"Mom, have you heard from either one of my sisters?"

"Nothing much from Ally." The adults looked at each other meaningfully. They didn't want to say much in front of the kids, but it was pretty much what they expected. These past few years, with her big job, Ally had ghosted everybody.

"I did hear from Jennifer."

"How is she doing?"

"I think she misses the family here, living in Toronto. You know, she seems very happy with her job and her new husband."

"Do you like him much," asked Ashley.

"Actually, I do. I'm getting to know him on screen. He seems to honestly love her. I'm just frustrated because she lives so far away. Hopefully we'll be able to get together here, or there, soon."

"I know you miss her, Mom." Her middle child Jennifer had moved away three years ago after a rather abrupt separation. "Look on the bright side, you've got us."

"How true!" Kara winked at the children with the joke.

"Wait a second, I'll get some more bread." Ashley went out into the kitchen and reached into the oven to fill up the plate.

She was pleased to listen to the usual banter of her family. Jhonian was shining on to his mother about a local furniture reno business that had got fined for illegal disposal of waste. The owner had been charged with hiding the waste fabric inside the reupholstered sofas and chairs.

Jhonian was always trying to impress his mother. The two of them had a generous, warm relationship. Like Ashley's love for her son, Jhonian would always be Kara's boy. She was infinitely proud of his business of refurbishing furniture. He had a small factory where he bought used pieces and remade them to his style. His signature was to take old mattresses apart and use the foam, spring, and wood to make modern looking sofas and chairs. Although there were more successful artists in the major cities, he was still very successful at producing low-cost renovation pieces that were available in local stores at a fraction of the cost of new. They were very popular with people setting up their first houses or just not in a position to get a loan to pay for furniture. Lots of people just couldn't afford to buy new. In order to meet the lifetime standards, manufacturers were using materials that raised prices to levels that made new furniture a major investment.

Ashley returned to the table. "Kids, I remember when I was your age that people would just leave their old furniture at the end of their driveway and hope people would pick it up."

"You mean people just left their stuff anywhere," asked her son. "But it's not garbage."

"That's right. I remember that people would get tired of what they have, or their kids would grow up and they wanted to get the kids new furniture. So, they just left it out on the lawn hoping people who wanted it would find it."

"That's stupid. Why didn't they take it to the recycling centre? Or post an ad on the community centre bulletin?"

"Paint it purple!" offered the four-year-old.

"Great question," Jhonian said in his best dad voice. "But it gave me the idea to start my business. And now we make a living out of it."

Jhonian looked over at his mother's jawline for the familiar sign of tightening as the family digested their dinner and this anecdote from "the bad old days." He knew these scenes frequently provoked gut-wrenching guilt in her. She could get irrationally angry, crying out to anyone in earshot that she should have "done something real and used my voice years ago." Now she had to cope with the fact that life for him would never be as easy as it was for her. The irony was all her guilt and sadness didn't really help now. It could just ruin something pleasant.

Suddenly Ashley remembered she had to make an announcement. "My Mom is coming," she said.

Utensils that had been scraping plates and serving dishes stopped. Jhonian and Kara looked up with a look that spoke of their panic.

"When?" Jhonian asked with what he hoped was a neutral tone in his voice.

"In a couple of weeks, I got a phone call today."

"A phone call?" Kara questioned. "Who does that today?"

And so the old tension started.

After some reflection and a few sessions with a marriage negotiator, Ashley and Jhonian had come to terms with this explosive combination.

Ashley's mom Rachel was about as far away from Kara as you could get. Two personalities put on earth to provide the stark contrasts that they did.

Rachel complained about everything that was post-consumer. She longed for the "good old days" of picking through dress after dress on store racks until you found the right thing. She amazed the kids by wearing perfume and dressing in a different set of fanciful clothes every day.

Rachel had a pretentious way about everything. Big things, or small considerations like Jhonian's name. He winced internally about how he'd have to listen once more to Rachel torture it. "Hoe-ne-ah." Something like that. Said in a breathless manner to indicate that mastering his name was unreasonably exhausting.

He was used to it and he often gave a little allocution lesson when he greeted someone new. "Hi, I'm Jhonian", he'd say, giving them a warm smile and a handshake. And then he'd wait for the look of confusion and add, "I know, it's Spanish. My dad was from Mexico. Yoh-**ni**-an." Most people would get it. Sometimes, when he was in a mood, he'd add, "It means "gift of the gods." It was his little joke. He had no bloody idea what his name meant.

Jhonian gave his mother a 'how you doing' look. She was doing her best, but he knew that Kara would soon crack. She'd complain to Jhonian when others were out of hearing. "That woman Rachel spends too much time on her nails, and not enough time on the world around her." Kara would wonder aloud if Rachel was a good influence on her grandkids. "She sets up expectations for a life that those children will never know. She might as well promise them a trip to Mars!"

Yup, Ashley's mom was an unapologetic narcissist and strident shopper. She'd turn their world in directions they'd not planned to go.

Their house would quickly become Rachel's domain. The kids doted on her because she arrived with old toys that she had found somewhere and told wild stories about the old days like they were still a reality. She had a loud, irresistible laugh. Her mission was to make any place she's at fun. As Rachel would say, what kid wouldn't want a piece of that?

Ten

It was a Friday in autumn, and the gardens were overflowing.
Kara Asher spent a good part of today at the community kitchen,
helping out families with their jam and canning.

In the big kitchens in the back of the hall, she stood at the centre of a
group working on their weekly dinners. She was surrounded by
young, impressive people. Everyone was young to Kara now. Boiling
water vapour from the stove-top sterilization process made this warm
work. Shiny pots of peach, plum, tomato red, and basil green stood in
rows on the cooling racks just beyond the worktable. They were
preparing the food for brining pickles now. This particular group was
more experienced, so the work went quickly. The cleanup would be
easy. That was good because she was expected for dinner.

She was grateful to share what she learned as a child. "Putting down"
food was another of those old domestic skills that the young people
wanted to revive. Greenhouses and vertical farms supplied a lot of
what used to be trucked in. But some veg had to be preserved when
they ripened. You simply couldn't count on finding fresh food like
pears and fennel in the winter.

That's why many city dwellers were overjoyed when local authorities
expanded their services with large commercial kitchens, gleaming
with all the equipment needed to make large amounts of food quickly.
Sure, you could make it all at home. Some foolish hold-outs did,
deluding themselves about their rugged self-sufficiency.
Notwithstanding these peculiar individualists, prevailing sentiment
was that life's drudgery overwhelmed you at home. The chores go
faster, and it's more relaxing, working with your friends.

Kara, with her folksy manner and shock of white hair, was a fixture at
the community centre now. A couple years ago she'd wandered in
and started chatting with the young man behind the welcome desk.
He listened politely as she freely offered her opinions on how people
in her community could work together to make family life easier.
Usually he tuned out the old timers; this time he'd been impressed
with her experience of doing things he'd been desperately trying to
learn about since he got this gig. Making jam, repairing clothing,

cleaning upholstery. He'd found a solution to a problem. Old people knew this stuff and were willing to work for free.

At first her shifts volunteering were unsettling, even disorienting. People were coming and going with a lot of ruthless purpose. These people all wanted to get straight to whatever task or obstacle that needed sorting out. Stressed-out people were brusque, some were even bullies. Most didn't care that she was just a volunteer. Fortunately Kara was charming company, thoughtful, hale and very generous. People remarked that she had an ease about her that made her pleasant to be with. She could create calm by entering the room and simply smiling.

It surprised her how much people needed help. Kids came together to learn something new. She often taught them herself. How to make cookies or how to fix a broken toy. Parents needed her help. Who to call to repair an appliance, when to plant vegetables so they would be ready for fall, or how to remake a wedding dress into something modern. They looked to her to help them get it done so they could get back to their homes and families.

Now it all was comfortable. Comfortable not just because she could look around and feel with ease where everything was stored. She had either used it, cleaned it, or made it over the past couple of years. Its comfort also came from knowing that good happened here. Working with young people made Kara feel useful. Success here, in a small way, made up for what she hadn't done in the past. She'd spent the afternoon listening to parents prop the virtues of making your own at harvest. Kara felt relief that someone's life was now a tiny bit easier.

But this bit of atonement wasn't enough, not by any measure. She craved more to do, to blunt the burn of regret.

Before she retired twelve years ago, Kara had worked for 35 years as an executive at an ad agency. She had managed large amounts of money and equally large amounts of people. As the years passed, she had her own agency; it paid her well and its proceeds supported her well now.

For the first twenty-five years of her career she made her money the old way; selling any new product like it was revolutionary. Expounding the buy-more philosophy. Strangely, she did not fight it when the time came to reposition advertising because it encouraged consumerism. She worked as an advisor on commission after commission to create the post-consumer restrictions. She openly admitted it was a kind of censorship. Kara often asserted it was a necessary evil to stop people from buying and consuming things they really didn't need.

She became an ardent spokesperson for the new reality. In the second act of her career she spoke frequently in the public discussion spaces about why she was part of the PC movement and why it was important to give forward. Whatever she got into, her time and opinion were soon central to the success of the group. Kara found she enjoyed being a leading figure and intuitively leveraged her success into wider and wider networks online and across town. She convinced herself that her contribution could make a difference to the community. She could help to save the planet. People believed her when she said she knew how. Her posts were highly subscribed and respected. Ironically, her advertising company still made her money. There was lots of opportunity to sell people the new way of life.

Now in retirement, she turned to this more hands-on approach. Her kids and her grandchildren were a big part of life. She offered as much practical help as she could. It pained her so much to watch them when they struggled.

She spent a great deal of time volunteering anywhere that wanted to teach cooking, crafting, and sewing to the younger generation. Kara could go on for days about how we were losing so many skills that the people needed to make them more self-sustaining. She was asked to sit on boards of local community groups. She was invited to moderate online panels. And so, she also enjoyed an active social life. She was even asked to run for the Greens in local government, although she turned it down as it required her to give up too much.

True, she could be a bit overbearing when she got started on another of her "work together as a village" lectures. She preached her less-is-more philosophy, the post-consumer ethos that connections, not consumption, made you happy. She would share the information she liked about eco-advocacy through conflict and the positive effects of the restoration of the link with nature. She believed it all and was convinced that it was the best for the future of the people she loved.

90

This sort of talk bemused Ashley and Jhonian. She had options that most did not. Jhonian knew that when she got a bit short, his mother could cash out some of the green bonds she'd bought years ago. She was worth the forbearance as he found life more tough and chaotic than he expected, and he was comforted to have her near. Their live-in arrangement meant that the grandkids got to know her. "Mom," he shared once at the end of another of his long days, "I'm so grateful you're around to help me out."

Those were tender words that made her flood with regret. Maybe she should have done more when she was younger. But what? Voting. Advocating. Protesting. She always thought she was on the right band wagon. If she looked out for her kids and was willing to support the prevailing wisdom, that would be enough. But now she was convinced that she was just going with the flow. At the end of a full life, no matter how much she crammed into her week, she had lots of reasons to wonder about that now.

Eleven

The Ottawa headquarters of Department of Citizenship and Consumerism had the grandest gym in town. It was a landmark on Kent Street, a curving, multi-level glass structure on top of the office tower that overlooked the Parliament Buildings.

Its amenities included several health pools and a network of private and open rooms for workouts and training consultations. The conversation floor was studded with large fake rocks carved into benches and laced with coffee dispensers and make your own protein bar vending machines. There was even a retractable glass ceiling so that on fine days people on the top floor could use the cardio machines in the open air.

Anybody, including many tourists, were happy to pay to enter. Almost all of the department's employees took advantage of the gym because they had free access. Like every Canadian, they needed to get to a certified gym on a regular basis to log exercise credits. Those who were negligent faced daily messages from government agencies; over time these messages changed from polite-but-firm to menacing. Finally, you lost your health coverage. But this had never happened to a departmental employee. They'd never dare. These were the people that set the standards for citizenship.

It was a frequent gripe that key parts of the gym were closed on Mondays, Wednesdays, and Fridays from exactly 10:30 a.m. to noon. The reason given was that the gym required periodic, thorough sanitization to guard against viruses. Ally Asher had been sympathetic to complainers throughout her career. It was helpful to nip down and exercise when it was quiet rather than face the lunch crush. That was, until the day, several years back, when she assumed the top job as the deputy minister for the department and found out that these closures were for her. Buried in the package about the new DM job was a note about the departmental gym. She had to read it twice. She had exclusive access on Monday, Wednesday, and Friday between 10:30 and 11:45. There were trainers on standby if she needed them. All she had to do is ask.

Her arrival in the deputies' club had brought certain liberties, such as the ready access to drivers. Private elevators and bathrooms. And the early pensions. Less publicized were the host of exemptions from the duties of citizenship. Exercise exemptions are given to somebodies: the military, doctors, nurses, paramedics, police, firefighters. The principle was that they already needed to exercise to keep the job. Deputies, likely because they influence the rules, added themselves to the list of somebodies.

It was a little pretentious, but it now made sense to Ally.

Deputies can be peculiar, mysterious creatures. Deputy watching is a sport for many aspiring public servants. Ally had been privileged to work closely with several deputies over the years and that had given her a taste of the job. You always have to show up. You're always 'on.' You are expected to be hyper-articulate; able to be the public face of their department, explaining whatever is new or controversial with data and recent anecdotes. Most important, you skillfully have to do all that, while avoiding giving an opinion of your own.

Every deputy minister had a brand that helped to make them seem approachable. One wore fine wool sweaters instead of suit jackets to communicate informality. Another unfailingly talked about shared values, to reinforce the importance of content over style. The Clerk of the Privy Council was an old boy who emphasized education as part of his pursuit of the best and the brightest.

Ally had her own brand now. It was a rare day now that her face or her name didn't appear somewhere on a social media feed or on a committee somewhere. She always talked about healthy living. She was known for it. Saying not much but communicating stability. She was inspiring at acting her part.

The hours on the job were punishing. Ally spent seven days a week in long discussions with her Cabinet Minister, advising her or simply just listening. The Minister told her what the party in power wanted to achieve. The time left over was consumed with making something out of this grab bag of new policies, political ambitions and vague election promises.

So, in her private life, it was better for the department that she avoided public places like gyms or community centres, where staff might run into her and ask a question she dare not answer. Or worse, run across someone who cared about the department's issues and wanted to spar for a debate. Cameras were everywhere. When she was off the clock the last thing she craved was to meet more people in those precious hours. Her work days were overflowing with obligations to people with whom she wouldn't likely have more than a transactional relationship. Her life was filled with a huge cast of characters who let her see a snapshot of their problems. Her job was to understand them, fix their issues quickly, and move on to the next.

But exempt or not, Ally never let her guard down, modeling the best of citizenship. People murmured she was an effective deputy because of how she conducted herself. Keeping your composure under enormous pressure from angry stakeholders. Asking the thought provoking questions at the appropriate times. Keeping an upbeat attitude at all times, or showing up to champion the right causes. Equally important was the soft, unspoken stuff. You always had to be camera-ready. Smile at the right moments to convince people you are pleasant. Dress modestly but youthfully, to look good. Keep a level of language that reflected her position. There were lots of dos and a sad lot of don'ts.

Newbie deputies worried that the content of their decisions would come back to haunt them, but Ally learned that was less of a concern. Most bad decisions could be explained away fairly easily with a few contextual points. Nobody set out to make a bad call. What was much harder to cope with was a sudden burst of human failure. A terse word, a breakfast stain on the blouse, a question that unknowingly contradicted some new government policy. These were the minefields that Ally tried to stay out of. Everybody in the department, and beyond, watched her every move. One bad day was like a radio wave rippling through the consciousness of thousands of people. Neurotic organizational rumours of cutbacks and dissention started with less. Her goal as a DM was to create an environment of order and permanency so everybody else could make the department flourish.

Ally stood in her office and glanced up at the time. As it always was on Wednesday morning, the empty gym was waiting for her. If she hustled, she could still make the fitness group from Paris to which she subscribed. She liked getting into the gym because exercise offered a chance to think. She strode out the door of her office without making any eye contact, gym bag in hand, making her way to the empty change rooms and the gym floor.

As she entered the gym, Ally waved at the gym's only other occupant, Salim the caretaker. He was cleared to sanitize when deputy access periods were scheduled.

Over the years, she had come to know this gentle man. His lean, tall gait, the scar on his cheek, and the missing finger told Ally that life had been harder on him. She had heard some of his story, his journey to Canada from Ethiopia, the hunger, the hope, the work to reunite his family. He did not speak of the difficulty of getting settled. But Ally assumed that his story was the same as the many new Canadians she'd encountered.

By now they were friendly. It was not in the man's nature to be silent. He felt it awkward, impolite to ignore her. He would never be so rude as to ignore a fellow passenger on the journey of life. And so, he always tried to strike up a conversation. He did not presume with her, but he did not defer either. He treated her like an equal; most likely unaware of the department and its rules and personalities. Ally was simply the nice lady that was always in the gym while he did his rounds.

"Hey Salim, how are your kids," Ally asked.

He laughed as he spoke, as he often did. He was spraying down the treadmills with a square fog of hot steam and disinfectant. He pushed down his mask to speak. "They are very good. I had all of them with me this weekend."

There was something extra sunny about Salim today. "My son just told us that they will be blessed with a child."

"That's amazing! Is it your first grandchild?"

"Yes." His happiness at his good fortune shone through the blue mask he wore to protect him from the disinfectant. His infectious laughter turned up again. "My wife is already getting the baby bed ready. They are already out shopping."

"Congratulations Salim. Next Spring will be very exciting for you."

"Indeed, Ally. The baby is due in June. We had a party to celebrate."

"I bet that was loud with all the happiness," ventured Ally.

"Indeed. My wife can't stop laughing and singing." Salim stood back as the fog from another machine settled.

There was a familiar buzz. Ally's attention was distracted by a message on the cardio machine as Salim joined her. A reminder that she had to be back in the office for a meeting at noon. Apparently her Minister had an urgent question. She looked up at him as he took off his mask with measured gestures that signalled a need to ask her a question.

"Everything okay," Ally asked, still a bit distracted as she clicked through the words to answer another message from Mark, her second in command.

Salim stood very tall. He was nervously fingering the mask, and touching his pocket with the other hand. She rarely saw him in this worried state of mind, looking at her, hoping not to offend. "I need to talk about something very important. Can I share something with you?"

Ally stopped the machine and came over to stand with the man.

"I received a letter from the government, and I need your advice. I am worried I have done something wrong. My wife said I should ask you about it. I think you work for this department. No?"

Ally nodded her agreement. "Do you have the letter? May I see it?"

Salim took a well-worn piece of paper out his pocket and unfolded the message carefully. She took it gently from his extended hand.

Ally read it over quickly. Many people feared letters in the mail. Sadly, these letters could cause a lot of unintended misery and it wasn't shocking that it had caused concern for Salim.

Ally looked up at the man and tried to relieve his worry with her smile. "This might be good news!"

Salim looked confused as Ally filled him in. "Did you apply for a job in the government? Maybe months ago?"

"But it says it is for an interview. About citizenship."

"For a job at the citizenship department. Did you think there was about a problem with your citizenship?"

"We thought they might need money."

"No, Salim," Ally replied kindly. "It's the opposite. They want to meet you and see if you can work for them." Ally still felt Salim's disbelief. "Tell you what, I know someone in the department who can help. Can you trust me with this note and I will have someone get back to you?"

With that, the man smiled broadly and gave a little bow. A modest gesture, but Ally felt his sincere appreciation. They made some quick arrangements and Salim left directly, no doubt to share the good news with his wife.

She straightened up and went back to the cardio machine. She still had time for a run before noon. Her Executive Assistant had sent her another four messages that had flashed on the across her cardio machine. One caught her attention. Her daughter Tanya needed money, and she called her back directly.

Tanya's pretty face now filled the screen. She was wearing bright gold earrings that skimmed her shoulder as she spoke. Ally was relieved to finally connect. For the past few days, repeated messages to her daughter had failed to get a return. The drill was familiar. Ally had assumed that her daughter had lost her screen or didn't have money to pay the bill. Maybe she'd taken a road trip and was wandering, signal-less in the woods. The details of the silence were left to stew in Ally's imagination.

"Hey Mom. Sorry to interrupt you at work. I need some help."

"What's up? Why didn't you answer any of my messages?"

Tanya paused. "I couldn't. My screen got crushed."

"Crushed? How?"

"There was a fight. No big deal. But I don't have the cash to get a new one. I'll pay you back as soon as I have the money."

"Hun. Um."

"I can't go without my screen, Mom. What if someone needs me?"

The story danced on the high wire between credibility and manipulation. Her daughter managed her young life like a circus. "Mom," said Tanya plainly, I don't know who else to ask."

"Geez."

"Mom, it's tough right now for young people. It's not like when you were young."

"Okay. I'll send you the money this afternoon. Everything else good?"

"It's all good otherwise. It's just this issue with my screen. Thanks Mom, this is a lot of help." Tanya's voice was sincere. Ally gave her daughter a big wave and the conversation finished on a positive note.

Ally looked at the empty screen for a second. The interaction had been brief, and it was pleasant this time. But she still felt the familiar pangs of panic and pride about her only child. Tanya was always into some scrape or another, trying to be different.

She shook off the exchange and tried to focus on the run across Paris. The familiar image of the Arc de Triomphe was on the screen. She kept walking powerfully, but flipped to the briefing material for a meeting this afternoon. It outlined the reasons she was pulling her support to a project that a colleague in Parks department had let run seriously over budget.

She could hear herself make her point of view plain. "Yes. Frankly, I'm shocked to see the price tag. There's no way I can agree to that. Furthermore, I do not believe that the public wants to spend that."

It would be another difficult exchange. She was used to giving people bad news. So went the job.

She thought about Salim's words as he thanked her. "You are most kind." Each one of her days were filled with people who needed her to succeed. She played her part and accepted whatever emotion they shot back at her. It was rare that people used the word kind.

Twelve

Phillipe was the country's top bureaucrat with the archaic and grandiose title "Clerk of the Privy Council." His likes included monitoring the political broadcasts, squash with his old school buddies and eating lunch with the incestuous gang that hung around the powerful.

Ally sat in her usual chair at his massive solid oak round table. From here she could look out over Parliament Hill and around his immaculate office. The Clerk had tasked the installation around the room of his gleaming career and lifetime awards and recognitions. It added to the gravitas of the oak panels and flooring. Everything about the office would make the casual visitor think they were in a significant place.

"What do you mean?"

Her question was a delay tactic. Ally was pretty sure what he meant. She'd heard rumours on her personal networks and seen the Party launch the trial balloons. The polls showed some public interest in the proposed policy, a policy that wasn't new, just more of the same. Nonetheless, the Party was moving up in popularity because of this facile, pre-election, packaging trick.

He'd want her to invest obscene amounts before the election, convincing people the policy was new and necessary. Once the election kicked off, the Party would invest even more obscene amounts advertising their track record. It would give the Party the bump it needed from bigger numbers about the progress they were making cleaning up the environment.

Phillipe was the elite incarnate, genetically detached from the day-to-day life of the average person. He'd come late to the public service, straight out of law practice and already branded as one of Canada's "forty under forty." He shot up through the ranks with the support of a system convinced that pedigree meant superiority. True to the legal profession that trained him, he knew how to employ his body to communicate his power. He spoke deliberately, with a forceful, energetic cadence that sounded like battle orders. His chiseled jaw melted into his overgrown shoulder muscles. His linen shirt routinely gapped with the strain of his chest as he moved. Ally wondered how long he'd been using steroids.

In the decade or so that their careers had intersected, she'd never felt she'd achieved anything with his support. He was supposed to be on the side of reason, impartial. He spoke the talk. Still, she hated the covert way he was a yes man for the government. He had no qualms about passing on any request, no matter how political. Today was the same as many others. His office had requested that she "come over and chat in about an hour." This had put her staff into a frenzy of scheduling, as meetings were reorganized and relevant briefing materials were suctioned from all areas of her department. She'd run out of the office without a jacket, which she regretted. Fall was heralding its arrival; it was a nasty chilly day.

They'd already spent the first ten minutes dancing their way through the usual chatter about the news and her departmental files. At a point the Clerk deemed appropriate, he adjusted his buttocks in his seat and looked at her directly in the eyes. She was familiar with the signal. He was ready for the real chat to begin.

"It's so good that we get to talk face-to-face. I really should do this more," he began, lowering his voice slightly to confer confidentially on the information she was about to receive. Ally maintained her composed, receptive face.

"Well," he explained, "the Party wants to see the economy produce more carbon savings, create some room for future consumption reductions, so if targets aren't met in the future, Canada will still be ahead of the game."

Ally held her breath for a second, reflecting. As always, the Clerk had barged ahead on a topic without a scintilla of context. But she knew the Green Party was preparing for the fall political session, and the election next year. And he called it a "game." She thought it the perfect choice of words. His gentle way of expressing himself, betraying his dearth of understanding about the reality of who got hurt or how things got done.

"You're talking about the views of the Party about the heating policies? They want more savings?" The Clerk raised his eyes in agreement.

"In that case," Ally continued, "there's bound to be some hardship for people. They've absorbed a lot of change over the past two decades. The latest reports from the northern regions show that people were very upset with the current heating rationing quotas. And of course, there have been alarming increases in the protests against some of the more recent restrictions. It's been more than usual."

"That is as it may be, Ally. The Cabinet is very aware of this, and there are a number of action plans to address it. Some very interesting developments." It was his way to try to make her feel like an ignorant peasant.

Ally took off her glasses and rubbed the spot on the right lens that had been obscuring her view. "Fucking bullshit," she thought indignantly. They both had seen the data showing that the people on the margins weren't making it. Whatever the Party had in mind would be asking Canadians to pay more and make more sacrifices. It was ludicrous. People had nothing left to give. Furthermore, weren't things on the carbon front getting better?

She straightened herself in her chair and replaced her glasses. She looked at the Clerk and smiled with acceptance. "Well, what can my department do to help?"

He beamed. He had worn down her resistance for today. He began to give a few details of the project that she'd have to deliver in time for an announcement in the new year. "It will be a big commitment in your department's annual plan. You'll see a big bump for you in the Budget." He wanted to buy her support with promises of more departmental money.

Ally knew it was pointless to argue right now. The man was both her boss and the head of the public service. Best to take a longer-term view. Because that was the way to get something done in the public interest. More to the point, she had no intention of giving anyone what they wanted, without first knowing exactly what was required. Although she had no doubt this jackass would.

So, there it was. She was now in charge of a new government project. She didn't know much about what she was being asked to do. But she knew those details would stream in later. Through her very efficient departmental staff or in hints and interviews in the media. From her Minister's own people. Soon she'd be flooded with demands. But for now, she could go back to the office and focus on something else.

It was after seven and almost dark when her car pulled into her driveway. Her mind was inundated with the demands of another brutal day, filled with the relentless pressure of dealing with everyone's problems. A day of putting her thoughts and feelings second to a host of outsiders: ambitious climbers, idealistic advocates and the average observer. The meeting with the Clerk had been the low light. Ally knew she was paid to take it. It didn't make the daily prospect any more rewarding.

It was going to rain and the sky was dark. Ally watched the lights of the driver's car pull away. The dark hall illuminated as she opened the door and she listened to see where Derrick was.

After all their years of marriage, she could tell her husband was home. She could feel the pall in the house. Too few lights were on. There was the smell of some reheated dinner and a hazy voice of a broadcast signal in the distance.

In the shower she spent a few extra minutes letting the hot water run on her throbbing back muscles.

She pushed a window open to free the cloud of steam and grabbed a comb to tame her wet hair. There was a thought cloud creeping in, more serious than simply dealing with the realities of her career. Lately she found herself wondering about the point. And by the point, she was wondering about her life, but also about what was happening to everybody she knew. The questions persisted. Can you take on so much you can break? How far can you go before you are too isolated and too cynical to recognize the good? Was all this about suffering or about joy?

She reached the family room doorway and saw him in the old, worn-out reclining chair he loved so much. Representing the stereotype of the angry, depressed, middle-aged white guy.

"I installed the new recycling system. I hope you like where I put it, at the side of the house. It works. You can feed the stuff into it from the kitchen."

"Thanks," she replied. She would have said more, because she was grateful, but things between them weren't that way.

She waited there, looking at him and wondering about asking him about his day at work or what he was watching.

"I heard from my brother," Derrick offered, glancing at her quickly with disinterest. "He's in town for Thanksgiving."

"This weekend." She was about to ask if they wanted to get together when her husband jacked up the sound on the broadcast. He leaned forward towards the screen with rapt attention. "Live from New York, it's the U.S. Fight Club Championship. Tonight, it's the long-awaited battle between two absolute heavyweights of the no-rules fighting scene."

Ally waited a minute more, leaning on the door frame. He turned to her, his sardonic smile making his intention to her clear. "Did you want to sit down and watch the fight with me?"

She smiled sweetly and declined. More confirmation of what was dead between them. She turned away and bitterly thought to herself that he was just another asshole. If he had been listening carefully, he would have heard her mutter bitterly, "you fucking cruel no-balled bastard. When do you die?"

SECRETS

Thirteen

Janey pulled the cold metal handle of the door to *Robotz*. Gotta hand it to Tanya. Anywhere she goes, it's a party. There was some pretty loud EDM. The club vibrated to the beat of the music and noise of the ton of people there. Janey looked around and knew this was going to be a not-so-PC night.

She stood in the dark, musty entry and gracefully folded her trench coat, watching it magically disappear into the small pouch in her purse. Janey shook her shoulders to smooth out the black lace dress she'd bought in New York last winter, pushing her bra up to showcase her assets. She studied the line of guys sitting at the bar. All dressed up. Sliding between them, she looked over the dancing crowd trying to get a clear line of sight with the bartender. The guys all smelled of cologne. That meant they were looking to score. So was she, so hey, they had something in common. The bartender stretched over and shouted they were selling real tequila. She held up two fingers to order a couple of shots.

She caught a snippet of her cousin's voice over the din. Tanya and her crew occupied the round table against the wall, at the far end of the bar. It was dark, but that was Tanya for sure. She had on a familiar chambray shirt with hand-etched 'tattos' in black and red permanent marker. The shirt was tied at her waist and open to reveal a black leather bustier. A red, white and black bandana was artfully pulling back her bleached, wavy hair. Her cousin held up an arm to salute Janey's arrival, giving everyone a full view of the ample rings of silver and black metal decorating her arm.

Janey pulled over an empty chair. Tanya was wired, as usual, surrounded by a crowd, emphatically recounting a story about the results of her 21-year-old future health screening. Her sarcastic style, her sense of fun, merged with her naturally raspy, deep voice to turn this antiseptic event into something brazen, riveting, and verging on the edge of sordid. Her cousin was a breed apart; she ended up partying her way through Fridays, she bummed food from everybody, she got her guy friends to drive her where she wanted to go. She couldn't name one recent government waste reduction program, although most people could rhyme off ten.

Tanya-style, she'd dodged the messages and official summons for several years. But the results were worth the wait. The doctors had found no predisposition to Alzheimer's or diabetes, or any other of the diseases they screened for. Then she got a laugh by loudly calling the doctor a zero-watt bulb for predicting that she'd like put on weight as she got older. A list of vaccines, hormones, vitamins and when over the next fifty years she would likely need to take them sat unopened in her purse. There was a download of info on environmental cautions and genetic info that might affect her kids. People at the table giggled as she play-acted the doctor's discomfort about the test's insights on her gender orientation. He gave her the talk about exercising to keep your health insurance. Here Tanya leaned into the crowd and recounted in hushed tones how one of her old boyfriends fudged her records to get her the right number of exercise credits. Finally she wrapped up telling everyone to avoid alcohol. Like anybody does, Tanya hollered to the room. Janey ordered the group another round. Time to celebrate that Tanya was with them for the long haul.

A guy came over to speak to Tanya and took her away to dance. Janey started to feel the effect of the tequila and ordered another. She caught the eye of the cute guy at the bar and he came over. Damn, she thought, it never is this easy. What a night. They went out to the dance floor and partied. He seemed like a good guy. Not like they were talking or anything. The music was loud. They stopped for drinks at the bar and Janey lost track of the table of friends. This guy seemed nice enough and they tried to half talk over the noise.

Sometime later he slipped his hand around her waist. She knew the night was going to end well. She leaned up against his body and he leaned into her. She smiled a lot, not concentrating on what he was saying. I'm very drunk she thought. Bliss. He kissed her. It seemed good. He tasted like bourbon and coffee. They danced, grinning at each other with conspiratorial confidence. Shortly after, they left.

There's something spiritual about the walk of shame the next morning. Dragging your fucked-out body onto the subway, dressed in whatever you choose to wear of what you wore last night. It's early, hardly anyone is up, except the people who weren't wasted the night before. They're busy opening up the fresh food markets, making bread, cleaning the streets. And there you are, walking along thinking that surely someone notices that your bra is almost hanging out your

purse. But you don't care about being tagged as a bad girl.
Something good finally happened. You scored, in case anybody asks.

Fourteen

Ally arranged everything carefully around the room. This week she'd made sure the evening would want for nothing. She'd had to steal bits of time because her deputy minister's packed schedule. She messaged Pete once, quickly in breaks between meetings, to ask him what time he would arrive. She got a very spare "6:30" as a return message. But no matter, she knew that he wanted to be here.

She hung the provocative black lingerie on the back of the bathroom door. She put the toys and oils in the bed stand. She organized the hotel room to make it as homey as possible. The bottle of wine was taken out of her case and on ice to cool. Then she hid the can of Coke and a bag of chips under his side of the bed. Both were convenience packages and cost her a small fortune.

She sat down and waited. Patience wasn't her strong suit. She had waited for three weeks for them to find the perfect his-and-her excuses for tonight. She had lied and told Derrick that she was travelling for work. She had no idea how Pete had managed to get away. Their arrangement was such that they didn't tell each other how they lied to their spouses. For good reason, they didn't want to throw away their precious time together with more lies.

She flicked the screen system on. They were in a decent hotel, but they had a crappy system. Probably some restraint or recycling program in action. She tried to put it out of her mind. Thinking about why was shop talk. She flicked past the news about yet another environmental program. It would be the same old thing: either good news about reducing consumption, or bad news about a pending reduction or a program gone awry. She tried to find something that would remind her of the good old days. A sit-com about boy meets girl, and they have sex, boy and girl start fighting, and they get married anyway. They have kids and hang on past the relationship expiry date for no good reason and a shit load of excuses. She turned off the TV system. She was living the comedy anyway. And most of the good old programs were banned because they encouraged consumerism.

She flung her housecoat over the sign in the bathroom that berated her to be kind to our environment. "Every gesture in the bathroom makes a difference," it advised. It was one of the hundreds you would see in a day. She ran a bubble bath and floated back into it. She tried to remember how Pete would smell, what he would feel like. He was younger than her, stronger and manly, with seemingly unshakable confidence in himself. He was what she so wanted in her life, someone who was fun, who didn't worry about life's small stuff, who could take the ordinary out of her routine and make her feel something wonderful.

The card in the door rattled and she could hear him come in. "Hey baby," he called out to her as he found her in the bathroom. She looked at him with a wide smile that ranged from the look of a kid on Christmas morning to a sex-craved slut. There were always a few minutes at the beginning that felt awkward but hid a kind of child-like happiness. If there was a kind of a karmic scale of right and wrong, they felt too electric, too connected, to be on the wrong side.

He got a towel down from the rack and held it out while she got out of the bath, drying her off slowly, keeping his gaze on her eyes. She leaned towards his lips and they kissed while he pulled her hips closer. It was peace she felt first, like fresh cool water through her and then desire, which overcame them both as they made love with a kind of technical lust. It was if they had to do, be, and try everything all in this one night. This had to be memorable.

Later, they both lay side by side on the bed, lost in their thoughts. "Any chips?" he half-joked, feeling under his side of the bed. "Everything's coming up Milhouse! There's some Coke too!" He propped up all the pillows on his side, including the one currently under her head and made a kind of royal resting place for him to lean back and enjoy his treasures.

"Thank you, thank you very much for stealing my pillow!" She rolled over to watch him eat and offered a fake pout. In the half-light of the room in profile, he was beautiful to look at, his body chiselled by the sports he'd played over the years.

"Ally, anything I can do to make you happy. My pleasure!" He leaned over to give her a chip and she caught his hand and licked the salt off his fingers. "You are such a slut," he said smiling and shaking his head.

Ally snuggled closer to his body, organizing the sheet and lying so her body touched his all the way down. "So how is everything with you, Pete? Kids OK, business..."

He gave her a quick smirk of amusement. "Hum, why do you ask?"

"I dunno. I thought we could try what normal couples do. You know, chat about their lives."

"Okay," he nodded while looking at the bottom of the little bag for another chip. "The business is great really, can't ask for better. Sales of the new bio alloys are ahead of projections, I was looking at the numbers yesterday."

"And the kids, well, I took Mikey to his first boy-girl party last weekend." Pete crumpled up the bag and threw it on the nightstand. Then he turned to lie with her so their bodies leaned against each other. "I think he didn't move off his chair for the entire time, scared a girl would kiss him. Funny how things move. He didn't want my advice afterwards. He's growing up and I feel both kids needing me less and less."

He took a breath and lowered his voice. "I know we have this thing where we don't talk about our other lives, but I just have to share this one thing with you."

"Sure. What thing," Ally gently nudged.

"A couple of days ago my other half and I were having this blow out argument about something the kids asked for. Very stupid. And all I could think was, I wish I could be with you. We wouldn't fight like that.

"I feel like I never do a thing right for her. If it weren't for the kids, there are nights I just don't want to go home. Truth is, whatever this is between us, it keeps me going. These past couple of weeks, I wished that I could have called you. I just wanted to hear your voice and know that everything was going to be alright."

Ally reached up to kiss him on the cheek and put her arm around his chest. There it was, the bittersweet truth. It had been a year now. It was supposed to be casual, but relationships can't escape change. It was easy for her to ignore the pain of her marriage. Her daughter was gone and she easily found excuses to avoid her husband. Pete, with two kids at home, couldn't find the same escape route.

They both sat up silently and Pete picked up the remote and flicked through the sports mindlessly. Ally finally broke the silence. "I don't know what to say. I do care about you. I was in Toronto for work and went to dinner with some friends. It was fun and the food was great, and I wanted, for all the world, to have you there beside me. But this casual thing is all we know about each other. Right now we're bending the rules. Are we talking about breaking them?"

They were both sitting up beside each other now and she looked him in the eyes. They were beautiful eyes, brown pools of masculinity that she would lose herself in. She had even caught herself sketching his eyes at work during those tedious group-think management meetings.

He leaned over and caressed her shoulder before kissing her. "I don't know what I'm talking about these days." he murmured in her ear.

His tone punted the question down the road without another word. Better to live the moment they had right now than dwell on possibilities that can never grow into reality. They passed their evening deep in happiness, lost in their own company. And although they were both exhausted, the next day he called her at work, just to hear her voice.

Fifteen

"Kids fine up there?"

The men were thankful when Frank raised a hand to signal "yeah."
They'd been looking forward to the next hour or so of adult time.

It was Saturday night and this neighbourly trio of couples were pot-
lucking it together with their flock of young children. Experience
showed that if all the kids decide to get along, then they had a good
hour before they would be drawn into their drama.

"I put out the new projection playground," said their host, Frank.
"You can walk around the mat and play with the holographic
characters that appear in the room. They ask the kids to say what to
do next and they go on this adventure story. It lights up when you
sing and dance. It's kind of fun. I wish we had those when I was
growing up."

"You don't have to miss out on your childhood, Frank. We can still
give it a go!" laughed Jhonian.

The three men were in Frank's kitchen getting a handle on the food
while the girls had gone back to Jhonian's place to get the wine and
frozen pies. Jhonian and Ash had come directly from the hockey game
and had forgotten their contribution. As was their natural habit, the
women travelled together, so the guys had offered to get the dinner
ready while Ash, Frank's wife Selma, and Ted's latest girlfriend Maeva
went to forage.

"I guess it's safe to put the lawnmower away for the winter?"

"Tough call. I think we're safe. Should we get it tuned before we put
it away?"

Frank volunteered, "I can just give it some oil before I put it in the
back of my garage."

"I guess we're going to dig out the snowblower at the same time."

None of the guys had any real issues with sharing their equipment.
They could get better stuff that way and share with repairs and
storage. But it meant sometimes negotiating details and being square
about what needed to be done. On the plus side, it also gave any one
of them a ready excuse for time away from the kids or coffee on a
Saturday morning.

"Did you hear that asinine thing about Carbon Credits going up?"

"What's up with that? I just heard a bit on the news."

"Apparently, there's some speculation that they might introduce a
fine if you use too much heat."

"What? That's bullshit! I thought things were getting better." There
were shudders and groans from all three. No one wanted to pay the
government more.

"Did you hear that the Backstreet Boys are being beamed live to the
Civic Centre?"

"Aren't they like 70 years old?"

"Older. They've had a lot of work. They look pretty good."

Frank stopped and looked at Ted with the same disbelieving shit face
that he used to scare his kids.

"Yeah OK, I am full of shit. They look ridiculous and I don't want to
see a 70-year-old boy band. But they are being broadcast live at the
Civic Centre. Tickets will set you back $500 each."

"That's like a month of electricity. Who's paying that..."

The doors opened and the laughter of the three women could be
heard in the hallway. They had been gone forty-five minutes.

Jhonian went over to take the food and wine from his wife. She
smiled at him as she peeled off her thick sweater. As she popped her
head out of the collar, he reached over to smooth her hair. "Stop for
coffee," he teased. "Did you talk about me?'

"You. You. You. You're worse than my mother," she teased back softly. "I showed the girls all the hard work you've been doing in the yard, and then we got to talking."

"Well, I'm glad you had a good chat."

As their wives and girlfriend entered the kitchen, Jhonian and the guys headed for the fridge to draw another beer from the keg. They had got most of the dinner in hand. While the dinner finished cooking, the guys had the better part of an hour to themselves. "I have a spare set of eyewear, if you forgot yours," Frank called out. "The game is all set. All of your characters are compiled already into *Halo*."

The evening passed. Sweet relief that would recharge all their batteries for the week. Funny how the harder things got, the more you needed each other.

Returning home, it was well past nine o'clock when the kids finally got into bed and Ashley had her house right-sided. She was taking the time to breathe and sat at the kitchen table for a few minutes. The screens were off. Tea was still hot. The silence gave way to what she always seemed to crave: time for her thoughts.

She started as she often did, with a few positive affirmations. She closed her eyes and listened to the silence and dwelled on good things she had to be grateful for.

Seconds passed. She waited patiently for her mind to find something interesting.

Her mind filled with images of her husband and kids. Not very creative, but true.

"Oh, come on brain," she extorted herself. "Surely there's something else. There's more to be grateful for."

The word "grateful" triggered an idea. "OH, *Yolo-Hooray*," she exclaimed triumphantly to no one, getting up to fetch her screen from the buffet.

She scanned through the index of her apps and clicked on the app with the diagonal YOLO! in vibrant yellow script.

The screen lit up with the face of her avatar, a middle-aged woman, her hair drawn back into a messy knot. Not too pretty, projecting an admirable amount of self-control; she could be your cool aunt. *Yolo* gave you a lot of avatar choices, from Queen Curious, to Zen Master, to their most popular, the Side Splitter. But Ashley had customized her avatar, and cheekily called it Good Rachel after her mother.

"Hello Ashley," the avatar welcomed her in a voice with an Australian vibe. The voice reverberated in the empty house. She didn't want to wake the kids.

"Hello Good Rachel, can you speak a bit quieter? The whole house is asleep."

"I'm sorry, Ashley," the avatar responded, speaking louder. "I didn't catch that love."

"Love?"

"I'm sorry, was that too personal? You can always adjust my settings."

"Thank God," Ashley replied, fumbling anxiously to find the volume setting. The app screen was very cluttered. These days even the simplest functions were hard to find.

"What do you want to do today," the avatar continued with its cheery, empathetic tone. The avatar paused for what felt like four of Ashley's heartbeats. "Would you like to go back to where you left off?"

"Good Rachel, I won't need you tonight. Put me on to the silent screen. Thanks." Avatar continued to look at her, blinking and nodding knowingly. Nothing happened and then the auto-tuned *Yolo* sting played at full volume.

Ashley continued to move a few of the widgets on the screen, hoping to find a volume button. "Rachel, how about flipping me over to the main screen. Let's not waste time."

"I understand Ashley. What do you want me to do?" Ashley sighed and studied the screen for inspiration. "Rachel, why is everybody with your name so difficult?"

"Are you under stress tonight? *Yolo* can help. Let me tell you about our services, to help you decide. Your time is valuable."

Ashley buried the screen in a nearby bin of unfolded laundry, as a stop-gap measure to deaden the sound. But the avatar automatically turned up the volume and seemed to compensate by screaming.

"Ashley, we are here for you. You can sit down with one of the four psychologists and five counsellors on standby. Choose your rate by hitting 'something to share' button. Rates are posted on the welcome screen."

"Oh, damn," Ashley thought. Ashley looked over to the kill switch in the kitchen, and then remembered her husband was probably using his screen in the bedroom. "Last thing I need is for Jhonian to catch me."

She bent over the laundry, in overdrive toggling through all the icons and letters, and pushing her children's tiny socks and underwear onto the floor in the process. "Hi, Ashley, let me know how *Yolo* can help you today." The avatar sang the app's name again.

She was interrupted for a second as she thought she heard Kara's footfalls. They advertised the life out of *Yolo*. Everyone recognized the voice of its autotuned high-low "yo-lo" sting. It would be worse if Kara knew.

She finally found a tiny "I" in the lower left of the screen, revealing the mute setting, which she configured to private, just as she heard "hey there, are you still…"

In a flash, the avatar was replaced with a generic welcome screen. Ashley flipped a few socks in the bin and sank back into her couch, a little winded.

She was safe. Then she looked over the dashboard which told her she'd already spent sixteen hours on the app on the past week. Some of that was idle time when she'd started something and had to put the screen down. But the time was creeping up. She read about how this happened to people.

Then she pushed a few buttons and started back with her "establishing positive dialogue through reframing" exercise. She responded to a question about how she felt with "My life is filled with many challenges, but I have the skills and know-how to move ahead."

She pushed the button and the app assessed to her effort. "Not bad," it responded. "But go for a more positive tone. Try substituting the word challenges with opportunities."

She let out her breath in frustration and rolled her eyes. It was like banging her head against the wall.

"Everything good here?" Jhonian pushed his head around the corner of the living room. "You ready for bed?" His optimistic tone was a relief as she put the screen aside. The time for synthetic connection was over, she was ready for the real thing.

In the half-light of the bedroom, Jhonian fucking did look like a Mexican film star. Saturday night and his expectations were high. His was a sustaining presence and she was so grateful for him. He was a gentle giant of a man and she couldn't get by without him. Even if she felt like a shadow of what she could be, he always saw her as something much more.

Sixteen

Kara peered into the recent satellite detail of coast line where she usually spent her winter vacation. The shape of last year's coast was traced over with a white line on the image. She picked up a second tablet with the pictures from a decade previous. There was probably a way to call all of these images onto a big screen, if she knew how. Instead she extended her arms to hold both out to compare for changes, paying special attention to the beach where she usually rented her condo. It was a gated community, right on the water. Best she could tell, the erosion still hadn't taken over the beach. She'd already looked at the water and temperature reports. She was delighted to find that the worst of the damage from rising ocean levels had still managed to evade her little corner of South Carolina.

She put both screens on top of a couple of paper books and got up to refill her glass of water. The motion was enough to send the pile to the floor. Her white hair came annoyingly loose as she fussed with her hair and bent over to pick it all up. She had the fleeting reflex to chuck all this clutter for a modern set-up for her work space.

Jhonian often suggested it when he had occasion to visit her basement apartment. "Mom, I can build you something more efficient. With a large screen across the room and everything cabled behind the wall. You could get a virtual keyboard near the couch. A better voice recognition system. I can build a cupboard so it looks like it's part of the wall. Get rid of all this…" His eyes would wander over her bookcases with paper stacked neatly at every end of each shelf. Past the open cardboard box with spent technology gathering dust. Around the small table with a stack of antiquated metal biscuit tins crammed full of souvenirs. He knew if he had the courage, he'd likely find pieces of his childhood artistic triumphs there. To the tower stand on the floor which had been with her for ten years now. It had a backup of all her data. Just in case.

"It's okay dear, you've got so much to do. I'm happy knowing where everything is." Despite the occasional wish for something else, her old-style office arrangement with a desk she could sit behind suited her much better.

Her son was never quite content with her rebuff of his standing offer. "I get it Mom. At your age, it's cruel to make you change."

She'd give him a dose of the hard stare of motherhood to challenge his good-natured dig. Squinting her eyes with her hands on her hips; they didn't need words now. It was the same stare for nearly forty years. He'd return her stare with a look of familiar affection. "Okay Mom, I'll let you get back to your retro century office. Or should I say your command centre for your efforts to rule the world!" Somewhere mid-sentence he'd jog up the stairs, demonically punctuating his departure with "ha, ha, ha." His laugh was so much of his father.

His father she had loved so much.

Her first husband, Stuart Asher, was someone who was just there. They were too young to understand the commitment they'd made to each other. She soon realized that she'd married for convenience and this made their time together uninspiring and monotonous. They didn't fight, they didn't connect and the only things they created were her two daughters, Ally and Jennifer. The relationship came to a blissful end about seven years along. The ensuing years proved that both parents were better off apart.

She'd been content to be a single mother of two until a fateful trip, alone to a sunny piece of paradise. Years ago, when going south was something that people could do. It was that Mexican sojourn where Kara learned what love could do to a person. In Mexico she fell completely for her second husband, Kelvin Bernal, and would have gratefully walked over broken glass to see him. Despite the demands of her company and the responsibilities of her two daughters, Kara and Kelvin kept up a torrid relationship. They told their families very little, with her going back and forth between her kids in Ottawa and her new life in Mexico. As much love as she had for her daughters, she only felt whole when she was in his company. His love was food for a starving soul.

Then the day came that they both planted their feet in Canada. They married simply and set to the idea of building a life together in the snowy north. So it happened, and Jhonian was christened not long after.

Life for mother and husband number two started well enough. Half-sisters Ally and Jennifer joined them every other week. But eventually, the homesickness that creeps up on many immigrants hit her husband. His language skills held him back, and he hadn't bargained on raising three kids, two of which did their best to make him feel incompetent. In a couple of years he was back in Mexico. Later the sad news came. There had been a tragic construction accident.

Jhonian remembered little of those times, he was too young. Kara knew little Spanish and less of her husband's family. Ties between Jhonian's Mexican side never flourished. His name, and his laugh, were the few ties to his dad and Mexico.

Her son philosophically accepted that he'd never really know his dad. Still, she found herself making up for her son's loss over the years. Sometimes her amends were intentional, like accepting to move in when Jhonian asked her.

Some things she did unconsciously, like always making the kind of pie that he preferred.

She looked over at the screen. Terry would call soon. She didn't talk about her latest relationship with Jhonian. Every year, in the depths of the hard, frozen months she escaped with Terry to the Carolinas. He was someone she'd worked with years ago. After her divorce they'd confided in each other and grown very close. But back then they were never lovers; she'd been too immature to trust what she felt. Despite both of them finding new partners, discreetly they had kept in touch. When his wife had passed almost a decade ago, their feelings came back to life.

The discussions about both moving to something more full time in one city or another sat unresolved. It meant one of them would not be there for their kids, and that was unthinkable when the grandkids were growing. For better or for worse, their annual hookup was what their obligations would allow.

Terry had been a hidden fact of Kara's life for some time now. She had never said a word to Jhonian, the one man that really mattered more than any of others. It might scar him more and that would be another pain she couldn't bear. Better her son trusts that his own father was significant to her. Better to avoid the question whether she ever loved either of her kid's fathers. Better it was all left a secret, so safely hidden that if something ever happened to her, Terry might not find out.

Kara sat down and took a sip from her glass before clicking a few buttons on a keyboard. They'd agreed to talk this afternoon. Terry was on screen in an instant, standing in his living room in a dark blue suit; his pear-shaped frame was balanced by the cut of the jacket. Others might see an older man with a kind smile. Kara focused on what had been with him since his youth: the wavy hair, his blue eyes and fluid way of moving.

"Hello you. How is everything in Winnipeg?"

"Brutal!" It was his habit to start all their conversations with a good-natured weather report. "We had to scrape the cars this morning. They were covered in frost this morning."

"Sorry about that. You look very dignified in that suit. What's that about?"

"Oh," he looked down as if he was unaware of what he was wearing. "I guess I still have it on." He looked back up at her. "I was at the bank today with Michael. He's looking into a mortgage and I will need to help him out."

"What a spectacular dad you are!"

"Better to help them now, when they need it."

"True that. Go okay?"

"Dunno. We've gone through all the automated stuff, the credit reports, the price histories, everything. I think I sent a screen shot of everything I know. I was waiting for them to ask for an income statement from Mr. Bigs over there!" He pointed to the cat sleeping peacefully in a round ball on the couch behind him. "This is the last interview. I thought the suit would give me a bit of leverage. I don't understand half of what goes on now. It's all dumb bureaucracy anyway. They have access to every transaction online. They're my bank."

"So frustrating. I went through that with Jhonian. The waiting was a killer. They acted like they're doing me a huge favour. I almost went online and looked at one of those fast cash places."

"The rates aren't much different. Anyway. It's almost done. Michael and his wife are very happy. That's what's it's about."

"You need one of these." Kara pressed a button on the bottom of the screen and it filled with hearts that danced around the edges of surface before racing into to the centre to make up the word 'hug' in large purple letters. Then it disappeared like a puff of smoke.

"Thanks. Very nice. But you know what I'd really like." He paused for a moment to gaze at her. He leaned closer to the screen, as if he was getting closer to her. "I can't wait to see you. I hope the next two months fly be."

Kara gave a soft chuckle of agreement. "Terry, sweetie, I'm looking forward to waking up with you too. But don't wish your life away." A woman with three major relationships can't help but compare. Terry was the easiest to be with. Maybe not as passionate, but lovely and easy. It was like this that the month would pass. Eating, laughing, fooling around, and talking with old friends about stuff that only old friends would understand. Kara loved it. Most of the year, when she was knee deep in grandchildren and volunteer work, she needed to know that this world existed. An elegant respite from the real world.

"I checked everything out at the property. Waterline looks good. I think we are safe to reserve in our usual spot."

"Great. I can come down for three weeks. I'm hopeful I can add a week, if I move around a couple of things I have to do here. I looked and they have space late January."

"Do you want to reserve, or should I?"

"You go ahead. You like to get there first. I'll let you do your routine and set the place up. Just let me know what my half will be and we'll make the cash transfer."

"Thanks. Time will fly, you'll see," Kara reassured him. "How are you doing otherwise?"

"I'm still shaking my head at what happened at the bank."

That wasn't like Terry. He'd been a university professor until he retired. He was generally ahead of her. "How so?"

"It was a young guy at the bank. And my kid. Between the two of them, they were talking some sort of code. Made me feel so out-of-date."

"I hear the kids do that sometimes. They talk like they game. What's one of them? 10X."

"I know that one. That's been around forever. Means thank you. It was a new one today. I had to ask Michael after we left the bank. They kept saying BDE and smiling at me. I just grinned back like an idiot."

"I know that face!"

"Ha. Funny. I wish I was there to say F U in person."

Kara stuck out her tongue, with a playful leer.

"As I was saying, before you insulted me...."

"Sorreee...," she sang with a contrite automated voice.

"Better. To finish my story, BDE means best dad ever."

"I guessed that."

"You lie, you had no clue."

"Okay. You're right. I had no clue. But you are the best dad ever. Happy now?"

"Yes. TTYL?"

"Of course. Tomorrow is another day." Kara pressed a couple of buttons and a large heart floated across the screen with the numbers 143 in script.

"Very clever and modern. I love you too."

"You've got to stick with the lingo, buddy. You mean 143 2."

He shook his head. "That's enough of you today," he chuckled kindly back, in a voice that he might use to jolly along his faithful old cat. "I'll stick to words." He blew her a kiss and his image disappeared.

THE STANDARD OF JOY

Seventeen

Janey was prone on the floor of her living space on Sunday morning. Her arms were strewn over her head while she stared at the ceiling, reflecting on the situation immediately in front of her.

Inside, guts were turning, slowly, painfully. Movement was risky, as another wave of nausea ripped. "Please not again." She'd heaved once already this morning. A good portion of the club sandwich she'd eaten late at her local diner, and probably most of the bottle of reproduction tequila in her stomach for company.

She winced at the hazy panorama of last night's glory; like stumbling loudly into the diner with Tanya and her entourage. Tanya waved them all to a table and ordered another round.

"Except not for my cuz, over there," she'd laughed, directing attention to Janey, who was sitting face down on her folded arms. Beyond that, she tried to remember if she'd made an ass of herself. "Nobody will remember," she told herself remorsefully. She sighed, knowing she had to face the truth and the diner staff again.

It's sweet when you party to rebel. The shitty part was the next day, putting in the time to recover. Her personal screen lay out beside her. She'd already checked for any uncomfortable pics that showed up where her mom and dad could find them.

In the half-life of this, the next day, as the fake joy expired and other real-world thoughts flowed in to be dealt with, she began to wonder bitterly about the ambition to get so shit-faced. It was the silent standard set out for all young people. Not an expression of some political outrage or bigger cause. Nothing so complicated. The next morning, remembering her head in her arms at the diner table, it just seemed like a pathetic quest for amusement.

Traveling in the States, she'd noticed they had so many other options for entertainment. There, with a little ingenuity, you could find a fresh way to act out. Fun didn't have to be all drugs and alcohol. You didn't always need them to go crazy. Buy a gun and wear it out to dinner. Speed down the highway in your vintage gas guzzler. Scream hate anonymously at someone online. How dare you say I put a filter on my dog's balls? They are that big. The options for senseless distraction were boundless.

Not here. Alcohol was choice number one. "Have a beer and forget about it." The advice she heard repeatedly as she coped with being an adult. In the media, from coworkers, hell, even once from her doctor.

She had a vague bout of gut regurgitation and then some nausea. "Stupid." She tried to lie very still.

Why did she ever try to keep up with Tanya? She was far more experienced in the art of rebellion. Janey screwed her eyes up tight against the light and observed herself standing in some dark void. Feeling way too gross to process much beyond that.

This would be a Sunday on the couch, absently flipping through the video screens and ignoring all the beeps from friends and fam.

Lots to do and nothing would get done. She'd have random panics as she'd be overcome by her thoughts telling her that she was missing out. What would she rather be doing?

Hiking through the hills, making fall bonfires with mysterious friends who also like such things.

Taking in a lovely ballet streamed live from New York or Berlin in a room full of grey hair.

The panic of choice. If only she could have more. But it was oftentimes hard when presented with too many great options. Maybe choices make you unhappy. If she only had one right option, it would be simple. Janey contemplated being simply happy. Or happy simply. Maybe she had too many choices. Maybe we all did.

A pounding started in her head that promised to be relentless. And then it hit her, she was drying up.

There was always fifteen minutes of intense philosophical introspection between the effects of alcohol leaving her system and the pounding hangover headache. She was dallying in this illusion marked by a lot of 'deep' thoughts. She'd written a couple of well-reviewed essays in university based on inspirations in this state of withdrawal. But most of this profundity would soon be forgotten, and if remembered, would be found on sober reflection, to be objectively not very deep.

How much did she drink last night? And why? And why did this always happen when she went out with her cousin?

She got up from the floor quickly, in time to wretch in the toilet down the hall.

Laying back down slowly, she focused her thoughts on a spot on the ceiling. Much safer. She closed her eyes, but before her lids touched she noticed the red flash through her eye lashes. Maybe she should reach up to the sofa table and check her screen.

Instinctively she folded herself upright and fumbled blindly. "Incoming video call from Byron Larssen," it reported. "Fuck," she yelped, pushing the 'call you back in ten minutes' button. That wasn't enough time to look good, but at least she could get out of these ratty pajamas and splash some cover-up on the circles under her eyes.

Byron, was an old school friend who now lived in New York City. They'd kept in touch after high school. The virtual back and forth died out over time. However, when she began her annual winter treks south, they made a point of getting together. It had been fun for both, and, as adults, they had got close. She'd give him glimpses of her austere post-consumer world and his childhood. She got to witness his striving to measure up to NYC wealth.

Her thoughts, hungover as they were, lingered as she thought of him. He'd been in town recently visiting his family, and they had got together.

He looked fine now. He had a thin build in school and dressed geeky. The city had given him style and age had filled him in. At six foot four and with his broad shoulders, he was the kind of guy that Janey found quite striking.

They had gone out to dinner locally. He worked in a notable hotel in NYC, and she had been a bit reluctant to show off the local PC eateries.

Didn't matter much. It was a nice night. She'd seen him over the years in his element, but he adapted well to hers. God, they could talk. Hours went by and they still had more to say. They walked out of the restaurant and sat at the Canal talking for quite a bit more. It wasn't like her to be so into a conversation. She was more inclined to observe and add the odd comment so as not to seem without opinions. But Janey and Byron, as Kara would say, had chemistry.

She looked at herself in the mirror, hoping she didn't look like hell. She felt a little better. The prospect of good chat had pushed the hangover down. She sat down at the cleanest spot in her living room, picked up her screen and pressed the call back. "Hey, sorry about that. I was busy for a second."

"No worries. How's it going?" He was in his apartment, dressed in Sunday sweats. His sandy hair looked like it was still wet.

"Going fine up here. Same old. How about you?"

"Like you say. Same. Work's good. Busy enough."

"That's good. I'm coming down again this winter. I was about send you a message to see if you wanted to have dinner or something.

"Of course I do! I'm really looking forward to your visit. I'll check out what we can do. Are you going to your Grandmother's first?"

"Yes, first. I'll send you all the dets." Kara had this deal where she got away every winter to a sea-side cottage in South Carolina and Janey would join her for a week. She looked forward to this time away every winter. She'd take a train out of Montreal and stay for free with her Nans. And that was fine by her because they got on. It was better than no trip at all.

On her way back, she would switch trains in New York City. Janey stopped in the city every year. She would tell others that she found some gadget or other that would make life better or has some positive environmental impact. She would rationalize that she needed something for one of her hobbies. She clipped articles on this or that throughout the year as she saw things and put it in her wish box.

Then she would book into the same hotel and wallow in the ease of New York life for a few days.

"I was thinking that we are both going to be twenty-nine this year."

"Yes," Janey agreed. "It sounds so old. Almost thirty."

"It's not old. It's just a number." They started talking about this milestone and what it meant. The ups, the news, and the profound stuff. She looked at the time on the bottom of the screen.

"Hey! I just noticed we've been on the call for an hour."

He grinned back. She thought he might be blushing. Hard to tell for sure on the screen. "I'll look out for your trip dets. It'll be great to see you again."

"You too." She smiled back at him as if to share the unspeakable. They signed off. Still, it felt like they had so much more to say. She sat on the chair in silence and looked around at her life. A tingle of adrenalin came up from her legs to her head as she let out her breath. Closing her eyes and smiling, she mused about being face to face with him soon.

Eighteen

She walked into her offices and staff were aflutter. Ally and all the heads of ministries had been called downtown.

"You mean, physically," she asked her staff in amazement.

Almost all meetings of the departments located across town, except for the Friday deputies' breakfast, were streamed. She could remember, even longed for the days, when she would get into a taxi and drive to a meeting. Now her time was considered valuable, so no one would dare ask her to come to their office. Her office became a benign prison, rotating around the corners of the room. To the video station, to her desk, to her meeting table and then to the computer. Her portable screen was always in front of her. Lighting up every few minutes with some new piece of information. There were days now that she would feel she had physically met a great many people, while, in fact, she had not shaken one hand.

However, today was different. She guessed it was about what the news streams were calling the heat refugees. Winter was approaching and a new wave of northern Americans was making their way over the border. These were the poor. Still mostly tied to carbon fuel, and unable to heat their houses at US supply prices, they were sneaking over the border to get housing with government backed energy incentives.

As Ally walked to the elevator, her staff scheduler walked alongside, going over the plans for today.

"Can you just tell me..." the anxious voice of her scheduler tried to squeeze in one more question as the elevator door shut. Ally waved and yelled back "I'll call from the car." She remembered that she also needed an upload of the briefing materials on the government's latest energy plans.

No matter how you managed it, energy sat at the base of every environmental issue. Energy saturated the public discussion. Long ago, carbon-based fuels had lost their favour, although sometimes, like in the far north, they were the best sources. So then, what was the best source of energy? How much energy did it cost to produce food, or was it "good" to invest the energy to ship goods from one end of the continent or other? Was it "right" to use petrochemicals as raw materials? Were large scale energy projects that caused enormous changes to the watershed or bird population "acceptable impacts?" What was the most "efficient" energy source? Solar was popular, but you needed raw materials and energy to make it too. Turned out that you need energy for just about anything.

Across the developed world, the approach was different, although the challenge to reduce or replace the carbon-based energy we all needed was the same.

The Green Party in Canada squeezed out every drop of energy in every sector. It hurt, but Canadians took it on as a "for better or for worse" PC life commitment vow. Sometimes it resulted in satisfactory alternatives, like hothouse tomatoes or strawberries in February. Sometimes it meant that things disappeared. Exotic fruit was just that now. Packaging restrictions seemed to regress the food industry to an earlier era. Frozen homemade leftovers in their specially designed containers were modern convenience foods. In a country familiar with minus 40 degrees in January, home heating was rationed to reduce energy use. The argument went that it was fair. Everybody could afford to stay warm and we all made a contribution.

For our closest neighbours south of the border energy costs rose to "fair market value." It hurt as the price of just about everything skyrocketed. There was lots of innovation; companies grabbed at environmental problems with new products, but the response was chaotic. Nobody knew what choice was better than another. People grew weary and retreated to making sure they had their own. People chose solar panels because they matched their roofs. They bought electric vehicles based on the untested claims of manufacturers. Every news cycle brought some new research to solve the undefined climate crisis. To the world outside their borders, the U.S. approach missed some central direction.

Still, the American argument went, the market had to be free. And someone had to make a decent, and every so often, indecent profit. The Canadian idea of working together and making sacrifices was held up as a sort of socialist hell. The thin edge of dictatorship that detractors claimed lead to death and anarchy. Lately, that meant Americans without means were much worse off. It was forcing people to make ridiculous choices. Like the heat refugees. Sad and embarrassing for what was once such a wealthy nation.

About an hour later Ally was listening to the discussion at the deputies' table. Her suspicion for the urgent meeting was right. She was sitting around the table with her colleagues in charge of the other government departments reporting on progress.

She knew the dance. Culture and propaganda were her domain, so this wasn't her issue to solve. Ally spent the time watching the drama of the thirty or so of them. All the departments were expected to do something in support. She looked with some empathy at her colleagues who were the leads on this file. They looked confident as they presented their usual stories about what they can do.

Truthfully, what they could do was round up these unfortunate people and put them in holding cells. When the weather got a bit nicer, the Canadians would ship them back.

It was the venerable Phillipe, Clerk of the Privy Council himself, chairing the meeting. He already let people know that he was going to carry some weight as the lead on this file. In his most forceful, clipped tone he told his soldiers that he'd be getting hands-on, leading the development of the briefing materials and cabinet presentations. Given the anticipated per cent of news stream coverage and the fact that borders were reporting higher than usual crossings, she had no doubt the Prime Minister was putting the pressure on daily. The government wanted this to go away. Our relationship with the Americans was important and this was an unfortunate irritant.

The meeting dragged on without a conclusion. There was a full hour of ritual servitude and codependence where the Clerk told them, again and again, what was required. Each department head had to give a few points about what they could do to support this "serious, life-threatening" situation. Staff had shot what she needed to her personal screen while she was at the meeting. Some publicity at the border to ask Canadians to greet warmly and report any of these refugees.

The lead departments told the group what arrangements were in place to find out more. International was handling the liaison with the

U.S. Consulate. Warnings about handling any media centrally. Same crap as the last few years. One day the Americans will wake up and do something about this. She liked visiting the States, but they were living in a dream world thinking everyone can pay for what they needed.

The Clerk was his composed, forceful self, but he made a few forgetful mistakes. He proposed some changes that everyone knew had failed last year. Then he suggested follow-up for the Canadian embassy in Washington, although these suggestions had been discarded earlier in the meeting. He was unsure how to create something worthwhile out of the jigsaw puzzle of people's unmet needs and daunting expectations.

Like everyone in the semi-circle facing their boss, Ally smiled politely. She enjoyed the comedy of the Clerk's trip into her hands-on world as he grasped for his own practical ideas.

"I wonder if we've considered all the potential fall-out from this idea, given how dramatically the data fell last year, after implementing something similar." It was Hector from Environment ever-so-diplomatically reminding the Clerk how his current idea was a repeat of last year's failures.

"Join us in the real world anytime, you son-of-a-bitch," mused Ally to herself.

As the meeting broke up there were a few nods of greetings and chatter about shared projects. People had their game faces on, looking upbeat and focused. As she drove away, she asked staff to set up meetings with the two leads on the project. She liked Hector at Environment especially and wanted to give him some moral support.

Nineteen

Ally paused for a second at the door to her executive suite and looked around. People were already in full swing for a Monday. She neatly draped the fine tweeded wool of her coat over a hanger in the entryway closet and walked without making eye contact to her private bathroom. Inspecting her face in mirror, she put on some more lipstick, then adjusted her burgundy outfit, finally brushing a few specks caught in the silk of her vintage dress. Satisfied with her appearance, she said hi to her staff in the outside office before closing the door and gliding into the most comfortable chair to start flipping through her messages.

Requests from people had piled up in her inbox over the weekend. There was nothing all that urgent, and that let her mind wander back over the last forty-eight hours. Saturday evening Ally was invited to the home of a deputy colleague who was celebrating his son's engagement. The room was filled with the achievers in the Ottawa public service. The deputies, the Chief Advisors of a long list of Stuff, like Science, Climate or Leisure. The next-in-line. And the spouses and the occasional elder child as a plus-one getting a taste of what was in store.

Derrick had ultimately agreed to attend and delivered a satisfactory account of himself in public. Beforehand, she'd cajoled and pleaded for him to join her at the party.

"Why?" he had questioned her. "You know that half those people walked over me on the way to get where they are!" He'd ended his career with his retirement three years ago. Despite his striving, he'd never got to the top of his specialty of geology, as far as the organizational hierarchy was concerned. He was still a respected scientist and went into his lab on a regular basis. But his personal ambition to be a head of a university department, or a senior public servant, had never really happened for him.

Ally had countered, reminding him calmly that he knew why. "That's our deal. And you're going to put on a show, and not embarrass me. Get it? That's how this gig rolls."

Derrick was used to her threats and insults. Nothing hurt like it used to. She'd stopped short of stabbing him with the worst truth. Most of the people he resented were entitled to their success. Sometimes you're not worth the rewards that you covet.

In the end, she endured his nauseating transformation from "Derrick the pitiful" to the persona of "Professor Emeritus Derrick Green" that she saw so rarely. Making toasts and small talk as if he cared about anybody or anything but himself. Enjoying himself. She smiled warmly through the usual comments about how much everybody just "loved" Derrick. Ally, they said in their naiveté, was so lucky.

The idea of her bad luck put a familiar chill up her back, shaking from side to side to fling the anger out of her. She closed her eyes and changed the channel to much more pleasant reflections. She lingered over the memory of yesterday afternoon with Pete. Pretending to run into each other at the half-decent sports club at the other end of town. "Yummy Pete," she closed her eyes and drew her breath as if she could still smell him. The comfort of playing some tennis and having a civilized meal together.

Her scheduler put her head in her office. "You ready," she asked politely. "You'll have to chair the meeting yourself. Mark's not here."

"Ah, crap," Ally said to herself. Today's meeting was scheduled so Ally could bless her department's new citizenship campaigns before they went off to Cabinet for approvals. These campaigns had been crucial to the success of the environmental movement. You couldn't turn a country around from a nation of buyers to a nation of savers without a solid investment in what she called communications. Or what others called propaganda.

Last night, Ally had spent several hours going through her briefing dossiers for the week. She'd put aside all of the briefing material for this next meeting, and they'd sent lots of it. She'd counted on Mark, her second-in-command, to carry this meeting. Now she'd have to wing it.

Walking out of her office towards the boardroom, she asked her EA where Mark had got to. A deputy's life was comprised of thousands of decisions about the details. She'd forgotten she'd sent him to Washington because embassy staff wanted to know about our citizenship programs. Mark, who often stepped in for Ally, was the propaganda master. The Canadian government's propaganda machine was envied throughout the world and Mark's expertise was much sought after. It was to his credit that Mark's team was hard at it as she strode into the room.

Khristin sat at that opposite corner. She looked so young; when they first met Ally mistook her for a teenager. Her group worked on defining the new citizen, which meant keeping track of all the old and new programs.

At the end sat Regine, who ran what was essentially a sales team. They got out and sold the ideas to others: schools, mayors, advertisers, community groups.

Ally sat down beside Louis, her money man. The government had poured money into all this activity for decades, happy to campaign on this achievement. Louis made sure to complete all the interagency formalities so the money flowed and she didn't have to worry about it.

Mark's team used the media in ways that were so original, other countries wanted their secrets. They were a confident bunch. Unlike the rest of her department, they did not fear her. They respected her and humoured her. When you're internationally recognized, you don't need kudos from the boss.

They got started talking about the grants, deciding where to put government dollars into provincial, city and local programs. Putting the federal "*We're moving ahead!*" stamp on every aspect of a Canadian's life.

Regine told the group that with an election coming, the government wanted the volume turned right up. They looked over the spreadsheet with its largesse running to about ten dollars for each Canadian. A lot. Soon every athlete, library, school child in a little league, fitness club, community centre, arts program, yadda yadda across the mighty land would have a new video display and logo for their sportswear.

But the truth was that the whole team knew that this would have little real effect. The government had been at this for three decades now. The money and slogans were expected, too familiar. It had no effect on Canadians anymore. Nobody ever read a sign with the too-familiar *"We're moving ahead!"* logo on the top. It was as banal as wishing your neighbour "a nice day."

They moved onto talking about the special campaigns. These were different every year and targeted the areas where the government assessed that Canadians still had more work to do. They were important years ago, because Canadians demanded to know what needed to get done. Like explaining price increases for local manufacturing, or converting meat production away from agri-food. Whatever, there was a long list of big stuff coming out of the Post-Consumer Royal Commission. For Ally, these were the best part of the job, because she could see the difference she was making. Whether it was sports sponsorships, lotteries or t-shirt giveaways, she was key in designing the communications to make the changes real.

But change stabilized and ideas from the Royal Commission dried up. These campaigns became less essential and more political. Ministers started to insert their vanity projects that would help them get reelected. Special interest groups lobbied for projects that would support a favoured cause. Ally had to give them special attention as they were less about being PC but still had the power to nudge Canadian's behaviour. Some of that nudging caused more irritation than good.

This year the first campaign supported housing conversions, where families carved up their old-fashioned cavernous suburban houses into smaller apartments and rented out parts to family and friends. There was government support for this, as interest rates had been rising, and the water and heating systems needed upgrading.

Ally had wondered at first if the government had any right to muck about promoting what was essentially a family affair. Yes, it had been a good idea at first. People could stay in their neighbourhood. Cities could avoid tearing down these big houses and replacing them with high-density housing. The issue was that while this sounded like a good idea at first, in practice it seemed to rip families and friendships apart.

She said as much to her colleague at Canada Housing when he asked her to run this campaign. But he wouldn't back down and told her

140

that her support was required. According to him, there was a risk of violence if they couldn't get the population to accept the program. He cited the recent events where a father had burned a house down that was 80% converted when he learned that his kids expected he and his wife to live in the basement.

She thought that was an isolated incident until a young couple befriended an elderly pair and were later charged when they tricked the old folks to renovate, and then got them to sign over the deed.

She got on board with the campaign when she'd observed the focus groups. As she sat on the other side of the two-way mirror, the problems were clear. The younger generation felt that this was a way of moving back in time to their parent's era. But people from Ally's generation felt they were giving their kids a hand up, although they had reservations about the reduction in living space and privacy. More to the point, the oldest generation was moving back in too. Three, sometimes four generations could be living together, maybe even with old friends and other relatives.

Ally knew she had the best people working on this assignment, but even they were stymied.

"We have tested this twice now," shared Regine. "We know that there are numerous issues with this concept and don't know where to begin to unpack it to develop the campaign. We are definitely not ready to send this off for approvals."

"I suspected as much," responded Ally. "What seems to be the major challenge?"

"Where do I start? There are marked differences, depending on the age group. It's as if this issue is a lightning rod for what's bad or difficult about this stage of post-consumerism.

"The younger generation is happy to make this work, but if they are married or if they have kids, they want to be the alpha members of the pack.

"The older generation regrets ever getting into this. They feel they are already making more sacrifices and giving up a lot right when they wanted to retire. As the transition moves along, they wish they could renege on what they call 'the whole mess' and move into an apartment.

"If we advertise this program hard, we will get a backlash. It'll be even worse in ethnic communities that have more tightly woven family dynamics. Even after all the gains we have made, we can't go against the flow of generations. Kids are supposed to leave."

"Did the Housing representatives see the tests?"

"Oh yeah, they were stunned. They had heard about these problems from their field people. But when they saw the tests, they told us good luck coming up with a campaign."

The delay in the campaign was not going to be good news for the Party. She would send a signal up the line and buy some time.

They moved on to the next item, the ad campaign for changes to the government heating program. This was going to be equally challenging, but there was no possibility of a delay. The regulation was coming into force quickly.

"Tell me that the heating campaign is on the rails," said Ally.

It was the new kid, project manager Drecina, who answered. The modern trend to name your kids after house plants had not been kind to Drecina. Yet she seemed to flower under the ridiculous moniker. That was just one reason Ally had been impressed by Mark's young charge. It was not so much because she reminded her of herself. She didn't in fact. Ally didn't grow up with Drecina's obvious confidence. However, Drecina possessed an uncanny marketing edge. She could make a successful campaign out of anything.

"Yeah, this campaign is going to come in on time. We're going to build on the existing creative approach for the Carbon Credits. The government is saying it needs more action to reduce carbon emissions. We'll use some of the messages from the principle of a balanced economy. One way is to reduce the heat standard."

Ally suddenly felt quite angry. Ally had not yet made the mental leap between this campaign and the task that the Clerk had given her. Her voice slipped deeper into her low-key, commanding manner as she looked over at her. "So the storyline is to tell Canadians to reduce their heat consumption even more over the winter, or pay more to the government for the privilege of staying warm?"

"Yeah, really sounds a bit perverse. We were already advertising an 18-degree standard. Now we are going to 17 Celsius. There's a new twist this year. They're going to let the provinces levy fines on people who go over the standard."

Ally tried to understand. "How would that work? It's not a sin to use alternative energy to heat your house beyond the standard. You've just pay for the credits."

"I'm not that clear on the logistics. I'm still waiting for the details."

"Who put these ideas on the table?"

"They came about after a meeting with the Clerk's people. They say the government is going to be pushing the Carbon Credits thing really hard this fall and they strongly feel that our heat campaign should support it."

"And the provinces are going to collect fines from people who heat their houses more than 17 degrees? I assume they're counting on the smart thermostats in everybody's houses to determine who gets a fine? What's the principle behind that? Just giving the provinces a chance to grab some cash?"

"Not sure," replied Drecina, with a slightly chipper tone. "But the provinces love this. Before they would charge people at standard rates for the costs for the extra hydro. Now they'll have a great new source of revenue with the fines. They might not call it a fine though. They are thinking about if they need to come up with a better name."

"Jesus." Ally looked around the table. The faces were hard to read. She wondered if everybody was buying this shit.

"I thought we had all agreed that we were raising the heat standards because there was less need to ration heating. We were supposed to advertise the success in solar and wind conversion. More people than ever were off the grid. Hydro projects working at maximum efficiency. That kind of stuff?"

Drecina looked at her as if Ally was not in the inner circle. It was an impassive look that showed that Drecina had spent too much time with the Clerk's people. Bought out by the thrill of ready access to "insider" gossip that dulled her sense of right and wrong. Ally now regretted not reading her briefing material. But that did not change things much. It would have only made her fume overnight.

Finally, Ally spoke. "We can't launch a campaign like this. It's dishonest. We should be telling people that things are getting better. Not worse."

"Well, best of luck Ally. The government has its eyes set on the election. Getting better doesn't help them much when they are the Green Party."

Ally wondered if there was something about Drecina's character that she had missed. Nobody calls her by her first name in the office.

"Not sure that's my view," said Ally, straightening up and assembling her material to signal the end of the meeting. "This campaign is not ready for approval with the prime minister's people. Please tell Mark that I will need a status report on this issue by the end of the day."

Drecina gave her a withering look that said that Ally "would see."

"Drecina, I know that you think there is no point discussing this and we must bow down to people at higher levels, but that is not always the case. I count on your discretion to let me pass along our department's feedback on this campaign. I will see those notes by the end of the day."

Ally dismissed the room with a practiced "Thank you, everybody."

Ally had had much higher expectations for this meeting. Now she was livid. For once her people went quiet and watched her respectfully as she left the board room.

Twenty

Jhonian threw off his fleece sweatshirt onto the hook of the stuffy greenhouse. He loved to eat homegrown vegetables, but they were work. He was planting another few rows of spinach, hiding out, trying to avoid the inevitable. Soon Rachel, his mother-in-law, or MIL, as he named her in his thoughts, would arrive.

The kids loved her. MIL enchanted them in a way his mother never could. It struck him ironic as Kara cared deeply about their future and Rachel often mumbled when recalling either of their names.

Ashley usually went into this remorseful kind of dementia whenever MIL visited. His wife was normally tall and confident, dressed happily in whatever came to hand, often her pyjamas. This lack of style was the kiss of death for sex appeal to many of his buds. But he loved the way that it made her cuddly.

But when MIL arrived, she changed, and he figured it was to impress her. He had caught her looking in the mirror at her stray gray hairs. She had spent some of her valuable time doing her nails. She had dug out an outfit that made her look serious and a bit stern.

Ash was a dear sweet thing. It was difficult for her to process when people were just screwing with her. Especially when Ashley, as a parent, would never do the same to her kids.

He steeled himself. "Only for a couple of days," he psyched himself.

"Hi! Hi!" he heard her call from the porch. She had a way of using the upper register of her voice to create an affected mid-Atlantic accent that grated on him. And she was loud, with a sugary, confident tone that resisted interruption. Assured that all anybody wanted was her arrival. Her movements were heavy and deliberate, as if they were blocked out by a stage director to impress an audience.

And then the commotion started. Kids screeching "Grandma!" on cue. Adult footsteps of his wife as she opened the door. "How is everyone! Oh dear! You two have grown!"

Kara came out back, stopped at the greenhouse threshold and said two words: "she's arrived." She made it sound non-committal and casual. She watched as her son pretended to ignore her. She had time to notice that he'd planted most of the bins for the Fall.

Eventually, Jhonian stood up and gave her a look that he hoped said, "I know mother that you detest this woman and that she stands for everything you despise. But can't you see, mother, that I am caught between you two and I'm making the best of it for my family's sake. What's more, I want you to try. By the way, stop hoping that I will take your side."

Kara snorted her reproach. "I have dinner plans this week. Just so you know."

Kara's son shook his head and gave her a watchful smile. It was only for a couple of days he told himself.

They both went inside and joined the family. Jhonian took the bags upstairs. He reflected that once again MIL was packing rocks and sandbags as he dragged them to the room where she'd be staying. It was one of the kids' rooms; the kids were bunking in together.

He reflected that the tone of the house had already changed. Whenever MIL came to town it seemed like his family changed from a modern mid-century family to throwback to 1992. That was because MIL was a throwback to that era. He knew it and lived with it. From the first days he had met her and she had shown him the photos of her wedding. Her next wedding. Her trips. Somewhere in there was the birth of his wife. The boyfriends. The parties. The excesses that today seemed like she had been sailing on a yacht for her whole life, getting first-class service, all the while entertaining the crew.

He was part of her crew right now, pulling up the suitcases to her room. He would watch his wife become part of her crew too, but a kind of below stairs crew that would never measure up. In bed before they slept, she would rail at the crap that her mother would pull. He would do his best to make peace.

His mother would refuse to join in, and still pull him aside to try to get him to speak ill of his MIL. He mutely resisted because he knew it was the right thing to do, a sign of marital health. He let it all roll off him as in the end, her visits were short and infrequent.

The kids were the audience, not crew. Spectators. They would revel in Rachel's countless stories of the past and "what it was like then." They would get a priceless chance to know what the world was like before it got so screwed up that we all almost drowned and froze to death. Such was the magic of families, a perfect combination of conformity and ritual that leads to both stress and comfort.

Back downstairs he went into the kitchen. "Who wants something to drink? Rachel, I'm sure you have a million ideas you want us to try!"

She flashed him that smile that was mildly inappropriate since he was married to her daughter. "I do indeed. Last winter I was in Thailand and they make this fabulous rum punch with coconut milk! We sat around the deck and looked over the ocean and drank them all night. We got ever so tipsy. We should all try some while I'm here. They went so well with the papaya mousse that they served and the fish that we all liked. I can't remember what that was called."

Jhonian looked at Kara. He thought he heard her snort, but she appeared to be smiling with interest. MIL was just getting started and already she had broken about ten environmental guidelines. For one, Thailand had not signed the environmental convention, so MIL must have left from the U.S. Jhonian admired MIL for finding the money and the loopholes for all these exploits. The closest he would get to Thailand in his life would be the virtual travel exhibit at the mall.

The kids listened with their usual rapture. They had never seen a real coconut. They asked her questions about the plane ride. How long did it take? Did you feel safe? Did you get claustrophobic? Imagine if you could buy coconuts in Canada?

Ash suggested that they all go out to the living room while she made them supper. Her mother stayed behind in the kitchen to help.

At bedtime, Jhonian would hear from his wife how MIL had sat at the kitchen table doing not much while chatting loudly. His wife would tell him how she listened while trying to maintain self-control.

Ashley would recount how MIL had stood around, expecting to be waited on while she rushed to assemble a simple but filling meal of salmon, homegrown beans and potatoes, and strawberry mousse for dessert.

"You know Mum, we don't have any coconut milk or papaya anymore."

"That's a shame. Oh well, I guess we can try something else. I don't know how you kids put up with all this."

"Don't you mean why?"

"I know why. Look at your mother-in-law!"

"That's over-the-top mother, but I will let that go. Times have changed. And Kara helps us a lot."

It was the trump card that Ashley always played when she wanted to slow her mother down. Rachel couldn't argue the point.

"Mum, it's Jhonian's fortieth birthday next year. Can you plan to be around for that? I was going to organize a surprise party sometime in May. I want to do it just before his real birthday."

"Yuck. May is such an undependable month up here. It can get cold and rainy. Not sure if we can even get outside. Why can't he have his birthday later when we can do it on the porch?" Rachel cast her eyes in disbelief through the window, to determine the potential. Their porch was piled up with overflowing bins of onions, carrots, and drying herbs.

Ashley started the Mixmaster to drown out her indignation, thinking "how can I be related to this woman!"

Calmer, she poured the mousse into some dark blue pottery bowls. "Mum, I don't think he can change his birthday. And it would be wonderful to have the whole family around. Where were you going to be this winter?"

"I've been invited to Morocco. My friend Jean is a bit frustrated these days because he has this big house, but with all the travel restrictions
148

in Europe, he is roaming around quite alone. So, he will pay for me to travel from New York. It's that just I can't stand the train, so I am trying to find a drive there."

"You don't worry about getting fined by travelling so much?" Ashley would have been better to change the topic. The answer was obvious and her mother's answer was going to push another of her buttons.

"At my age, I want to experience life. Can you blame me? You are my daughter and I admire you for fighting the good fight for mother Canada. It's not for me. I have pluck."

Pluck, pluck, pluck thought Ash.

"It's nice for you, mum, that you have dad's money and these choices. I didn't grow up travelling the world for my job. And even if I could, I still wonder what's the best thing for my two kids. It's their world now."

There was silence. The self-absorbed normally can't be reached from the outside. They don't say they're sorry. And they don't feel remorse.

Then again, sometimes maybe they do. "Pass me those beans," Rachel said quietly. Ash looked up at her mother and was shocked to see her looking thoughtful. "Let me cut them up for you. I was thinking I would take the kids out and buy them some new shoes. Would they like that?"

Twenty-one

"**Aren't you a bit freaked** that all those bottles are going to make the cupboard smash off the wall?"

Oscar looked over at Tanya moving stuff into his place and then stopped to admire his vast collection of beer empties stowed on top of a good-sized length of kitchen cabinets. The bottles lined up to fill up the entire space between the top of the cabinets and the ceiling. A nearly perfect brown composition of glass standing endwise about five deep, embellished with more bottles piled sideways on top.

"Can that happen?"

"It might. Who knows? That's probably pretty heavy," Tanya suggested. She shifted a small cardboard box in her arms while looking upwards at the ribbon of shiny glass. "Last night while we were talking, I figured that had to be about four hundred."

"N'aw. Can't be."

Tanya shrugged and left briefly to put the box in the hall outside Oscar's bedroom and rejoined Oscar in the kitchen. They both concentrated on the bottles for a couple of minutes until she broke their reverie. "It's quite an achievement. But it's worth a whole bill if you take 'em back."

"Really. One hundred bucks?"

"Sure. There's probably another bill stacked up over there." Tanya waved in the direction of the old white fridge where old cardboard boxes overflowed with wine and whiskey bottles stacked up against it. "It doesn't bother me. I'm just crashing here for a bit. But if you're ever short of cash!"

Oscar smiled broadly as Tanya went through the front door. Clad in black shorts, and nothing else, he was a big dude with a steady laugh and playful eyes. "You're the clever one of us, girl! You really think? Two bills for doing nothing."

"Two bills for getting trashed," she called out as she reentered the apartment. Tanya now had her well-worn gym duffle slung over her shoulder, wheeling a suitcase. She made her way down the hall again and dumped them both right beside the box. That was all she needed in the world. A cardboard box, a duffle full of sheets and towels and this beige and black plaid suitcase that someone in the family had given her years ago. "To inspire your adventures" was still inscribed on a large brass luggage tag that hung off the handle.

"Hey, thanks for letting me hang for a bit," Tanya told her friend as she made her way back to the kitchen.

"Hey, it's no problem. It'll be slaps to have you around," replied Oscar, who was now leaning over the open door of the near-empty fridge. She checked out the intertwining vines of ink running all over his back and onto his neck. The tattoos were masterfully planned so the bright colours jumped off the contours of his dark skin where his muscles flexed. He closed one door and opened up the freezer to reveal a long thin box. "Want some pizza?"

"Perfect."

Tanya went over to the living area and fell down onto the couch. It was pretty sturdy. Last night she'd slept here okay, using her coat as a pillow. Maybe for once she'd go a buy one. Yeah, not the first time the thought came to her. It was a lot of commitment to stuff. So probably not.

She opened the lid to one of the cigar boxes stacked on the dusty coffee table and took out a joint. "Want a drag," she said to Oscar.

He came over and bent to take a hit as she held it up to his mouth. He straightened up, gave a little laid-back smile of satisfaction, and turned to saunter down the hall.

Tanya took a few more drags and grabbed the remote to flick on the screen across the room. Like everything else, it was covered in a dust that misted off the screen as it came to life. Oscar wandered back and took the joint from her casually. "Do you mind if I hook up my screen to this later," Tanya asked him.

"No, not at all. I don't know where my screen is. It's lost somewhere."

He put a plate of ripped up pizza in front of them and flopped back onto the couch beside her, while she casted through the scant offerings for something to watch. They sat around until Tanya tipped the last of the joint into the plate full of roaches and grabbed the other cigar box. She flipped open the lid and looked up at her friend in surprise. "What the fuck happened?"

The young man slapped his hand on his knee, laughing. He kept it up for a bit, pointing at her, savouring his accomplishment. Finally, he calmed down enough to speak. "I put all that shit away. You go through it like water!"

"No! I just want a hit. I'll get some more tonight."

He laughed again, but this time with a firmer undertone. He knew she'd never deliver. "Maybe later."

"Fuck you!"

"Maybe later too."

"That'll be the fucking day."

He looked at her again, chuckling still. But he'd made his point.

She threw the box back on the table and started to cough.

"You okay," Oscar asked.

"I'm fine. I always cough. I'm fine." She spoke through her coughing and then paused to regain some composure.

"No, seriously," asked Oscar. "You okay?"

Tanya gave him a gesture to say 'of course.' "Just one hit?"

Oscar got up and rubbed his hands on his shorts to distract her. If he gave in, he'd soon be ripped and never get out of the apartment to the rally this afternoon. That was the thing about Tanya he'd forgotten about. Her priorities.

"Alright," Tanya eventually said. But she hadn't given in. He knew it.

"Come with me this afternoon," he said. "You'll like it. There's lots of people who know what is happening."

She looked at him greedily. Her eyes roamed his body up and down. Thinking about what to say. Or do. To get what she wanted. She waited for some inspiration, but she was dry. Finally, she gave in. "Where are you going?"

He pointed to his sleeve of thickly drawn tats. It was mostly stuff about his family, lovers, and anime characters. There was some nice art that didn't really say much to her. "What?"

Then Oscar pointed to the marks on his wrist. "Ah," she exclaimed quietly. "The Triple X. I didn't peg you as a Freedom Party supporter."

"There's a protest today. You should come."

She looked up at him dutifully, hoping to avoid an argument. "Sounds like it might be awesome. But I gotta go and see a friend. I told her I'd help her dye her hair. She's got a job interview in a couple of days. She doesn't want to scare them away with the freedom red and blue."

She chuckled at her own joke. He had to suspect it was a lie. So, Oscar ran with the Freedom Party. She'd run into a lot of people that fell for this wet-behind-the-ears, let me do whatever I want libertarian bullshit. They could be stupidly insistent. Promising anything to get you to show up. It had to be bullshit. She was still waiting for the day when somebody did anything she actually needed for free.

Oscar was stoically standing over her, so she stood up in front of him. "Think about it." Oscar had an insistent tone. "I'm leaving in a bit. It will be good for you to see what we do. We want to fight back against the oppression. The government suffocates the creative spirit."

"So ya think," Tanya thought to herself. She stood there silently, patiently waiting for his disappointment to set in. She let him wander back down to his bedroom in silence, waited and then heard the shower running. Feeling a little relieved, she grabbed another joint, leaned back with the smoke firmly in her grip and sighing. This gig with Oscar was going to go to shit. Fuck. Soon he'd be nagging her to get out off the couch and follow him. She'll argue that her ambition is to focus on the essentials. He'd ask her what that meant. She'd say something dumb. Why does everyone need a philosophy? There's an irrelevant line between believing something matters and just living. She just wanted to be. You might as well just live. Then he'd yell something about money. That would be the end. She might be able to drag this out for a few weeks if they fucked. But he was just another guy with an angle. She'd have to start already working on Plan B.

"Maybe he'll get arrested soon," she mumbled to herself.

"What's that," yelled Oscar.

"Nothing. I just said I like this tune."

Tanya looked outside and saw the sunlight. The temperature was too cold to walk around, but it was better outside. She put on her coat, grabbed his keys, rummaged through the cigar box and bolted without a word.

Minutes later, Oscar sauntered back into the living space, dressed for the afternoon. The cigar box was open and almost empty. The couch had a dent where she'd been sitting.

"That bitch," was all he said, shaking his head and smiling.

PRINCIPLES

Twenty-two

At some point Ally had let her fandom for *Star Trek* slip and it stuck to her. She'd received gifts of t-shirts with "we're giving it all we've got" and staff had once used the campy science fiction theme for a birthday party. When she moved to the deputy's suite, staff had very quickly renamed this room her "ready room." It was a deliberate reference to *Star Trek Voyager*. To the people in her department, she was the Captain.

Before Ally took over, this room was simply called the deputy's private meeting room. It'd always been an intimidating place; entered through a small set of double doors inside the DM's private office. If you were here, you knew you were part of the A-team. You'd spend a little extra care on your outfit the days you were meeting here.

The room itself was small, not much larger than the average person's dining room. The luxurious, reddish-brown mahogany panelling made it feel more intimate. The wood finish was a hold-over from the 1970s and was long since banned. But it had been left up thanks to the protests of generations of deputies who grew to appreciate its effects.

The spare room had a round, heavy wood table surrounded by very utilitarian chairs. The only adornment was the usual health, safety, and, more lately, environmental prohibitions, such as no single-use plastics. These were posted on delicately engraved brass plaques and covered the wall beside the door. In most government meeting rooms, these warnings were hastily posted in dog-eared paper or flashed across the screens that ran all the time. The visual impact of these brass plaques was extraordinarily different. Each plaque was uniform in colour and size, affixed with two small brass screws. The positioning of each made a uniform grid. The earliest, such as the fire marshal's edict "Maximum of 10 people in this room at one time," or "Please return chairs to their places" ranged across the wall at eye level. Subsequent messages came below, like "No scents are good scents," "Please take all your garbage with you" and "No straws, plastic bags or other single use plastics." Most recent entries were things like "Please stay home if you feel unwell" beside "No near field communication" or "Animal protein free zone" were in columns further and further down the wall. Staff had often remarked that it was a beautifully presented monument to the sterility of modern life.

Ally was in another pre-brief meeting with Mark's citizenship campaign team. Mark was thankfully back from his trip from she didn't remember where and tricked out in his usual private school ring and tie pin. He'd brought along Khristin, the positioning geek, Regine, in charge of sales, and beside Regine sat Louis, the finance person. Drecina was absent, as Mark had very likely asked her to sit this meeting out.

"I don't see a way around it for the moment."

Ally was sharing her game plan with the players around the table. She knew they were trained to avoid secrecy and anticipated that they would be uncomfortable with what she was going to ask them to do. Ally would be honest about the political pressure. It was one of those ugly, no-win situations, the kind that most bureaucrats steer away from. The kind that would make each of them think, "I'm glad I don't have Ally's job," and mean it.

Since she'd been dragged into the Clerk's confidence a few weeks ago, she'd seen a flood of briefing materials coming from every direction. She'd seen a transcript of the Environment Minister's speech at Davos. She carefully reviewed the source documents themselves, and the point of the government's exciting new idea to increase the Carbon Credits was clear to Ally.

Publicly, Ally had voiced neutral support for the proposals, asking to see more. But in private, the proposals put her into a rage. She'd gone back and forth between anger at being asked to lie to people to wondering why this time she cared. After all, she'd been asked to deliver a lot of bullshit over the years. There was the tree planting program that was supposed to be delivered by fundraising cash from celebrities. She found out later that the program was a disguise for politicians who wanted to hook up their kids with the famous. Another beauty was the announcements to unveil historical plaques, which turned out to be deep cover for liaisons between her cabinet minister and his mistress. She found out about that one when the minister's wife called her to leave a message. "Tell the bastard not to come home," she'd screamed. Ally had a lot of stories to tell.

It was her job to make the best of it, arguing for changes to mitigate the worse of it. Negotiating to maybe get something out of a bad idea for the public benefit. And for every program that was a steaming pile, many, many more programs truly met some public interest test. They helped people.

But this new steamy was in a class apart. For days she'd had trouble getting to sleep. Thoughts about putting this new plan into place intruded as she felt herself drift off. And then she'd spend hours lying in bed in a half-dream state, where fantasies of burning Green Party headquarters or taking over the news streams with a broadcast about the failing intellect of the Clerk of the Privy Council seemed like real alternatives. She'd wake in terror until she realized it was a nightmare. Maybe all her years of service had been catching up with her. Maybe the oppressive rot in the system had reached a crescendo. Did it matter? It was driving her crazy.

But it wasn't tortured sleep that had provided some relief. It was a remark overheard at one of her countless meetings, on an unrelated topic. Last Spring's rationing program got a lot of public criticism because it had lacked front-end planning time. It was the way the Party was blaming the bureaucrats that caught her attention.

It inspired her words as she sent the Clerk a request for more time, say a few weeks, to allow for better planning of the increase in the Carbon Credits. Surely, she argued convincingly, no one wanted a repeat of last Spring.

She was confident that the Ministers would buy it, as the timing would bring them closer to the election. And what they wanted was election equity. They wanted this new program to be fresh in the minds of Canadians, so they could confidently say that they were making a difference.

For the foreseeable future, her goal was delaying this announcement through a steady, slow, painful negotiation of each detail of the roll out with the Party. Who was the target audience? What was the essence of the message? Each government rule on focus testing, purchasing, or transparency would be painfully applied, dragging the process well beyond the expected launch date. This would have to happen while acting fully committed to their plan.

Ally was silently jubilant that she'd sold her own steaming pile of bull back to them. It gave her time to break open her own plan.

158

Somehow, she was going to find a way to create a counter-narrative, to undercut the government's intention, and make it politically unsaleable. She'd not quite figured out how to do that, but she had created the time to come up with a plan.

Marshalling your support in the bureaucrat's playbook meant executing based on the onion principle. That meant layers. You start at the easiest layers and peel them off until you got to the nugget in the middle.

Her meeting today with her key staff was the first layer. Ally looked at her people and said simply, "I know that we don't like the government's idea and that it doesn't track with the data. I am following the government's direction. What I am asking you to do is to quietly move slowly. You guys are all pros, so I know you can get this idea to market in weeks. But the fall data from the Environment department will only be made public in two weeks. I want our plans to drag until then. Can we all do this?" Ally saw nodding heads and some discomfort.

Ally continued. "I think the data will help surface the disconnect. The government wants a proposal by the end of the week. I need to delay our deadlines for an extra week. Any ideas on how we can explain it?"

Khristin looked up and scratched her head from behind. A tell of discomfort. "It would have to be credible. We are never late."

Mark offered that normally they would send this to testing, but that they can't give the focus group the data to make choices. And the Party probably wouldn't agree. What if the focus group results leaked?

"Our money isn't fully approved," piped in Louis. "We can't actually begin a campaign until the Treasury weighs in."

Ally nodded. "That works for me. I appreciate your usual discretion and I know this is difficult."

A chime sounded and Ally got to her feet. She was due to congratulate the latest group of new hires. As she left the room, her scheduler was already waiting with her jacket.

"Mark, you want to join me?"

Mark excused himself and joined her at the elevator. Once the door closed they were alone. "Are you sure you want to do this?"

Ally pushed in her private code that told the elevator to descend, without stopping, to the conference hall floor. She thought pensively before she replied. "You've seen the data, the briefings, like I have. When does bad become corrupt? I think we're seeing the line being crossed."

Mark didn't have time to reply. The elevator doors opened as staff greeted both of them warmly and whisked them through the crowd to their designated positions. From her place at the podium, she watched Mark work the room from his spot near the back. People deferentially greeted him, while others signalled his presence with a respectful wave. She was seeing a glimpse of the future, as her protégé would almost certainly have his time commanding the department.

Later that week Ally listened online as Mark and Khristin ran through their presentation about the roll out of the Carbon Credits to the rest of the staff. They were clear and convincing. If there was any doubt among either of them, it didn't come across. But she knew that the newcomers to the file would have questions.

She flipped through the comments the staff had already posted and took her seat at the camera. The first question came in. What was new about this change?

Mark answered that it would pick up on themes from previous campaigns. Khristin added that it was part of our challenge to make it new. Creative ideas would be needed.

Next, the question about how partisan to make the campaign for these changes. Wasn't it more about the ideology that we had to accept that we needed to make more sacrifices? Ally answered simply that they were not to take partisan positions. The campaign should relate to all Canadians.

Finally, the question about why? A hardball question disguised as a lob. Didn't the real effort, if they were going to make any difference at all when you consider the most recent data, need to influence other countries to come on board? Regine answered that they were looking for ways to expand their international relations. It was an incoherent answer to an obvious question.

In a bureaucracy, when you ask all the good questions and you get universally stupid answers, you know the game.

They got down to the effort of today's meeting to design a new campaign to announce the changes. For the next half hour they kicked around possibilities. It was a credible effort and by the time they were finished, Ally almost thought that increasing Carbon Credits was the right thing to do.

The unspoken truth languished in a corner, ignored. What had started as an important idea had morphed into a dangerous political ideology. They had become the comedians, making this all seem right.

Staff signed off, privately praying that somewhere above their pay grade there was a plan to stop the insanity. But if not, at least their efforts could mitigate the damage. It was the bureaucrat's prayer.

Twenty-three

Ally passed the time reflecting about the call with her sister
Jennifer in Toronto. Their relationship was almost totally virtual, and
yet they were great friends. In fact, in those rare opportunities when
they got together in-person, the exchange felt stiff and awkward.

It was a great freedom for Ally because most often she was
surrounded by staff or colleagues where she had to maintain the
armour of a deputy minister. She'd connect in the off hours when
they both were available. Even though the rest of Ally's family were in
Ottawa, she saw her brother's family and mother rarely. She was
most available to her sister.

It was their habit for Ally and her sister to pick a topic and debate it,
based on what they had seen or been reading. Ally, as a deputy had a
lot of data and insights from work that she could share.

Her sister tended to topics that made her a bit opinionated. Lately,
they had been talking about what was popularly called the fourth
dimension. When she was a kid, they would have called it paranormal
phenomena. Back then it was a domain of the fringe -- loons and
your odd family member. Today, physicists and celebrities alike told
apparently credible tales of the weight of the human soul, the
explainable influence of dark matter, the reaction of atoms in large
scale colliders producing a reaction that defied measurement by
known methods. Society seemed poised to recognize that our
thoughts have collective energy that lived outside our brains.

Her sister thought that some people had the brain juice to perceive
what others couldn't. Characteristic of her, she was trying to hone
these so-called fourth dimension skills. In turn, this gave Ally some
practice listening, without judging. Life was full of unpredictable
events and judging just didn't help get you through them. Still, she
was a bit worried about her sister taking this stuff too seriously.

The sheets groaned next to her. Pete was pretending to sleep. Ally
wondered what was in his head when he lay there. Pete was so much
more straightforward than her sister. Was he thinking about if there
was any food in the room? Was he getting up to take a piss? Was he
trying to avoid the conversation with her that terrorized him? Did he

really think if he closed his eyes and breathed like he was asleep that she would politely wait forever for him to leave his wife?

Their last few encounters, things had seemed to level up, or down, she was trying to decide. Small gestures grew irritating because they weren't enough. For her, she was ready to jump out of her crappy situation in an instant. Her daughter had to be aware that her parents' marriage was dead and probably wondered why Ally and Derrick didn't have the stones to do something about it. But as time passed, it was clear to her that Pete had tied himself down mentally to a loveless marriage.

She thought about when they first got together. It didn't take much to make her happy. It was pleasure to have something so intimate and someone so caring in her life. He made her feel like her old self, someone who appreciated the small gestures he would make. She was alive.

As time passed between them, she'd daydreamed a future for them. Now she started to see the flaws in her assumptions. In one of her calls with Jennifer, she finally told her about Pete.

"I kinda suspected that you and Derrick weren't getting along."

"I haven't wanted to say it out loud. I needed the illusion of my marriage. What could you say to me anyway?"

"Look, second marriages do work. I can attest to that. Do you think Pete will ever leave his wife?"

"Fucked if I know." Then Ally cut in on her own deflection. "I do know. He told me, right at the beginning, that he could never live a day without his kids. They are young. For him, he had told me, he needed to be with them every day."

"Hun," mused Jennifer.

"What?"

"It's an odd turn of phrase. You know, narcissistic. He needed the kids. Shouldn't it be more important that they depended on him?"

Ally had never thought about it. "That's interesting. But it's not like I can be judgey. I'm a party to the mess."

She had tried to talk to him about the future and the result was always deflections. He was content to live a compartmentalized life of Ally and their adventures – sex, friendship and connection, and the other life of his wife and kids. Pete was responsible, dependable and an over-involved father. Painfully, her logical mind didn't understand it.

And so, Ally came to realize that even clandestine relationships mature. Loving and attentive as always. But there was a bitter undertone of reality that struck Ally. Maybe he had an emerging sense of leaving his wife and his conscience weighed on him. Maybe the joy of having two women to please was wearing him out.

Even taking into account the faltering belief in their future, Ally couldn't bring herself to change what felt like a pretty good arrangement. Better with Pete, than without, she told herself.

She slid one of her feet towards his back. "Your feet are cold!" he groaned.

"Wake up! I want you to play with me!" She gave him a childish smile that she was secretly quite good at.

He rolled over smiling and grabbed her to give her a kiss. His warmth and the snugness of his arms around her made the bottom of her doubts fall out. Thinking about stuff was nice and all. But feeling something was so much better.

Twenty-four

Briefing notes are to public servants what seed is to farmers. As one colleague once told her, a man who eventually became a deputy, you needed a briefing note to go to the bathroom. Nothing got done without them.

Ally leaned back on the chair in her home office. She was wearing her loose sweatpants and a T-shirt with a hole in it. She was a lot more comfortable than she usually was in the office, where she donned a very narrow range of wardrobe selections. Earlier today she wore what she called her black widow outfit: black tights, black long sleeve top, and a charcoal gray skirt. With her dark colouring, she looked very impressive and intimidating, which was the effect she was going for. But often, and like today, she put on a Black Watch tartan shawl just to soften the whole tableau.

Now she sat there in the most comfortable clothing she owned, an old green tee-shirt with faded lettering that she got from some departmental event and black gym pants, grateful that at least her clothing wasn't causing her any grief.

Weeks had passed and her delay tactics were working. She was exhausted, looking at the tenth draft of a briefing note for Cabinet Ministers about the advertising campaign for the blessed Carbon Credits, the decrease in the heating standard to 17 degrees for all houses, commercial establishments, and industrial facilities.

Usually she could toss off a briefing note to staff as she walked. A lot of them now are mostly put together with the briefing note algorithm. This note was much more of a puzzle since she actually cared about the words. She wanted to find some inspiration, finish up and sleep. She massaged the tense knot at the base of her head, messing up her long dark hair in the process. A small section of her hair came out at the roots. "A-ha," Ally exclaimed to herself, "that's where the expression comes from."

The trouble was a new section on the messages about the options for penalties and fines. Some moron who was looking for glory had chimed in on the need to "encourage" Canadians to limit their consumption. Oh, the magic words! It was an important bureaucratic detail added by the Finance department on how people would be fined progressively more for every time they "overheated" their buildings. She'd heard the Clerk talk about how he saw the new policy changing for the better and growing strong branches. That was his way of painting an optimistic picture as he wanted everybody to get behind the proposal. Without tiresome questions.

The amounts they had listed on the chart titled "monetary consequences" were the most offensive part of what was to come. Her counterparts in each province had rammed their way into the fray, proposing increasingly more draconian fines. For what? Heat. Something everybody needed in the depths of winter. People needed to stay warm. They didn't just wantonly consume heat to improve their social standing. You couldn't throw heat around the neighbourhood for the sake of conspicuous consumption. Behind the drive for fines was the drive for more taxes. She knew each province saw this as a way to increase their revenue. But fining people out of their hard-earned money, just so they changed their behaviour, neither worked nor was an easy sell. To her, this proposal looked like a 13-vehicle pile-up at rush hour. The sort of thing that one deeply regrets being involved in, and sure as shit the sort of thing you don't want to be near. It was objectively corrupt.

She scrolled the note up and down on her screen. She'd have to figure out what she wanted to say before she went to bed, so this would be ready for the morning. Her office received an urgent call from the Clerk's office at late day. They were polite but insistent. They wanted to see the note tomorrow. If not, someone in her Minister's office could leak their commitment about the reduced heating standard to the media. The proposal would move from a thought to a done deal. If they forced her hand like that, it would be too late.

She ran over the options in her mind. The words were close, but not quite persuasive enough to convince the system that delay for more consideration was necessary. One paragraph stood out and had her vexed, about how an increase in Carbon Credits would increase Canadian's happiness. It went to the root of her anguish with this latest government proposal.

It's true that the happiness index was the core of the government's ideology, and the role of her department. It underpinned all the original principles of the P.C. platform.

Ally's eyes skimmed the briefing note one more time. Again, she stumbled over the paragraph that read that "a reduction in carbon emissions would ultimately support an increase in happiness for Canadians."

The line was usually boilerplate in most government memos. "Don't forget to add that line about carbon emissions and happiness," she'd loudly remind staff. It represented an idea so ingrained in the daily banter of her department, no one even read it over or questioned whether it still made any sense. "Sound management of carbon could only increase Canadians' opportunities in the future, not just for Canadians today, but for Canadians for generations to come."

In reality, did it make people happier? Why did we all think that? Long ago Canadians could heat their home as they pleased. But then came heat rationing so that you could only use so much fuel. The government started to promote incentives to make Canadians want to heat their homes with alternatives like electricity, solar, and wind. Added next was the concept of Carbon Credits, which was more truthfully, a politically palatable way to say tax. Yes, as a further way to curb Canadians' appetite for all things that ran on energy. Like heat to stay warm in winter, or energy to power vehicles.

A tax on consumption. We'd all be better off if we consumed a lot less, made our clothes go a bit further, chose appliances that lasted longer, drove cars that used alternative fuels. The government repeated for decades that consumerism had to be beaten and replaced by sustainability and a new sense of community. Even school kids believed that Carbon Credits were a way of paying for the change. And over the last couple of decades, most agreed it worked. An impressive majority of Canadians had converted to non-carbon fuels.

Ally had seen all the data. Carbon outputs were significantly down, the threats of floods and fires were past, and food supplies were stable. At least in Canada, the thirst for fossil fuels and consumerism had been beaten, and we had survived.

That's why it stank that her job was to turn the screws some more. Ally knew she could sell this crap. The impacts were perverse. She knew that if her team got on board, Canadians would believe, maybe even demand, more belt-tightening.

But the Party's illogical pressure on her to deliver told her something Ally didn't even want to consider. A new demon had taken over. What had started well, altruistically even, had been corrupted into the age-old problem of the pursuit of power at any price. Her department would spend tax money telling Canadians about our "achievements." Measuring happiness and telling them they were happier. The Party was stuck on its success; selling voters on the ethos of a Green Revolution. After thirty years, an environmental agenda needed to give way to a new agenda. If not, average people would suffer for it.

Ally had been reclining back on her chair and felt herself nod off. As she jolted herself awake and sat up, she accidentally spilled wine from the glass she'd been holding. She migrated over to the couch to find a dry place to work and looked at the note again.

For some reason tonight, an image nagged in the background from a past staff event. It ran on a loop, from an inconsequential annual broadcast of the Clerk's message to public servants. He was making a speech at a pro forma forced "fun" event for public servants. The event was followed, as they all were, by a series of pot luck lunches. Most public servants worked at home, but that day everyone filled the viewing theatres to see the Clerk.

People don't get to senior positions if they can't deliver a bit of comedy and pull off ten minutes on camera. This year he was impressive. When called upon the Clerk could make fun of himself in an apt way. Ally grudgingly gave him that. If you didn't work for him, you might think he was a decent guy.

The point of his message that year spoke about the continuing need for public servants to uphold their values and provide fearless advice and flawless execution. Canadian public servants were known around the world for high standards. The day featured green t-shirts passed around to senior managers with "fearless and flawless" inked on.

And now the Party wanted some flawless execution. Threatening her department, and her personal sanity, if they didn't get it.

Ally looked down at the hole on the word "fearless" on her shirt. And then it hit her. In a matter of minutes, she'd added a few points to the suggested approach. A small amount of public consultation about the success of the Carbon Credits program was recommended. It was slipped in with a couple of other points that the Party would never agree with. She would argue about the importance of all three but be willing to settle for the small consultation. The Party would love the idea of consulting about nothing on the taxpayers' coin before an election. And it would give Ally time to organize. She needed more time.

Twenty-five

"I hear your department is facing quite a challenge," Hector at the Environment department was speaking to her and trying to keep others out of earshot.

It was Friday morning following the ritual deputies' breakfast. She was taking in the air. It was the one dependable time she could count on being out of the office. Ally and a couple of the other sustainable resource and environmental DMs were walking back to the cars.

What challenge is that?" Ally had an annoying habit of looking for confirmation that other people, especially senior public servants, were talking about the same thing. Her rule was that this wasn't a team, it was a gang that operated with tribal rules. You had to check where you stood, before you voiced your thoughts. She had learned that the hard way on her way up by expressing an opinion to a close colleague on some inconsequential policy. The next day she saw the news stream coverage with the statements attributed to her and realized she had been unknowingly playing "gotcha!" You can't always know who your friends are.

"What I mean is, the push you're getting to promote more Carbon Credits. We had all assumed that we're past all that. We were going to promote stability, keeping on course. Where is the push coming from?"

Ally paused to read her colleague's eyes. There was no hint of guile. And she trusted and admired Hector, who was dependable, knew when to push and when to shut up.

Ally and Hector heard footfalls as Claude, the Deputy from Natural Resources, fell into step with them. Both men were now in the conversation.

"Does this mean your department is not on side with the campaign?" Ally ventured.

"Well, I don't see how it helps us," responded Claude. "We are reducing heating subsidies and are hoping to start withdrawing from the heating field. Promoting the credits will make us pull back our plans and we will have to eat the extra that this will cost our department."

Ally turned thoughtfully to walk to the car. The wind was picking up and it was chilly. She wished she'd worn her gloves.

"Listen Ally, we need to talk about this!"

Ally turned gracefully as if to offer to take the men to lunch. Her speech was soft, friendly. But there was no disguising her surprised look. "You don't think I thought of this? What would you have me do? I'm dragging my feet on this hoping the release of the Fall stats will make the idea DOA."

Hector looked expressionless except for the panic deep in his eyes. "We are getting some pressure on the stats," stated Hector bluntly. "They want us to issue them once a year. The Party has some idea about announcing that they cost too much to collect."

As Hector spoke Ally could see the Party was ahead of her. They must have realized that the data from Hector's department might undercut their plans. She needed a change of tactics.

"We should discuss this further. And soon. But not here." said Ally in the driest deputy's manner. She knew that people were watching. There were cameras everywhere.

"Should we meet," asked Claude in a tone that was more of an instruction than a question.

"I can set it up," volunteered Ally. "Just us, no staff. It will show in your calendars as consultation on upcoming promotional campaigns."

They all got into one of the shining black electric vehicles and let their drivers take them back to their respective towers, while calmly fuming about the work ahead.

OLD TIME RED AND GREEN

Twenty-six

The house was quiet. Ashley and Jhonian were at the market and the kids were napping in their rooms. Kara was upstairs at her son's place babysitting, as she kept an ear out for her youngest grandchildren.

Janey, her oldest granddaughter, had come over for a visit. The two were absorbed in sipping their mugs of tea and sharing details about the upcoming adventures. The white hair of wisdom sat across from chestnut hair of opportunity in the sun-filled kitchen on the main floor. Between them sat plates of homemade biscuits and ramekins filled with blue, red, and peach jam. Through the window some of the leaves were still hanging on the trees. They shone bright yellow and orange in the autumn light.

"Janey, you'll take down my Christmas presents for your mom and the kids when you leave for TO?"

"No problem Nans. I found a ride to share. This time there's lots of space in the vehicle." One of Janey's girlfriends was also going to Toronto to see her family and had access to a car. They'd drive down when the inter-city travel restrictions were eased.

"How do you think your mother is doing?"

"I think she misses the family living in Toronto."

"Do you like him much," Kara asked with a tone.

"Nans, you don't like him?"

"Actually, I do. It's just taken awhile. But I miss not being able to see her as much."

It was true Kara felt her loss. There was still lots of pain from the changes that happened three years ago, after a rather abrupt separation from Janey's dad. On the bright side, it had made her connection with her adult grandchild even more special.

"So, my dear," Kara continued, "you are welcome any time after I get settled at the condo. I'll be leaving soon after Christmas. I'm going to take the train to Toronto to spend a bit of time with your mom. And then I'm on a Canadian train to South Carolina."

Kara was getting prepared, looking over all her obligations, exercise credits, Christmas shopping, medical appointments, and the like. She put her blogs and media sites on vacation. Janey was looking forward to joining her. As always, they would travel separately, but there were details to figure out.

Janey was one of few in the family who saw how Kara was a different person down south. Easy-going and a bit aimless, she seemed to waste away the time doing whatever presented itself. She spent some quality time reading books and getting reacquainted with the neighbours at the condo community where she rented. She sat on a deck overlooking the ocean, listening to the wind in the trees and the waves lapping up on shore and drank a couple of margaritas and read. And Terry, her nice but shadowy boyfriend, would join her.

"I wish I could go sooner. I only get a two-week leave from plastics this winter. I'm going to wait until the third week of January. When is Terry coming down? I don't want to get in the way. I can see if I can change the dates if you want to be alone."

Kara deflected out of habit. This was Janey's third trip with her, and she knew Terry well. "That will work nicely. It will be great to have your company. Just remember I'm back here on the tenth of February. Are you coming down via NYC again?"

"No, I'm coming directly to you. I change trains in New York City, but it's a quick layover. I think I can afford a coupon for an American train, so the bumping will start right from Montreal. But I will do the NYC visit on the way back."

"Are you going to stay with your friend?"

"I've reserved my usual hotel. I love that place. It's all polished brass and red carpets. There's staff that help you with your luggage. I feel like a glamorous Hollywood movie star."

"How is that fellow, Byron?"

"He's fine. I'll see him when I'm there. We'll probably just have dinner."

Kara thought she heard some expectation in the voice, but she allowed her granddaughter her privacy. They were generations apart and yet so alike.

"Make sure there is lots of bourbon, Nans."

"I admire how you enjoy yourself. And call me Kara now. You're old enough!"

"Enjoy myself? Nans, I am the dullest twenty-eight-year-old I know!"

"And that bothers you? You are such a sensible young lady. I always tell my friends how proud I am of you."

"Yes, I'm the model PC woman. My grandmother thinks I am sensible. I spend my working days worrying about the plastic that people want to make. My exercise credits are up to date. What does that say about me?"

"It says you're like everyone else these days. Better now than in my day 30 years ago."

Janey smiled and let the statement sit. It was a pleasant moment and they were both just joking around, trying to make a few travel plans.

One day she might challenge Kara's pat answer to this too common and too philosophical conversation. Nans believed and her faith kept her sane. Easy for her.

Twenty-seven

The tee shirt hanging in the neighbor's yard was now a dingy
sodden mess after the flash storm of freezing rain. Worse, it was in
plain sight of their family room. On this sunny morning, with the
leaves off and melting ice dripping all over, anybody's eyes would be
drawn to this gray rotting rag.

"Do you think we could say something to Mr. Jazerhi?" Ash was
asking her husband, her gaze fixed on the shirt as she drank her
badly-needed coffee. The kids had woken her up twice last night.
Jhonian had done his best to settle the six-year-old in his own bed at
one point. She got up next to deal with the younger one. When she
woke up, they were all there in her bed. The rats were intertwined
between Jhonian and herself. It was just another night and neither
parent had slept very well.

"That's tough," replied Jhonian, dressed similarly in pajamas. "It's
hanging from their pear tree, so it might be there to scare the birds,"
he ventured musingly, reaching around her for his coffee.

Indeed, they had admired Mr. Jazerhi when he had carefully pruned
the old tree several years ago. The pears his partner Jeff had given
them were delicious. Still, Ashley thought she would get up the
courage to ask him about it. She spent a lot of time looking out this
window over the winter. The need for the t-shirt scarecrow was well
over. We couldn't abandon all our standards for the times.

Jhonian turned around to gesture across the room at the download
button on their oversized fridge screen and scrolled the images up
with a wave in the air.

"Why do they always start with the weather," observed Jhonian,
pushing the text up.

"I told you we could always just look outside," teased back Ash. "You
had to have all the gadgets."

He shook his head to disagree with her as they both scanned this
morning's announcements. An ad for a solar energy collector system
caught both their attention. It was half the price of solar panels and

didn't need snow removal because it was installed on the side of the house. With all the heat rationing, they both wanted to get off the grid as soon as possible.

"That looks like just what we need," said Jhonian enthusiastically. The ad flashed at them both for attention. "Wanna see how it will look on the house?"

"Hang on. We can't geek out with the Google this morning, honey. If we start, we'll be signing the contract in half an hour. I just can't this morning. I'm going in to work." Ashley waved her hand and the ad disappeared.

"Wait, I want to look at that!"

"I know, later, I just pressed save."

Jhonian looked at her in mock disappointment and then pointed to a reminder on the screen. "Did you speak to Pat and Frankie about the trip to the country?" This April they'd planned a house exchange with a family in a farming town about a couple hours out of town. Unlike the stories his mother-in-law always told them about picking up and driving whenever the whim hit you, today's standards, the price of the road tolls and the travel permits alone meant that you had to thoughtfully plan all the logistics.

"I did, and it sounds good. I don't know how much stuff we can bring through."

"We are still aiming for the third week of April," her husband asked. As he spoke, he'd moved smoothly to nestle right behind her, as he often did, cradling her small frame with the one expansive arm resting on the counter.

Ashley felt his hand run up her spine in that divine way he had, which she playfully ignored. "What are the chances that we will get caught if we take your great big van?"

"I'd rather take the new electric."

Jhonian leaned over to whisper in her ear. "The kids are still asleep." He pushed her hair to one side and kissed her shoulder, working greedily up to her neck. She felt a slow bump from behind, and this time Ashley couldn't ignore its magnitude.

"Yeah, I see. All good points." She turned to face him and reached to give him a kiss on that spot she loved on his jawline. "We've got time to get this organized," whispered Ashley.

He leaned in to kiss her as he guided her hips onto the counter. She leaned back and grabbed the edge of the counter as he thrust himself inside. She watched as his face transformed into the cherished ecstasy that only she got to see.

He pulled back and stroked her hair, as Ashley scrambled off the counter. He offered a couple of tissues with an idiot grin, as she slurped something off her fingers. Strawberry jam. "Must be stuck under the counter."

With a grateful kiss he told her he had to get going, "I'm late." Jhonian's voice trailed off as he went upstairs to take his shower.

She, too now, was about four minutes behind schedule. It was worth it. She grinned girlishly, still tasting the strawberry jam in her mouth.

She got some more coffee, calling up the food section of the download, letting the fridge suggest what she should do for dinner. It recommended a good deal on a beef-soy protein. Maybe she could pass by the shop after work and pick it up. Then she sighed and nodded no, clicking through the menu to have what she needed delivered. It was cold enough outside that it won't go bad waiting in her grocery lock box.

She went over to the buffet and pulled out the cereal and bowls for the kids. She thought she could hear them upstairs. A social media post that flashed on her fridge made her think that she wanted to go through all her kids toys to see what could be donated to a local charity. She would ask the kids to put stuff into the pull cart and they could help her drop them off.

Her eyes jumped from the screen with its flashing information to the t-shirt hanging from the pear tree.

Leaning into the same counter where she'd just had sex, and sipping coffee that had grown a little cold, Ashley continued to free associate the overwhelming number of must-dos, should dos, good intentions, and dreams that scattered about her mental desktop. And there was another thought somewhere. Something she was supposed to be paying attention to. The thought was gone. She heaved another sigh. If only she could clear her mind and get caught up.

When she heard the kids and his footsteps on the stairs she realized that Jhonian had long since left the shower. She started and ran upstairs, moving like a gazelle through the steps of the morning.

Waiting for her ride, her son at her side, she practiced some affirmations in her head. "I'm going to stay cool today. I'm going to focus on what's a priority for me. Every day is a treasure."

The postscript came later that morning, sitting through another chokingly boring meeting about transportation logistics. It was the dull, but necessary stuff her company did to stay in business.

Ashley had already tuned out the conversation when it veered down the usual path of work rage. She never got drawn in, because it made her a living. She looked down at her screen and saw the message from her husband. He'd made a little "he shoots, he scores" animation to amuse her, and she tried at the same time to suppress the laughter and appear to empathize with the outrage in the room.

She thought about him. Their life. Time was passing and Jhonian's fortieth was getting closer. She wanted this milestone to be special because she loved him and he deserved it. While others in the room vented about synthetic unfairness, she sent a message to his friend Alex to see if they could use his basement. It was chill; he'd turned it into his own pub, complete with a full bar.

The old-fashioned clock on the wall loudly clicked away the seconds. As she looked up, she focused past the chatter at the table to see that snow was now falling thick. It was a simple pure white that fell in fluffy flakes. A sticking snow that coats everything and makes the world clean.

"Look everybody!" she said to the room, nodding at the window.

180

The pity party adjourned as everybody went over to the window to joyfully marvel at the first snow of the season.

Twenty-eight

Like every Christmas with her family, this Christmas turned out to be first-rate. Jennifer, her mom, was a star at transforming their family home into a red and green fun house. It was beast. Life at its festive best.

That's how she remembered it over the years. Christmas was where all of Janey's memories were wonderful. Her younger self stood amazed in front of a tall, fragrant green tree that was overflowing underneath with red presents. Jennifer and her dad Nicolo together beaming as she and her siblings ripped into the paper wrapping around them. Each of the kids took turns shouting out their approval of the haul. "Mom, I got a superhero set!" "Dad, I got a bitsy doll!"

The kids would have been less excited if they knew about the empty bank accounts, parental wrangles, and sleepless nights that made the magic happen. It was a child's good fortune that they were joyfully unaware. Christmas morning was worth the excruciating wait.

As she got older the rituals evolved. These days she gladly redirected any limelight to her younger nieces and nephews. Now she was expected to give more than receive. Accordingly, this year she'd arrived with something for everyone.

As she matured Janey grew to know her mom as a person. She saw how Christmas put more stress on Jennifer, as her mother. December always was the traditional season of high expectations. As the years passed and the expectations changed as consumerism grew less acceptable. The appearance of excess was frowned upon. But the desire to recreate some Christmas magic was still there.

For most grandparents, the anti-consumer punch casting Christmas morning as an outdated consumer ritual was difficult. Her mom, house now filling up with grandchildren from Janey's siblings, was no exception. She turned into a Christmas confidence woman, explaining away excessive gifts with crazy excuses, such as she'd won them in a raffle.

What's more, her mom was still getting used to her life with her new husband. After so many years with her dad, where the arguments, roles, and stresses were familiar, she was throwing herself into a new life. Her new husband had kids and grandkids of his own. Janey liked this new family; they were easy to get along with. But there was still an undertone of irritation because Janey's mom had "broken up" their family. And for that, she pushed herself harder to impress them. It made Janey wince sometimes when she overheard her mom seek their approval.

Most striking, now that Janey was an adult, she realized that her mom was her own worst taskmaster. No one was harder on her mom than Jennifer herself. Her standards were predictably unachievable. It didn't matter what she tried, she would plan and research her project in extreme detail. Planning and structure were her mother's curse. She would look at all the options until none of them looked any good. It frequently left her exhausted and down on herself.

This effect was accentuated by her parents' divorce. Janey could see now that her father had softened the edges of their childhood. Bedtimes could stretch or rules could be negotiated. But without him now, they frequently dealt with her mom's high expectations.

She figured too, that over the years Kara had been a steadying influence, and Janey could see it more with the physical distance. This year Kara had not made the five-hour trip, and it was true it was her son Jhonian's turn. Janey compensated by working extra hard to make her mom happy.

And it was simple. All she had to do was arrive and be ready to listen. Frequently she'd help her mother just by saying that everything was "perfect." Jennifer would stop, visibly reflect, and then smile with relieved happiness.

Her daughter knew that although she was armed with a thoughtful gift, her time and attention was what her mom really wanted. Getting into town a day early, mother and daughter had spent it puttering around in the kitchen and later watching a film together. Any other time of year Janey might have been overwhelmed by mom's neediness. At Christmas it seemed alright; Janey found she enjoyed making her happy. Funny how you let your guard down at times.

When Christmas morning arrived, they crowded around the tree to open the presents. Janey watched as the younger children pulled off the tea towels and pillowcases. She helped her mom with the dinner. The house smelt amazing. Real turkey and all the best of the larder pulled out for the feast.

When the meal arrived and the family sat down, she didn't even mind that her step-dad gave a bit of a speech about how happy he was. He was very happy, having started with the mimosas at breakfast.

"I'm so proud of all my kids," he stammered.

"Cheers Dad!" His kids nodded at each other, smiling at the maudlin spectacle. That's happiness for you.

On December 27th, her friend pulled up to pick Janey up for the long ride home. As she loaded the car, her mom came out with an offering of food. Homemade sauces and jellies. Some meats and pies that were carefully homemade, freezer wrapped and packed on ice. Her mom hoped the kitchen treasures would remind her daughter later of how much she loved her, even when she was far away.

As they packed the car, her step-dad took her aside to ask her how she was "doing." Small word with a big meaning. Her step-dad's one-word's approach to checking in with his new daughter.

"I'll be up your way soon. If you like, we can have a nice cup of hot chocolate and a skate."

She told her step-dad she was doing "fine." Which compacted in one word how she was fully employed, paying her rent, taxes, partying only lightly, and generally having fun. He would see some of that when he visited.

"Love you both!" she sang as the car pulled away.

She traded stories with her friend about their time with their fams as they drove. Her life seemed a bit colder the farther away they got, like the temperature outdoors. The red and green faded. She was back in her world again.

Tomorrow new colours would take their place. Probably electric youthful ones. Meanwhile, she reflected lovingly about the familiar bounty of red and green.

184

Twenty-nine

A few passengers glanced down at her quickly, obliquely. Others passed by her, sitting on the platform bench as if she was invisible. Some would read her sign and press on, gazing straight ahead. But despite their pitying glances, Tanya had confidence that this crowd at Berri metro station was in the Christmas spirit.

A pair of giddy children dumped four coins in her hat. A decent number relented and came back to throw in a buck or two. Business for the past hour had been brisk. Her buddy in Ottawa was right, this was a reliable way to make a couple of bills in short order. It was working out nicely, all part of her goal to give herself a sizzling Christmas present. Step one: cash.

Only thing was the boredom of the dull, slow work of sitting for too long. She'd locked up her screens and anything that could provide her some distraction, along with her real clothes, at the nearby bus station. She stared into their faces as they filtered past. Pairs, groups of people attached to each other by an invisible tether. They drifted in circles and in lines, rhythmically exchanging words back and forth the as they shared, laughed, and giggled. She scanned for life in their eyes and found instead the ubiquitous force of obligation to each other. She didn't have anything in common with them. Thinking about their commitment to the rules made her a little sick.

What intrigued her were those who had a clear, focused goal that they reached at any cost. She observed these people carefully as they ran from the entry way to the platform or they fussed impatiently at the coffee line. Sometimes they didn't notice when they cut someone off, or made a fellow passenger swerve sharply to avoid them. They were headed somewhere. They had a mission; they were going to get somewhere today. In her experience, most people take more than they give. She was more like these people with purpose, wanting to get something out of the moment.

Christmas always pissed her off. She loved her crew, but truth, when something like Christmas comes up, they were hypocrites. She'd been deserted by them, one by one. They claimed they were into living free, but lately they'd all dipped to join conformity. This year, her ditsy friends all took a sabbatical from her, finding their family or spending time with some of their duller relations.

Where she'd been crashing for the past month, Oscar had asked her to get out for a few days so he could host his sister. So, Tanya spent the festive formalities with her parents. Tanya survived the 25th dinner with both her parents, Ally and Derrick, as well as the other two days where nothing happened. But at least her mother had given her adequate money, as a present.

Which left some space to come up with a plan, until things picked up at New Year's. That's how Tanya pursued interests a little further afield. She had a friend in Montreal who welcomed a little company, so she took a bus for a couple of hours and crashed on his couch.

She rubbed her shoulder. "Damn," she swore. It hurt a little; her friend's couch was old. That was only one shitty thing about living with her kind of freedom. And it screamed to her when she spent the nights at her mother's. Having a real bed, where you can stretch out and flop down every night. It would be so basic to have a comfortable place to sleep. But that's a slippery slope towards all the other turd that came with it. Like working. She rubbed her shoulder again.

"Thank you," she responded sweetly, as a well-dressed man put twenty bucks in her hat. Nice.

"Merry Christmas," he wished her as he walked away. "Indeed," she told herself as she took the bill out of the hat and put it with the others in her pocket. She made a mental tally. She now had enough for step two.

She got up from the bench and steadied herself against a pillar. Getting to her feet quickly had made her a little dizzy. The pillar was wrapped in a blue and silver ad that spiraled up from its base. It extolled the benefits of the Re-PR brand of sustainable cleaning products. Its photo showed each family member hard at work cleaning various parts of their imaginary house. Through the walls there was a yellow beam of what was supposed to be happiness. "Fucking shit," murmured Tanya as she straightened up.

She took a deep breath and noticed how tired she felt. It would all get better, pending the execution of step two. "Suckers," she sneered at the pillar, and went out to the front of the metro station.

A blast of cold air greeted her, and it was welcome after the stuffy station air. Tanya looked over the waves of humanity for the local guy her Ottawa stooge had recommended. He arrived as promised and she handed over a fair chunk of the money accumulated this afternoon. He had a small bag of white powder that promised to make her happy.

Then she left the station and galloped up the road to the bus station, grabbing her bag from the station locker. She went to the bathroom and dumped her stuff on the floor outside the stall. She peed to convince anyone who was watching and took a deep breath to relax.

Then she went out to the mirror to check to her nose and to change. It was starting to feel normal again.

Women looked at her as she stripped down in front of the baby change table. It didn't faze her, in fact, she enjoyed making them uncomfortable. She put a dress over her head that floated softly on her figure; her stockings shimmered gold. Then she turned her efforts to her makeup, bending close to the mirror and making each stroke carefully. A woman looked her over as she stuffed her case with her afternoon attire and a sign that said, "homeles, need $ for food."

"Merry Christmas, ou Joyeux Noel," she drawled to the woman in her deep throated voice, as Tanya inspected the final result at full length. The perfect haircut that she'd got with her mother's Christmas money was bougie AF.

Leaving the bathroom with a flourish, she pushed her case back into the locker, dropping in a few of the coins given by the cheaper donors to her Christmas celebration.

Then she tripped back to the nearest metro station. As she walked, she hummed the chorus of a song stuck in her head, repeating "I don't want to live like that, but I don't want to die." She strolled along catching people's eyes, imagining herself singing the song aloud, performing it to the passengers streaming by towards the station.

Now hopping on the downward escalator, she switched to a Christmas carol, singing it loud to tease the fellow riding up beside her. She could hear the screech of the wheels pull at the metro platform. The buzz from the white pulled her together. Like magic, Tanya disappeared on the train, off to explore Montreal's charms. Step three.

Thirty

"No," replied Ally.

"Okay, well, what about setting up a feed in your office."

"No again. I need to meet with them in person, in my boardroom." Ally caught her scheduler's eyes. She was past frustrated with Ally's request.

"Everyone is telling me it's impossible."

"To meet in person?"

"Three deputies? Together in a room? Yes, I'm getting a lot of negative feedback."

"I don't understand the issue. Just find a date when we are available and send out the invite."

"I'll have to write a memo about why first and submit it to Shared Services."

"Do what you got to do. I need the meeting. Soon." Ally watched as her scheduler shrugged her shoulders sullenly and turned to leave the room.

Ally's task of organizing a meeting with Claude and Hector had turned into a comedy of technology and timing. Their schedules over the holidays were very full and already they were looking at time in January.

She kept hearing that it was just not done. But the next step was to get together in a room to map out a way forward. They had to meet where there would be no records of what was said.

And then came the questions from her own heads. It was unusual that all three would want to meet without staff. What sort of briefing materials would be required? Was she sure?

In the end, she'd almost wished she'd made a private arrangement. A restaurant was out of the question. Too much appeared online almost the instant you did anything interesting. And just as instantly the Clerk would want to know more.

Her instincts told her they had to meet soon. There'd been ominous silence on the file that made her worry.

There'd been no sign from Treasury that they'd approved the money for the advertising buy she'd proposed. This could be a signal of trouble about the plan itself. Or maybe Treasury had their own misgivings. For once Ally wasn't messaging her counterpart to lobby them to get on with funding. Nothing about this file was like usual.

No words of pressure from the Clerk. The Party wasn't overacting to the delay in the launch date. She'd been working her network to find why things had gone silent. She didn't want to mistake a lack of feedback as disinterest.

The Party had two speeds when it wanted something from her department. Speed one was mysterious indifference. That's when you give them what they want, and instead of saying thanks, you got eerie silence and an echo chamber of feedback to what you provided. For the past month, they didn't seem to care if they launched the changes to heating standards in the Spring. They'd stopped talking about it in the media. Let the story go cold.

Those with experience knew that suddenly the Party could move into their second gear, a level of diabolical preoccupation. Every public servant learns about this early. You go from crickets to blistering messages about where everything is. Why isn't it done? That's when you get your ego handed to you. Dressed down because you had no right to take the Party's lack of feedback as an excuse put down your tools.

Yet, the fact they hadn't expressed intense interest at the start of the heating season gave Ally some room to herd the system in her direction. And it made it more obvious that the real need was the Party platform for the Fall coming election.

She thought about her colleagues Hector and Claude. It was a relief to think she found some support within the gang of deputies. She
190

wasn't the only one to have some gut trouble with the Government's plans.

Hector had circulated a message he'd received from the Clerk who had asked about the timing of the data on carbon levels. The message didn't say much more than that. There was so much caution about public access to physical records that the public servants, especially at the most senior levels, rarely put anything in a message.

Claude circulated a report his team had sent him on the reduction of carbon levels in the various countries. It wasn't shocking that Canada was up at the top with the Scandinavian countries and Chile.

Later the same day staff had sent her an urgent message to review the latest versions of the explainer video for the Carbon Credits campaign that was in now production. A broadcast quality, three-minute marvel of animation and charts that brought another dull government idea to life. It looked professional as always. So convincing that even she wondered if she should take the easy way out. Just roll over and let them have their way.

Ally was headed home. As she put on her coat she asked her scheduler about her progress in setting up a meeting. She seemed happy enough to report that after what felt like a heroic effort of coordination, a date was selected in mid-January.

"Bunch of clowns," Ally scoffed at the date they'd found. Friday, January 13.

BRISK CANADIAN WINTER

Thirty-one

In January every Canadian craves the light, and nature gives you a sliver of what you want. There's often a week where the sun shines and the snow melts and softens. Temperatures push to the point where you can forget your mitts and wear your coat undone. It's a tease because the cold will return, rendering the sidewalk slush as hard as concrete.

But while you're in a thaw, it does you good. Odd teenagers wear shorts. Terraces open up briefly and people happily drink their coffee and beer on cleared patios. Grandpas enthusiastically chip and scrape away the unwelcome ice and snow on their driveways.

Spirits thaw too. Neighbours feel free to walk over for a convivial chat instead of the quick yell of a greeting while running indoors, head down against the wind. Kids can be heard laughing as they play in the yards. It's a feeling of escape from winter. Time stolen from the routine. Nature's way of teaching you to live in the now.

Even the redoubtable Clerk of the Privy Council seemed a bit buoyed by the turn in the weather. Ally expected Phillipe to overreact once again and deem this thaw a chance to showcase the diligence of public servants. Perhaps order a full-scale statistical analysis of January weather, with special detail on warmer weather trends during the month. Assess whether this week was a sign that climate conditions were turning for the worst. He'd ingratiate himself with the PM, sending the data and attaching a detailed Q&A in case there was a question from journalists or a scientist or even a Parliamentarian.

But at this morning's deputy heads call, when Hector at Environment held his breath and asked what was needed, the Clerk replied distractedly that nothing extra would be necessary. The government had come to terms with what were normal fluctuations of weather. "Hmm," thought Ally. Was the Clerk distracted by bigger sport?

Later in the day, it was thanks to this January thaw that both Ally and her second-in-command Mark chose to sit outside at lunch.

As Ally enjoyed breathing this outdoor air, she added this experience to the growing list of unusual events that had crept into her world. Her typical workday sealed her inside the office, but today she had

made another exception and scheduled lunch at a local bistro. She
wanted the privacy. There was an additional layer to peel off in her
plan to deal with the Government's drive to increase Carbon Credits.

Mark sat across from her looking at the menu on the tablet. She had
selected this spot because it guaranteed a fully local menu. It also
had real people serving and preparing the food. It cost a bit more,
but it felt good to know that someone was getting the tips.

"So, what do you fancy?" she asked him. It was small talk; Mark was
a man of intense social convention. And she would never tell him
that. He wore his school tie often, which made her wonder more than
once if he didn't have a wardrobe of school ties. His shirts were
monogrammed, featuring conspicuous French cuffs with what looked
like passed-down-from-father cufflinks. He curated a slight English
accent that got more pronounced under pressure. Not a lot, but just
enough to give him impeccable diction.

There was wealth of old school in Mark. The pinstripes and the suits.
The references to trips to the family retreat at a well-known resort
town. The brother who was an academic at McGill in the medical field.
Brogue shoes. Mark, she had always assumed, was old money. But
old money or not, he was an asset to any team. He thought
impressively quickly on his feet.

"I'll have a cobb salad," he answered her.

"Why do you even look at a menu!" She laughed.

"I've had cobb salad all over the world. It tells me much about the
place I'm in."

"What place are we in right now?"

"Odd question Ally. I assumed you want to know about the status of
the communications campaigns about the heating programs."

"Not directly. I was going to ask about how that trip to Britain went.
How impressed were they? I heard that the British want to change
some of their energy use programs." She paused for a moment and
then tilted her head to him with genuine interest. "Could you tell me

any more about their proposals on international standards and major emitters?"

"They gave me a couple of documents on some of the parts of new policy. I will share them with you. But basically, they agree with us that there is only so much one country can do on its own to get the carbon levels to where we need them to stay. And they're all worried about the economic parity."

Mark continued, "it's simple math. If Britain, Canada, France, Germany all cut back another couple of percent on carbon emissions, it's quickly lost when emissions slide backwards in places like India and the U.S., where it's cheap to use carbon-based technology to stimulate economic growth. We lose some flexibility to grow our own economy and they have an economic advantage."

"Sounds so old, redundantly ancient," retorted Ally, "worrying about economic growth."

"That's the challenge in a nutshell. We now have two very distinct value sets in play across the world. One that is some model of ours, looking societal happiness and longer-term sustainability."

"And one that is more short-term, which means that using carbon is okay if it gets you where you want to be," said Ally, completing Mark's thought.

"Yup, you got it."

Their salads arrived and they both spent a few silent minutes dealing with their food. They looked up at points to nod back at departmental staff who offered deferential greetings.

"Oh, forgot to mention the other day that I got a call from Hungary." Mark looked up at Ally hoping she would get the hint. He'd never been to that part of the world.

"How was their English?" answered Ally.

"Pretty good. Surprising really. They wanted some more detailed info on original campaigns when we introduced Carbon Credits."

"Aww yes. You'd be the right fellow for that. Which campaign were they asking about?"

"More doesn't mean better."

"A classic. That seems so long ago."

"It was. Wrapped up twelve years ago. I downloaded all the files to refresh my memory. You were there, in charge of the project. I worked on the school programs."

"We got a lot done in those days. I still see people wearing that t-shirt. You know, the one we targeted at seniors."

Mark nodded agreement and picked up his screen, elegantly pushing around icons until he turned the device to Ally. "Here's some of the images I found from the campaign report."

She smiled as she scrolled through, stopping on the video of her old team, each one clad in the multi-coloured shirts. They bore a sizable, fall-coloured maple leaf with the words "Get your head into it" sprayed diagonally.

"That was the tag line that seemed to stick," Ally recalled nostalgically. "I thought it was a dull cliché; and I argued against it. But it worked."

"It worked because it was perfect timing. Older people were holdouts, and they needed a good shove. I remember touring the old folks' homes with our "More doesn't mean better" roadshow. We'd hired hundreds of high school kids to make these presentations across the country, about how we had to consume less, reduce our economic footprint. Success was the growth of happiness. Canada's new social roadmap. I don't have to remind you."

Ally passed the screen back to Mark, who continued. "Most of these seniors were well past their years of buying stuff. But they all voted. And they liked the shows. Somewhere around Thunder Bay I realized that the kids liked the shows too. The slogan was a missive from one generation to another. I noticed how the kids would bellow "get your head into it" at the end of their presentations."

"I went to one of those shows. They were low key, until the end where the kids lined up and grabbed each other's shoulders and sung that song. Who wrote it?"

"I can't think who it was. I didn't see it in the file. But they made a lot of money with our slogan."

"Staff would change the words and sing it at staff meetings. It was hilarious. But I was the boss, so I had to tell them to stop. Even though I was busting a gut trying not to laugh. It stuck in my head, and I remember mis-speaking "Get some head out of it" at a senior management presentation."

Mark smiled. "Ah, I heard about that. It was astounding the ideas they'd let us try. Mostly it worked. Remember how that kid passed out doing the door-to-door canvas?"

"I do, indeed. And I remember all the coverage in the news stream. She was campaigning about the heating programs."

"Yeah, that's right. It was the middle of winter, and they were supposed to be in pairs, but that day her partner left early. She finished up knocking on doors. She was passing out the toques with the "Get your head into it" slogan, along with program info to the homeowners. She fainted and banged her head out on the street. A local found her unconscious reported it to the police."

"That's right," Ally confirmed. What a mess. I spent two long weeks cleaning that one up."

"Kid was okay?"

"Fine," Ally replied. "I think we settled. So, she did okay."

Mark nodded knowingly. "Still, those face-to-face campaigns got results. They created a lot of grass roots activism."

"You're right. It made change hard to ignore. But giving people $10,000 to buy a new electric vehicle or turn in their old car worked too!"

"I mentioned that in my briefing to the people in Hungary."

"Good," said Ally. "And they were suitably impressed?"

"Oh yes, they were. But they asked me a serious question. One I think we are wrestling with right now."

"What's that?"

"They asked me what the end game is. How do you know that you've done enough? When you can relax and say you won."

Ally took a few bites of her salad before replying. "Yes, Mark, I think you are right. I'm wondering about the end game, and whether we are here. I'm not sure everybody, though, is in the same place."

"I think we both know they aren't!"

Ally looked around for a few seconds, taking in the flow of people leaving the restaurant. "I don't know if you share my view, but I always felt there was always an implied contract here. At least I assumed there was. All us government types would get on board and sell the change, but at some point, the numbers would show we've done enough."

"I see what you're arguing. We all understood that some of this hard sell and sacrifice would be temporary."

"Yeah, there'd come a point when we could take the pressure off. Relax some of the rules and let people have some freedom."

"Some would argue that it's not our job to decide when that could happen. Elected officials decide. We execute."

"I agree, some would argue that. But there's lots of very informative points in history where that logic falls apart."

"And we are here?"

"I can't be sure. But I worry that the people with the power to make the best decisions, the right decisions, are too conflicted to see it. I mean, you said it yourself earlier, Canada can squeeze one per cent, ten per cent more carbon savings. But it won't make a difference."

"I can't message the people in Hungary that!"

Ally looked at Mark and smiled. "Insights like that are better said in person. So now they want you to go over and make your standard presentation?"

"Well yes," said Mark, smiling at Ally. "They do. I guess it would be possible to make it with hologram projection. Avoid the travel. However, I always have a little more leeway to be frank and I get so much more out of being there."

"Okay, I'll say yes this time, even though I may have to twist a few arms to justify this. Just remember, it's a favour." Mark nodded with understanding.

As they ordered the bill and prepared to leave, Mark mulled over what had just happened. Ally's pointed comments were markedly less circumspect than usual, capped with an unexpectedly overt quid per quo. Ally was lining up a few pieces that would be needed for later. He'd have to think about how he would respond when the time came. But it was a surprisingly blunt ask.

There was no downtime for a deputy, except when you physically got away from the country. It was a job where you were always on. You had to look the part, demonstrate a thorough knowledge of all your files, and act with the impassive impartial demeanour that was the hallmark of a perfect deputy.

Ally played the part to perfection. But he was close to her for hours in a week. Lately, although most couldn't tell, he knew that she was having trouble staying in character. Mark had assumed that with Ally's age and with her increasingly perceptible contempt for the Party, it was only a matter of time before she retired. Maybe she was considering her own personal end game.

He wanted his kick at the job. To see if he could maintain the role. It was a sacrifice he was intellectually curious about. Mark always observed Ally closely, but he thought that now would be a good time to double down on his efforts. Ally was a great role model, but Mark had the profound confidence that he would show the system a few new moves himself.

200

Thirty-two

The sun was strong on her face, poking fun at winter at its
coldest. Ashley stood out on the porch, pulling her sweater closer to
her body and tilting like a sunflower in the direction of the warm rays.

These past few years most people began to accept that winters were
getting a bit more predictably cold. But January always held a few
surprises. Today the bright sun was one of them. The rays felt like
heat from a fire, even though the screen said it was freezing. The sun
was so inviting that Ashley had to take a break from the morning's
tasks to see what was going on outside.

She took a sip of her hot coffee, breathing the crispness of the
morning. Then she stretched out, a cute animal in her element,
looking around at the piles of snow in every direction. Ash made a
note to thank her husband for shoveling off the porch. Yes, he had
done it so he could reach the BBQ through the snow that had
accumulated the past couple weeks. But she was delighted that she
could benefit. She welcomed the peace.

Overnight the wind had drifted the snow up softly so that it sparkled
like candy. She could hear cars in the distance making their way to
the shops on the Friday home day. But the snow deadened the
sound; you would think the movement was happening very far away.
Squirrels found the courage to peek outdoors. A pair chased each
other across the fence directly in front of her. She listened as the
married couple next door climbed into their car. Even with the snow,
and even though they were speaking their native Mandarin, she was
again amused by the familiar nattering of the two of them in the
middle of a disagreement.

She took the last hit of coffee, now chilled with the winter air. The
day had started well. Friday was always a blur of things to get done.
The trick was getting up early and to stick at it without getting
distracted online. YOLO had sent two messages with updates. But
she'd held strong and resisted, attending to the necessary stuff first.

This morning she had checked on her government dashboard and
reviewed what the bots had done on her behalf: renewals of the
driver's licenses for them both, completion of a permit for the

upcoming trip later this Spring, and there was a report that assured her that all their exercise credits were all up to date. While she was there, she looked at some recent medical tests and made a follow-up appointment for her six-year-old. Nothing serious, but they'd left a note that they wanted to see him again.

Then Ashley had spent a few minutes clicking through all the monthly reports from her home inspection bots. Nothing to report. The sensors in the dryer vent showed she was lint-free. They'd sent a series of camera images. Why had Jhonian paid extra for the camera? He could never say no to the extra gadgets they sold you. And she was happy to see that the sump pump was operating normally. A sudden thaw and they might need it.

Finally, Ashley checked the app that monitored that problem with the kitchen drain. The info on the app confirmed her suspicion that the enzyme levels in the drain were down. No wonder it had been running away slowly. She pressed the reorder button so the plumber could deliver more.

Dinner was already in the slow cooker. The kids liked beans. The laundry was well on its way, and she was finished with the time-consuming task of sorting the weekly garbage. She'd schlepped a carton of recycling outside and carefully done the triage. It was difficult to be sure she got it all right against the rigourous *Kamikatsu* standard, with its forty-five categories of recycling. Regardless, she did her best, carefully sorting the trash into piles of high-nitrogen and other compost types, folding the papers carefully and crushing the cans with her feet.

Her review of the download of the grocery specials found real meat at a good price on her way to her husband's shop. It was a small butcher, hopefully there wouldn't be a line-up. She was helping out Jhonian this afternoon and would stop on the way and get some for the weekend as a treat.

The cold was beginning to hit Ashley as the sun disappeared behind a rare cloud. She could see her breath. So she slid the door open and let the warmth of the house welcome her back.

She was walking over to refill her coffee when it happened. The beeping on the kitchen screen. The alert there was an incoming call from her mother.

"Hi, hi!!" Ashley heard her mother call from the screen. She turned dutifully towards her mother, hoping that her face looked bright. She waited for it.

"Oh, hi dear, there you are."

Ashley stared at the image as she tried to hold her smiley eyes in place. "Oh hi, Mom. Good to see you." Her mother was sitting on a sofa that looked more like an exotic carpet. Behind her was a bank of palm trees that to swayed in a gentle breeze. Rachel was wearing a kaftan that was no doubt original to the country she now found herself in.

"Good to see you too dear. What time is it there? And what are you wearing? Don't you have any makeup left?"

"Oh yeah, thanks Mom. It's 9:00 in the morning here. Everyone's out. I'm just catching up with stuff to do in the house." Ashley thought ruefully that until five minutes ago she was enjoying being alone. Now she prayed that someone would walk in so she could fob Rachel off. Then she felt badly for letting her mother get the better of her. "Be positive," Ashley told herself.

"Well, no matter," said Rachel acting as if she was accommodating her daughter's fragile state. "I thought I would give you a ring to see how everyone is doing."

"Come on over here Jean." Rachel turned to someone off-screen and waved them into view.

"Ashley, you know I told you I was going to Morocco this winter. This is Jean. His place is just fabulous."

"Nice to meet you, Jean," Ashley said. She heard her mother say to Jean that normally her daughter looked better, when she made an effort. Then Rachel added that she was so happy to be away from Canada, concluding with a meaningful "you'll see what I mean."

Ashley continued on the high road. Experience taught her that it was the best place to be if she was talking to her mother. "Oh Mom, I didn't think you were going to Morocco. I guess there was a change of plans." Her mother was nowhere to be seen. Jean was looking back at Ashley waving. There was an uncomfortable pause as Ash realized her mom was avoiding her question. She pressed on.

"Where are you from Jean? Have you always lived in Morocco?"

The next seven minutes passed while Jean proudly told her his life story. It was a typical story of privilege and squander. Eventually he took a breath.

"Well, it's nice to meet you. You two seem to be having a nice time." Ashley waited for it.

"Oh yes, so much nicer than the snow. Do you have much of it? And what are you doing today?"

I'm trying to be a good citizen and contributing to saving the planet, Ashley wanted to say. "I'm working at Jhonian's shop this afternoon. We're all eating dinner here together tonight."

"Kara too?"

"She's left for South Carolina. It's just the family."

"I told you she never does very much," she heard her mother tell Jean. She added off-screen that he wouldn't like Southern Carolina.

"What's that Mom?"

"Did you hear that?" Rachel asked with a twinge of embarrassment in her tone.

"Mom these new video calls are pretty good now. I can hear everything."

"Oh."

More of the uncomfortable pause. Again, Ashley continued. "Looks beautiful there. Is that a hibiscus in the planter?"

Her mother came into view and pointed to the plant, saying she wasn't sure.

Ashley turned the camera on her screen without waiting for an invitation. "The snow is very beautiful here today. Want to see?"

"Yes, looks nice. Almost looks like the sand. But I assure you Jean, it's bloody cold." Then Rachel doubled back to look at her daughter. "Look, I'm calling about my return travel plans. Is Jhonian's birthday still in March?"

"You mean the party?"

"Yes, yes, the party. Is it still that soon?"

"No Mom, wrong month. His birthday is still the same. Early May. Can you make it back? The kids would really like to see you."

"I am seeing what I can do. I will probably come back via France to New York. Then I can catch a train. They make it all so difficult. I got these miniature carpets for the kids that are so special."

"Okay, thanks for calling and letting me know. Try hard Mom. If you can't make it, at least Kara will be back."

She regretted it as it left her mouth. That last fact was a petty dig at Rachel. A clear turn off the high road. Ashley had almost made it through the call without letting herself down. Another banner day in her relationship with her mother.

Jhonian would tell her later that she should let it go. "Your mother knows how to make you feel bad. But you're better than her. Just let it slide off and forget about it."

Ashley wasn't built that way. She would feel the sting from her chat with her mother for the rest of the day. She nodded along for a few more minutes, said her goodbyes and ran upstairs to get a shower.

Thirty-three

Ally had her driver drop her near Centertown. She got out and walked east. The houses got a little more run-down as she crossed the intersections. Instead of proper drapes on the windows, some places used towels and sheets, pegged up as a cheap fix.

As she walked, she compared a paper with a number that she had scrawled on not a half an hour earlier to the numbers on the houses. She went up to one of the front doors and looked for a buzzer. There wasn't anything, so she knocked and the door opened on its own. The smell hit her, mostly marijuana, but there was an undercurrent of mold. A staircase in front of her had a dirty, worn carpet running up the centre. The place was old and not very well looked after.

Her daughter came to the door, holding an eyeliner pencil. Tanya looked good, but a stark contrast to Ally's polished office appearance. The eyes were outlined in black in a cat's eye style that reminded Ally of an old Hollywood movie star. Her daughter's nails were particularly dramatic. They were long and featured some sort of rose crafted in three dimensions at the end of each nail. The rips and tears of boring government outfit were arranged to accentuate her waist. Ally wanted to give her hug, but she held off.

"Hi dear!" she tried to say cheerfully as she followed her daughter into her ground floor apartment. She walked into the main room and opened her coat.

"Back in a minute!" Tanya abruptly left her standing in the middle of what must be their living space. Ally heard her close the bathroom door and hurl violently into the toilet.

She looked around as she waited. It was cold in the room; the windows seemed a paper-thin defense from the snow accumulating on the ledges. Near a large screen sat a huge penis-shaped bong. In front of her was a heavy-looking coffee table that had probably been rescued from the garbage. It looked like it had recently been wiped down. On the table sat a stack of small boxes. She could see a small pile of ash beside the box on the bottom. The top one was open showing off a collection of bud. She bent over to replace the lid. She could guess what was in the other boxes.

"You okay" her mother called to her daughter.

"Why?"

"I just heard you puke."

"Oh, you heard that. It's nothing. It always happens when I drink. We were drinking last night."

Ally decided not to pursue it now. Her goal today was to be responsive to her daughter's request. Show up and let her daughter know that she cared. A lecture on her daughter's alcohol habit, and some of the other more mysterious habits would drag them into an argument. Ally heard the water run in the bathroom. "Whose place is this?" she asked.

"I know, you don't like it. I'm staying with Oscar again. He's a lot of fun."

Ally looked over into a corner. There appeared to be broken rubble of three chairs. "Well, the location is good. There's a pretty good grocery store around the corner."

"We go there sometimes when we have money, but a lot of times we go to the Food Bank."

Ally wondered if that reference to the Food Bank was an effort to make her feel guilty. Tanya frequently asked her for money. Yet her daughter had been raised in relative comfort. She couldn't imagine her choosing to hang out where poor people need to go. Ally reminded herself of her plan. That's not what she was here to do. She was here to show she cared.

"Did you need groceries? We could always go out right now and get some."

"God, you're always trying to fix things."

Ally sighed with well-meaning resignation. Tanya marched back into the room, with an expression that looked as if her mother had slapped her across the face. "I thought we could get together and just talk. I even made tea and some cookies. It's useless. You just don't give a shit about me."

She was wrong about that. As often happened when she was with Tanya, Ally felt powerless. It was killing her to see her daughter struggle.

"No, no." Ally tried hard to keep the pleading out of her voice. "Please, let's sit down and have the tea. You called me to ask me to lunch. I want to spend time with you."

Tanya turned towards the table in the kitchen and picked up a tray of food incongruous in style to the rest of the surroundings. It struck Ally that everything on the tray, including the tray, had been recently purchased.

"That looks lovely dear," Ally volunteered without thinking.

"Do you like it? I used a gift card I got last Christmas from Aunt Jennifer and went and bought all the stuff. It's so pretty."

Ally carefully commented on each piece on the tray, as if it was a child's tea service.

Tanya beamed as her mother noticed the details. It gave her pleasure that her mother appreciated what she had tried to create for her.

"Thank you, dear, for the tea. The cookies were delicious. Can I take a couple for later?"

"If you want. Everybody loves my baking. I tell them I get my talent from you!"

"Well, these days I don't get much time for baking."

"I know Mom, you're always working."

"But I make time for you though. I hope we can see each other again soon."

"Of course, Mom! Why do you say these things to me?"

Ally didn't know what to say. Anything she could come up with seemed like a provocation. "Oh, a mom always likes to see her daughter! Let me give you a big hug before I go."

It was an awkward hug, like she was hugging a board. Tanya kept her shoulders dead straight. Despite the apparent ease of her daughter's tone, she had felt the stress of the encounter too.

Ally left the apartment and got out onto the street, messaging to find her driver.

She walked to the rendezvous point trying to unpack her mind. The January wind helped her to focus. It was going to take a while to process what just happened. She had responded to Tanya when she had asked her to drop by. But she left wondering if she knew how to connect with her.

Ally reflected that the pressures of the office would soon take her away from these thoughts. She made a mental note to return to this moment. She didn't know what she felt while she was walking away. Apart from the screaming obvious -- something was wrong and she needed so much to make it all right.

Thirty-four

Ally looked up from her seat at the sizable conference table to greet Hector and Claude as they entered the meeting room. Normally there was space for 60 participants, with extra chairs for support staff and observers ringed around the walls. Today the three of them were alone in the cavernous space.

They exchanged pleasantries as they served themselves lunch from the table at the far corner.

Hector took his jacket off and draped it on the back of his seat. He had a lean, muscular form, the shape you get when you play a sport for years. "Look, I don't know what to tell you. I have argued with the Clerk I don't know how many times, but he just insists that this is the direction that the government wants to go."

Ally had organized this ménage à trois as promised. The premise was a discussion about the newest citizenship campaigns. Staff had put together briefing materials for the meeting. The intro pages flipped uselessly on the screens in front of the deputies. The true reason for this meeting was to figure out what to do about the infernal Carbon Credits.

Collectively the three deputies had sizeable influence. Claude's large department ran all the resource programs for oil, gas and mining including the Credits program itself. Hector's environmental department issued the statistics that showed the results. Scientific stuff like carbon production from industry and warming trends. And Ally could assure the public with her happiness index and propaganda team.

Claude, renown as a man who loved a good meal, had balanced his full sandwich plate precariously on the stack of documents he had carried in. "We all know what the data is going to show. There will be no need to ratchet up the Credits. If the public finds out, it will be political suicide.

"Claude," asked Ally, "You were at the meeting with me. Did I overhear that there is now a plan to publish the names of businesses that heat their buildings over the standard?"

"Correct. Apparently the brain trust in the Party came up with it. I was told that smart enforcement is one of their themes for the election. They asked the Public Safety department to make an app with all the names of non-compliant businesses to encourage people to stop buying from them. Not just on the heating standard. Any time a business is non-compliant, it will get on the app. The idea ticks off two boxes for the Party. Smart enforcement and transparency."

"Transparency. Groan." Hector retorted. "Transparency is the devil at work on any stupid idea."

Ally continued. "Did the folks at Public Safety agree to this?"

"I was at the retirement for the Chief Statistician last week, and I asked our counterpart. Of course Public Safety doesn't agree. But they're worried that if they raise the issue, their Minister will go on and carry out his promise to cut the funding for services in the north. And that's more important right now. So, they're waiting to see the outcome of the election. It's the least harmful of all the stupid options."

"Every time I hear about this proposal, someone's added their own nasty twist. Soon we'll be rounding up people and putting them in camps," said Ally.

"I fear that things are even bleaker," responded Claude. "What if the government is successful and the public is brainwashed? You know, manage to convince their voting base to once again make a sacrifice for the environment. The government gets free rein to ask for anything it wants. And those that can't afford it won't get enough heat. HEAT! Christ de merde! Don't they know where we live!"

Claude made a few more salient comments in French, waving an egg salad sandwich as he spoke. Ally nodded in agreement.

He lowered his voice, trembling a bit as he added, "when I was kid my family didn't have a pot to piss in. We were poor. I remember the days of the twenty-degree standard. We never heated our house more than that. We couldn't afford to pay for more. We had this old wood-burning stove and Dad would have us cut wood from our lot. On the really freezing days, he'd burn it, ranting that someone was going to report us. Although we all knew no one would. I used to stand close to the stove, hoping to heat my hands through. For months I just never got warm."

"I guess I was lucky growing up in the Philippines," reflected Hector. "When we immigrated here it was the nineteen-degree standard. My parents were shocked. We spent a fortune and wondered what the hell we'd done coming here."

"This file makes me want to hit something," added Claude. "For years I have willingly done the government's bidding. I accepted that I wouldn't get rich or famous, but I could make a difference, doing what I believe in. But now I know I'm being lied to. It's corrupt. And I'm supposed to turn this around and lie to my people, to the scientists. And where will it end? I do this and what's next?"

Claude's sentiments were a bad omen. Up until now their discussions had been brief and heavily coded. It was the first time Ally had heard her colleagues voice their own anger. Part of her had hoped that she was wrong and that her judgment was off. That things were really okay. It felt much worse now she knew they were all equally incensed.

"So, what can we do," interjected Hector. "The media and lobby groups won't know what we know. They won't let a couple of facts get in the way of a good narrative. Most of them are so in love with the current hype that they'll question the validity of the facts, if the facts ever see the light of day. And the facts show we don't need to reduce. We've met our targets. It's time to change course."

Claude got up and wandered to the back of the large room to help himself to another sandwich. "Nice egg salad," he mused to himself. "Does anybody want anything from the table?"

His colleagues didn't hear. They were pensively reviewing the charts in front of them.

Claude regained his chair and sat down thoughtfully. "I don't see a solution but to get the data released. Not just released but put in context. Show the contradiction and let the questions get asked. I've been going over some scenarios..." He let out a dejected groan.

Ally was thinking out loud. "Somehow we have to embarrass the government into releasing the data. And the only thing I know that will do that is a half decent scandal. Something that will drag down the government to the point where releasing the data is immensely preferable to living with the political fallout."

Hector, Claude, and Ally all looked up at once. They went over the bin of material that could lead to the required scandal. There were the personal problems, the drugs, the sex, and the financial issues. Those were discarded because it would be too easy to crucify the bureaucrat concerned.

"We need something big that touches everyone," said Claude, thinking hard.

Hector started in his chair. "I don't know why I didn't think of it. The data on manufacturing in the country has been running flat out for two quarters. My people brought it in to show me. They were quite excited."

"So?" queried Ally.

"That means that there is a huge upswing in the amount of stuff that qualifies as made in Canada, or locally produced. It's a great sign that the economy is meeting its target for reducing the environmental footprint."

Ally and Claude still looked puzzled.

"For such well-paid public servants, it's too bad you two never paid attention to statistics in school! Basically, if this indicator is running hot, you would think the others are running hot too. It's new. The government has been struggling with bad numbers for years and things are turning around."

Claude answered slowly, considering what was heard. "We could give this to an opposition member on the Environment Committee. I still don't know what the deal is."

Hector shook his head. "Look, it's simple. The government has been claiming that the data is bad all over. Everybody takes their word for it. Nobody ever looks at the detailed data. It's time they did. We could put together a package of positive results. It will tell a different story than what the public hears every day."

"Somehow we need to get this into the right hands. Someone who'll ask the right questions publicly and force the government to release the other figures."

Claude was still fuzzy. "Do you think that will make a dent? You're asking a lot of people who are already overloaded with information."

Hector shrugged. "Hey, you know, this week my Minister stood up in the House of Commons and told everyone that there was no way the country would meet its carbon reduction targets this year or next. I messaged her press secretary and reminded them that our internal data shows we almost met the target last year. We likely will meet our target this year. I didn't hear anything until I saw the press secretary give an interview repeating what the Minister said in the House. They've got their own facts."

Claude looked a bit clearer. "Alright. I hadn't realized it was as wonky as that. Now I see why the Party doesn't want to release the latest numbers. As long as we can get the message across..."

Hector didn't give him time to finish. "We'll wrap it up in a big red bow, give the numbers enough context so the disconnect is screamingly obvious. This will work. We just have to leak it to the right people."

Ally smiled. "I agree. You guys work on the data. I'll work on getting it released. I know just the guy who can make that happen. Leave it to me."

AWAY FROM IT ALL

Thirty-five

A quick five-minute walk from Ashley's work was the only retail showroom left in the city, at least on her side of the river. Here the bigger retailers displayed their better-selling products along an indoor corridor of booths. In the space that used to be filled with stores there were services: a large depot that specialized in managing retail returns, a gym centre for the kids, places for haircuts or repairing broken stuff. In the middle was an old-fashioned food court, with its mix of pizza, pasta and fried foods. Ash loved it for the hit of nostalgia alone. A cartoonish splash of yellow and red communal tables, that greasy smell of mixed carbohydrates and the satisfying gurgle of lots of people laughing. Germs and joy together again for what, these days, felt like something special.

Seyyal and Emma, their puffy coats open and flapping askew, were strolling down the retail corridor beside Ashley. They were friends and coworkers, all moms in their mid-to-late thirties, outfitted in some sort of office attire that said they were aware of the fashion rules and trying their best. Together pretty, in a harried kind of way. As was their habit on days when the three were in the office, they'd carted their lunches through the snow to sit in the food court to eat. It gave them a chance to attend to errands and more importantly, just relax and talk.

At one of the booths Ashley lingered to pick up a red silk tie from the rack of men's wear and showed it to her two friends. "What do you think of this for Jhonion? I could get out a photo. Try it on him and see how it looks."

"Seriously? That as a birthday gift?" retorted Seyyal. "A tie? For his fortieth?"

"There's the party too," Ash responded a bit defensively. "Don't forget that. He's always saying he never has anything to dress up in. He wears the same worn-out jeans everyday for work." Ashley put the tie back as if it had spontaneously caught fire. "Crap. I don't know what to get him."

"Yeah, that's clear. Maybe you should order a little something for you. You know what I mean. A cute bit of red satin and lace from the 'ain't we naughty' boutique at Walmart!"

"I don't know about clothes, for a guy, for a birthday," piped up Emma. "Wouldn't he want a tool or a gadget or something for his system?"

"Then I'll make him feel like the guy stereotype," replied Ash. "I'll keep looking. I've still got some time. If you geniuses think of anything, let me know!"

The three moved out of the booth and kept strolling down the indoor street.

"If you want," ventured Emma kindly, "I could send you some ideas for the party. I've been thinking about it. You want to make it a stand-out night, so you've got to create the right atmosphere. Everyone should leave talking about what fantastic night they had. Have you thought about some sort of private fireworks display, or hiring a tattoo artist to ink some special birthday design on whoever wants it? It's in May isn't it? You could go with an outdoors theme and hire a company to build a beach outdoors. Wouldn't be too expensive. It's the fine touches that'll make it an event."

Seyyal puffed out a grunt of disbelief. "Sure, right. Ash, you should get on that. Or keep it simple and go down on him after whatever little celebration you've got planned. It's all in the dick, that's what I say."

Ashley laughed, waving off her friends' suggestions as she did. "If I needed any further proof, it's obvious you two don't know me at all! You, Emma, fail to appreciate the minuscule amount of energy I have these days for, what did you call it, 'the fine touches.' Truthfully, I'm not sure Jhonian would notice them. Even if the fireworks went off under his ass. He's a 'where's beer, my dear' kinda guy."

Ash took a few steps and then relented. "You know what I mean, my husband is a great guy, he's just not into a lot of fancy stuff. He'd feel embarrassed that I went to all that trouble. And as for you Seyyal, I think you've got your own issues! I got the dirty side well covered!"

The issue was closed, but Emma was unconvinced. Ashley always talked a good game, but when the time came Emma worried. Knowing Ash would find an excuse to avoid that last bit of effort. "Well, I'll put a few thoughts in a note and send them to you anyway. And I'm happy to help you set it up. You should get the invitations out soon."

"Okay. You're right. I should do that. What is that?" The three women were steps from their usual table in the food court. Ashley directed them to a new booth full of workday helpers. They spent a few minutes looking over an intricate plastic tray with take apart containers. It wasn't cheap, but Ashley dug out her screen and posted a photo on the inspiration wall of her organizer app. Anything that promised to save time made the women happy.

They finally sat down and quickly unpacked their greenery and grains. "I didn't see you, Seyyal, at the meeting this morning," remarked Emma.

"I was five minutes late this morning and I didn't want to interrupt the meeting. It would have looked obvious that I was late."

"Kids are sick?" asked Ashley.

"No, just fucking disorganized this morning. It's Thursday. But tomorrow it will be better. I booked a consult on decorating. I want to redo the living room. And I need to exercise. Let's pray that I get a few minutes to myself before the kids get out of school."

"I'll pray for you," promised Ash. "I am helping Jhonian all day at the store tomorrow. On Saturday I have some tournament with the kids and we'll have to walk to it with all the play equipment unless we get all the stuff out of his work van. Plus, you're right Emma, I should probably send out the save-the-date for the birthday party. Sunday I have the usual. Laundry, dinners to make for the week, kids' homework." Ashley sighed. "I really hope Jhonian can help with some of it! I can't forget to go to the community centre and raid my mother-in-law's pantry for the week."

"Your mother-in-law has left?" asked Emma with some empathy.

"Yes, last week. I will be glad when she's back," exclaimed Ashley. "But she left me the keys to her stuff. She got a bomb shelter's worth of food squirreled away over at that centre. It's helpful. You should see all the jars lined up on those wire shelves. She's got peaches and pesto and all kinds of soups."

"My mother is the same," said Emma. "She takes a lot of pride at the look of her pantry. Gives me something every time I go over to her place. I come back home with a heavy bag of those jars."

"You guys are lucky," interjected Seyyal. "You've got it good. I'm jealous. My parents are useless. Not going to lie, they don't do anything but complain."

"Well, I will trade you for my mother," scoffed Ashley. "She's a pain in my ass. But Jhonian's mom is the exact opposite. She really tries to help. But it's not like I don't want her to enjoy herself while she's away. She calls Jhonian and seems to be really happy down there. There's this old guy that comes down to 'visit.' We don't ask too many questions. She's this strong dour old broad with us and I love her for it. But when she leaves for South Carolina, it's like she leads a secret life."

"Good for her," said Seyyal. "I'd trade some of my boredasm for a bit of mystery. Maybe there's some truth to what they say on YOLO. There are more benefits when you get old!"

They laughed.

"Did you see what that guy was going on about last night," Seyyal continued.

"You mean the story about the family feeding the coyotes," Emma said dramatically.

"I saw that," Ashley added. "I just scanned YOLO last night and read the first bit. About the neighbours complaining that it put the local kids in danger."

"Ha, I caught you both! I thought you didn't spend much time on the app!"

"Seyyal, you're a pill!"

Ashley chided, "don't lie, you look at YOLO too! I bet you spend just as much time there."

Seyyal didn't respond, opting instead to change the subject. But the friends all knew she was just like them.

Thirty-six

"Look at the end, near the rocks. The sea level has risen again this year! Last year you there were more rocks further out on the point. But this year they're gone." Terry pointed out to the horizon to a striped lighthouse stationed where the coast curved out and jutted into the water.

It was his first night; he'd arrived this morning. Kara leaned into him happily as they took their walk along the beach. It was what they always did late in the afternoon. Sometimes they'd walk so far that they could watch the sun go down. An orange flare would cast its colour throughout the evening sky. But today the sky was much darker than they'd expected. They'd made their way beyond the circle of quaint blue clapboard bungalows through the white wooden gate, past the large sign that restricted access to the renters at the resort. While they'd walked the wind had come up suddenly. Waves crashed and splashed loudly.

"I don't think the water's any different," Kara insisted. "I've done this walk every night since I got here a week ago. It looks the same to me. There's a storm coming up. It makes it look higher. See the break of those waves!"

He looked at her and then softly reached over to push a lock of her white hair out of her eyes. "I dunno know my dear. It's happening all up and down the coast."

"Not here. It can't happen here. It's the storm, and high tide. This morning the bay was filled with boats and wind surfers. They are all in now. It will be back to normal once the worst of it passes."

They walked along barefoot in case a lap from the ocean caught their feet. She fussed with a large scarf she'd brought along over her bare arms. "It's windy. I wish I'd brought a sweater."

They kept wandering, but the worsening whistle of the wind and the angry ocean made it hard to hear. Terry steered them both away from the edge of the water and onto the strip of green where the sand ended. They found a bench and knocked sand away as they put on their sandals, their eyes fixed on the shore. Nearby the fuss of the birds devouring garbage made a deafening racket. But that didn't stop either of them from the fascination of the force. They gazed as the waves scrolled up and broke near the shoreline.

"It's so beautiful. It's one of those shows that nature puts on to entertain us. I could watch the waves for hours."

He held her closer as she shivered against the wind. She leaned into his warmth.

"It's always work to get here and sometimes when I'm back in Canada I wonder why I bother. But as soon as I see the shoreline again, hear the ocean, I forget all that and feel its joy."

Terry grinned at bit at Kara's philosophical outlook. "Well, if you won't say it, I will. I'm happy we're here."

She looked up at him, his wavy hair caught in a gust, blue eyes fixed straight out at the horizon. "Of course. You're right." Then she turned her head to where he was staring. "What do you see?"

"I'm counting the rings around the lighthouse. There's nine. Last year there were ten. The water's definitely rising."

'I counted them yesterday."

"Darling, you can try with your mind, to carve out this little corner of the world. Insist to yourself that it's different than the rest of the country. That you can protect it because it's yours. But's all this is connected. No matter how much the people here do to remediate the shoreline, use solar or conserve energy, this piece will soon be gone too."

Kara kept her eyes on the horizon, not wanting to answer. "I know, I just don't want to admit it to myself. This is our place. We've got years of memories invested here. It makes me so happy."

"Me too." They watched the waves for a few minutes longer and turned towards their place. He tried to steer away her melancholy. "You said seafood tonight?"

"I did." Kara brightened as she thought about their first dinner together. "The menu tonight is some lovely steamed clams and sweet potato fries. Followed by your favourite. Chocolate mousse cake I made earlier."

As they moved inwards they could hear some kids playing at the condo development next door. Not the screaming kind of noise that demanded sorting. It was a happy, summery, peace-bringing noise. What would it be like at her son's house right now? The chaos and clamor as everyone came home and got about their dinner. Talking to her daughter-in-law about how to stretch the spartan menu. Debating with a six-year-old about spelling. Putting some laundry in the machine so it could get hung up overnight to dry. There was always something.

In comparison, tonight was calm and delicious. After their splendid dinner she took her place on the chaise, lying in the late day sun. At her feet was a paper book that she'd just bought at a local thrift store. She liked leafing through the paper; it had a distinctive smell. She looked around at the room and saw that it was in perfect order. Later, they would go to their friends a few doors down and play an old-fashioned game of euchre. And enjoy each other's company over those martinis that their friend Max always seemed to have ready. It was like this that it normally went during her month or so away.

The sunroom door slid open gracefully and Terry walked out with two glasses of the wine from the bottle she'd bought from a winery not far away. "I think it's chilled enough" he said as he passed one to her. She looked at him and felt the familiar *frisson* she had looking into his eyes.

She took a sip of the wine and he bent over her neck and kissed her. Like they used to do when they were young, before they married other people.

"You were thinking again!"

"OK, you caught me. I'm feeling a little guilty. I'm here doing sweet FA, living a slice of the good life, pretending that everything is great. Soon all these buildings will have to close."

"Yes, I know dear. But you don't have to be on guard all the time. The way I see it, if we're the last ones, we should enjoy life like it's the last dying days of summer."

"Terry, I love you. And I know you're trying to cheer me up. However, you can't compare now to the halcyon last days of summer. We enjoy those days because we know that summer is coming back. Here it's too late. This town is dying. What if we're the last generation here?"

There was no answer to the big question. "I'll stick with I love you," he replied, with that familiar smile on his face which meant he had had a plan. He stroked her behind the ears in a way that he knew she liked.

"What time do we have to get to Max and Shelia's?" he asked.

"We've got some time. They are getting home about eight and want us to get started a little later," she replied.

He smiled and she caved. His eyes. The bright blue with a fascinating ring of green. They cleared her thoughts. Even now they had a physical connection that most assumed is the province of the young.

Thirty-seven

Janey had stayed in the Canadian car even after it joined the
American train at the border. Since she'd left Ottawa she'd been
wedged into a seat so small she had no idea how anyone with a
weight condition managed to take a train anymore. Lucky that her
fellow passengers on either side were average.

She'd paid the extra to be able to roam the American side. There was
a heavy beat coming out of that part of the train; it was bumping and
packed. As always it offered a bewildering variety of entertainment.
She could hook up her personal screen to any of the entertainment
servers that her family allowed her to use. She could pay for the
service on board. Or she could join the crowds in the virtual cars.
Take a trip on a trip they say. It was tempting because they had the
Tahiti program running in one car and the rain forest program in the
other. She could join the party in the bar and observation lounge. It
was filled with northerners getting a jump start on a winter vacation.
Or she could hang around in an available sleeping pod reading. Or
perhaps chat with a few friends on the large screen on the ceiling of
the pod.

Instead, slow to get into her vacation, Janey opted for the Canadian
lounge car with the stupidly small seats with her headset tuned to an
old playlist that she found. She wished there was food for sale on this
car. Even though it would be expensive and plain.

She bought an egg sandwich from the vending machine and bided her
time. She still had hours to go before reaching South Carolina. Kara
had promised to pick her up at the station.

She looked forward to time away. All those small pleasures. She
couldn't wait to taste grapefruit again. After the years going down to
Carolina, it still felt both familiar and fresh to her.

It was a great arrangement. Nans was discreet and never got in the
way. She would always find other people her age down there
escaping the weather for a few weeks, lapping up the solar spit. Nans
liked this place because it was an environmentally harmonized, gated
place. Janey knew it didn't have all the nightlife that she would be
looking for, or the shopping. She would have to share a drive into

town for that. But it had a good selection of pools and hot tubs, other young people, and it was within her means.

These rides used to seem long, but now they passed swiftly. It meant passing through New York City. You knew you were getting close to NYC by the smell. Burning gas and garbage, a smell that was so intense. Kara called it the smell of the old days, but to Janey, it was the smell of adventure. As you got closer to Grand Central Station there was always a kind of hum that vibrated. And finally, you saw the buildings, the cars, the energy. It was guilty pleasure, a nirvana of infinite contradictions; you wanted to stay forever and leave as soon as possible.

Janey would stop there every year. This year she saved it for on her way back home. She had already paid for a few days at her beloved hotel. She loved its glamour. The ease of asking for a service at the concierge desk and knowing they would trip over themselves to help you.

New York City was the best and worst of everything. The city could be remorseless. She'd been shocked to see people walk over a well-dressed man passed out in the street. Walking home late one night she watched a taxi driver whine to a policeman that his hack was a write-off. He whined while the guy in the other car sprawled lifeless out the side, his blood pooling on the pavement.

The best was the plenty that surrounded her: room service, taxis, rental cars, food from all over the world, people travelling in and out on those crazy-fast high-altitude planes. She had seen a lot of the museums and attractions. There was always something amazing to do, if you had the cash. She would squirrel away cash for this leg of the trip. She loved to pretend she was rich enough to be part of it all.

She would take a taxi to the Lincoln Center and see whatever was on. To see real people perform curiosities like opera and ballet made her feel like a member of a secret society. Ballet especially transported her. The elegant flow of its synchronicity coupled with the pain that the dancers must surely feel. It had no point, but it seemed more real and emotional than her everyday life.

And the city still had shops. Clever, cozy, or sophisticated. She treasured the time spent browsing the boutiques and experiencing the merchandise. Then there was the food. So much selection. She would spend time imagining the tastes and get the catered meals at *Dean & Deluca*, staring at the city lights while eating in her room.

She would study the menus at restaurants that she passed by on the street and settle on one that offered the most elaborate dishes and specialties from faraway places. She would go to the antique market and pick up trinkets for everyone, and then hide them in her socks to bring them back over the border.

Over the years she met other young people, residents, and found herself invited into their world. She remembered partying at a beach house with the extremely wealthy. People with some celebrity would be there. They wore perfume, jewelry, and fancy clothes like it didn't matter. She got a little tipsy and for a few hours imbibed the ease and grace of the fabulous.

Her friend Byron had brought her along to events as his plus one. Like the time she found herself at a wedding reception in Soho. A small restaurant filled with the happiest people. They all looked like they came from somewhere different. But in truth they were all the same: rich, privileged and benefitting from the fruits of other people's labour.

That's what Kara would say. "These people are rich and don't make the sacrifices the rest of us make." Or she'd say "those free riders live in a bubble of wealth while the rest of us sacrifice to make sure that we don't all drown from melting ice caps and swollen oceans or dry up from sun exposure and fires."

Janey pushed the dour thoughts out of her head. She made sacrifices 363 days a year. Two days a year she supported the Sodom and Gomorrah that was NYC. If Janey wanted to make the point, she could say to Nans that her generation had lived to excess for their whole lives. And when they got old and too sick to enjoy anything, they relented and created their world where sacrifice was the sport. Which was fine for them since their bodies were giving up anyway. Nans couldn't eat anything anymore; fat, carbs, sugar and alcohol made her sick. So what kind of sacrifice did they have to make anyway?

The smell of perfume lingered as a well-dressed woman passed by. "Smells sweet," thought Janey. "She might get a fine if they catch her." More curious still was that she was on a train at all. Perfume was the stuff of the rich, and they usually flew.

Her trips to the U.S. opened her eyes to life of the wealthy. The real life. It was more than the trashy feeling of consuming anything. She realized that the fabulously wealthy were the ones that defined the fine edge of life. She wondered how it would work to really be one of them. It would probably have its own problems. The world for the rich was getting smaller and smaller. And seedier too. More and more of the famous and well known were climbing on the post-consumer bandwagon. She imagined that if you didn't really care how you dressed, and what you ate, the post-consumer world could offer a pretty good personal branding. And you still had your money.

Not everyone though. From time to time you heard about celebrities who used to be rich and tried to keep up appearances. That got tough after a while. Tragically one day they would come out of the closet and join the rest of us. Why pay for things like heat and medical care when you could get them paid by the government?

Her personal screen came alive and she saw it was her mother. She was checking in. Mom was fine. The biggest news was that Jennifer was having a few people over for dinner and was serving fresh peaches she found at the farmers market in Toronto.

As she put the screen aside, she thought of the weeks ahead, times on the beach with Kara and that elusive boyfriend of hers. Car trips with the other adult grandkids at the resort. And NYC on the way back. A visit with Byron and whatever he'd got planned. It would be good. And rich or not, she had a pretty good life.

Then Janey got her stuff together and left for a virtual car. A flashing sign told her that a rum company was sponsoring a free dance party in one of the American sections. They called it 'All in for Azure;' promising to plunder her booty with its synchronized beat mixed with the treasure of a blue and white neon atmosphere. She smiled thinking she'd made it again to the States. It was time to move. Time to get her blood and bones into the spirit of her vacation. Her ass had gone numb in these chairs.

228

Thirty-eight

Something second-rate had taken over her favourite hotel. This was her fourth trip, and the chic vibe that Janey waited for all year was only here in fits and starts. The free coffee in the paper cups was gone. They now charged $3.46 for disposable cups, and then $1.54 for the brown refreshment. She could have brought her own cup, but honestly, the coffee tasted better when the cup was free.

The sound in the lobby had changed too. She listened to the people come and go. That always pleased her, a soul-warming change from the almost monastic sounds of her city. But the hotel now seemed to want to drown out the cacophony of real people, the rich mix of languages and accents. There was droning music in the lobby, some horrific remakes of songs she had learned in the choir at school. With a lot of WTF peppy trumpets.

This morning she'd installed herself in one of the armchairs in the lobby. The hotel had staged a grand living area centered around a great big wasteful gas fireplace. This year tragically the overstuffed furniture had been replaced in spots. It used to scream old-world luxury, with its soft brown leather and black glossy arms. But the new stuff they'd added had a kind of post-consumer, recycled look about it. The style was still aiming to capture the luxury of the 1960s, but it was lightweight and scant. It didn't fool.

And finally, the staff. Well, the doorman was the same and the concierge was the usual helpful, spirited guy. They knew how to make her feel special while she was so out of her element.

Terribly, the front desk had adopted an attitude of incompetence. The power of suggestion that used to result in whatever she'd hoped for, say a drink on the house or a complimentary shuttle, only seemed to yield a withering look and an insistence on the wrong answer. She wanted the magic to come back, where all her dreams could come true. She feared that the dourness of her world was starting to arrive in paradise. What shit.

She read over the news on her tablet. First, she looked at the NY bulletin. There was a small travel advisory for the Wall Street area scrolling across the very top of the page. Flooding had submerged many the streets south of Beaver Street and it was expected to continue for another couple of days. It was part of the same storm surge that Janey had lived through in South Carolina. But most of the screen was happy stuff. A story about a party at the museum, an ad about a new car, and some fashion news. She breathed it all in and enjoyed it with guilty gratitude.

Then she checked her own local bulletin. It had its rational, measured feel, like it always did. Stuff on the economy and politics. With the undercurrent of government PC cheerleading. It was cloying, even if she was a model citizen and believer. Away from it all, she wondered who was its intended audience? Who was that ill-informed, information avoiding person, who everybody assumed existed somewhere, but was nobody's acquaintance?

Byron was now sitting in the armchair next to her with his own cup in his hand. They both needed the coffee. She grinned slyly at him and turned off the bulletin.

"Wait. I was going to look at that." He leaned over to her and his smell transfixed Janey. She clicked back on the news from her hometown and passed him the screen.

 "I think it's hilarious that you don't have service reports on your internet," Byron remarked as he pushed the content up.

"I guess we don't have problems with supply. We have this fair use provision. I don't know what it does."

"Here we plan our day around when you'll get the best service. Everyone reads the service forecasts every morning. It can be the top news if service is choked up." He scrolled quickly for a minute and passed the screen back. "Otherwise, I see that things haven't changed since I left," he remarked dryly.

Their annual visit had taken an unexpected turn. It started as soon as her train pulled into the station, where he was waiting to surprise her. Seeing him standing on the platform, so confident with his hands in his pockets, scrambled her thoughts. Waving at her, as the train pulled in, shocked her agreeably. He stood there patiently waiting, as she realized that everything was different. She felt overcome with gratitude, as she unloaded her luggage onto the platform, her eyes

230

fixed on his smile. He walked over to her as she found a cart for her bags. Then he helped her steer everything out of the station to the cab stand. They didn't say a word to each other, preferring to smile and walk together. Finally the silence was broken when he told the driver the name of her hotel.

That was the beginning of it. The point when everything changed for the spectacular. He'd taken time off from his job and they hadn't been apart since she'd arrived. For the last couple of nights they'd been together on all manner of adventures. Looking out together at the midnight skyline from her hotel bed. Lunch on a rock in Central Park. Whatever they had done it was fun, passing fast. The things you'll remember for a lifetime.

She lingered silently over what was left of her coffee, trying not waste it with talk. There was everything in this connection, with him, right now. This morning it all still felt delicious. Still fresh, loaded with the chemistry of their new connection. As any romance addict could tell you, they were at that fucked-out, intimacy loaded point that anyone with a heart craves.

She was scheduled to leave and they both were there thinking separately about the next few days. He wondered how he could ask her to stay. He didn't want to pressure her. He watched her timidly glance down at the ground and then raise her lovely face to smile at him, making him feel simply like some sort of genius. All he wanted was to spend more time with her.

She contemplated the excuses she could give to her work; they expected her soon. What money could she tap into to pay for this hotel for a few more nights? Was staying the proper thing? God he was good looking.

He spoke first, looking straight ahead at a point behind her head, "do you have to go today?" What he had said was out there, hanging, while he continued to fix his eyes on the same point on the wall. Then he leaned over her and spoke quietly. "OK, listen, I know that this is probably odd, but why don't you stay with me for a bit. I want you to stay."

There it was. A choice. A choice that presented itself like the train taking off at the station. Not sure where it was bound, she was running alongside it, figuring out whether to jump up before the train picked up too much steam and was gone, out of sight. This time the train wasn't going home, back to the familiar. It was travelling someplace else.

Byron was still leaning towards her, his breath and his hopes palpable. "I'd like that," she replied simply, knowing it was what they both very much wanted. Then she stood up while he straightened himself. "Let's do something great today," she said as she took his hand.

Thirty-nine

Janey walked down the crowded street, casting her eyes around at the faces. Some were chatting to each other, their hands in front or overhead to emphasize their points. Others, withered and small, walked forward slowly with eyes blank with pain. A car stopped, letting a man in a fine grey suit dart across the sidewalk, to then disappear into a glass front. Many others talked to someone through headsets. She overhead the collage of their speech as she passed them, obscured sometimes by the parade of cars honking pointlessly down the length of the road.

She was on her way to another of her New York rituals, where she shopped in person for what she dared not dream about back home. Colourful, processed foods. Spices and mixes of all kinds. Kitchen gadgets. This would normally be one of the highlights of her trip. This year she'd had to fit it in while Byron reluctantly dropped something off at work.

She stood at the entry to the grocery store and imbibed the smell and the feeling of abundance. This was a special place; it was where the 'foodies' blogged about. She knew the aisles well now. She walked in and started to pick up a few essentials. Dark chocolate covered biscuits and a bottle of aged Bordeaux. A six-pack of champagne in little bottles. Italian blood oranges and muscat grapes. Cheese from France. A dozen oysters to share with Byron. And a couple of magazines made out of paper that were laden with pictures about being rich and buying "the latest." Didn't seem to matter what: clothes, dinner reservations, travel. She only ever saw these magazines in the finest stores; they certainly weren't available in many places. The pages were colourful and shiny. Bits of fancy text with addresses sat in corners like a secret code to the wealthy.

Janey moved to the aisles and stocked up on her favourites. Cumin and chili powder. A mix that made curried rice. Powdered ginger. Chinese five spice. Food colour. Jelly beans. And then a trip to the clothing aisle where she could find shoes and lingerie. Makeup. Fancy stuff, with names like "Pretender" and "Naked Lies" so unlike the drab crap at home. She stood in front of the rows of colours and tried to imagine what they would look like on her. Such luxury. It was hard to choose. Overwhelmed, she forced herself to pick something because she would be stuck with the three or four government authorized colours for the rest of the year. When it comes to nail polish, the government was wrong. Less was just less.

A week's salary lighter, Janey left the store and got into her ride-share. As she rode back to Byron's place, her head was filled with her trip.

By now she'd stayed an extra week in New York, but she felt internal pressure to be sensible and leave soon. To think things through. It was nothing but magic with Byron, the man was so comfortable to be with. There was no dead air. He knew who she was and appreciated her; she liked who she was with him. Her feelings for him were starting to challenge her own unshakeable commitment to what she wanted out of life.

Back at Byron's, she bagged up all her contraband and stuffed it in with her dirty laundry so customs wouldn't dare. She left room in her case for more loot from the new liquor store that Byron liked.

She sat on his couch looking at the magazines, waiting impatiently for him and his wonderfulness to get home. He didn't work far, but it was huge hotel and he'd most likely been detained a little longer by staff. Flipping from one glorious curated image to another, she felt the pleasure of the anticipation of him. It was a nervous feeling, but not like a job interview or waiting for a test result. More like waiting for a dress from one of these magazine images to arrive at her doorstep. She knew it'd be good. She smiled as it dawned on her what she was feeling. She'd always loved him.

The door rattled as Byron unlocked the double bolts with his keys. His place was small by any standard, so she had time to scamper to the front entry mirror to check her face and bolt back to the couch, before he finally opened the door.

She expected him to drop whatever he was carrying and make his characteristic joke. "Honey, I'm home!" Or "whatever your making, that smells delicious!" Dumb, folksy, stuff.

Instead, he took three steps into the apartment and froze with a gob smacked expression.

"What," insisted Janey playfully.

234

"You'll never guess!"

"You're right! You look like you've won a lottery. So why don't you just tell me."

"The best thing happened. I went to my hotel to deal with that report they wanted, then ran into one of our good customers on the way out. He walked right up to me and offered me these two tickets for *Roiling Republic.*"

"Really! That's insane." Janey stood up from her seat as if shocked by an electric current. It was the hottest show on Broadway and they'd tried hard and failed to get tickets. "What did he want for them?"

"Nothing! He said he didn't want cash, he had to leave town early and he just wanted them to be used. Apparently I did him a solid one day, a while back. I don't remember it."

Janey ran up to him and grabbed his waist in joy. "That is the best! Show me!"

Byron grabbed his screen from his coat pocket and proudly flipped to the tickets as she took the screen and went a bit giddy. "It's for tonight, and look where we're sitting," she squealed. "We'll be right up front with all the bling. God damn, I can wear that dress I bought today! This'll be so much fun. What time will we go to dinner?"

"Woah there, partner. You just settle down a spell!" He took the screen back and laughed as she twirled around the living space. "The curtain is at eight o'clock. We can make dinner if you're quick getting ready."

She was already down the hall before he was finished. He grinned with a mix of pride and amazement. He'd have a forty-five-minute wait before she came out again looking so hot he'd rather stay in. She didn't need the dress or all the work to transform herself into something beautiful. Still, it made her happy, so he contented himself with pouring himself a glass of wine and checking out the news.

Glass in hand, he sat patiently on the couch, instructing the wall screen to make the dinner reservation. Then he spent a few minutes reflecting on whether it was better to tell her before or after the show. After, he thought. In case the fact he was moving back to Canada would somehow upset her and ruin what looked like a pretty solid memory.

Forty

Janey could leave a message for her cousin and not hear back for days. Not odd for Tanya. Janey was used to waiting, sometimes abandoning her efforts, to speak to her cousin.

This morning was different. She had to share with someone familiar ASAP. She woke up next to Byron before the sun pierced the blinds. He didn't stir while her thoughts exploded. A fleck on the ceiling of grayish-white reflection was her focal point while she lay flat as a board, reliving the joy and jitters of last evening. The marvellous glamour of the show with its velvet elegance. The refined audience and its cultured restraint. The heartfelt applause that drew two curtain calls. The drink at the lobby bar on the way out. Byron's silence, which seemed so natural as her departure was drawing so near. His suggestion that they walk the few blocks back to his place. This was different. As they walked he held her hand tight. And then he did something that cut her mind in pieces. "Janey," he said confidently, "I've been considering this for some time. Moreover, your visit has affirmed my view that it's time for me to move back." The memory of his quaint pronouncement, very upfront, very precise. However, whatever she stammered in response was as muddy as, well, her thoughts right now.

Janey wasn't unhappy. More like confused and annoyed at being blindsided by her own lack of imagination. How was it that she never dared imagine where they were headed? Missed spotting how fast life can change? His feelings were obvious, rolling back the week. Now her own feelings were a chaos of prospects, unanswered questions and fear. It was as if he'd opened a door to an unexplored world that promised to be both dangerous and exactly what she wanted.

"It's exactly that," replied the voice in her head, smugly. "You want this, you're just pissed you didn't see it first."

"If you're so damn smart," she replied to the voice, "you could have let me know sooner!" She groaned a bit involuntarily and then remembered Byron asleep next to her. So Janey crept out of the room and closed the door behind her to find his coffee maker.

A conversation with Tanya would help. She cradled her mug, pacing the floor, wondering if it was safe to call now. Tanya would recognise how Janey feels. Have some inspiration as to what do next. True, Tanya could be unpredictable with views way outside of conventional boundaries. Probably tell her to get wasted too. Then she prayed Tanya would utter some unconventional insight that would bring Janey back to normal. Some idea that hadn't yet made its way to Janey's agitated brain. Something that only someone with Tanya's keg of youthful life experience could dispense.

Byron was up now and kissing her goodbye. She stood up from the couch and stared distractedly at one of the skyscrapers that could be seen through the wall-high windows. She didn't get the fascination with this view. It was nothing but a dungeon of tall structures. Each designed to make you feel small and insignificant. To her Canadian sensibilities, all she wanted to do was break out and find some open space where she was the tallest thing around.

She sat back down in his main room and tried to make peace with the disquieting quiet. The walls seemed to creak. The agitation had made time fly by. Byron had left about half an hour ago to spend the morning at work. She'd already showered and eaten some breakfast.

She picked up her personal screen and scrolled through her contacts. His main screen lit up as she moved the information up and down to call her cousin. No answer. There was a blaring staccato sequence of ads. While she flipped through, she did her best to ignore the hard sell. The ads were so unlike what she heard at home. These ones tried to make you feel guilty for not being part of the crowd.

She tried to call again. There was no answer at Tanya's last known number. A subsequent call to their mutual friend revealed that Tanya had moved, but where was unknown. Finally, in desperation, she called her Aunt Ally's place. She was going to leave a message. She didn't want to get involved or contribute to the obvious disappointment of Tanya's folks. It was 9:30 a.m. and Tanya picked up on the 2nd ring.

"Hey, chickie! How's it going," exclaimed Tanya. Janey saw that it was the unadorned version of her cousin. No glamorous movie star makeup. Her hair looked like she'd just washed it. It was combed straight back neatly and framed her face. She looked a little pale, but

238

that might be the video screen. Her eyes had a blurry look, with dark centers in her pupils. She probably had a buzz on.

"It's going great. Are you staying with your parents now," asked Janey. "I left a message at the number I had for you a few months ago."

"Me? Yup. I'm chilling with the 'rents for now."

Tanya took a good look at the scene behind Janey. "Where the hell are you?"

"Byron's. Remember that friend I told you about in New York City."

"Awesome! Are you having fun?"

"Yeah. We've been crazy busy. Byron knows all the places to go around here."

"Well, that's good to know. But, how's…?" Tanya made a crude gesture, exponentially emphasized by the large screen. "Are you and the boy having lots of fun?"

Janey blushed. "I'm having the time of my life. When I'm with him I don't notice the time going by."

"How romantic! I see why you're not back already. I hope you're getting a good pounding out of the whole thing."

"Did anybody ever tell you, you're crude? Since you're keen to keep score, for the record, every hour," Janey projected calm, although a little annoyed. "So, moving on. I wanted to ask you something."

"Sure, but before we get to that, don't forget to have at him every chance you get. When are you coming home?"

"That's a good question. I've already delayed my trip back for over a week. Has anyone said anything about it?

"Not that I've heard, but I'm hardly the most plugged into family group chats."

"Oh. Well, that's good. So, what about you? How come you're staying at the parents? It's the last place I thought you'd be."

"Yeah. I know, I don't want to be here either. It was my mother's idea. She signed me up at some school courses and I'm supposed to be tuned in about now. I log in and then dip. I just need a place to crash until I can set myself up somewhere else."

"And if I'm asked, what are you not studying?"

"Same thing I always pretend to study. Physio. It's so boring. A bunch of old people and their diseases."

Janey thought a bit about what to say. Tanya was one of smartest, canniest people she knew. Still, would Tanya ever settle into any job? She was in her mid-twenties now and still wandering from couch to couch.

"I guess I'm the boring one of the two of us. I just can't imagine not having a salary to depend on."

Yeah, well, that's the shit. You sound a bit like my mother. She tries so hard. She's driving me fucking up the wall. I can't smoke anything around her house. All she wants to do is talk about my future and our *relationship*. If I don't come home at night she wants to know where I was. And I think she's been going through my stuff. So, I've had to keep my real shit in the basement."

Tanya stopped and took a drink of something in front of her. She looked up at Janey, about to make a point. "And she's such a fake. All the time she thinks I don't know that she's fucking this married guy. And she's on at me about my future. Like it matters. And like she fucking cares. Whenever they're here, all I wanted to do was sleep. I don't want to hear another fucking lecture about my life. The other night I screamed at her to shut up and slammed the door on my way out."

"Sorry Tanster. That sucks."

"I don't know how you do it every day," answered Tanya. "The straight life ain't for me." Tanya took a breath and looked around the apartment again. Janey went over to the window and opened the blinds to reveal the city.

Tanya quickly sucked in her breath. "Oh my God. I'm so jealous. New York City! What sort of shit can you get there?"

Janey overlooked the real meaning of the question. "That's one of the reasons I called. I wonder if there is anything you wanted me to bring you back? Down the block there's a warehouse place with returns of stuff people had made for them, custom. You know, where people order a design they input on some clothing app, only it looks like shit to them when they get it. There are bins on bins of the stuff piled up that they are just about giving away. We can't get this custom stuff at home."

"What about some good shit? Can your boyfriend there hook you up?"

"I'm not going to bring any of that back. Anything else?"

Tanya laughed laconically. She'd been pushing the envelope, but it didn't hurt to try.

"No. It's okay. Wait, can you look for a pair of jeans? Something really colourful. And some decent eyeshadow pallets. I like that 1960s, last century look, light blues."

"I know what you mean. I'll see what I can find."

"Hey thanks for thinking of me. That'll be -- awesome," Tanya replied, singing the "awesome" in a theatrical manner that didn't suit her. The inauthentic blast of comedy was covering up something very dark. She wanted to challenge Tanya, but it wasn't the right space. "You take care of yourself," she said, meaning to wrap up.

"Always do! I'm out tonight. Looking forward to the buzzzzzz."

"I'll be home tomorrow. Let's get together. Save a space for me real soon. I can fill you in about my trip."

"Sure, if I'm still around."

Janey pulled her finger away from the exit button. "Where did that come from? Are you okay?"

"I'm joking, I'm joking!" Tanya laughed to reassure Janey.

"I hope so. That's not something to joke about! I guess you're feeling a bit more bummed than you're letting on."

"Maybe," offered Tanya. "It's more like I don't see the point anymore. I see how you fit in. But there's no place for me."

Janey tried to shake the surprise from her voice. She'd never heard her cousin express less than enthusiasm for her lot in life. "I don't know about that. It's not like I did anything special. Sometimes you just have to make a choice."

"That's the problem. Nothing excites me. I'm tired, I can't get motivated. I have a headache all the time and I just want to sleep. The world is fucked."

Janey sat there for a second, powerless. Tanya's face was on the screen in front of her, larger-than-life. "If I was there beside you, I'd give you a big hug."

"I'd like that."

"Well, wait for it. I'll be back shortly."

After she'd hung up, Janey remembered she wanted to talk to Tanya about Byron and him coming back to Canada. But Tanya wasn't in any shape to offer advice.

The apartment went quiet again, but Janey didn't notice. She wondered how her cousin had reached such melancholy. She would get out to see her as soon as she was home. She wondered if maybe she should share what Tanya said at the end. But with whom? She reflected on the reactions of the people in her family. Telling her own mother or father would be telling a wall. They wouldn't know what to do any more than she did. Kara was probably her best bet. She sighed to herself and promised to think about this later.

242

She sat back on Byron's sofa and considered her own worries. The call had put Janey's concerns in perspective. The anxiety was gone. Sometimes your problems aren't problems at all.

Tanya had a real problem. She was facing a choice and her choice was to come to terms with the sober life. Right now, this didn't have much appeal to Tanya.

Janey's problem was much more pleasant and conventional. She could choose to try and make a life with a man she knew she cared about. She wasn't the first to make this type of decision. It just felt like it. She took a breath and her world settled.

Forty-one

She'd only paid to sit in the Canadian part of the train home, so there would be no wasteful fun. Just lots of the old reliable. For example, the limited selection of food that was well prepared and in decent proportions. Janey went with the cultured pork in an apple glaze with roasted potatoes.

Janey ate in her seat in the day car and then read for a while with the others. She chatted with the man beside her who was reading *Raising Poultry and Rabbits on Scraps*. She borrowed it for a minute and saw it was a reissue of a Penguin handbook published in 1941 at the height of the English war effort. The gentleman was very pleased to have found it on a popular book site and was going to try raising animals himself. Janey listened, half wondering what his kids would think about the idea. They were going to love their dad for slaughtering their pets. Oh well, whatever helped.

They were coming close to the border and Janey was getting a bit nervous. Not that she had ever been caught with her haul of contraband, but there was always a first time. She was sleepy, but she had to stay awake until they crossed into Canada. Janey conferenced mom to catch up. They all looked well. Mom said nothing about her stopping longer in New York. One of her mother's gifts was to understand when to bring on the inquisition and when to tread softly.

When Byron saw her off at the station, her thoughts had been blurry, mostly from serious lack of sleep. These two nights she might have closed her eyes for two hours. Last night the two of them had gone to a converted factory that was now a huge, slick club. The understated, but loud music and the gold sparks of the lighting produced a honied other worldliness. They'd danced for hours.

Her senses, both overwhelmed and deprived, put her on a sort of autopilot on the train. It would take a few days to come back to earth. The euphoria would wear off and one of two feelings would remain. She would either miss him as if a surgeon skillfully removed her heart, or panic would set in and Janey would contemplate talking him out of his pending visit. He was coming home soon so he could talk to his folks in person about moving home.

Time seemed to drag. Two more hours and she would be home. She looked at the landscape going by. Northern New York State was a dump and looking poorer and poorer. Soon as they were over the border, it would look groomed, clean, and comfortable. There would be greenhouses blending in with the snow. There would be wind and server farms, ski hills, and government buildings. It would have a hard worn and hardworking patina. A country of purpose and balance. She was looking forward to getting home. Getting some sleep. Tomorrow was a work day.

PITCHING THROUGH SLUSH

Forty-two

"What the hell does that say? Does that really say *Plan B*?" Ally was talking to herself under her breath as she unplugged the car and threw in her bag. She'd driven herself home and kept the car at her house last night, instead of asking the driver to drop her off. It was morning and she was in a rush to get to a breakfast meeting. She grabbed the box for the morning-after pill and went back up the stairs.

Her daughter had moved back into her old room. She was here for a little while finishing up some classes towards her degree. Tanya had called her a week ago pleading with her to stay for "awhile."

"I'm tired Mom. I just can't get enough energy to find a job. Maybe if I come home and try some courses online, I can look for something when I'm done."

Ally wasn't sure what to trust, but she said yes. Since then things had been going surprisingly smoothly.

Last night they had taken the car and gone out to play tennis at the indoor courts. Then they stopped for coffee. Ally had bought a big chocolate chip cookie that appeared to make her daughter happy. Everything had seemed so pleasant. Tanya was her little girl again.

She knocked on the door and waited for her groggy answer. Stepping in Ally knew she didn't have to raise her voice on this one. "Isn't *Plan B* the morning-after pill?"

Tanya seemed to go rigid under her covers. She looked at her mother to assess how the next few minutes would go.

Ally continued, trying to keep the sarcasm out of voice. It was tough, because as embarrassing parental gotchas go, this was first-rate. "You spent the evening with me. Did you take the car after we got back? I think I would have noticed this box on the seat of my car yesterday."

Her daughter started to stammer. "My birth control expired..."

"Look, you are twenty-five and you need to concentrate on those classes. I thought we agreed to this. I am too young to be a grandmother. Don't take for granted that you can always fix this!"

There was silence from the rigid form in the bed.

"Are you feeling OK? We'll talk more about this tonight. I have to get to work."

"That was fun," Ally thought slightly gleefully as she drove away. She wondered if this was the most excruciating thing that had happened to her daughter.

And then the grim reality set in that the little girl of last night who played tennis with her mother was likely an act. In part at least. More to the point, Tanya had been out acting reckless. Where the hell had she been in her car? She'd found the key fob in Ally's purse and helped herself. "She could have asked me," Ally ruminated to herself. Then she ran over the past few weeks together, at the river of bitterness flowing between them. Ally had ignored what was happening, explaining it away as Tanya's choice. But this morning had forced her to be honest; Tanya didn't feel she could count on her mother. The realization threw Ally's glee into a pit of sadness.

Driving, Ally dwelled on the miserable way that they had grown apart. She was Tanya's mom and her daughter deserved better from her. She thought she'd always know her daughter, be able to protect her, and figure her out. Here was proof that she didn't know the woman her daughter had become. "If this was the crap she was willing to show me, there has to be worse that I don't see," Ally mused. For once, she didn't jump to conclusions. She didn't know what to think. Or how to fix it.

Forty-three

She heard Derrick go upstairs, presumably to his study. Good news, because once he was settled in, he rarely left. Now Ally could safely pretend she was all alone and that he didn't exist.

So far today she'd managed to fake it through the day. It was a work-from-home Monday and she'd puttered through some briefing material from the office in the morning. Small wonder she got anything done; she'd been up most of the night with Pete at their dependable hotel spot. She'd slunk in the early morning hours and crashed on the couch.

The briefing material included a manila, double-enveloped package from Hector's department. It had been hand delivered late Friday, with a signature required from her executive assistant. For extra security, it was marked, "Business planning forms." She recognized Hector's handwriting. Ally admired the touch, just the right amount of bureaucratic mumbo-jumbo. The man was gifted. No one is going to be curious enough to open it before it got to her.

She'd reviewed the contents this morning. It was table after table of data about where the country was headed. Probably someone with more background would get all the detail out of it. But Ally got the gist: things were getting better. The percent of locally produced goods compared to imports were up over expected benchmarks. Conservation efforts to preserve biodiversity had moved this indicator back into the positive. The percentage of houses and cars using renewable energy was well over the targets established decades ago. And civic participation in community activities was way up. Ally sent a two-word message back to Hector. "Looks good." Their plan was well on the rails. This data, once leaked to the right person, should surely create enough of a scandal to embarrass the Government. It should raise a lot of questions about why Canadians needed to sacrifice any more. This, in the face of an election, would be difficult for the Party to explain. It was in Hector's hands for now. But in a few weeks, not long now, she'd be stoking the fires of this scandal. Dealing with the heat.

At lunch she fixed a sandwich and then sat down at the kitchen table to watch her screen for a few minutes. It was the first stream that she stumbled on; an older fellow in a bright blue t-shirt and a pony-tail talking with an air of authority about mindfulness. She listened distractedly at first, but soon she paying attention. It intrigued her.

The man was talking about finding your joy. A strange word to her. Who thinks about joy these days? Joy, claimed the man, was a result of unconditional gratitude.

This last assertion jogged a thought. More of an intuition that bubbled up from her inside. Ally hadn't developed the idea enough to make it a slogan. She wondered if just being grateful was enough to make you happy.

His talk about joy brought her back to her vacation last summer, to the familiar county with its small-town life. To the charming landscape that made her first consider trading her job for retirement. "Could I retire here," she posited as she watched the locals. She quickly realized they had such a confident and positive outlook. "People are so damn happy." At first she found it simple, facile. She railed in her head that they did not see the complexity of life. Modern life with its challenges and sacrifices and discipline.

Then she stopped fighting the truth and moved on to wondering why. The answer was simplicity. And that they were grateful. They enjoyed farming, food selling and life at the beach. They figured that city people were missing something nice. They had a kind of attitude that you might want to seek out and enjoy.

One antique dealer took her through his barn filled with everything old. He was there five days a week and more in the summertime. In material terms, he was small town, with so much less. But he brimmed with an enthusiasm about his work that she found off-putting and disquieting at first. Ally came back later during her stay just to talk with the man. He loved his life. He was confident that he was moving in the right direction, doing what made him happy and fulfilled.

Since last summer, Ally noticed the word joy everywhere. People talked about it quickly, in snippets. With a reverent longing that caught her attention but also felt out of reach. She started to wonder if the joy in life had been pounded out of her, her colleagues, and her fellow city dwellers. Such a small word, but joy is the distance between longing and fulfillment.

Her sandwich finished and still lost in pleasant thought, she bent over to find a spot for her empty plate in the dishwasher. About then, Derrick wandered into the kitchen. She snapped up to attention, as if to defend herself. He avoided her eyes and moved around her to get a spoon.

"Oh," Ally said, trying to step aside.

"You were hoping for someone else," he asked sarcastically. He grabbed the cutlery and a jar of yogurt from the fridge and went back upstairs.

Ally closed her eyes and shook her head, sucking in air as if to cleanse herself. "What the hell was that about," she asked herself. But even as she asked, she knew. Even Derrick with his limited powers of observation must have noticed when she got home.

There had been a time when she cared enough to let his bitter remarks suck her into a vortex of guilt. But now she knew that it was best to own up and pace herself. She was out with Pete. He can languish in his anger. No need to take on his feelings. She quickly transitioned to cleaning up the kitchen, ordering some groceries and organizing some service people to come by in the week.

Tanya arrived home later, before dinner. She moved wordlessly around the house, going to the laundry room to find a change of clothes. As she moved, Ally could smell the perfume hiding the sickly smell of the pot. Ally watched as Tanya rooted around in the fridge to find something that appealed to her. Finally settling for soy hot dogs, they both sat silently while her daughter made herself something to eat.

Finally, Tanya broke the silence. She poured a glass of apple juice and then asked "where were you last night?"

"What do you mean?"

"When I left last night at midnight you were out. Where were you?"

252

Ally looked at her daughter trying to figure out what she was playing at. It had never occurred to her that Tanya would notice her comings and goings. Her daughter taken a hammer to the solid brick wall in her mind. The one that stood between Ally's need to get on better with her daughter, and her desire to leave her failing marriage.

"I was out with a friend."

"Oh," replied her daughter knowingly. "Just like me Mom, I was out with a friend too."

"Why don't we sit for a few minutes and talk about this."

Tanya scoffed at the suggestion. It was as if her mother suggested something tactless. "Nobody really likes being supervised by you Mom," Tanya responded. Not waiting for Ally's reply, her daughter quickly put her stuff in the sink, ran to the door and grabbed her coat. Before she left, Tanya yelled back, "I don't work for you!"

The exchange had lasted a few minutes. Her emotional turmoil lasted another few hours. Ally reflected on a loop that something was wrong. What had she done? Why was her daughter so offended? The situation called for action, but how to reach Tanya? She fantasized about picking up her adult daughter by the shoulders as she used to when she was little. Years ago, she would sit her in front of her on the kitchen counter and give her a talking to, followed by a snack or a treat. The bitter truth followed by the sweet support. Ally ruminated on Tanya, but no solution came.

<h1 style="text-align:center">Forty-four</h1>

Phillipe was nonplussed, as only a private school boy could be. It was hard to tell his moods from the outside. The bottled-up anger and cultured deference had created an emotional armour so thick that his smile remained about the same on days he politely fired someone as when his first grandchild was born. As the Clerk of the Privy Council and the nation's top bureaucrat, he no longer had to try to be outwardly impassive. He just was.

Internally, though, he could get himself in all kinds of situations. He could feel a rage that would have him pound the walls of his bathroom. He could feel the pangs of his old nemesis as he admired another young woman much younger than his wife. Dedicated Phillipe watchers knew the signs beneath the armour. When Phillipe avoided eye contact and kept his head down, turning pages while he asked what sounded like off-topic questions, staff would book off afternoons. When excuses were made to his wife about a cancelled engagement, they knew not to gossip.

Thus, staff had simply left and closed the door behind themselves when they gave the Clerk his daily briefing materials. Suspecting trouble, they had left without waiting to see if there was any follow up required.

He was reviewing each sheet one by one. Mid-way through the sheaf he came upon the hand-written note from his executive assistant. "PM wants to speak to you about the support from the Heritage department on the CC."

"Blast! The damn Carbon Credits again!" he exclaimed to himself. He grabbed the note and wadded it up in a ball before he pitched in the wastepaper basket.

He thought he had it all under control. He knew Ally would question his direction about pushing the credits. He had shared her concerns. He had challenged the PM, pointing out the problems and the ethical issues. Even he had thought this was beyond the pale since we all knew that the next thrust had to be outside the country. But the decision was made at the very top and a bureaucrat's job is to execute. That was Ally's job. He had made that plain. And now something had gone awry and he had to fix it.

"Get Ms. Ally on the line, would you?" He had called his assistant on the intercom to hook him up. He began to compose himself again. Despite his suspicions, it was best he got a few insights from Ally's side before he dialled up the PM. Might be some very justifiable issues that are causing the stir at Langevin block.

Forty-five

Funny how you can have an almost unconscious connection to someone. A connection that drew him to look across the street as he walked up to the pub. As Peter Haque was about to grab the cold metallic handle that stood in the way of a beer and a couple of rounds of pool, he saw Ally looking at him.

She was getting into a black government car, probably driving from one meeting to another. He knew so little about her day-to-day, or why she was there. But what he did know, as he stood on the sunny side of the street, was that Ally had her frosty side. She looked at him vacantly as she got into the car and drove away. She was like that. Pete was convinced that she rarely got a moment to thaw out. And those rare moments were in private, with him.

He stood for a minute and watched her drive away down the road with dirty grey snow piled neatly on both sides of the road. This year there had been so much more in town. It framed the dark car as Pete watched it vanish. He wondered if she'd turned to look back at him through the tinted windows. Then he hurried to get inside.

The bar was crowded. He hoofed it to the back to get a table. His friend would arrive soon. It was warm and lively. He would quickly rationalize and forget the cold shoulder from a woman who spent her off hours with him, groaning under the sheets.

His table secured, he moved to an old-fashioned pinball machine. He loved these things. His dad had shown him how to play. There were three similar machines in the bar and they were all filled with guys over forty. They were the perfect distraction.

But thoughts just came anyway. The first thought was about getting tired of a double life. This thing with Ally, it started before he considered what he was getting into. At the time, like now, things with his wife were not great. She was, and always is, pressured, comatose by 10:00 every night and complaining of what she had to do the next day. He tried and tried to do whatever he could around the house. If he took her away for a weekend his wife would assume it was for sex. Maybe it was a bit about sex, but he had really wanted was to get their thing back on track.

And then he was hit with the wonder of iceberg Ally. At some forgettable association function that they both attended.

Ally spent the first few minutes of the function chatting up the head table crowd. She took a chair at the reserved table facing the guest of honour. He watched as she toured the table shaking hands and chatting. It had a ritual feel to it, she was well regarded in this company. Her figure was eye catching in a dark, beautiful way that is reserved for an older worldly woman. Aloof some would have called it. Self-sufficient in a very hard shell said some others. Not one to give an air of needing much from anybody. He couldn't help but watch until he lost sight of her.

Some minutes later he found himself at the bar. She sailed up right beside him and waited for him to order. "Same," she said. Then he felt it. An unmistakable pull. There had been so much research recently on why attraction happens. But for most, you don't know why; you only know when you feel it.

He felt it when he saw the crack in her armour. A look inside at the real her as she fumbled for her card to pay. She smiled and shook her head. It was a kind of patient pause as both he and the bar keep looked on. And then a crazy, fun look came over her as she dumped a pile of cards on the counter. "I don't see it guys. Help me out and I'll get you one of what you're drinking!"

Pete found the card quickly and handed it back to her. "I think I have what you are looking for."

"And so you do," she smiled with a hint of something he tried to ignore. Pete waited there fascinated, wondering what was happening. But then she offered to buy his drink, and they found a table at the back of the room

He didn't know why he did it, but as they got chatting, he omitted his usual reference to being married. His rule when he saw a woman that made him stand up was to mention his wife at the first available opening. "My wife and I just downloaded that party play pack for our kid's fifth birthday" he would hear himself say, rupturing any chemistry and chance of flirtation.

Until he had figured this rule, not saying you were married at the outset only led to grief and awkwardness. Not telling Ally he was married was a choice, and he found himself disassociating with himself, lapping up the possibility of pursuit and sexual conquest, while a voice inside of him blathered on in a panic. "What the fuck are you doing? What if someone sees you? You have kids, stupid."

Two years had passed since then. It took six weeks from the day they first met to when they managed the sweet relief of sex. Six long weeks of waiting and planning. At first the panic voice was strong, waking him up at night and nattering. Then he had to have her. There was no other way. And then the disassociating stopped completely, and he felt that nothing mattered but Ally. He could leave and see his kids part-time. They would be happy.

The thing went on at a vigorous pace. Pete was distracted at home. About a year ago his wife insisted that they all needed to get away on a trip to see her parents. Two weeks away from Ally, down south on a train with the kids to his in-laws.

Setting out, he thought it would kill him, but the effect of being together day in and out created a counter pull of what he had with his wife and family: a sense of steadiness. Not love or passion, but a consciousness of the return on his life's investments. The panic voice returned.

A year had passed and now the panic voice didn't stop. He used to sit on the couch trying to drown out the demands of his family by imagining he could smell Ally's hair. Today, seeing her across the street made him take a breath to clear his confusion.

And even if Ally was not in the least demanding, she had started to assume he would be there for the long term. His alter ego started to play little games, pointing out her imagined faults and slights. She was taking advantage of him. She didn't really love him. Pete just made her feel good. Helped her as she dealt with the pain of her dick of a husband.

And yet even as he tried to pull away, and even not counting the sex, which a guy like Pete does with great difficulty, he knew he would rather be with Ally. He wanted both still he knew he couldn't.

He rolled the images of breaking up with Ally in his mind. He couldn't bear it that she would hate him. She would rebuke him for being so short-sighted and selfish. He'd be remorseful that he hurt her.

Pete's hands hurt from hitting the flipper buttons on the pinball machine. He had been playing hard. His buddy would arrive in a few minutes, and they'd play a few games of pool and stay clear of anything personal. That was unfortunately because he was busting to talk to someone about what was going on. He was more than willing to be scolded that this affair had run its course.

<h1 style="text-align:center">Forty-six</h1>

The lights changed on the other side of the street and Tanya stumbled across quickly. It was nothing new, but her head hurt worse than usual. She could tell she was dealing with some sort of transition state from stoned to hungover. Hopefully the cure for that was in her pocket.

She'd been pushing herself for a while now, even though an irritating piece of her screamed for attention. It was normal to feel some sort of pain, like this stupid pain in her chest and she worked hard to push it down, down, down. It made her think twice about doing things, wondering if her plans were dumb. And still, this nasty little piece of her kept screaming its warning from within. Today it was blaring. It was tangible, taking the human forms of the people walking alongside her in the street. Looking at her with a mix of pity and judgment. Trying to tell her something that her ears managed to keep out of range.

She could always stop a bit behind one of those buildings and burn a fat one. But then she might be too loose to work. Tonight she had to make at least six bills to cover what she owed to her stooge and to pay her wireless signal before they cut her off. Didn't matter what she made, it was never enough. The buzzless pot that you could buy over the counter was fuckin' robbery. If only she could grab a ride and head uptown to her peeps and down a few shots. Get back to normal.

The back room of *Savannah's* is known officially as the VIP room. You had to be a special friend of the bar to get in. Those few knew that it is one of the last of the titty bars in town, where girls danced and guys dreamed.

Further back, and even less well known were the champagne rooms. Tanya was now one of the older girls, but still could make some decent coin there. She had a long track record with the bar. The owner let her work whenever she wanted.

She had been sixteen when she was first introduced to this world. It seemed exciting. The lure of the sudden cash was overpowering. It got easy to make fast money a night or two a week. Now it was just a job. The bar stank of booze and sweat and Christ don't want to know what. Filled with losers that hung around hoping to find the right girl.

As she walked in, she gave the bouncer a sweet smile. He got the message. She was here to make the bills. For sure she was getting paid bonuses for every lame guy. No one was getting a freebie.

She popped the stuff from her pocket while she got into her outfit. She was going to dance a set and then bring every sucker she could find into the CR. She wanted to get in and out of this place as fast as possible and back downtown to tequila and the dance floor. She poured on cologne to drown out the smell of the marks.

She almost tripped getting up on the bar as the pills kicked in and it was dark. She gave 'em a good show, trying to put her mind on autopilot. They cheered.

Three hours later she was almost done with the last mark. As she grabbed his shaft she heard him groan "oh baby, oh god" as she went to work. Then she flinched, as a sharp stab of the other world came in. She heard a crash of chairs in the distance and felt her body floating up towards the ceiling.

The noises grew fainter and all she could think was fuck, fuck, fuck, fuck, fuck.

Forty-seven

Kara called at 4:00 a.m. through the emergency line of her screen. It came to life at her bedside and repeated its loud howl until she connected.

"You and Derrick need to get to the Civic Hospital. Tanya's here. They just called me. I'm on my way."

"What's going on," Ally asked, consciousness growing with each word.

"I think it's best to talk at the hospital. Get here as soon as you can. She's in Emergency. I will meet you there."

Ally got up quickly and pulled on her clothes. She threw together a bag of essentials: water, snacks, some work, electronics. Then she wandered down the hall and knocked on Derrick's door.

"What," growled her husband.

"It's Tanya, she's at Emerg at the Civic."

"What?"

"Our daughter's at Emerg. I'm leaving now. The car is here. Call a car. I will meet you there."

She heard a stir in the room. "Okay?"

A few seconds passed and Ally heard a thud. "Okay?"

"Okey dokey," Derrick mumbled, his voice either halfway awake or halfway back to sleep.

About an hour later she sat with her mother in a hospital waiting room for people like her. People who urgently needed answers. There were no windows in the small, stuffy room, no clock. You only had to look at the drowsy, sad looks on people's faces to know it was the middle of the night. Her mother scanned her screen and gave her daughter optimistic glances. Ally willed herself to stay still, knowing she was one more story in a room filled with people waiting for news from the medical staff.

Derrick still hadn't shown, but that was easier for Ally anyway. He would bring his unhappiness with him, flapping his gums about scenarios drawn from his grim imagination. And Derrick was unhappier than ever. She didn't know why he was unhappier. Like everything connected with Derrick, it just was. His choice, it didn't have to be like that.

"What's wrong with Tanya?" Ally asked tersely under her breath.

Kara turned to her daughter, watching her as she glanced around the room as if she was caged. "They'll be here soon, and we'll know more," her mother reassured her.

Ally sat straight in the chair, banging the back of her head slightly against the pasty beige wall. She thought about picking up her screen, but she couldn't concentrate on anything but the panic in her gut.

"Get out," she heard the voice say. Ally got up and stood at the doorway of the stuffy room. A bored technician in green scrubs wheeled a cart with supplies for drawing blood.

"Get out," said the voice again, more insistent. Ally was tired, too tired. But she realized this was a voice coming from inside her head. Yelling about some stupid notion about running away. From what, she wondered? The hospital? She mustn't leave. She was needed here.

"Get out," it screamed. "Right now."

A nurse came to the doorway and called out a name. Ally took her seat again as a group of people got up and followed the nurse wordlessly.

Ally turned to her mother. "Our turn must be coming next."

"No doubt dear. Just be patient."

"I'm sick of being patient, mother."

"I know. It won't be long."

She watched as another family arrived and filled in the seats. The mother, Ally presumed, was guiding the younger woman into a seat. Her voice was gently comforting. "It's going to work out. He'll get patched up soon, and then we'll be out of here. You'll see. He'll be as good as new."

Ally closed her eyes. "Get out," she told herself. Now she knew what it meant.

A cart rumbled by, pushed by two orderlies who were clearly tired near the end of their shift. The main doors to this wing of Emergency opened, and several medical personnel entered, chatting loudly to each other. At the central nursing station there was a different hum. People were standing around screens, pointing and discussing cases. The morning shift was coming on.

The mood was stark in the waiting room. Everybody wondering about their future. Kicking the floor or studying a spot on the ceiling. What would happen next? Good news? Sadness? It wasn't a place for daydreamers and idle chatter. It was a place to face up to pain and reality.

Her bitter truth was she had to stop toying with ideas. Or putting up pointless barriers. It was clear now, it was time to act. To get out and move on.

Pete was never going to be part of her future. She knew that now. It was pointless to blame either of them. It was best to let it go.

There'd be the ritual announcement of her retirement in the news stream. And a big celebration. That would be Derrick's last duty call for her. She would move out shortly afterwards. She already knew she'd move to the lake where she liked to spend the summer. All she had to do was contact the relocation service to suggest some options.

And then she thought about Tanya and what the hell was happening. The regret of the unknown heaved her forward. Failure fell heavy on Ally and she grasped her head in her hands and sobbed. Kara did the only thing she could think of, wordlessly rubbing her daughter's back.

FAMILY TO THE BARE WALLS

Forty-eight

Routine is a tonic when you like what you are doing. As it was with Janey, who got off the transit bound for the office. She was wearing some of the jewelry from the trip to New York. Fancy silver stuff that fell ostentatiously around her neck against her plain white shirt. It would surely get a rise out of those in the office today.

The walk from the light rail station to the office was remarkable for its quiet and cleanliness. Against the memory of New York, her city seemed like little buildings posing as skyscrapers, recently bathed in detergent. The cars, the people, all looked so purposeful, but there were simply fewer. Yes, it was a city, but every time she returned, its scale seemed laughable.

Tonight she was going to the hospital after work. She hadn't been surprised to learn about Tanya. It was sad but it confirmed her worst suspicions. She was anxious to see her cousin and hopefully catch up. It sounded like a lot of the family would be there. She debated whether she would say anything about Byron, but it was best to say nothing. There would be a flurry of questions and she didn't have many answers.

She had only been back home about fourteen hours now and she had already heard from him twice. He was coming in a couple of weeks to visit her. When she left, she hadn't felt any sadness; she was certain there was some sort of future.

Into her seat and already the computer rang. She beamed when she saw his image and turned in her seat to be alone. He wanted to know how her evening had been.

When she closed the chat with a series of heart emojis, she turned back, and then distractedly hit a stapler. It was made of a new vegetable plastic that she knew would never make the grade. She was pleased to see the stapler break as it hit the floor. She was only a low-level plastic goddess, so her opinion about its durability got lost in the evaluation process. And there it was, all greenish and smashed on the floor looking like, well, she didn't say it to herself. She was trying to keep the positive feelings going.

"It must be so nice to have someone message you like that. At the office, after so long of nothing."

Unusually, Janey's daily saga had attracted her colleague's interest. "Fioria, are you serious? Do you really think that my life is one bad meme away from tragedy?"

"Fer sure! But look at you now! You're crushing it!"

"Sure, true." Janey was happy. She felt it. For once she played along with her colleague and her teasing. "Okay, I admit I look forward to hearing from him every day. There. Happy? And here's more hot tea for you. We've talked about it, and he is going to move back here. We want to move in together as soon as we can."

Fi smiled a little righteously at cracking Janey's PC armour. Janey could run rings around her at some stuff, but her track record with men wasn't normally something to envy.

"Umph," Fioria said respectfully. "I am happy for you. Byron seems like a great guy. I like him already. I think he's got balls."

"Yeah, that's true." Janey ignored the straight comic set up.

Fi took the hint and changed the topic. She came over to lean on Janey's cube. "Did you see what happened to YOLO?"

"You mean that app that everyone's on?"

"Yeah, not me or you. We're too young. But my mother goes on about it."

"I know it. "Yolo? You mean Yo-lo?" Janey sang the familiar jingle.

"Yeah, that one."

"My Aunt Ashley is always on it too. Every time I see her, she tells me about it. What happened?"

Fioria recounted a story in the news stream about a couple that paid for the YOLO twelve-step program of self-help counselling on coping with OCD. It promised to cure the problem for a hefty fee. Then she drew a breath before getting to the point. "Well, it turns out that this was just another fake app."

"What," sputtered Janey. "How can that be? Millions of people are on it."

"I was reading more about it this morning. That couple wasn't happy, so they called their credit card company. They hired a forensic digital investigator. You know in the YOLO ads how they tell you to hook up with their certified counsellors?" Fioria mimicked the tone of the ad. "We have highly-trained, certified professionals located in major cities. Not true! They were just a group of fraudsters living in an apartment in Finland."

"But there had to be thousands of people calling every night."

"Yes, but most of those people were actually speaking to some sort of AI."

"Oh my God. And nobody noticed?"

"That couple finally did. They got suspicious when the 'counsellor' kept forgetting their jokes. That was the giveaway."

"Sweet Jesus."

"I know, crazy right? And it gets better. The app was managed by a group of three computer hackers in Malaysia. They were making billions of dollars. The U.S. and Canadian governments shut the app down. It's been taken down everywhere. It's just gone. Pouf!"

"How did so many people fall for that," Janey wondered.

"It's amazing what people will buy online. Nobody checks the medical qualifications to sell something if you've got reviews saying it works."

"You should. Geez, we have so many other rules, you think they could fix that."

"I know. Stupid right? My mother is going to be devastated. They've got all her information."

268

"I hope she's okay."

There was a pause. The women both knew they had work to do.

Fioria caught Janey by the arm. "You seem lit. Congratulations. This thing is something sig and I think it's great. It's such great news that he's seriously thinking about dumping the good life in New York and coming back to PC hell."

Janey smiled musingly. "He's giving up his job and going to re-certify for hotel work here. He says anyway that New York is quietly changing over. In ten years, things between the northern States and here will be so homogenized.

"Progress. Damn. Where will your kids get away from it all?"

Forty-nine

The two women huddled against the plexiglass windbreak that was inefficiently positioned at the front entry of the hospital. Gusts grabbed the edge of the plastic and magnified the howl of the wind. A few stray pieces of debris whirled noisily against the brick wall.

"Did you see her," Ashley enquired of Janey, as she shuffled sideways, grabbing her hair to keep it off her face and, pulling her trench coat tight around her slight frame to defend her from an astoundingly frosty draft. The weather had turned quickly; this afternoon Ashley noticed through her back yard window how the dead brown of winter was beginning to green away, revealing parts of the garden. She'd left the window open a bit and listened to the birds call to one another. Rich and melodious, a hopeful Spring sound. Now with the evening darkness came a wintery blast that threated to undo the afternoon's thaw.

"No, sadly," replied Janey, as she shifted a bit from foot to foot, pulling her arms in to her chest to protect her from the cold. "They wouldn't let me in to see her. Apparently, Tanya's still out of it."

"Oh, that's a shame. Not sure I can do much then. Maybe they don't need me here."

"No, no! Go on up! Everybody else is there just hanging out in the hallway. I was worried about getting in the way too, but people wanted to talk. I stayed longer than I thought I would."

"Great!" Ashley sighed and smiled uncomfortably at Janey. Hospital duty calls can be a tough assignment.

Large glass doors slid open with an institutional bleakness, while the wind came up again to battle with a countervailing warm, antiseptic blast from inside the hospital. The two women stood wordlessly as three people, eyes fixed to their screens and dressed in coats and scrubs, passively ambled by.

"Well, my ride is waiting over there," concluded Janey, pointing at the pick-up point. "Go on up, Kara will be glad to talk to you. Glad I ran into you and I got to say hi."

"Yeah, me too. I should get out of this cold. Good to see you too. I'll have you over for dinner soon." Ashley waved goodbye and made her way inside, very stuffy and loud. Families hung around in bunches, circling people in hospital gowns seated in wheelchairs or attached to monitors or IV stands. She negotiated around the line-up at the information desk and found the elevators.

There was a ping and the doors opened and Ashley recognized a familiar head of white hair. Kara waved, happily intercepting her daughter-in-law.

"Oh perfect. I'm glad you're here."

"Yes, I just arrived. I saw Janey on the way in."

Kara didn't hear what Ashley had said, instead focussing on the panels suspended overhead. Ashley loosened her coat and watched, bemused by Kara's intentness. She took in the effect of her mother-in-law's matriarchical drive, set-off by the grandmother attire of a pink plaid shirt and light brown, loosely-fitted pants. "What are you looking for Kara?"

"I always get a bit lost down here. I need to get some tea."

"I'm pretty sure it's that way. Looks like it's open for another hour."

"Where do you see that?"

Ashley pointed to the pictogram of a teacup on the wall at the corner. "It's got 8 -7 listed on the panel. I think that means the cafeteria closes at 7:00. You'd better get some now."

"What good are signs without words? I mean, good gosh." Kara started to dart towards the cafeteria and then stopped to collect her daughter-in-law. "Come with me. Please. I could use the company."

"Okay. Alright. Tea would be nice," Ashley stammered back. "But I don't think I've got the time. It's already getting late." But then she stopped. "Kara, I think I've got to pass on the tea. I'm going to go up and say hi to Ally. Then I've got to get back. The kids need to get into bed."

"I know. That's why I asked Jhonian to get them ready tonight."

"Oh. That's alright then. You're a step ahead of me."

"Sorry if I overstepped. I wanted to talk to you. Have a chat with a friendly face. After all the doctors and rigmarole. You know."

"I can imagine. You're probably exhausted too, Kara. Jhonian told me that you spent most of the last night at the hospital."

"I did. Tanya's not doing well. Come on, I'll tell you all about it. There's lots. But first, let's get the tea." She waved at Ashley to move as she spoke. It wasn't her usual command. It had a comic frailty that surprised the younger woman; the stress had begun to wear on Kara. She'd suddenly got old.

They waited patiently at the cash with two mugs of tea on a tray. "Did you eat, Kara? Maybe you could use some food." Ashley looked around and found a cooler with some sandwiches and yogurt and leaned over to put something on the tray.

"What happened to your shirt?"

Kara looked down at the pink plaid stains at her waistline. "Oh, that. Tanya threw up all over me this afternoon. I thought I got most of it. Next time I'm home, remind me, I need to bring a change of clothes."

They found a seat at a nearby table in the seating area that was mostly empty. "So, I'm getting the impression that things are really tough."

Kara picked up a sandwich and poked angrily at the container. "Not sure it gets much worse."

Ashley gently took the sandwich out of her mother-in-law's hands and steadily pulled at a corner to open it. "Here. I hope it's fresh for you," she said as she passed the food back.

Kara took a bite and chewed quickly. She'd been hungry. She got down half the sandwich before looking around the cafeteria as if noticing where she was for the first time. Then she turned back to Ashley and leaned closer. "My granddaughter is in a world of pain."

"I'm really sorry Kara. That's terrible for everybody. How is Tanya doing?"

"She's sedated a lot of the time. The doctors say the nausea and shaking is withdrawal. It's pretty bad."

Ashley picked up her mug, blowing on the tea to cool it. She took a sip and then spoke. "We always knew she liked to party. But I didn't think it had got this bad. Do we know what she was using?"

"We don't really know. She had some pills on her, and cocaine. But we all knew about the drinking."

Ashley watched as the rest of the sandwich disappeared, thinking how all she really knew about Tanya was her commitment to a good time. Now life had crashed her party hard and put her in a place no one would choose. "And the cancer, it's non-Hodgkin's lymphoma? Why didn't the doctors catch it?"

"They wanted her in for tests months ago. They told Ally that they even wrote to her months ago." Kara shrugged regretfully. "She's a functioning addict, she didn't follow up."

"Geez, I have trouble keeping up with their notices. I'm not surprised. Ally must be devastated."

"Yeah. But you know my daughter. She's a mess and doesn't know it. She's upstairs right now with Tanya." She stopped and balefully looked at the snow now falling beyond the window. "I hope they won't get into it while I'm away."

Ashley collected the debris from the meal carefully and put it on the tray, thinking about the long road back for everybody. It was time to ask the unaskable. "But do they think they can help her?"

Kara looked up at Ashley. "You know how it goes. The first stage is denial. When she's awake, Tanya's trying to leave the hospital and says she doesn't want any treatment. But the doctors say that's the drugs and the withdrawal making her loopy. There is a treatment. It's fairly new and complicated."

"But there's hope."

Kara smacked open the yogurt jar with enough strength to spill a little on the table. Ash reached over for a napkin and wiped it away and then extended a hand to touch her mother-in-law's arm. "But there's hope. Right?" she repeated. The older woman looked at where the yogurt had been, confused about the gesture. "Kara, I know you. You know there is hope."

Kara closed her eyes for a minute, breathing in deliberately. Then she opened her eyes and smiled, returning to form. "Yes, of course, dear. You're right. Thank you for reminding me. There's always hope. In fact, the treatment is fairly new. She's lucky to get this now, not twenty years ago. I just have to focus on that."

Ashley looked at the woman who she always assumed never had any doubts. She'd been washed away by a flood of sadness. "I'm always here, Kara, anytime you want to talk," offered Ashley, wishing she could come up with something better.

She stood up and disposed of the tray. Kara was standing by the doorway when she returned. The food had brought some colour back to her face. "Do you want to see her? I'll take you in for a minute."

"Yes, of course, let's go up," Ashley offered as she extended an arm.

Tanya's room was dark as they opened the door. The florescent light from the hall shot across the bed as they went in. Her single bed centred the room. The curtains were drawn across the windows on the far wall while monitors flashed and beeped quietly.

"She's sleeping," Kara reported as the door closed behind them and she switched on a little lamp in the corner. Ash noticed the arm chair on the far side. It was the grandmother's station; books, a package of biscuits and electronic equipment were neatly piled on the ledge behind.

Ash looked over at the rumpled pile of sheets and blankets, finally finding a hand with an IV pick and tape across the hand. She drew closer and saw Tanya asleep on the far side. She was pale and thin. Her hair was wet with sweat and her expression pained.

Ash looked up at Kara, nodding. "Probably best we let her sleep." Kara nodded back in agreement. Ashley's words were a deflection. As she would tell Jhonian later, Tanya looked like hell. Poor kid probably didn't want any of us to see her like that.

Kara came over and took Ashley's arm, kindly leading her closer to the door. "Thanks for coming," she whispered. "I'll let Tanya know you were by."

Ashley nodded once more and smiled back. "I will see you at the house," she whispered back. As the door closed behind her, she closed her eyes in a second of quiet, guilty gratitude.

"Hello Ashley. Thanks for coming." It was a familiar, firm voice. Ashley opened her eyes and saw Ally sitting on the vinyl padded chairs on the other side of the hall. Her coat was folded neatly over the back. A black leather satchel perched on the floor filled with files and a portable screen.

"How are you doing Ally?"

"I'm fine, I think." But her drawn, tired face said Ally's answer was more autopilot than real. Ashley went over to the chairs and sat in an empty space. "Has the doctor been by? I was talking to Kara and she filled me in a bit. Do you know what's going to happen next?"

"They've given me a lot of information. But the gist is that there's still some tests to do to figure out the best treatment plan for her."

"I guess this is going to take a while. Must be hard for you, to be patient."

"It's easier when you know what you want. I can't wait for Tanya to get well and get out of here. It will be the time for both of us to get out. Make some big changes."

Ashley nodded gently, not wanting to challenge the strange answer. They both loved some of the same people, but there never was the time for a friendship between the two of them. If there was, she might like to put her hand on Ally's shoulder, hoping to reach her with her touch because Kara was right; Ally was in denial. Her tone declared she could will her choices to happen. But her eyes were crushed, red and anxious. Not the usual steel blue. It was the most emotion she'd ever seen in her in all the years they'd known each other.

Ashley sat still, waiting to see if Ally had more to say. Her eyes wandered down the bare walls of the hospital, with their grim beige hue. A grey metal window at the end of the hall revealed a washed stone roof top and countless dull black metal vents that crowded out any sunlight. Just like her, families were clustered at the doorways conversing quietly in their languages about what was going on in the rooms of their loved ones. Waiting for nurses to walk out after attending to the people they cared about. Hoping for a bit more detail about the path forward. Some looked relieved, perhaps nearing a happy end to their journey, while others looked sad, expecting the worse. Ashley realized her family was at an early stage, confused about what lay ahead.

"Ally, Jhonian and I are here, if you need anything." Ally looked up, acknowledging the offer.

"Can I get you something from the cafeteria? I'm going to head out soon, but I can bring you something before it closes."

"I think I'm okay."

"Alright. But how about I get you a sandwich. In case you get hungry later."

276

Ally shook her head, wordlessly saying no.

"Okay." Ashley got up, tightened her coat, then turned and took a few steps.

"Ashley, hang on. Some coffee would be great."

Ashley looked back to find that Ally's eyes regained a bit of life. "You like just sugar, right?"

"You're an angel, Ashley. Thank you for being here."

"It's no problem. Really. I'm serious. Anything I can do to help. Just ask."

A few minutes later she was back in the cafeteria line, now moving slowly as people had rushed in to buy food before it was too late. It was noisy as workers energetically pulled the last of the food out of the display cases and piled it up on steel refrigerator carts to close for the night.

Ashley reached for her screen in her pocket and pushed the button to order a car. Then she looked down at the bologna sandwich and wilted salad that she'd managed to snag for her sister-in-law. Not very appealing, but it was all they had left. That, along with the coffee, was better than nothing.

She waited in line, sizing up the assortment of choices that make up a life. Both the rational ones, and the ones you throw in without much thought. How you set a course early in life and keep true to it because you're sure you want to. You think you're on course with what you want, until something like this happens. That's why Tanya was here; life randomly came up with a whole set of painfully different choices. Nothing she'd ever asked for; she'd never have stood outside this building and screamed 'let me in. I want to humiliate myself in front of my family.' But here she was anyway. And it was a very short list of people that would choose to take her place in that hospital bed.

As for her, she got the chance to leave. In about twenty minutes Ash would be home in time to give her kids a big hug. She could imagine their warmth in her arms, asking their silly questions before they finally let her settle them into bed. She sighed to herself, this time with a bit of genuine happiness. She'd take the silly questions any day over the stale bologna.

Fifty

She was still getting used to this. Janey stood outside her apartment door fumbling for her keys. She could smell that he was hard at work, up to something in the kitchen. She stood there for a minute trying to guess, Italian most likely. Then she got a strong confirmation of basil and garlic. It beckoned her to come in.

She turned the key in the lock but found the door was already open. Ridding herself of her coat and bags, she noticed the tidiness of her apartment. It was pleasant, but it was also unsettlingly new.

Byron had moved in a couple of weeks ago and with him came a lot of stuff. She never thought much about the size of her apartment, but now he'd arrived and taken up a decent bit of her personal space.

His first challenge was figuring out where he could find a job. Canadian hotels were paragons of environmental virtue, with an almost proletarian feel. He'd been gone ten years and most management jobs in the hotel industry had insanely strict environmental regulations. He'd have to pass a PC certification before he could apply, and that meant aggravating time online trying to figure out how. She prayed he'd be working soon and he'd be happy. He wouldn't have either the salary or class of his old employment.

While Janey worried, Byron proved to have a naturally optimistic nature. She wondered if the blind optimism she found in Americans had worn off on him. He passed his time catching up with people he'd not seen in a decade. He lived in the moment, happy to tend to daily domestic things. It nettled Janey sometimes when things were moved around from the way she had left them. She was adult enough to know that it was okay. For Janey, change was a welcome challenge with generous benefits. Still, it was unexpected and different, demanding she keep an open attitude and sometimes keep her opinions to herself.

She went off into the bedroom and donned her sweats. Not a romantic look, but relaxing and comfortable. Then she collected all her stuff to be washed from her work bag and joined Byron in the kitchen.

"How was your day," she asked joyfully as she snuck up from behind and gave him a cozy hug.

He turned from the pasta sauce and hugged her back. She buried her head in his chest and drank in the excitement. This too was new for her. It felt both awkward and beautiful. Then she pulled back and reached up to kiss him on the cheek. She tweaked his nose with her finger as was becoming their playful bent. She had to reach on her toes as he was taller than her, especially without her heels.

He put his arms around her and pulled her up almost off her feet, kissing her as he did so. "Day was great! I leaned in and finished that application for recertification. Now that's moving. Then, as you can see, I took a load of our stuff down to the locker.

Janey could see that there was a bit more space in the apartment. It had an airy feeling now that some of the stacks of boxes were gone.

"How did you manage to find space in the locker? Last time I was down there it was full."

Well, there's a bunch of stuff in there that I kind of rearranged." He looked across at her to see if that upset her. "Plus, I donated a few things which looked like they hadn't been used in years. Stuff like old garden equipment. We can always find new things when we get our own place. Someone had given you a lot of lawn and garden crap years ago. That's all gone now."

Janey couldn't remember that stuff and told herself it wasn't anything important. What was important was being able to walk across the apartment without hitting themselves on boxes.

She considered whether it was time to offer that they should go through their stuff and look for duplicates to donate. They wouldn't need two grill machines or espresso makers. Instead, she fled to safety. "Thank you. It looks much better. I look forward to getting up in the middle of the night and not falling over something!" They both giggled. It had become their running joke.

"That's the spirit! It's only stuff anyway. And this is only temporary. Hopefully, my certification will come through quickly and I can get a job at a hotel downtown soon. Then we can look for a place together that has enough space for both of us."

"You've got it all planned!"

"What? You don't like that plan?" Byron was joking but there was an edge or at least a question in his voice.

"It's a great plan. I'm just trying to get my head around it!"

"You mean you're not sure?"

Janey pretended to not hear that last question and moved around some chairs into their living area. She went over to their main screen and spoke a request to her personal screen, trying to find some music to stream.

While she fiddled though, she reflected on her hesitancy. His plan was hers too. Yes, definitely, she wanted him to stay. If they could have as much fun as they did in her cramped apartment, she was convinced that they had something good.

But what kind of life was he signing up for? He'd been away for a long time and lost track of how confining the PC world could be. He was making a big change to be with her, giving up things he'd come to take for granted. Things that might not matter now but may become painful later.

Asking him to stay was asking him to take on so much less. Maybe they should be really honest with each other. The problem was her words; how to express a muddle of passionate happiness and self-doubt. The nagging doubt that she would not be enough; that she was going to hold him back and, in the end, make him unhappy. All that and the fact she loved him.

She turned back to him to watch him stirring the fragrant mixture. He took a pinch of salt and threw it in, so optimistic, so incredibly capable, that she was suddenly confident that he would find his own way.

He looked up at her and asked her again. "What are you thinking?'
His brows arched and his tone said that he knew that she heard him

the first time. It freaked her out that he already got her that well. She stood calmly for a minute and watched him get the spaghetti in the colander. He did everything with a professional precision that showcased his skills. It would be cool to be married to someone who trained as a chef.

"Whatever you're making, I can't wait to taste it," she said, nodding at the pasta. Then, more softly, eager he'd know she was genuine, "I hope you will stay around."

She went over stood beside him and put her hand on his back, rubbing it softly. She surveyed his dinner preparations. "I see you have cleaned off the kitchen table. I'll set it for you." She kissed him on the cheek. She hoped, hoped, hoped that her future was his.

Fifty-one

Kara sat at Tanya's bedside. She watched as her granddaughter slept, heavily sedated, praying she'd stay asleep for a bit more. It was time to have a serious talk with Tanya, but Kara was still figuring out what to say and how to deliver it.

Talking to her other granddaughter Janey was easy. It was like talking to herself. She'd say the first thing that came to her mind and she could count on the exchange going okay.

In contrast, even at the best of times, talking to Tanya was a minefield. Whatever Kara said, treading lightly with a casual suggestion or venturing the direct route, it never landed well. Her granddaughter could go off with a snide comment or sharp, sarcastic remark. Kara had gone too far, offered too much advice. Then the discussion was over.

Now Tanya was like dynamite, constantly angry since she arrived at the hospital. She was full of explosive anger that scared her, Ally, and the hospital staff. Sometimes the anger took the form of silence. Sometimes it was a barrage of caustic and not very cogent observations about their relationship. At times it hurt, and other times she told herself that it wasn't what Tanya meant. No matter what, it wasn't easy. More to the point, she had a good reason. Kids her age shouldn't have to deal with cancer.

Progress was complicated because Tanya still had the hunger. Within twenty-four hours of admission, she'd woken from the heavy sedation and left the hospital in her hospital gown looking for "smokes." A policeman had found her and brought her back. She spent the next few days in restraints.

When Ally came, often towards the end of the day, things would get worse. If Kara was at least able to respect Tanya's anger, Ally was clearly in as much of a mess as her daughter. She continually tried to discuss 'the situation' with Tanya, making what she must have thought were helpful suggestions and observations about Tanya's condition. There was an air of guilt and panic in Ally's demeanour. It offended her daughter.

What Ally failed to understand was becoming clear to Kara. Tanya didn't want to get better. She didn't want to be in hospital, she just wanted to live the rest of her life.

But what the doctors kept telling Tanya was that lymphoma was quickly overtaking any quality of life she had left. Her choices were limited.

There was a groan. Tanya lifted her head from the bed and looked around the room. She watched her grandmother reading in the chair next to her.

"God damn," Tanya finally exclaimed to the world in general as she wriggled up in the bed to sit.

"Let me help you with that," said Kara as she got to her feet and adjusted the pillows. She had a firm touch and spent a minute making sure Tanya was comfortable.

"Thanks," said Tanya.

"You were smiling in your sleep."

"I was having such a great dream. I was with the girls at *Social* downtown. The bomb. Then I wake up in this shit hole. I can't wait to get out."

Kara stood at the side of the bed looking at her granddaughter. She was relieved that she seemed to be calmer today.

"We all can't wait to get you out of here."

"I'm hungry. Is there any food?" Tanya reached out a hand to grab the glass of water in front of her. It shook as she reached for it, so Kara helped her hold it steady as she drank.

"You haven't eaten a lot."

"I would've puked it anyway. Today's better. I feel more settled." Tanya pushed the buttons on the screen beside her bed, asking for food. Then she smoothed her blankets around her and raised the head of her bed.

"Nans, what's it like getting old?

"Were you dreaming about getting old?"

"I never thought about it. Before I got stuck here. I just lived my life. It was great."

"I know." Kara didn't really understand. Everything she'd learned about her granddaughter's life up until now had shocked her. She didn't mean indignation, it was more that everything in this young girl's life was beyond Kara's experience, or even imagination. One thing was sure, Tanya's mind was as jumpy as a cat locked in a box. But this was progress. They were talking.

Tanya looked out the window at the sunlight. "But now it's not so great."

"For now. But you've got some good options. It's not all gloom."

"I don't have a choice, do I?"

"You mean about getting treatment?"

"And staying here and everything."

"Well, if you want to get out of here and live yeah, that's your choice."

"I'm going to lose my hair. I'm going to look all bloated and weird"

"That might happen with the chemo. But the doctors told me they have new targeted ways of doing it. They have therapies that don't give you as many side effects. You'll recover. You're beautiful now. You'll be beautiful again."

Tanya paused silently, reflecting. Kara could see her adding up what she knew.

"Maybe," Kara offered, "you could speak to the doctor again. They told you a lot since you got here, but you haven't had much time to really ask questions."

"Fuck I wish I could smoke a joint."

Kara paused for a minute, searching for the right tone. Push too much and there might be more anger. And Tanya, from all the medical tests, didn't have time for much of that.

"That sucks," Kara replied.

"No, it's worse," Tanya joked. "It blows ass."

Kara and Tanya both laughed. It felt good. Relief that Tanya was coming around. And relief that Kara finally said something that helped.

"Do you want me to see if a doctor is around now, dear? I can step out and you two can have a private chat."

Tanya looked a bit hesitant. Then Kara played her trump card. "Oh, would you rather do this when your mother gets here later on this afternoon?"

Tanya's eyes widened. She'd not thought about the prospect of discussing any of this in front of her mother.

"Yeah, okay why don't we see if the doctor is around. Might as well get this done now. You can ask him if he'll prescribe some weed!"

Fifty-two

"Is something the matter," Jhonian asked. His tone was tender, not sarcastic or frustrated. Not meaning to critique her performance in any way, as he might have. Instead, he leaned against the doorway, wearing a jacket with his gym bag in one hand and watched her patiently, a pinch of worry in his eyes.

For the past thirty minutes his wife had been squatting on their daughter's room floor, sorting through clothes to find those that were too small. No doubt this job needed to be done. But it was so unlike her. It was already mid-Saturday morning, and she usually demonstrated a dogged devotion to the routine. By now on a typical Saturday, she'd be yelling at everyone that time was racing by. The kids should be on their way to swimming. She'd be moving them all along with a mix of exasperation and efficiency. This morning there was none of that. He watched as she let a t-shirt she'd been folding drop from her hand. She looked up at him listlessly before she responded, "nothing's wrong, I think. Why do you ask?"

"You've sorted those clothes for a while now."

"I can't stand the mess in here. I need to figure out how I can sort it away."

"Okay. I understand that." He looked at the piles in front of her that appeared about the same as thirty minutes ago. Ashley slowly picked up one of his daughter's sweaters and smoothed it lovingly into a perfect square. She put it back into the same drawer it had been in and stared at it for a minute longer. "You know, sweetie," offered Jhonian, "I can help you with that when I get back."

"Really?"

"Sure. Look, I have an idea. The kids are almost ready and I was going to workout while they have their swimming lessons. Why don't you grab your gym bag and come with us?"

Ashley heaved up from the floor and stumbled slowly over to her husband, opening her arms and giving him a bear hug. "That's a great idea. But I think I need some silence to collect my thoughts. You go, and that will give me some time to get a few things I've been meaning to do done."

"Alright," he replied, squinting his eyes to gauge her intentions. "But promise me you'll get whatever's bothering you off your plate." He kissed her on the cheek and gently replaced a stray piece of her silky hair. "Leave that shit there, I'll help you when I get back. I think it's time I built something to keep it organized." Then he called out downstairs. "Kids. Where are you? It's time to go. Swimming!"

Now the house was delightfully silent. Ashley did as her husband asked and went downstairs to stare out the kitchen window. There were ripples in the puddle of water on her back porch left behind by the overnight rainfall. They entertained her for about ten minutes. She watched the wind push the water while the old clock on the wall clicked to mark the seconds. She looked back at the breakfast trappings strewn over the kitchen counter and sighed as a plan for the next hour and a half came into focus. There was work to do. Tidy up. Get showered and out of her pink flannel pyjamas. Most of all, message people about the plans for Jhonian's fortieth. It was coming up fast and the arrangements needed another push. Thankfully a lot of people are helping. Some people at work are bringing food, Jhonian's best friend was handling the music and a lot of friends offered to help with decorations.

She padded over to the counter and pulled two cereal boxes off the counter to stow them. A few flakes fell on the floor, and she bent over to get them, her motivation unbroken. Soon the rest of the breakfast mess was away and she felt vaguely better.

She took a step to head upstairs to find some adult clothes but froze in the middle of the kitchen, closing her eyes and clenching her fists. Suppressing a scream. Because that would surely be loud enough to bring Kara upstairs. Kara, she remembered, hadn't left for the hospital. Fucked if she was to going to get her worried about her too. Let her know that she'd been plain stupid. Ashley closed her eyes and took a slow, deep breath. Sigh. Another breath. She could do it, she told herself. Oh, Christ, where was her screen? What irony that the thing she craved to make everything good again was the thing that had driven her crazy.

"Okay, just for a couple of minutes," she thought as she rushed over to grab her screen off the kitchen table. The bright yellow letters came on the screen and she slid her index finger slowly over the welcome lettering. YOLO. She felt a nice hit of energy as she saw the letters again. It was too soon to delete the icon. Not yet. Just looking at it made her feel okay again. Back to when she could shelter herself away from the family and feel connected again. But it went nowhere now. She could press the icon over and over and shit would happen. Nothing. If only she could curl up on the couch and spend a god-damn hour with it, she could feel right again. What a relief it would be to escape into its details of everybody's else's problems. Talk to strangers about her complaints. Let the minutes flow by feeling like she was making something happen. But it was gone. No warning. Nothing. Just one day fucking gone. She stood at the kitchen table staring at the yellow letters, sloshing around in the uncomfortable guilt.

The chirp of a bird made her look up at what was happening outside. The puddle was still there. A bit smaller as the sun had come out. She gently put the screen back down on the table and looked again at the clock. By her calculations she'd made it four hours without thinking about the app. That was better. In the six weeks since the app had died her cravings had got less persistent. Now it was just a couple of times a day. She could almost contain the withdrawal. Soon, she knew, she'd have the guts to get rid of the icon on her screen. She was almost ready for that.

Getting hooked on an app was stupid and she would have laughed off the suggestion that it could happen to her. Until it was gone, she never believed that YOLO had become her go-to spot for escape. Everyday. A couple of times a day. Many hours in the week. It felt great to be a frequent flyer, checking-in to find out who else was there. And if something was brewing inside of her, she knew she could troll through the content to find a line, a bit of discussion, that could set her right. Like the time she'd been pissed with her mother about forgetting her daughter's birthday. She'd found a thread where a bunch of grown-up daughters vented about their self-centred mothers. She'd joined in, happy to find out she was normal. It all seemed so real, and helpful.

She'd furiously read all about the trio of crooks that concocted the app to drag the dopamine receptors of overworked moms in rich countries. Like her. She'd quietly paid the government to find and delete her information. Thank God they found it. Now it was safely ground out of existence. All that was left was her cravings.

Jhonian clearly suspected something was wrong. But she couldn't confess to him. She'd rather let him imagine what was happening than tell him this. That she'd spent the last couple of years retreating every day to what he must believe was a fantasy. You can't tell the people you love that you've been ignoring them and blathering away about your life with the anonymous likes of @Swedishhandigurl2000.

At least she wasn't alone. The social sites were filled with people sharing how they were coping. YOLO's disappearance had left them floundering. At first it soothed her to scroll through the forums and sometimes see a familiar avatar. But after a week of the ex-YOLO community, she felt the seduction of the group-think and chatter, and willed herself to just stay away from the forums and chat rooms for now. Nonetheless, for the past six weeks with her mind unravelling, just knowing that others had fallen prey to the same goddamn scam helped her deal with it.

If losing YOLO had set her off her hinges, there was something worse. She suddenly had an abundance of this other fucking thing. Four new letters that dominated her life. TIME. An extra hour or two that magically appeared and demanded that she fill it. She was struggling hard. Writing list upon list on her organizer app. Trying to list her three main goals for the day as soon as her eyes opened. Every day was a new adventure in the world of deciding by herself. It was clean, less anxiety-ridden. Almost boring. She'd realized that it's a skill to be in charge of your own life, without depending on constant validation from strangers.

"What you decide on your own is important." A while back she'd written that down on her screen in large, fancy script so she'd see it every time she picked it up. She'd been tempted to post it online and see what others thought. But that made her laugh because that wasn't the point. It was kind of slowly coming back to her.

So, on to this Saturday. The kids were at swimming. Her husband was out. She sat down and looked at her screen to find her organizer app. In a half-hour she'd confirmed the invitations, ordered a cake and some clever decorations for the upcoming bash. She looked at the list of food to order and added a couple of ideas that had come to her this week. "See, that was simple," she assured herself. She shut the screen and got up to get dressed, nodding as she did that it felt good to be organized. In fifteen minutes she'd be dressed and all tasks accomplished. What next?

In truth feeling this organized wasn't as great as, say, joining in the venomous antagonism of the WE-R-ALL-FIREFLIES chat room. Assessing the pros and cons of all their perceived grievances. Filling the tedium of chores for hours with thoughts on what Ashley really felt about the group-think. Testing out lines for how she would respond later. Looking forward to chiming in with the Greek chorus of followers on the YOLO pages. "Ha," they would say. "You're doing your best. Don't be too hard on yourself."

Was any of that real? Ashley was starting to wonder. Standing in the middle of her kitchen on Saturday morning, she wasn't sure what was she supposed to do. What was she supposed to feel? And did it really matter what all the others thought?

It was all a fucking headache. The key seemed to be to keep trying. Trust herself. And trust Jhonian too. He seemed immune to group-think. She could be pissed at his oblivious confidence, but he seemed happy enough. He'd found the border between his life and the fiction.

Fifty-three

The sky was still dark when she got into the back seat. It was an early start as there was a lot to do before her first meeting.

"Thanks for getting here on time," Ally apologized to her driver.

"You're always hard at work," he just shrugged and smiled. "How is your daughter?"

"Better," she replied with her warm authority. "Very kind of you to ask."

"That's good news."

She was already opening the purple file in her hand and leafing through its contents. "We're through the first round of treatment and she's done well. We're happy to have her home."

It must be a relief to know she is on the mend."

"Truthfully, we are not out of the woods yet. My daughter is finding the side effects difficult."

"As would anyone her age, I imagine. I have a teenage daughter myself. She would be a little bit sticky about losing her hair."

Ally looked up at him and smiled. "Sticky is a good word for it. Still, we are all grateful for the progress. There's a lot more hope now than when we first got the news."

"That is good to know. May I just add that everyone at the car service is hoping for a speedy recovery."

"Thanks. That's very kind. Please pass on my regards to everyone."

She nodded respectfully at the driver who continued down the empty street with no further discussion. Ally returned to her purple file, reserved for the early morning ride when she was most focused.

Her life, her expectations had changed so materially with her daughter's illness that this next twenty minutes had become prime work time. Her evenings used to be filled with hours of work. Evenings were now more like last night when they'd watched a movie together at Tanya's bedside until her daughter had nodded off.

But the churn of her work carried on at its usual pace. The world knew she was dealing with "troubles at home," as her boss the Clerk had called it. But she was a key part of a large machine, grinding away day after day. It didn't slow down for her. A year ago she might have been angry with her circumstance, but it was different now. Furthermore, with her retirement looming, Ally knew that she'd be extracting herself from the machine. She'd be leaving the decisions to someone else soon.

This purple file was the only one that mattered now. She'd been busy working with Hector and Claude to finish this package that could bait a potential journalist. Soon the package with its story about a tired, dishonest government would be ready to leak to an opposition member of Parliament. From there she'd make sure it would find its way to a journalist or two, and they would figure out what needed to be done.

Soon Ally realized that she'd be in for a few tense weeks. There would be a furor amongst the insider crowd, crowing about transparency and accountability. There would be questions about the Party and what it was planning. How could they justify not making life a bit easier? The Party would defend their plans but it would soon be plain that they never had an exit plan. They weren't going to let people pay a bit less or consume a little bit more. They didn't have the creativity to figure out how to let that happen, and stay in power. So, they'd opted for a hoax.

As they had in the past, they had counted on the compliance and stupidity of those that served them to make their hoax a reality. They expected loyal, unquestioning execution from a civil bunch of servants. Which was where the Party had made an error in their thinking. They took the lazy way out of their conundrum. Inside the machine, people had finally taken notice.

For the past couple of weeks, Ally found herself constructing her own hoax, finding credible excuses for delays. A logical puzzle of bureaucratic missteps to hinder the government's plan. She was surprised how easy it was for her to continue to lie. She thought the stress would do her in; instead, she was rather enjoying the play. Mostly though, she tried to say as little as possible. She knew how to start a sentence, take a pause, and let the listener fill in the gaps. There were online records of most of the conversations these days, and she preferred that her actions were invisible.

But her dance to create delay was getting harder and harder to sell. Her creativity was causing some tension between her and Mark. He'd groaned within earshot when she told the morning meeting that he would complete another version of the briefing note that explained the delay.

She knew that they were coming to a point where she needed more than lies to keep the pressure off.

A few weeks back, Ally had a frantic call from the Clerk about the progress on the upcoming communications campaigns. He calmly stated that he was concerned that she was not "onside." A brutal stab to label her the bureaucrat's term for a traitor.

"I'm sorry if I gave you that impression," replied Ally, with a consolatory tone. It'd be bad if he went away thinking she was not "onside."

"I'm sure that you're doing everything you can to deliver Ally. But things need to move faster. The Party is looking to launch in the next month. I'm getting a lot of pressure; if we really can't deliver, I need to tell them a good story."

"That must be very difficult," Ally commiserated. "But I'm getting some push-back at my end from some who wonder if we are doing the right thing. I can give them a push on your behalf. They keep pointing out that moving ahead with limiting people's access to heat over 17 degrees was unnecessary and contradicted what the Party has been saying about reaching our environmental goals."

Phillipe let out a sigh. "I know that." His tone changed. He'd lost his private school boy affectation and Ally knew that for once she was talking to the real human being. "For Christ's sake, I've told them all that. They don't care. They want to position themselves for the election."

"I don't get it," replied Ally, also dropping the façade. "I don't see how this works for them in the long run."

"Neither do I. But I don't think they give a shit about the long run. It's just us who obsess about consequences. But ultimately, it's our job to give them what they want. If we don't deliver, then they'll think we're not onside and they'll punish us with cutbacks and crap that will make it more difficult for us. We don't need the problems. And what does it actually mean for the average person? It will be colder in their houses but they'll keep getting their heat subsidies, and maybe they'll save a bit of money."

Ally understood the Clerk and empathized with how he was stuck in the middle.

But nothing in her plans had changed. She felt for her boss, but she couldn't shake her gut feeling. The Party was about to cross a line. No doubt she'd be told that it wasn't for her to judge where that line was. But she knew, Claude knew and Hector knew. That was good enough for her. She wouldn't agree to do what's wrong. It just wasn't going to be her legacy.

When the leak was known, there would be alarms set off in every government office. "Whoever released that info was on a career suicide mission," many public servants would murmur quietly to each other. But she had accepted that her time as a public servant was at its end.

Once the data told its story and the political madness happened, she'd step up to take responsibility. There'd be questions about her loyalty. The likelihood of legal entanglement was small as she was willing to go quickly and quietly. If her plan fell into place, by then the government would have bigger problems to solve.

Fifty-four

Little Rachel was upside down, swaying back and forth with her tiny arms flapping in a mix of joy and effort.

"What are you up to," Ashley called from her seat at the edge of the playground.

Her daughter didn't answer, preferring to giggle gleefully. She tossed her head a few times to feel her dark ponytail hit the ground. Then she wrestled off her coat and cast it an impressive distance. "I'm hot," she finally offered.

Her mother went over to retrieve the little girl's coat, brushing off the dirt as she folded it on her arm. She stepped over to her daughter to look her right in her upside-down eyes. "My dear, you missed the mud. May I suggest that next time you throw a bit harder."

Rachel laughed at her mother's silliness. Then she bent herself forward and grasped the metal bars in front of her, letting her legs slip off so that she now hung off the ground right side up. Her mother kept one hand ready to avert a disastrous fall while she admired her little one's supple, easy way. A thud followed as Rachel let go and landed neatly on the ground. "I'm hungry, when are we going home," she demanded.

The two wandered back to the seat where Ashley dug out a round container. Soon her little girl was into the circular, crunchy snack. Ashley looked over to the small hill at the end of the park and watched her son play with some of the other boys. He was playing a familiar game where the boys folded their arms and then tried to knock one another over. They would end up rolling down the hill in short order and get up laughing, only to repeat it all over again. He would tell her all about the game on the way home. The strategy. Who won. How he'd managed to score a few points. That a couple of his friends worked together to roll down at once, creating a "gia-ganic boom!"

She picked up her daughter's snack container from the seat and shooed away a bird intent on scoring the crumbs that her daughter had dropped. The gentle breeze tickled with a welcoming softness,

296

promising warmer days ahead. The sun was strong enough to explain why people were casting aside the jackets they had all worn for the walk over. "Do you smell that, dear?'

"What Mommy?"

"It smells green."

"Green is a colour, silly."

"This is what green smells like."

Her daughter looked at her intently, going over the options in her young mind. Was her mother joking, or simply stupid on the matter? Then she looked around and saw the group of kids seated in front of an outdoor screen. There was a popular kids' program playing. Their intermittent laughter broke up the otherwise passive scene.

"Can I go watch the show?"

"No, Sweetie. I'd rather you played on the slides. We're outside. Screens are for inside."

"But you have your screen.""

"Yesss. But I am expecting a call from your Grandma Rachel."

"Don't be mad at Grandma, Mom."

The exchange took Ashley aback. What did her daughter observe? "What's that," she asked her little girl.

"Ohhh," Rachel squealed in response. She'd caught sight of one of her friends coming over the crest of the hill at the edge of the park. The matter was decided. "It's Alice. Can I go?"

"Of course! Say hi to her for me!" Ashley saw the two girls light up in the joy of childhood as they met near the slide. They held the arms of each other's sweaters and jumped around in circles. "Do you want to..." Ashley overheard Alice say. Then, in a perfectly equal exchange, they opted to try the biggest curving slide in the park. Soon they were tearing up the ladder and racing down together; landing and laughing in a pile at the bottom.

Her screen buzzed in her lap. Ashley picked it up, suddenly hit by a familiar queasy feeling.

"Oh hi dear."

"Hey Mom! How are you doing?"

Rachel senior appeared, balanced on a dark blue velvet couch. She was stylishly dressed in a finely knit sweater; it had ribbons of the pale pink and lavender knit design swirling up and down her front. Bits of silver thread sparkled in the light. Her head was bound in a matching scarf, so that tufts of her hair poked out the top. Ashley studied the scene behind her mother. Where was she now? "It looks like you're in Canada."

"Not exactly. I'm at a farm in New Hampshire. Just south of the border."

"Oh, that's funny. That means that you're only about one hundred and fifty kilometres away. Why are you staying there?"

"It's easier. I'm staying with someone I met in Arizona. He's letting me stay here in the off-season."

"For free? We might have liked to come down too!"

"No, no," Rachel waivered. "I've made an arrangement."

"Oh." Ashley didn't stop to think about what sort of arrangement her mother had made. "Are we going to see you soon?"

"That's so much pressure. I'm not sure."

"Pressure? Oh, okay. But you're coming to the party for Jhonian's fortieth. Right?'

Rachel's face froze. Then she threw herself into explanations. "It's just that I think I'm going to have problems with the exit visas. There are so many rules. I have to see what I can organize so I can travel later this year…"

Ashley interrupted her. "Everybody deals with that crap somehow Mom! I was looking forward to seeing you."

Rachel took a breath and bent slightly forward. The look on her face altered to an expression of concern. "You look good in a little makeup. How are you doing?"

"Nice," replied Ashley flatly. She quickly spun her screen away from her mother's view and screwed up her face in distain at the deflection. She sensed more excuses coming. She flipped the screen back to her face, composed again. "Humm. I'm okay. Thanks for asking. Just saying."

Her mother sat back on the couch with indignation. "Just saying what? Why do you make everything so difficult? All my friends have daughters that talk to their mothers. But not me!"

"Sorry Mother. You're right. Let me try again. You were asking how I am doing? I guess I'm doing alright. Work's about the same. I'm busy getting ready for Jhonian's party. The best thing happened. One of our friends said we can have it his house…"

"You mean you're having this thing at someone's house?"

"Well, yes. What were you expecting?"

"I don't know really. I just assumed it would be at a hotel or some nice place."

"It will be nice. That's what I'm telling you. This house has the perfect basement. The bar is huge. The walls are covered in wood. It feels like you're in a real pub."

"Basement? To be honest, I'm not sure it's worth the trip just to stand around in someone's basement."

Ashley shook her head, gesturing bitter amazement with her hand, to ask what her mother meant.

"Oh, come on Ashley. How is that going to be any fun! Did I ever tell you about the last time I organized a party? I had it in the courtyard of the villa where I was staying. It had a huge fountain in the middle with a lovely statue. I had local band playing all night. I barely had to pay them anything. All the local people came out and danced until past midnight. That's a party! You should try to do something like that."

"Mother, it's …"

"I went to this other party recently and the couple that invited me had rented the ballroom of a palace. It wasn't a big palace. When I was in Morocco."

"Palace?" Ashley felt the anger shoot up her spine so fast she almost jumped in her seat. She worked hard to keep her composure. A thought came to her that had never occurred before. "Why the hell do I put up with her?"

There was a brief pause while both women decided who would be first to break the silence.

Ashley exhaled. "You know what, Mom. Come to my shitty little party. Don't come. Either way. My life will go on without you."

"But… You're being dramatic. What are you saying?"

"I'm saying that you do whatever selfish thing you want to do. Your grandchildren really wanted to see you. But I'm fed up with trying to make you seem important to my family. You clearly don't want to be in our lives."

There was more of a not unexpected silence. Finally, Rachel took a breath and continued. "It's not that I don't care. I want to be there. But I can only leave the country so many times. It's just that it's so complicated."

"It's not complicated Mom. If we are important to you, then you will be here. Point finale."

"Why can't you be more accommodating?"

"Oh, seriously, piss off," Ashley thought. "I am accommodating Mother. I'm always here to look into whatever administrative problems you've got and I take care of stuff here so you can wander around the world however you like. I ask for this one thing. I'd like you to be here for the party. But everything I ask of you is always too much effort."

"That's not true. I think of you all, often."

"Oh seriously, Mother, piss off. I can't listen to your crap anymore." Ashley slammed the screen down so that Rachel couldn't see her face. She looked around for her kids. Rachel junior was still racing down the slide with Alice. But her son was making his way back to the bench to check in. She knew that look. He was hungry.

"Ashley, don't hang up! I know I ask for a lot. But I need you to check something about my health insurance."

Ashley picked up her screen and looked at her mother. "No, No. You don't get it. I'm not going to do another thing for you. You decide how this goes. It's time you got back here and deal with life like the rest of us."

"I don't know what's got into you but call me when you calm down. I still need your help."

"Don't hold your breath Mother. But remember, I'm expecting to see you soon. You know the date."

Ashley vigorously pressed the hang up button and slammed the screen face down again beside her. She rummaged through her bag for the Tupperware with her son's sandwich. He arrived without a word and gave her a hug to say he missed her. He quietly took the container, sat beside her and opened it, smiling as he did. "Chickpea! Thanks Mom."

"Glad you're happy son." Ashley heaved out a sigh.

He leaned in to rub his head on the outside of her arm to show his affection. Then took a bite and chewed as he nodded his head and beamed.

At least he'd learned a little gratitude, Ashley thought.

She smiled back at him, nodding back in rhythm until he laughed.

"Let me know if there's anything else you need," she told him. "Anything. I've got more snacks and a drink if you want it." Anything he needed, she would get for him. And she meant it.

Fifty-five

Mark was seated near security in the basement of the West Block, waiting to sign in and get security cleared. He had seen movies about people in his situation. He had imagined them anxious and worried about their safety. Not true as it turned out.

When he swiped his Parliamentary Precinct pass at security, he informed the guard he was going to attend a Commons Committee meeting on something related to his field. But once inside he made his way to the cafeteria. Mark had been to very good schools and his contact list showed it. He looked right at home in the halls of the House of Commons, so no-one stopped him as he poured some coffee into the white porcelain cup.

Sitting alone at the far end of the room was Mark's school acquaintance, now a member of Parliament for the opposition party. He'd be happy to see Mark; they would chat for a few minutes. Then all that was needed was to leave the envelope with the data in the MP's hands. There were no notes or markings outside. His school buddy would be intrigued with what was inside. He'd know what to do with it.

For good measure, Mark went to the visitor's lounge for the Committee meeting and spent the first half hour exchanging with a reporter he had known for years. Asked him what he had heard about the credits and increases. Primed him to ask the government about what data they had. The reporter admitted that he had been very busy on a couple of files, and then there had been the Spring Break. He'd look into it, he promised.

For a clandestine operation, Mark found this one fairly easy.

Fifty-six

She'd wasted a lot of time this week looking for the right restaurant. For once she couldn't blame it on the PC way of life.

Most people from Ottawa can tell you when they had a lovely meal out. They could regale you with stories of impressive menus, exotic foods, spectacular ambience. Rarely, though, did the stuff of legends happen in their hometown.

In many ways, Ottawa still operated as a small village, full of government workers conscious to their core about efficiency and their impact on the rest of the country. This fascination with all things outside Ottawa had, in many respects, left their own city a little underserved. An illustration was the lack of a world-class restaurant selection. Yes, there were lots of good places to eat. But if you asked around about a place for a spectacular evening out, you'd get a confused stare back. Why do that in town? The world is full of better options.

That's why Janey had wasted so much time choosing a place to spend this evening. A place where they could linger and maybe relax and talk. She wanted the night to go well.

She'd finally settled on a French-Canadian farmhouse. Janey had eaten here many times over the years with the family for birthdays and such. It was part of many mellow memories.

Except about a couple of years ago, when she'd been here with a guy who bored her so much she plotted out the nearest emergency exits, in case she lost her mind and needed to escape. It wasn't her at her best, but the guy was brutally dull.

Janey assessed the scene around the two of them. The table linens, candles and polished silver added a sense of luxury. But otherwise, the venue was folksy, like a trip to a French bistro of a past century. All it missed were the baguettes and garçons in berets snapping at the busboys.

She'd landed on this choice because they were the local darling of a mixture of vegan-cultured and local farm-slaughtered food. Byron's latest preoccupation. And the atmosphere would be calm and unhurried.

They walked side by side as the waiter led them to the table she'd reserved near the window. She felt a rush of excitement as she took her seat. Tonight brought the promise of what she liked best about the two of them: their conversation.

Byron took her jacket to the coat check. He folded it expertly over his arm, beaming with the chance to show his skill. He was getting into the spirit and wanted to make the evening special. She watched him walk away, reflecting on how they'd been living together for a whole two months. She had fallen in love with him, but also with having him near.

Despite that, there was a power struggle she was starting to see, just under the surface. It flowed from feeling she had the upper hand in their relationship. After all, he was joining her life.

It was hard not to weigh this relationship in terms of winning and losing. She'd never been in a situation where someone was giving up so much while everything got so much better for her.

Janey imagined herself riding a fulcrum of power. Bad days or good, the fulcrum was always looking for balance. There were many days where she compromised and gave him whatever she could; she wanted him to have good days. And then a few painful days where nothing seemed to keep the balance.

She'd tried ignoring the fulcrum. But that didn't work so well. It created insecurity that drove her delusional. What was he thinking? Was it bad news? She'd sit at work and feel waves of nausea when she'd recall an odd comment or look that he'd given her and wonder what it meant. She imagined all manner of nasty answers from "I can't stand the way you smell any longer" to "I miss my old job and I'm going back."

Then the troubled sleep. Simple nightmares at times. Twice she'd started out of a deep sleep sweating and anxious. It was the same dream. She'd been looking for Byron at a gas station that was about to explode into flames. She'd run up to the door and it wouldn't open.

She realized she was alone and stuck on a deserted highway. Only she could save him. But where was he?

He never said it, but she could feel that he wasn't completely comfortable with his new life. His PC certification in hand, he'd quickly found a job with the Canadian branch of his old hotel chain. But he felt like an environmental dinosaur and would need to take training course after course to catch up. Now he must be feeling like he was moving backwards.

Which was why Janey kept arguing with herself about the question. It arrived in a purple neon envelope flown in by four neurotic demons each holding a corner. What was their future? What was fair?

And if Janey could stop feeling responsible for Byron's discomfort long enough, she recognized that they had something special. When they were alone, she could connect with him like nobody else. In the mornings, she would roll over and absorb him sleeping peacefully. The sex was intuitive. And private. She avoided her coworkers' and girlfriends' attempts to pry as a devotion to their intimacy.

When they were out in the world, having him around made even the dullest tasks seem fun. He had an inner calm that balanced her structure. Shopping with all its packaging issues and transportation challenges would drive her over the edge. But he took some pleasure in making a list and putting together all the containers and labels. He had a vein of congeniality built into his DNA. He stood in line peacefully as harried mothers and fathers would unknowingly push each other to get access to the same vat of peanut butter or pie filling. Lately, he had taken to shopping at odd hours to avoid the line-ups. He had the enduring kind of practical self-discipline that was required to make it in the PC world.

Most telling was the reaction of her grandmother, who took a real shine to Byron. He had plied Kara with his boyish charm at one of her endless Friday jam making sessions. Apart from taking home some very nice berry confections, he also got an invitation to her house to guest blog with her about making food. Janey had never gotten that invite before.

He was a confident adult who knew what he wanted out of life. She, too, was a confident adult and they wanted a lot of the same things.

306

But the guilt of the transition was there, attempting to strangle the joy. Questions repeated without any resolution. How can she be so happy when he was not? Was it fair to ask him to make sacrifices when she didn't have to make any? Did he love her enough to stay?

Her father took her out for coffee and asked her how it was going. How did he know what she was thinking? He told her in his gentle manner that whatever she was worried about, she needed to trust that he knew his mind. Byron is a good young man; he will find his way. Give him some space to get adjusted.

Which is where her father's knowledge of women fell apart. Janey had an overmastering need to make things right. It was human nature, deeply embedded in female DNA, that a woman can't rest until her family was in harmony. A family can't be unbalanced. It all had to be fair.

She'd been studying the cutlery and hadn't noticed that Byron had returned to the table. He was discussing the wine choice and the positioning of the ice bucket with the waiter. She looked closer and noticed it had a gold wrapper and a cork.

"Lovely choice! I love sparkling wine," she told him.

"I know. I thought it would fit with the evening." He looked at her with his every man's usual look of a mix of two parts respect and one part lust. Today she noticed that there was a capful of trepidation.

He sat down rather elegantly. "Maybe it's a bit out of fashion, but can I say that you look beautiful tonight."

"Of course you can! I never mind hearing that!" It was flattering. She was wearing a dress that she'd found on her last trip away. It was made of printed chiffon that felt delicate on her skin. And it was infinitely better than anything she'd find here. Again, not so much a PC problem. You can't find a decent dress in Ottawa to save your life.

"You look handsome tonight too."

"Thanks." He put up a hand to deflect the compliment. "Seriously, I was walking back to the table and looked across the room. You took my breath away."

307

She beamed back. Coyly and with appreciation, she hoped. There aren't a lot of words that seemed right. Then she picked up the menu.

What to do? Maybe this was the opening to dive right in. Ask what he wanted to do with his life. But Janey felt that no matter what she said next, she would get the same reaction.

"I'm really looking forward to trying the lobster. The chef himself told me, as we came in, that it was shipped yesterday from Halifax."

Byron looked up from his menu and replied wryly that he knew that she had not brought him to this restaurant simply to eat lobster.

And there it was. That thing that had no physical dimension in a relationship, but always seemed to take up a lot of space. Power, on the fulcrum. Moving from one side to another.

She had really wanted to have a nice meal and to forget about their power struggle. She had prepared a mental list of topics that were safe. Hockey results and perhaps going to a game. Food. They both loved it. Stick to those and shoot around the fulcrum and avoid its unbalancing effects. She had led with the lobster and failed to make her shot.

"I assume that you have organized this dinner, which is marvelous by the way, so we can talk about whatever is bothering you lately," said Byron, doing his best to sound like a basket of adjectives: objective, casual, friendly, open.

Janey's thoughts sorted through a variety of options. How did she feel? Did she want to risk an argument?

"Did I tell you about what happened this week?" Janey launched into a mildly interesting story about plans for a new type of plastic. She took the specs into the lab to get an assessment of the composition. Her punch line was that after all that, she finally used a sample of the plastic and realized it was so hard to clean, no one would buy it. It got certified anyway.

Janey looked up. She had intended to deflect Byron's question. There was no way he was going to buy that what was "bothering her" was the certification of some plastic at work. Why couldn't she just say what was on her mind?

He caught her glance as she finished the story. He was grasping to find what he would say. He had the body language that men get when they're about to communicate a heartfelt emotion. If she wasn't paying attention, a girl could confuse it with the symptoms of gastrointestinal distress.

"You know that I *do* love you." She had never heard him say the words fully clothed before. She was struck by his words and the courage it took to say them. Tonight, knowing that they followed months of change and sacrifice from him, they meant a lot.

Unexpectedly, the words came to Janey. "I know you do. And I feel the same way. I love you till the ends of the earth. It just seems right that I would build my life with you. I want to get married. But I want to know that I'm enough to keep you here. In fact, I need to know."

He looked at her softly and took her hand. He looked around the room as if that would give him some energy for the next pitch. "I complain all the time about the job. But don't think that I am putting that on you. I'm here because I want to be. It's taking some getting used to, but I think we have a great future. Just give me a little time."

Janey exhaled a meaningful, pent-up sigh. Byron looked at her and grinned. A bit too smug, she thought. But no matter. The invisible fulcrum returned to a state of balance. They both ordered the lobster. She realized that he too wanted this evening to be peaceful.

IT GETS BETTER

Fifty-seven

It was odd meeting out in the open. Pete and her just hanging around in the atrium. The large central meeting area at his college, where he worked.

"I didn't imagine it would be like this."

"What? My school." Pete was right to clarify. Most of the discussions about the issues between them that could get started that way.

"Your school." Ally looked around. It was getting to be final exam time, and the campus was full of college kids finding out where their exams would be held. Or finishing labs. It was a disorienting feeling for the kids. So much of their course work happened in chat rooms and alone at their screens at home. Occasionally some courses required regular attendance to use labs. But most college kids these days only met their fellow students during exams.

"You can feel the stress. And what's with all the fuzz?"

Ally was referring to the clothing. The trend was to wear brightly-coloured, thick, furry pajamas. A girl walked past her in a fuzzy dark-pink top that made her seem like a lumpy kitty. A series of small fuzzy toys swayed from her screen case. For extra effect, she was wearing large black-rimmed glasses with matching dark-pink eyebrows.

"I don't know. I heard it's for self-soothing. My labs are up on the sixth. You can look down from the railings and see what looks like large stuffed animals walking around in groups."

Ally stared straight up from where they were sitting, up to the sixth floor. From their table on the ground they had a clear view of all the floors above them. The architecture of the building had one of those open plans, so that all the floors above the main were open in the middle. Each floor had its own heavy wood balcony that ran around the walls and looked out onto the main floor.

"We stand out here." Ally was wearing her dark work outfit. Pete had left his lab coat in his office, but he still had on his olive-drab scrubs.

"How's your daughter?"

"It's about as bad as it can be." Ally drew a breath and took a sip of the coffee. Pete watched her, observing how this small effort was sapping all her energy.

"The doctors have already done the genetic tests, and there is a therapy they would normally use. But they say she needs it right away, and even then, they aren't sure they caught it in time.

"The worst was when she was going through withdrawal from all the crap she's been using. My daughter took a long time to think straight. For a while she kept telling us she wanted to stop with the treatment and get on with her life."

"Sounds like classic denial."

"Yes, you're right. But thankfully she's come around."

Pete looked up at her. "Only to get another dose of drugs, poor kid."

Ally put her mug down, clasped her hands and stretched them back behind her head. It was an awkward movement. She was dealing with her own denial.

"Yeah, okay, I don't look like the mother of the year here. You don't have to say it. I thought she was just difficult. I saw the symptoms, but I thought it was her lifestyle. I didn't even consider she might be sick. Cancer? I no idea how bad things had become for her."

Pete nodded, thinking he'd heard the whole story. But he hadn't. Ally was too ashamed to tell him how they found her outside that bar on the ground. How they'd found her dressed in a dirty dress. That the policewoman had gently suggested that her daughter had likely been "working" in the bar and had passed out. The bar owner had called 911 and moved her outside to protect his patrons. They'd called it in as an overdose.

And then at the hospital, how she'd found out it was worse. Tanya had passed out because she was sick. Non-Hodgkin's lymphoma. What was this? Ally sat there stunned as the doctors told her about what to expect. They identified what they thought was the type. Told her how the bruises and fatigue were common symptoms. Tanya had likely been experiencing them for months, but her drug dependency had masked a lot. They'd been kind, but most of what they told her washed right over her. She just heard the words: drug dependency, suspected lymphoma, trying to avoid chemo and then far advanced, and that hopefully there's a chance.

"Yeah, things are difficult. Bottom line, I wish I'd paid more attention to her. I was so busy analyzing when I should have tried to act."

Ally glanced down at her coffee. She thought about Pete. Before the news of Tanya's illness, she'd accepted they were over. He'd never leave. She had to make the first step. She didn't feel the strength to deal with Pete now. All she could do is tread water.

She told Pete about her pending retirement. "Just as well. I'll need some time to look after my daughter."

She had looked forward to a clean break. Ally was going to move on and start again. That was her plan. But Tanya had put a torpedo through her plans. No. That wasn't fair. She'd pretended her kid was invisible for a long time. Now, her kid needed her.

"What are you thinking?"

Ally shook herself out of her thoughts. "Sorry I haven't seen you for a couple of weeks. I got your message last week. I didn't know what to say. I wanted to tell you in person."

"No, I get it, I can't imagine how difficult this is for you."

In truth, Pete felt relieved that this problem wasn't his. His kids were safe. He felt sad for Ally who had to deal with this daily, and he wanted to listen to her. But at the same time, there had to be rules about this. There had to be limits. This wasn't what he signed on for. He felt a bit angry that this thing had arrived and that it would complicate their time together. It made Ally seem needy and unattractive when she had been so strong and fearless.

"Look, my day is wrapped up here. I don't have to be home until after dinner. We can go somewhere where we can be a bit more private."
314

Ally looked up from her mug of coffee and gave him an enquiring look.

Pete leaned forward. "You know there's that decent hotel just a block away. We could think about something else for awhile."

"Aw, that's tragic," muttered Ally dryly.

"What?"

"You. You're tragic."

Fifty-eight

The party could be seen from down the street. The lights blazed as every room in the house was illuminated. There was a deliberately careless arrangement of LED light strings overwhelming the bushes in the landscaping on the front lawn. There were multi-coloured lights extending to the top of an old pine in the corner of the yard. This morning, the host of the party, Jhonian's friend Alex, had snaked his lean, tall body up the length of the tree with strings of lights in his teeth. He'd spent a lot of time putting out his whole collection of LEDs. He would almost certainly get a friendly note from the public utility about his monthly resource use. "Heck," he told Ashley as she arrived with the platters of food, "I'd like a note from the Canadian Space Agency asking about the bright spot they'd seen from their satellites. Damn the electricity expense, Jhonian is celebrating his 40th!"

The music, a lot of turn of the century classics, grew louder and fell away as people came in and out the front door. A group of pot smokers stood at the end of the driveway, chattering and laughing. For a May night, it was clear and warm outside. A gift from mother nature that made it possible for the smokers to enjoy themselves as they lingered and told one more story.

Jhonian came up the stairs from the basement, where the stash was laid out, to see if he could find his friend. He went outside and took a breath of the mild air. He thought for a minute about how this all felt, getting older, having friends, and the effort Ashley had gone to make this shindig happen for him. It was overwhelming. He felt both extremely lucky and a little embarrassed. For a guy who started out with no real plan, he was stoked to be doing so well.

"Did you see Alex?" he called to the laughing crowd.

"No!" they called back in amused unison.

He turned to go inside. As he pulled the entryway door closed, he nearly ran into Alex coming down the stairs from the second floor.

"Kids okay up there?"

"I don't know how with all the noise and people, but they're all down for the count," his friend reported. "How are you doing? Are you enjoying yourself?"

"I was just thinking that I am a lucky son of a bitch. Do you remember high school? We were losers with no plan, we just cruised from what was in front of us to what came next. And now we are here, still freaking hangin' out together, dads, kids, part-owners of a lawnmower."

Alex realized that Jhonian had had a few. Maybe he had tried the brownies that were out on the bar downstairs and they were beginning to kick in. "Are you surprised? Ash planned this for months and threatened to kick me in the balls if I said anything."

"Everyone's asking me that."

"About what?"

"You're a jerk. About whether I knew."

"And what are you saying?"

Jhonian responded with a sly smile. "You can't tell Ash anything. I figured it out about a month ago when Ash's mom called to tell me about her travel plans. She'd never come back to Canada so early if she hadn't been told to get back for a reason. And then one of the kids asked if I liked lots of blue balloons. Look, I am turning forty."

"That's funny." Alex smiled at his friend. He drew himself to his full height and gave a charming salute that ended with a comic flourish. "You deserve this celebration. I command you to harvest the pleasures of the night! Go downstairs and find yourself another brownie. I baked them so you'd get baked."

Jhonian grinned back while a thumbs up sign. "Dude! I know!" He gave Alex a playful shove and made his way through the crowd. People stopped to congratulate him. He saw his wife talking to her friends near the back porch door. Ash's look told him that she was enjoying the evening.

He felt a hand on his arm. Alex was standing beside him, clearly wanting to ask him something more. A new wave of his buzz hit him. He was having trouble keeping things straight. "Wha-at?" he asked Alex, with what he recognized was a bit of a stammer.

"Well before you become completely stoned, and don't get me wrong, it's your damn day, can you tell me who is that interesting lady who has joined us tonight?" There was a loud cackle from the direction of Alex's gaze. The loudest voice of them all was too familiar to Jhonian.

"That, Alex, I am happy to share, that woman leaning against your kitchen island is the elder Rachel. She's my mother-in-law."

"Well. What a surprise." His friend watched wordlessly as Rachel spun her story to the crowd. There was a burst of laughter as Rachel shrugged coquettishly. Alex observed the vignette, nodding at points, in an obvious effort of compassion. "I guess what I will say is that she is colourful."

"Ýup! That's one of the words I could use. Or deafening. Imposing. She certainly has made my married life interesting." Jhonian looked over where his wife had been, only to find she was making her way towards MIL in the kitchen. "Alex, you haven't lived until you have met her. You should go over and introduce yourself. In the meantime, I've got to get over there and save my wife."

Jhonian pointed in the direction of Ashley and weaved his way over.

As he got within earshot, he could hear Rachel telling her end of the story.

"They had on black armbands like, you know, what people used to have on after funerals. I've never worn one. And they were yelling at me."

One of the women leaning against the kitchen window bit on Rachel's line. "What were they yelling?"

Rachel raised her voice a couple of decibels higher than normal. "They screamed 'fuck you, grandma.' I just was passing them on the street. I don't know why they were so offensive."

By this time everybody in the kitchen had stopped to listen to Rachel. She plumped visibly with all the eyes on her.

Someone explained that it was common these days for older people to experience such verbal violence. People are mad that they are dealing with so much change. Especially the kids, and they take it out on whoever they see.

"I don't think that is right. They should put a stop to it. Someone's going to get hurt." Rachel was playing to the crowd.

Kara stood on the other side of the kitchen. She grabbed one of the carrot sticks that she had cut earlier and chomped it down in three bites. "Especially selfish people like you," she mused privately, "foolish spongers."

Ashley was in the corner of the kitchen, smiling patiently while Rachel held court. She watched her mother flirtatiously grabbing the corner of her chiffon scarf and twirling it between her thumb and index finger.

Then Ash caught the gaze of her husband, whom she could tell was near wasted. The sight gave her a balm of happiness; he'd let himself go and was having a good time.

He twisted his way through the crowd, getting the odd pat on the back and high-five on his journey. He finally arrived beside her. "One of us is swaying back and forth," he said and put his hand on the window ledge to steady himself.

But even through his inebriated state, he could feel what she was thinking. She leaned over and whispered in his ear, "Well, at least she showed up."

Jhonion looked back at her, grinning. He sensed a different edge in what she said. He'd later blame the next couple of minutes on the pot brownies, but nonetheless, he waded in.

"That was important to you? Her turning up?"

"Yes. I had to argue with her to get here. She had so many stupid excuses."

"And now she is here. Because you begged?"

Ash gave a withering look. "That's the point. I didn't beg. I insisted."

It was loud in the kitchen. Jhonian debated making a break for the brownies in the basement, but instead gently dragged Ashley by the arm to a quieter spot. "I gotta know. Why was is it so important for your mother to show up? It wasn't for me."

"It was for me. I wanted her to show up. Finally. For me. Stop making me feel like an after thought."

They both looked over to where Rachel was carrying on, unable to hear what she was saying over the crowd noise. Her hair was in some sort of puffy updo that wisped around her like a halo. Her tan had deepened so much over the winter she looked a step away from skin cancer. The effect was cartoonishly colourful, as she pointed out the window to demonstrate an important tidbit to her audience.

"Look, Ash, she's, she's never going to change. She's special. I don't know how you two are related. You're not at all like her. I think your mom's too special for us."

"She thinks she's special."

"Yeah, well, let it go. Just take a deep breath and do it. Let her go. I won't be offended if you go ahead and take her off our invite list." Jhonian was tapping on his forehead as if he was tapping the font of knowledge.

Ashley looked at him, ready to laugh. "You're wasted."

"Probably."

"That's okay. And I don't agree. I get it now. We're the special ones, holding the world together. All she's ever done is ride on that. That's so not what I want."

She leaned in and kissed him. "Happy Birthday! Sorry it wasn't a surprise."

Jhonian waved around at the crowd. "No, really, you pulled it off!"

"You're cute. The kids told me they said something."

"I love you."

Ashley smirked to return his affection and Jhonian smirked back, turning to weave his way back to the basement. He stopped mid weave, reaching back to her and holding out his hand. Ashley looked around the room at the happy crowd and took his hand.

On her way past her mother she heard what she was sharing. "Did everyone get to try the dates I brought?" Rachel pointed to an open container on the counter. "I got them in Morocco. Everyone should try them. You won't get them here."

Her mother's inspirations continued. "You know what we need right now. Where's Alex? Alex," Rachel beckoned over the crowd. "Let's change up this music! This party needs dancing."

Fifty-nine

She walked around the place and then went back to look through the large picture window with its peaceful composition. The water lapped gently against the dock while trees framed the windswept background. It was Spring, and there was a bright green haze on many of the trees. The water in the foreground looked inviting, but she shivered to think about its forbidding cold.

Ally felt disoriented, an unfamiliar rush of fear hit her as she contemplated life in this new home. She wouldn't be in control of this life; it would be in control of her.

"Ha, that's enough," she gave herself a pep talk. "Once you get here and you get into the rhythm, you'll know this is what you want."

Ally turned and asked the real estate agent how long the property had been on the market.

She could tell the agent was trying to soften the blow and not scare her away. "About a year," she said.

"Good. I like that. Maybe they'll be motivated on price."

The agent, who was used to much fussier city people, looked surprised and happy. Maybe this place would finally sell.

"I'd like to take another look around before we go," Ally told the amiable woman, who had already taken out her cigarettes and opened the door to find her car and wait.

She turned to review the front room. In her mind, it was already her living space. The room looked over the lake and had a walk-out to the balcony. In the corner was a stone fireplace, a lovely feature. Standing from the far end of the room she tried to place all her things.

There was space to elegantly place her sectional so it overlooked the water. She imagined places for the rest. Mercifully, one thing that would be missing was Derrick's recliner. That was her plan, a fresh start without him.

She told him as much the other day and he didn't even look at her as she was speaking. All the hateful anxiety she'd wasted thinking about the "I want a divorce" scene, and the only fight the little prick gave was his saccharin smile. He'd looked up at her and nodded as she finished. Then he walked away without saying a word.

To her shock, he was moved out within a week. A week later a set of papers arrived from Derrick's lawyer. She'd read it over quickly and it had made her blood boil. "What a piece of work he is," she had remarked. He'd been ready for this. He was petitioning for about half of her monthly pension to keep him in the style he was accustomed to.

But her lawyer was confident that the final number would be "much more commiserate with his financial contribution over the course of their marriage." Screw him, Ally thought, trying not to let it anger her.

She walked out onto the balcony from the living room and looked out over the lake. Elizabeth was right. The sunsets on this end of the lake are spectacular. It was late in the day and the sun was starting its descent. Elizabeth had been very content when Ally stopped by to tell her friend that they would soon be neighbours. Ally watched the yellow and pink shimmer from the setting sky, swirling as the water calmly rippled back and forth. The water had a rhythmic, hypnotic sound of motion. She would hear it every day.

Her eyes traced the structures on the property. There were stairs going down from the balcony to the dock. There was no beach on this side of the lake, but there was a lovely one within easy walking distance. Much of the land below was covered in trees. In this forest, on the far side and buried far from sunlight, was a discreet patch of leftover frozen white. The melting snow made a little stream of water running down towards the dock. It made a soft splash as it hit the water. This was an idyllic spot, so much more friendly than the natureless network of elevators and offices she knew. How would she describe this place to the people she hoped would be visiting soon? There were a lot of positives that came to her mind. In the end, she settled on restful and welcoming.

Farther along the balcony she found an entry door for the main bedroom. Once inside Ally's thoughts grew muddled. It was a big room for her alone.

It had been tough these past few months, but her perspective on being alone had eventually taken a hard turn. It wasn't just the split with Derrick. That was more of a relief than a cause for sadness.

Leaving Pete had left her overcome by crazy feelings brought on by grief, and the anger at how their affair had ended.

The weeks since the breakup she'd mused bitterly about the benefits of romance. She analyzed the problem as if she was researching a Ph.D. thesis. She hypothesized about what they could do to your brain. She fumed that your average person viewed relationships as a necessary evil, a way to meet their needs when they couldn't be met with family or friends. Like the need to talk about feelings and that sort of crap. And if you don't deliver, or if you dare ask them for something emotional in return, then you are made to feel you weren't all that useful to them. You weren't "nice."

At what turned out to be their final meeting, where Pete had so little to offer her, it was clear that he expected Ally to carry on with no future.

So it was there, out in public in the cafeteria where cameras were everywhere, when she serenely told him. She'd told him what she thought with a quiet force that stunned him.

He was selfish. He wanted it all ways. Or he'd do the honourable thing and deal with his marriage and move on.

And even though she correctly anticipated his answers, she'd asked him some simple direct questions for the record.

They'd been seeing each other for two years. She was ready to make a commitment. Did he have a plan? She expected him to have a plan. No plan. He sat, looking down at his empty coffee mug. Just stony silence.

"So, your plan," she had offered, "was to have your cake and to eat it too?"

He said, "no, it's not like that."

"What is it like then?" He shrugged. No answer. Likely hoping she would go, and the scene would be over.

Finally, she did get up and left him sitting pitifully staring at the table. And there it was, after two years of unexpressed and unexplored hopes.

Since that day she resolved never to see him again. Ally's resolve was strong. She didn't go back.

But ending two years of dependence on Pete hurt. Sometimes it hurt so much she could feel her chest caving in. It had been months now and the pain hadn't lessened. Every day she thought about messaging Pete and then told herself he was a bad habit she had to get over. The craving.

In the day, there was work: officially preparing for her pending retirement. And unofficially waiting for the consequence of the data about the Carbon Credits that had been leaked. She'd heard from Hector that the media were calling about the story. It was only a matter of time before she'd step up and take responsibility for the leak.

But in the quiet moments, or when she was bored at one of her countless meetings or getting driven back to the house, the craving would take over. All she could think about was Pete, his body, the way he seemed to care, and the fact of him.

She crossed the hall to a smaller bedroom that was still quite generous in size. It had a view of the lake, with trees spiraling up to the sky. She prayed this would become her daughter's room.

Tanya. The word interrupted her self-pity and brought her back to what really mattered.

She'd locked her relationship with her daughter in a box for so long. Refusing to see what was happening. Now even the pain of leaving Pete was dwarfed by Tanya.

It was killing her seeing her daughter bravely face her treatments. Holding Tanya's hand while she rested. Knowing that this should give more comfort to her daughter. Watching with remorse as her own mother took on the caretaker role that should have belonged to her.

It had taken her a full week to find the courage to talk to Tanya about her plans. About Tanya moving into this new place together. To give her time to get well. And to let her know that her dad wouldn't be there.

Tanya had smiled sweetly back at her as she talked. Although she had lost her hair and her colour was now the greyish pallor of the seriously ill, her expression was familiar.

"It must be hard for you Mom. I'm sorry. But in a way Mom, I think you were the last one to know that you and Dad were over."

Tanya's prospective room had lots of natural light. She tried to think if there was enough space for her to have her own seating area. There was a chair in the corner and she went over and sat down. The real estate agent came into the room and asked, "you okay?"

Ally brightened on cue. "Yeah, I'm great. This is a beautiful place."

It was a beautiful place and Ally was going to buy it and she was going to retire here. She had grand plans for the place. She hoped one day to see children playing here -- her grandchildren.

But Ally had also lied, she wasn't great. She felt overwhelming sadness as she thought of her daughter lying in the hospital bed.

She got up to leave. She was going to make the two-hour drive tonight and be with her again. Her daughter, her beautiful daughter, who had needed her so much. Who had been almost invisible. Treated like a disappointing inconvenience.

Now she was in the fight of her life. Ally applied the full force of her will to her recovery. Tanya was all that was important to her.

<h1 style="text-align:center">Sixty</h1>

Janey helped Nicolo with his jacket. It was a little threadbare. She discretely pulled at the label to find the size. As she put it away in the hall closet, she made a mental note. A replacement might be a nice gift for his upcoming birthday.

"Hey Dad! Thanks for coming!"

"Of course. I wouldn't miss this! I brought you a housewarming gift."

"Oh, thanks so much!" She gave him a kiss on the cheek. "Hope you don't mind, I'll open it later."

"No, that's no problem at all. I hope you like it. I ordered it from that site you always tell me about."

Janey smiled proudly back at her dad. She was eager to show him around their new place. She'd always be his baby, but more and more she wanted him to see her as an adult.

"Let me show you around."

She walked backwards in front of her dad as she led him to the far end of their townhouse. Nicolo followed, walking in a light tiptoe motion, as if he was worried about breaking the place.

She began the tour with an experienced tone of a tour guide. "It's all on one floor, but there is some space in the basement for storage."

"It's huge compared to your old place!" Her dad was looking up into a skylight in the hallway.

"We love it. We're not tripping over the couch anymore!"

Janey spared her dad no detail. She guided him through everything she liked about her new place. It had two bedrooms and a den that already looked gainfully employed as a home office.

"It's awesome. The setup of the doors at the front; it doesn't look like a converted suburban house at all."

"I know Dad, isn't that grand? I feel like I've got the building to myself. You barely hear anyone else in this building."

They wandered back into the kitchen and came upon the rest of the guests. Her dad remarked that it was nice to be able to stand side-by-side in this new hallway. He looked around at the guests to find familiar faces.

"Is Tanya here?"

Janey shook her head no. "I don't think she's well enough yet to make it." Truth was Janey hadn't even invited her. It was too soon.

Her dad looked at his daughter in the eyes. He knew she was lying. "This is sad news about her. It's just very sad. Tanya's always been challenging. I could tell that from the first time I met that family."

"Her challenges are pretty complicated, Dad. I knew she was in trouble."

"It got that bad?"

"Crap ya. I saw her the week before she went into the hospital. She looked horrible. Now we all know that it wasn't just her partying. All the time she was horribly sick too, and I didn't do anything to help her."

"How is she doing?"

"I heard from Kara that she still sleeps a lot. I don't know if she wants to talk to anybody. She must feel awful. I feel bad."

Her dad paused, continuing to look at his daughter. She was a responsible woman now. Still, even for most adults, this was a difficult problem. "My rule is that you are what you do, not what you say you'll do. Which means you should reach out. Speaking of that, I was meaning to call Kara myself," he offered, "and I'll Facebook you if I get more information."

"Thanks, that would be great. But Facebook doesn't exist anymore, Dad."

328

"Sorry! Sorry! I'm old. It's an old expression. I'll message you when I've talked to Kara."

"I don't want Tanya to hate me."

"Well, she might be angry for a while. But she'll be angry at everybody. Don't take it personally. In any case, if you care for her, you'll do what you can."

He gave his daughter a quick sideways hug. "Don't worry. It will work out. Now, what about this food!"

Nicolo walked into the kitchen and surveyed the scene. He recognized Fioria from work, along with a boyfriend. A couple of Byron's old school friends stood at the bar, munching something. Janey told him she didn't know them very well. Others were out on the back deck. A pair were vaping and chatting in the far corner of the yard.

They certainly had everything well organized. The kitchen was bright. It looked out over the backyard and you could see the patches of green coming through on the large tree visible in the window. It was a lovely day and the windows were open. The curtains that Janey said she'd just put up were moving back and forth with the breeze. The kitchen island that Janey had described as "life changing" didn't look very solid. When Nicolo looked closely, he noticed but it was on wheels and could be moved. That was clever he thought.

Byron was showcasing his culinary chops. The island was dressed with several colourful plates of food. A bowl with a large spoon had some sort of hot chilli. A pottery sign was attached to the bowl with the word "vegan" on it. On a table closer to the window was a selection of beverages.

Janey's dad smiled inwardly. It was a generous spread, but not too much, just enough to show you cared. His son-in-law-to-be was starting to get the hang of it. It was all about balance today.

He went over and took something that had a pastry top.

"I see Janey dear that you've had a bit of an upgrade in the kitchen."

His daughter agreed. "Oh yes, there's a lot more space to work."

Fioria piped up, "I don't think he was talking about the space."

Her dad laughed.

"Oh, you mean the food." Janey threw an admiring look at Byron. It was nice to see her so happy. "Yeah okay, that's an upgrade too. I'll admit it!"

Byron didn't seem to hear what was going on. He was absorbed in putting out some vegetable pate. He surprised everyone when his voice came from under the counter. "Nice to know I'm appreciated."

Then Byron stood up and wiped his hands before reaching out to greet Nicolo. "I see you tried the mushroom *vol au vent*. I was happy to find those dried mushrooms at a food place that your daughter recommended."

"They're excellent Byron." affirmed Nicolo.

The doorbell rang and Janey went to get it. They could hear another pair of young voices approaching as they entered the scene. Janey made the introductions, gracefully he thought. He was clearly the oldest guest at the housewarming. It was okay. He hadn't planned to stay long. He'd make his appearance and leave so the kids could have their fun.

He spent the next half hour circulating, exchanging stories and learning about the kids and their lives. They were all lovely young people. He admired their positivity and ambition. It was remarkable to hear the variety of languages being spoken. He recognized the French and the Arabic, but there were a couple of others that he couldn't peg.

At one point, one of the newly engaged couples talked about their upcoming wedding. He could tell that Janey was paying attention as they talked about the preparations. He was a bit shocked to hear that the pre-marriage rituals now included medical tests and vaccines. The couple had paid for a list of information on hormones, vitamins, genetic forecasts, including a forecast of their fertility potential.

He was leaning against the rail of the deck and looking intently into a neighbour's backyard. There was a pool. An old pool: it looked like a relic from his childhood. Still, it had been well maintained.

Byron came out of the patio door and went to stand by his father-in-law-to-be. He saw him looking at the pool. "That must cost a fortune to run."

"We all had them when I was a kid."

He turned to look at Byron. "The place is lovely, and I've never seen Janey so happy. Thank you."

Byron made an awkward smile that contradicted his confident tone. "You're welcome. That means a lot to both of us."

"How are you getting on at your new job? Are you enjoying it?"

"Well, not sure I would say I'm enjoying it. Officially I love it, but truth be told, I find it quite, hum, different."

"How's that?"

"Oh, where I was working before, in the States, the idea of a hotel was all about serving the customer. I feel here that I'm some sort of policeman, always enforcing rules."

"Yes, well, welcome to Canada. A lot of jobs feel like that now."

"The other day I had to tell a family that they had to stop using water or leave. They told me that they'd been bathing their three kids. I gave them a pamphlet about water use. It was a new low."

"Sorry," Janey's dad commiserated. "I guess that doesn't feel much like your old job."

"It's not even close! If I got a complaint before it was 'cause there wasn't enough of something. I'd have done my best to give them whatever they wanted."

"Now, every day, I'm explaining 'can't do this, you can't do that.' Hotels are filled with people from other countries, people who are learning about the country they're visiting! And the temperature! The complaints! It's never right. The AC isn't cold enough. And I hear that in winter we only allow thermostats to 20 degrees. That will be cold."

"I'd like to tell you it's going to get better, but I'm not sure it will. I think you've got to console yourself that this is the way we need to manage."

"Have you been talking to my parents? I've been hearing that a lot!"

"I guess I've lost track. I'm used to it now. I've been living the same thing for 20 years now."

"Well, it's all a fucking nightmare to me…" Byron stopped mid exclamation. His tone softened, remembering who he was with. "It's all new to me. I used to read how things were changing in the news or when I talked to my parents. Now I'm actually in the middle of it."

"I get it. Yeah, you're surrounded with propaganda, telling you to love your new reality. Everything will be better. Yet every morning I think about that old ad for razors, 'the best a man can get.' Today your improved razor, in truth, leaves you bleeding a lot more than that the old disposable kind."

Byron paused for a second to gather his thoughts and continued quietly. "It's not like I don't agree. I do. But it's easy when it's a theory. I'm stunned how hard it is to do it."

Byron's transition was going pretty much as Nicolo had expected. Janey's father led the discussion onto a positive track. "It's my kids that keep me going. And, you'll see, it will keep you going too. Rationing and travel restrictions and not being able to buy just anything you want may seem like sacrifices. I tell myself it's better accepting that now, than asking your kids to do more later."

Byron gave a low, meaningful sigh. "I know. Even when I was in the States, you could see that change was coming. Too slowly for many Americans. I worried they were going to hit a wall. I'm better off here. At least I know what the wall looks like."

The two stood silently, their hands still resting on the deck rail, staring straight ahead for a few minutes. They could hear Janey's laughter echo from the kitchen.

"You don't have to worry. I love your daughter a lot."

"I'm not worried. The more I get to know you, I see that you care. Just keep making her happy."

He didn't say anything for a minute.

"Can you…" her dad added. "You should talk to her about some of this. How you feel."

"I don't dare. She'll think that I don't care enough about her."

"Just figure out a way to do it. It will bring you both closer. You know, how you feel about my daughter and how you feel about your job are two different things. You can always change jobs. I hope you're not planning on changing my daughter!"

Janey's dad gave Byron a meaningful pat on the back as he turned to find his daughter to say his goodbyes.

Before leaving, he put his arms around her for a familiar bear hug. He grabbed her by the shoulders and told her kindly, as he had done so many times in the past, "Va bene! Va bene! I'm so proud of you. You're doing great. It's good to see it turn out okay!"

Later that evening Janey flopped down beside Byron. He was flipping through the choices on the video system he just finished installing.

"I can't watch a whole film. Got to get up early for work tomorrow."

"Me too," he said.

"You were out there talking to my Dad for a long time."

Byron kept flipping.

"What were you talking about," she persisted.

"You know your Dad better than I do. Can't you guess?"

"Okay, I know you were probably talking about me. What did he say to you?"

He flipped on a classic with Katharine Hepburn and Spencer Tracy. It distracted Janey.

"Oh, I love this one! She's so smart and strong."

"It's one of your favorites."

She watched for a minute while the two characters conversed, sparring romantically across an old-style oak desk. Then Janey turned her gaze back to her boyfriend. "I'm not letting you off the hook," continued Janey. "What did Dad say?"

Byron pulled her closer to him. She snuggled back in a familiar way he loved. "Your Dad's a smart guy. He loves you. And he wants me to be sure that I know what I'm doing."

Janey acted casual. She held her breath, letting him speak.

"I do, you know, know what I am doing."

"I'm sure you think you do. But you've left behind a great life. I worry you'll wake up one day and realize this isn't enough."

Byron reflected for a minute. "What you're asking is if I want all the old stuff I used to have. Over what we have?"

"I guess."

"Huh. I never think about it that way. I always figured I was part of an illusion. At some point I'd have to come back to earth."

His words soothed her like a cool breeze on a sticky summer night.

"That's a relief. I worry about it every day. Byron, you can't imagine how much I love you. How much I can't think about tomorrow without you.

He chuckled softly. "So that's what's been bothering you. So simple."
He sat up and looked at her directly. "I've learned what's important.
It's us. It's really you."

Sixty-one

At 6:00 a.m. Hector sent Ally and Claude a simple message.
"Breathe."

"Underway," she confirmed. They'd all had a short night. She'd been
up for a while, going over the schedule. It was D-day, the media were
already filing stories about the new angle on the Government's plan
to increase the Carbon Credits.

The Prime Minister had spent the last three weeks lying to Canadians
that more belt-tightening was needed. Ally wondered if even he'd
busily parroted the talking points, or if he knew what he was selling.

The average Canadian was well aware of the issue. The power of her
propaganda team had done their magic. Her ad campaign ran on
screens everywhere, 24/7. An intense fifteen seconds extorting
people to live with less.

Since Mark had delivered the envelope to the opposition, Claude and
Hector had been dealing with the follow up. Their media contacts had
taken some time to be convinced that the conventional wisdom, and
the government's line, was a fake. But the evidence finally brought
them around.

Ally stood in the front of the mirror, finishing her make-up. If she felt
anything, it was relief. She didn't have to pretend anymore. To staff,
to her best people, and to her mother. She'd spent the last couple of
weeks close to Kara looking after Tanya. She could finally tell her
mother about the big lie.

She already knew the political uproar this would cause. She would
take responsibility for the leak. Tomorrow she'd call a contact at one
of the better news services to give them the main points for why she
organized the leak. It was her alone and no one else, she would tell
them. One interview, and a simple statement.

It would be bumpy, but she was confident she'd be okay from here.
She'd made peace with leaving with her name being dragged through
the mud. Being called a traitor didn't matter much when the facts are
in your favour. But Ally wasn't looking forward to her final

conversation with the Clerk as a deputy. She imagined this conversation so many times. She wanted to lay into him. No yelling, just insubordinately cut him off mid-sentence. Calmly offer an acerbic remark about how he was both an oppressive, egotistical thug and an incompetent Party kiss-ass. It was probably better not to tell the Clerk how she felt. The scene would have to stay in her imagination and her statement would have to speak for itself. "It's better. At least people will finally know."

Today, Ally would excuse herself mid-morning and leave for the hospital while Tanya had more treatment and then ignore any calls or messages. The day wouldn't go that smoothly for everybody. Her choices would have consequences. "Mark is going to have a crappy day," she mused, looking out at the early morning light. "But then again, it will give him a chance to shine. Maybe he's a step ahead of us all, anyway." He had impressive foresight, and that was why he'd soon have her job.

She heard the first story on the feed playing during the drive in to work.

"The government today appears to be flip-flopping after the explosive revelation that levels of carbon appear to be well ahead of targets..."

"The opposition has already raised issues about the government's plans to increase Carbon Credits..."

As she walked into the office, Ally asked for a paper copy of the day's media review. She wanted to read all the stories from the first line to last. Staff had anticipated her request and handed it to her.

She read through while feigning disapproval with the top story. Page after page about the leak of government data that seemed to say that the outlook wasn't as grim as everyone had been led to believe.

Already, the opposition had indicated they had several pressing issues for Question Period this afternoon. They were demanding an explanation. They wanted more data to be tabled.

By 9:00 a.m. a message had come in from the Clerk, who had no doubt been woken from his slumber. "Ally," she listened to him say, "I've been in a meeting with the Party. They want to organize a counterattack, and there's a call about it later this morning. The Party wants strategies to support the government's position. Can you send your best? Oh, and ask Mark to pull the advertising. I've already asked Hector and Claude to get their communications people to call around to the media. Please do the same. Nothing written, mind. The Party thinks this story has some serious factual errors. Let them know. The faster the turnaround the better. We need to get ahead of this!"

She finished reading the news and then called Mark's office to let them know that she had to go to the hospital. Apologies, but could Mark be on the call this morning with departmental officials and the Clerk. Oh, and talk to the Clerk's people. They want to pull the advertising.

It was mid-morning when Ally called down to her head of Communications. She knew she had to stick to the Clerk's direction and ask them to prepare a response. She, Hector and Claude had already drafted a set of talking points for media. It was the government's line, but she asked her people to call everybody on their media list to tell them. Let them all know about the story. Maybe point to the existing coverage to fill them in. Her communications head didn't argue. She intuited that Ally wanted all journalists to pick up the story and spread the real data widely as soon as humanly possible. Time was limited. Before this insidiously corrupt government ordered them to stop.

And then she left for the day. Over the morning, she watched a barrage of messages going back and forth. She didn't answer, instead letting Mark take the lead. Phillipe was apoplectic, having been unable to report back to the PM's office with a usual speedy result. Media were calling their contacts in all departments for the detailed data. The pressure was real. The Clerk, she knew, would be unlikely to contain public interest. Some days it was difficult to do the government's bidding. And that bastard was going to have a difficult day.

By mid-afternoon the government finally surrendered and posted a lot of the data. Fortuitously, Hector's department had it ready to go early. To everyone's amazement, the data had shown a marked improvement. In fact, the Canadian environmental picture looked far rosier than the government had forecast.

The opposition was uncharacteristically prepared with their response. After Question Period, the media were scrumming questions about whether we should instead be looking for a softening of the Carbon Credits program. The opposition leader had gone as far as to say that this would be a key element in their upcoming election platform.

By dinner time, every Canadian was talking about this while they unpacked their day. There was suddenly a little optimism that life could get easier.

Sixty-two

It was early for her. It felt like a first to see the sun at this angle. The morning was cool, although the strength of the sun promised to make the sweater she was wearing unnecessary.

Everyone was sleeping when Ashley got into the car. Last night, Jhonian had insisted. He was sweet about it. "You never take time for yourself. I can handle the school rush. You've got the day off, and you've been on about getting that photo printed. You'll have fun. Just go!"

She wanted to turn the photo with its layers of red, sky blue and green into a canvas for the wall in the study. It was a scene from their recent trip away. She had come back home with plenty of photographic inspiration.

One particular photo was of a church. She had caught sight of it as the family had pulled out of a winery at sunset. The church sat high on a hill and was illuminated from behind so that the sky was framed with clouds in shades of orange. She snapped a picture quickly as they drove and then relented, nagging Jhonion to stop the car so that she could take some more.

She explored the scene from several angles while Jhonian entertained the kids on a nearby swing set.

"It's going to look spectacular," Ash told him. "I've finally found the perfect picture for that blank space. I wanted something that draws you in, that makes you want to be there."

When the car dropped her off at the corner she felt a mix of freedom and eagerness, strolling through the sunshine to one of her favourite places in town, the western branch of the library.

The library was a marvel, first because of its novel architecture. Instead of an economical box made of the signatures of the PC era— steel and wood beams -- there were repurposed regal white marble columns that felt grand. As she walked up the polished steps to go inside and admire the mosaic circle on the floor that divided the spheres of knowledge into colourful pie-shaped wedges. It was delicate and beautiful. Arguably, it was a waste of precious resources, but walking across the floor and interpreting the details made her happy.

The dedicated network of donors, bureaucrats, and politicians had created something pleasant, people-oriented, and fun. The library's slogan was "making all of knowledge accessible." It was a grandiose mission, but there was a marvellous truth to it. You could borrow anything you needed to make your life better, even books. Over time she'd used their musical instruments to test out her kids' nascent talents. She'd borrowed some coding tools to solve a problem with her home AV system. Their staff were constantly making recommendations about software and online resources. They had all manner of creative equipment, most of it too expensive for the average person.

Today she'd reserved the sophisticated paint scaping equipment. She signed in at the machine and set up what she needed to get the job going.

It wasn't long before she was leaning over the output printer as it did its job. The blossoming flowers outside the nearby window murmured that Summer was arriving. She speculated that they got more colourful every time she looked up. People walked by her window with their sweaters folded on their arms. The day had heated up already.

Her canvas was coming out beautifully. She stared at the nozzle as it went back and forth across the frame, dropping small bits of colour with incredible precision. Each colour went on one at a time. It was going to take at least sixty minutes.

"These printers don't seem to move very fast, do they? But they are so useful. It's amazing to have them."

Ashley looked around to see who was speaking. It had been just her and the librarian. She'd been so fixed on her task that she was surprised to realize there was another "maker" who had started to use the equipment. The man was carefully watching a 3D printer. He was printing what looked to be a small toy.

"What are you printing," she asked the fellow.

He looked up and smiled at her. A soft smile, welcoming. She wondered who he was, not for any other reason than she liked the look of his smile.

He picked up one of the figures and showed it to her, coming a little close as he did. She took a half step back and then took the figure from his hands.

"I make these toys. The kids love these things." He took the figure back gently as he smiled directly back at her. "You can get all the files for the drawings online."

"I've heard about that," Ashley replied. "But I hadn't thought about doing it."

"Oh yeah, I do a lot now whenever the kids get into a new cartoon or manga. And once the kids don't use these anymore, you can just use the melter to get rid of the plastic and reuse it to do something new."

"That's a great idea! I should tell my husband about it."

He looked back at her and smiled.

She went over to her printer and checked out her canvas. He put his figure back and then joined her at her printer.

"Your picture is amazing! Did you take it, or did you find that on a database somewhere?"

"It's mine. I used to do a lot of photography when I was younger. A lot less now that I have the kids. I love this paint scape stuff. I love how it gives the image dimension."

They talked for a while about her composition and her recent trip. He asked about the marbling technique in the image. He too did a little photography and told her about a local club. "Sounds fun. Maybe when the kids are older, I'll look it up."

"Why wait," he challenged her.

He positioned the next toy figure on the printer and pushed the start button. She went over to see the thread of plastic pour from the machine to form the base. They both checked the time remaining.

"Thirty minutes. Do you want to get some coffee while we wait? I'm Jake, by the way."

"Ashley." She stood up and nodded.

"I'm not sure if leaving stuff here is safe." She looked around. There was hardly anyone inside on this sunny day. "Let's go," she agreed. "They make an awesome cappuccino out in that Cup Cafe."

They went outside the library and stood at the coffee bar waiting to be served. As he stood next to her, she couldn't help feeling that there was something familiar about him.

What was Jake's story, she wondered? They had been chatting together for a good thirty minutes now and she couldn't shake the feeling they'd met. He was certainly a dad, so there was likely a chance they'd met through their kids.

He had this way of engaging her. Telling her to keep at it. He'd said it a lot since they had run into each other. She looked down at her clothing. She had worn the usual leisure/exercise gear today. She wished she's chosen something else a little more flattering. After all, she could look good if she tried. Jhonian seemed to never care what she wore.

The coffee came and they both sat down. He looked across at her and asked, "so what do you do for excitement?"

"What a question," joked Ashley, torn between telling him the crushing truth or making up some new reality.

She kept it light. "I work for a transportation company. I research transportation platforms for new delivery mechanisms."

He smiled back in that goofy way that he had. "You're hilarious!"

"Well, I don't think of myself as funny."

"You are! If we were a comedy team, you'd be the straight man always setting up the jokes."

Ashley stopped cold. "Are you Straightman40?"

He looked a bit stunned. "Yes," he confirmed with some hesitation.

"That's wild. So happy to meet you. You know, in person. I'm Strawberryjam2k."

"No! That's too much." He smiled at her, happy to see her. "How are you doing?"

"Okay, I guess. Considering." There was a strained silence while she stared at him. "This is weird, talking face-to-face."

"How did you recognize me?"

"I dunno. There was something familiar about the way you speak. I remembered you lived near here. I just took a chance."

They took a few sips of their coffee, trying to ignore the awkwardness. Memories flooded back to all their late-night conversations. "Do you miss it much" she asked.

"Yes, but I'm recovering. That's how it feels. I'm trying to stay away from the apps. Stay grounded."

Ashley nodded her head in agreement. It had been a long time since she'd been drawn back into the intimacy of the app. She lowered her voice. "I feel the same. But I miss it. Sometimes I just need it."

"I know." He picked up his cup and cradled in his hands. "I have to tell you; you saved my ass. I should thank you."

"Really. What for?"

"You bailed me out more than once. Remember that time I was fighting with my wife about whether my son needed help?"

"Yes, I think I called you a dick at the time. Sorry."

344

"Yeah, that part hurt. But you were right. I did what you said and told her I needed to know what she wanted. I listened. It got better."

Ashley sat back in her chair and looked at Jake intently. "Well, that makes me feel way better. Thanks!"

"How so?"

"My biggest YOLO regret is the time I threw away. Now I have some of the time back. I feel so much lighter. Except for the regret about what I did. All the time that was all for nothing."

"No!" He shook off her doubts. "You helped me. Several times. I mean it. It wasn't all a waste."

Ashley nodded her head ruefully. "What a relief." She sprung up quickly, impulsively surprising the man with a brief, awkward hug. He laughed at her gesture and she scurried back to her seat.

"This is great! Let's start again. I want to know all about you. The real you. So, Jake, how many kids have you got?"

He smiled a goofy grin. "Well, Ashley, I have three growing boys. I really love my kids. I love spending time with them!"

"Yeah, me too. I've got two. My son is about to turn seven and my girl is four."

He looked down at his coffee cup that was nearly empty. He lifted it up and sucked hard on the last drops of liquid like the cup might give him more if he did.

He slammed his coffee cup down on the table and quickly blurted, "Here's the truth. I'm in a rut."

Ashley giggled as he spoke and then held a hand up to explain. "I'm laughing because I know your pain. Everybody I know is in a rut."

Jake got up and collected their dishes. He shivered as he got back to the table as if to bring himself back to reality. "Sometimes I regret that we can't just be who we are online. Nobody told me I'd have to be the straight man for the rest of my life."

"I get that." Ashley went on empathically, "Maybe there's some place in the middle." She took a napkin and a pen and wrote Ashley Bernal on a napkin. "That's my last name. Message me if you want to talk. As Jake, in real life. I'd like that." Ashley smiled and then concluded, "thanks for the coffee and the chat. I hope we can talk again. Soon."

She ordered her ride, sauntering happily back to the library to collected her finished canvas.

She was still happy as the car pulled up to her house. She looked at the window in front of her and saw her husband and children setting the table. They were standing around it and looking at her little boy. Her son was jumping and clapping in place with his hands straight over his head.

They were laughing about his performance and pointing as if they were suggesting some other manoeuvre he might try. She recognized that he was doing the seal dance that he'd shown her earlier in the day. Nobody else would know what was happening inside but her. It was her piece of the universe.

From the way they were standing, she could tell they'd left a spot for her. She anticipated the scrambled greeting awaiting her when she pressed the door code and got inside. A yellow glow came from behind, probably one of the kids' toys that had been abandoned while still in operation. She watched and admired how the fuzzy light framed the scene. The front window was transformed into a screen from the story of her life. Not always easy. But hers. Warm and cozy.

Sixty-three

Ally sat on the deck of her cottage, taking in the summer sun and drinking her coffee. She'd always been a canny trailblazer, and this time it had paid decent dividends. She was finally on the path to joy. She had to stop striving to reckon how far she'd strayed. She was working hard to catch up. In other words, retirement suited her perfectly.

Still, you don't always get everything you want. She missed Pete, or at least his presence in her life. But the trade-up was the fact that Derrick was hundreds of kilometres away. If she was forced to choose between an affair, a loveless marriage, and her current state of independence and hope, she'd take what she had now.

It was a year later, and the Carbon Credits issue had rocked the government in ways even she had not imagined. She had seen the power of information and how average people, desperate for change and logic, can mobilize and create a new vision for the country. People were talking about a new era. Books by the Coupland Foundation had come out about life beyond the Post-Consumer era. Canadians were global citizens, leading the way internationally. The challenge was sustainable development for global parity. It was very interesting, but Ally was very content to let the younger generation lead the way.

Democracy was a tricky issue. Over the years Ally had heard her friends argue compellingly against it. Proponents pointed out that the information people need to make rational choices is never available, so others, better informed, needed to make the choices for us.

But that's not where her opinions landed after a career in the pursuit of rational choice. Democracy depended on a little participation. We should make some time to look for, and sometimes demand, the information we need.

From the government's point of view, changes to the Carbon Credits were a simple policy announcement. Not much work to be done. Just push a few arcane regulatory buttons et voila! An increase. Make your meme. Update the communications. Nobody pays attention.

Democracy is dead if we don't pull our heads out of our asses and start to want more. More than slick or pretty people with smiles and easy to digest ideas. More from ourselves too. The anger isn't good enough. Thoughtful and open-spirited involvement is going to create the ideas of tomorrow.

This thought reminded Ally of the beautiful bird that had alighted in front of her the other morning. Sitting in this very chair. She was retired now, and she had the time to dawdle over details, finding meaning in idle places.

She didn't know much about the bird, except it was beautiful, and that it was a chickadee. She was confident it was so.

And then, as she watched the bird, she realized that all she knew about birds, their names and their habits, she had learned in grade school. It was knowledge that was so abstract, and so carefully taught to her decades ago. So much detail that she had never questioned over the years. Chickadees. She remembered there were Redbirds. And Bluebirds. There was one on a tree not too far away. It was blue and a bird. It was a real thing.

But then it struck her that she should check again and find out what was happening with birds now. Maybe they'd changed their names. Maybe they no longer liked being identified by their colours.

Was this like everything she knew? Was her knowledge a network of absolute facts, or a collection of remembered maybes? Was the knowledge in her mind more precise than the knowledge in the personal screen on the kitchen counter? Was she going to take the easy road and carry on with what she knew? Or was she going to challenge it? Did she care enough to check? Was it worth it?

And that's how to fuck up a good idea like democracy. People run away from hard work. Lazy thinking. Lazy politics. That's where it begins. The system starts to rot from within.

That's some of what she thought about democracy. Worthful and work. Ally sent out a prayer into the ether that the next wave of public servants would try to have their influence.

And then Ally sat there in the sun, not thinking about her work, but her new life, her trip to joy.

From the interior of the cottage there was a thudding sound. Like a bear foraging through a campsite. The footfalls on the wooden floor moved around through the kitchen and drew closer to the patio door.

Tanya poked her head through the door. She was chewing a piece of bread, ripped off the loaf Ally had made yesterday. The colour in her face and the shape of her body looked healthier than it had in a long time. Her blondish hair was covering her ears now, regrowing after the treatment.

Ally laughed. Not at her daughter, but for her. "I see you're hungry!"

"I'm starving!"

"Did you sleep okay?"

Tanya looked around the lake. Her eyes were dazed, and she seemed to take in the mist on the lake, as the sun came over the trees. It was going to be a hot day. It had been six months since she'd been cleared from the disease. And it had been close to a year that she'd been forced to stop all her partying. For a while she'd been too sick to care. Then she needed every medical intervention available to get through each day. But now the days were easier.

"Did you sleep okay?"

"Oh, yeah, sorry. I slept great. All night. No bad dreams."

"I'm happy to hear it. That's a couple days in a row. Right?"

"I know." Tanya walked out onto deck and leaned against the railing. She stretched and yawned, still wrestling with welcome effects of sleep. "I woke up this morning and thought, hey, I should get up."

"That's my girl!"

Tanya scoffed gently at her mother, fixing her eyes on a point on the horizon. "Yes, mother, you're right. I'm your girl."

Ally stared out to where her daughter was looking at the other side of the lake. "What do you see out there?"

Tanya didn't answer for a minute. Ally wondered if she heard her. Then she spoke deliberately without turning her head. "I see the distance."

"Oh." Her mother let the quiet between them sit for a while and then got up from her chair. "I'm going to make breakfast. I've got some bacon and eggs from the local farmer. And you've found the bread."

Tanya nodded. "Yeah, sounds very tasty." Her voice had an undertone of amazement.

"Just to warn you, Kara is coming up this morning, so you might want to get dressed soon." The door of the cottage slammed. "She's always early," Ally called back.

"Nans is coming this morning?"

"Yes, with Janey and Byron. She sent us both a message last night."

Tanya came back into the cottage. "I haven't seen Janey in a while."

"Well, she really wants to see you. Maybe you three can go into town with her this aft. And it will be hot today, you can swim."

"Sounds delightful."

Ally stopped slicing the bread for a second and looked at Tanya. "Actually, it does!"

Tanya smiled at her mother. "It will be a party!"

"They're staying over tonight. There will be five of us. Kara said something about playing cards tonight. Do you remember playing euchre years ago?

Tanya was looking out the patio door at the lake. The mist had almost cleared. "We used to play euchre? I don't remember much."

"Yeah, we used to have fun."

350

"So, this is what I have to look forward to?"

Ally looked up from her breakfast efforts and gazed happily at her daughter. Her face had a conspiratorial expression, as if she was fellow hostage. "Well, I know from personal experience -- you don't have much choice. After all, you're one of us!"

A word from the author

I must begin with thanks to the early readers of this book, especially David Newman, Kathy Woodworth and Ann Marie Hussar-Lucas, for their insightful comments that helped me craft the final version of this novel. My thanks also to my editor, Aaron Kaiserman, for his skilled suggestions to improve the final product. Thanks to all the people, especially my patient family, who have offered me encouragement along the way.

I've been at this book, on and off, for ten years.

Over this time, I've seen climate issues grow in public awareness. Sounds obvious today, but back then the issue was more theoretical. I used to sit at the computer imagining what would happen thanks to unpredictable weather. Now, whether it's flooding, fires or extreme heat, I don't have to make stuff up. I don't have to imagine disasters to come. This issue seems dangerous enough for me. I don't want to see it escalate.

I got interested in this issue because it seemed almost impossible to fix. I had worked managing issues for the Canadian government for years. I'd read a few books (Ronald Wright's *Short History of Progress* for starters) and the dialogue piqued my professional interest. I wondered where this issue would wind up. It was big and amorphous. Definitely not easy to manage. It could easily be co-opted by outside interests. It could be conflated with other axes to grind. That was my big worry.

The more I read, the more I saw the problem. Every environmental interest seemed to have a horse in the show. If you were part of the anti-meat lobby you wanted to get out of meat production. If you wanted a new economic system, you wanted radical system reform. This was compounded by scientists who rightly worried that no one was paying attention. They tended to compensate by painting a threatening picture of doom and gloom.

The thing for me was that there was a dearth of solutions in these prognostications. They all wanted me to feel bad about our prospects, without giving me the optimism that solutions were possible.

But I was convinced we could find a solution. Every generation has an irretractable, impossible, global problem to solve. My generation was going to get bombed out of existence. Nuclear bombs were going to be launched by our staunchest enemies. Acid rain threatened our precious lakes. Then the ozone layer was going to fry us. The hole was going to get bigger and bigger until our atmosphere burned away. There were germs everywhere as we faced down Ebola, SARS and Covid-19.

But impossible problems find a solution. Even these real, big, seemingly impossible problems. We found a way to de-escalate nuclear tensions, we passed regulations to curb emissions, we developed international standards for chlorofluorocarbons, made vaccines in record time. I trust that behind all the panicked rhetoric surrounding climate change, that there are a series of solutions to this real issue of climate change.

I am convinced that the issue isn't technology. We need more of it, and we don't have it all worked out. But we have some of the best minds on it and genuine sustainability is a core value in the new projects coming online today.

It isn't really money. I am not advocating creating new currencies or that money is limitless. I am saying we can find money if our lives depend on it. Our response to the pandemic showed we have cash if we really need it.

Our challenge is our will power and the absence of a convincing plan. We trivialize the scope of the problem by arguing that individual action is the solution. But none of us feel confident we are working together. Our challenge is the lack of coordinated policy and the structural imperfections of short-term politics.

I realize that we have a series of international agreements, and they are a start. But they do not take the place of a well-thought-out plan. We are not going to muddle our way out of this. We need concrete, logical, gamed-out actions, like when we finally set up inspection programs for nuclear arms and started to decommission our stockpile. Or put scrubbers on smokestacks. Or put in place incentive programs to get rid of our old refrigeration and their ozone-depleting chemicals. Or stuck a vaccine in billions of people's arms. This is a time for a bias to action. And not just actions that make us feel good. Meaningful ones.

If you are interested in this issue, and you're committed, what you are wondering is what to do next. In plain language. And in a way that convinces you that someone with more brains than you has conceived of the big picture. What is the shortest way from point A to B?

We want to trust that we won't all buy electric vehicles and then have them all go down when the power grid is cut off because of forest fires. This is something that I worry about. Or we won't stop building pipelines only to need them in a hurry to ship hydrogen. We won't stop producing milk only to see childhood nutrition tank among the economically disadvantaged. I want to know that what I am asking my kids to do is worth it, because unfortunately they are going to bear more of this than I will.

In thinking about climate change so many years ago, it struck me that art was a good place to work through this challenge. I thought I could write a novel that would paint a picture of what can be. I tried to apply what I had read and heard about over my public service career and into retirement. It won't be a perfect picture of the science involved. I really wanted to game out our reactions. How will it feel? Who will be responsible? Where will we look for answers.

Throughout the process I was often reminded of Ebenezer Scrooge facing the Ghost of the Future. He wanted to know if he could influence his future. My novel is shadow of what could be. I hope some of it makes you think about the choices in front of us.

One of the most important challenges that I faced writing this book was coming to terms with how angry our kids and grandkids will feel about our choices now. An intergenerational challenge is looming that should motivate all of us who believe we love our kids.

It is up to all of us to work together, sluff off the chaff of the spurious arguments and get to the nuggets of truth that we need to build a sustainable future.

If you want to start to learn more about the issue, you can start at my website, www.rumbawords.com. I've posted info about books to

354

read and websites to consult. I've blogged about what we need to think about to use communications to push the issue forward. There's a place where you can share too.

Climate change must be understood and managed. We have the power of foresight. If ever our kids needed us to use it, it's NOW.

Kathy Trim